AN ORDINARY WONDER

A NOVEL

BUKI PAPILLON

PEGASUS BOOKS
NEW YORK LONDON

AN ORDINARY WONDER

Pegasus Books, Ltd.
148 West 37th Street, 13th Floor
New York, NY 10018

Copyright © 2021 by Buki Papillon

First Pegasus Books cloth edition September 2021

ISBN: 978-1-64313-781-0

10 9 8 7 6 5 4 3 2 1

Printed in the United States of America
Distributed by Simon & Schuster
www.pegasusbooks.com

For Julien. For Margaret and Samuel Olajide.
For Mubo, Jumoke, Muyiwa and Molara.

You are my beating heart.

Ṣey! Ọmọ omi-imọlẹ.

Duro, ọmọ olowuro.

Pẹlẹ, o! Ọmọ a lu igbi jo!

***

Hey! Child of the silver rivers.

Stay, offspring of the morning light.

Be well, daughter who dances to the beat of waves!

PART ONE

A person who sells eggs
should not start a fight in the market.

1

NOW

1991 (AGE 14)

My name is Otolorin. I've been called 'monster'. Within dark valleys of flesh I defy the given – a snake curled in upon itself, two in one, mythical and shunned. Yet, in that magical place between worlds, in the realm where the great mother gives milk to her offspring, I become like a goddess. There, in words unspoken, my voice is heard. I often wish I could take Wura, my sister, with me to visit that place where I truly come alive, but I cannot because Wura is normal, so it would be death.

Wura and I are twins. Like all other Yoruba twins that have ever been born, we should be called Taiwo and Kehinde – the one who came first, and the one who lagged behind. Even in this, our natural names, our parents kept us apart. Otolorin – *one who walks a different path*; and Wuraola – *a wealth of gold*.

Wura is everything to our mother, who will never have any other children because she is the woman who birthed the unspeakable, and my father has no desire to sire any more monsters.

Here in Nigeria, the road ends at my secret, but America, they say, is a land where wonders are created and the wondrous is made ordinary. Now that I have wedged one foot onto that path, I am determined to make it all the way. Because if I do, perhaps I, too, can become an ordinary wonder.

2

BEFORE

1989 (AGE 12)

In our house, there was nothing as dangerous as the truth. I'd slipped into Wura's room, though I was supposed to stay out of sight in mine. Backlit by the soft September sun, her party dress beckoned like a hibiscus to be plucked; pink blushing to rose at the hem, buttons like dewdrops down the back. A crimson sash. In a day we'd turn twelve.

Weeks earlier, surrounded by the freshwater scent of new fabric at Ibadan's Top Tailor, my twin sister had selected the exact dress I'd have chosen, had anyone asked. She would dazzle like a princess at our party and I would be the brother trussed up in a suit. Not that I hated trousers – they're useful for tree climbing and playing football – but I also longed to wear a dress sometimes. Okay, most times.

Surely, whispered a little voice in my mind, *Wura won't mind if you try the dress on. Just to see. In fact, she might think it fun!* And that was like Mother's driver denying he'd been drinking *kainkain* when the fumes on his breath could dry the water off your eyeballs. Wura would share her last bite of coconut candy with me, but if I touched her stuff without permission, her rage was roof-shattering, like Samson in the Bible. Yet, how we'd both gasped the moment Wura opened the catalogue page to that dress!

Minutes earlier, standing before my bedroom window, I'd seen Mother slide into the back seat of her Mercedes. Watched it shoot down the driveway in Mr Driver's typical gunfire fashion. Watched the huge truck that had brought dozens of rental chairs rumble sedately out behind it like a disapproving old auntie. The gateman shut the gate and I could finally escape. Mother would be gone for a while.

Wura padded silently in. This was the best and the worst thing about being twins: we rarely surprised each other. She smoothed the sash on her dress. Eyed me warily.

'Can I try it on?' It popped out of my mouth.

'No!'

'Just for a minute?'

Wura's lower lip vanished under the top one. It was unfair to ask. Mother said Jehovah God would punish us all if she encouraged my sinful habits.

I was maybe five the first time it happened. Mama Ondo, my grandmother, had been visiting. She'd set aside her wig, orange headscarf still tied on, while she napped on the cool verandah. I'd never realized till then that she sometimes wore one. I'd been shocked by the sight of her scalp bald all around the edges, as if someone had plucked her clean. I'd arranged the wig on my head, tiptoed to the hallway mirror and, as the world slid into proper focus, made the happy discovery that I was, in fact, a girl. I'd promptly named myself Lori, and raced off to spread the good news, confident everything would now be fixed.

'You're not a girl, Otolorin, you're a boy!' Mother had hissed. 'And if you ever repeat those words or let anyone see your privates, I'll lock you outside at night for *gbomo-gbomo* to steal!' That brought weeks of nightmares. I was never sure afterwards if I'd dreamed of my grandmother in a long white robe, standing before a small fire in the backyard, the wig she'd thrown on it spitting flame before curling up like a small, dying animal.

I'd tried my best since to forget about Lori but it was like trying to turn off a broken tap. The feelings just kept flowing.

'*Please?*' I pulled the big, sad eyes Wura could never refuse.

She'd hoped I'd say, *Never mind, forget it.* Then she'd exile herself with me to my room and we'd play snakes and ladders and pretend I'd never asked. But I couldn't. Because maybe if I saw Lori again, just for one sweet moment in that heavenly dress, then I could go back quietly to being Oto.

Her fists clenched, then released. 'All right then. Off with your clothes!'

I stripped immediately to my underwear before she could change her mind.

'Have you heard, skinny-bones?' Wura tickled my ribs. She was pretending this was a game. I wasn't trying to be someone else, just her silly brother playing dress-up.

'Heard what?'

'Opelenge fell on a plate, but he was so scrawny the plate felt insulted and refused to break!'

We erupted with giggles, knowing she might as well be poking fun at her own body. As she carefully slid the dress off its hanger, brows beetled with concentration, it was like watching myself. Big brown eyes with looping curly lashes, nose dabbed on like an afterthought above pillow-puff lips. Only my jaw was a touch squarer where hers was perfectly curved like the bottom of an egg. Her hair was done up in two beribboned buns, mine cut low.

As for the down-below parts, who knew? It was never talked about.

Wura's dress slid on like warm water. Impatient to turn around and see myself in the mirror, I looked down at my feet which, sadly, had always been a size larger than hers.

'I wish I had strappy white sandals.'

'Hey! Stop wiggling like a fish or the dress will tear!'

I heard a gasp. Mother stood at the door. She must have forgotten something.

Her eyes thinned to slits. Her face curled like lit paper.

Wura's hands trembled on my back, our hearts battering at our ribs. *I'm dead*, I thought.

'You wicked child!' Mother screamed.

In two strides she'd seized my shoulders, shaking till it was an earthquake and my teeth rattled like *shekere* beads. I broke away but her hand hooked into the neck of Wura's dress. Buttons pinged everywhere.

'No! Please! Wura's dress. It's not her fault!'

She slapped my mouth shut. Yanked harder. The dress ripped top to hem. Slap! Rip! Slap! Till I was cringing in blue Y-fronts and one torn sleeve.

'Mommy, please! Stop beating him!' Wura sobbed.

'You shut up and don't move! I'll deal with you later.' Mother pushed me out of the room, down the hallway. To the edge of the landing. The last time she was really angry, she'd hauled me to the kitchen, taken a wooden ruler to my palm, then made me husk a sack of groundnuts with my stinging hands. It took till the next morning.

Fast, like something mechanical, her hand shot out. I flailed, reached for a railing, found only air. Then I was tumbling. I hit the bottom with a squelchy crack and popped out of my body into a flash of light so strong, I was blinded. Then I could see better than ever before and the air around me was super-shined into a swirling silver-blue tunnel of tiny stars. I floated towards the big star blinking at the end. So beautiful!

A piercing scream made me wish I still had hands to clasp to my ears. Wura! I was rudely thrust back into the small body lying at the bottom of the stairs. Where did all the lovely blue and silver go?

Someone picked me up.

The ride to the clinic was a long, bumpy haze of pain.

'He fell down the stairs,' Mother told the doctor. 'He was too excited about his birthday party tomorrow.'

'Okay, Oto. This will hurt, but bear up.' The tall, long-faced man felt around my shoulder and pain swallowed me.

'Mommy! Mommy!' I cried, needing a mother to save me, to hold me close and tell me all would be well. The doctor mercifully let go.

Mother didn't move from her chair. Her face was twisted like a wrung scarf. I had a sick feeling that the switch in her head with my name on it, which used to hover around *bad*, had now flipped to *worst*. She'd never gone this far before.

'He'll be fine, Mrs Akinro.' The doctor swabbed my arm, smiling at Mother, mesmerized as a bug by the flame of her beauty. It wasn't an uncommon reaction.

Mother squeezed out a smile. She wouldn't leave my side for a second, but not for reasons the doctor thought.

He slipped a long needle into my arm. 'Be brave for your mother now, little man. No more falling down stairs in the future!'

My eyelids fluttered. The sharp white walls of the clinic wavered and faded. The table became a cottony cloud, wrapped itself securely around me and together we rose upwards, soaring above the trees and people who soon looked like ants on the ground. Somewhere far below was a doctor with his needle and a mother who hated her child, and I'd left them all behind.

My cloud disappeared and I was falling. Below, gentle waves caught the light and the sea shimmered blue-green-silver. I spun head over toes. I should be scared, but all I felt was eagerness. Sleek as an eel, I slid in. The water carried me with a strange grace, yielding yet supporting. I found my balance, stood upright. Turned and twisted to look around. Tiny fish darted by, unconcerned with my presence. I think one winked at me.

In the distance, I saw shapes that could be houses; pale, watery as though made of glass or ice that wasn't frozen. Nothing was what it seemed to be. Down here, the world gleamed brighter, sharper, clearer, the way it only ever looked when the sun came out after the first heavy rain that followed the dry season. Reds seared, yellows shone and purples looked wax-polished. Voices babbled softly, sweetly, in my ear, but I saw no one. I looked at myself in those glass walls and I was beautiful. Long plaits down my back, pearl shells on my chest. Bangles on my wrists. I searched my mind for the meaning of this. Where was I?

I must really be dead this time. No other explanation made sense. It wasn't so bad, after all, to be dead. Then, in the corner of my eye, I saw movement, quick as light, gone when I blinked. She played with me like that for a while, before she let me see her. She was a woman but then again, she wasn't. Her long slim arms gleamed with an impression of pearly scales. Shells covered her breasts. Her sweeping fins and tail flashed a multitude of colours – silver, red, electric blue – like the betta fish I once saw in a book. Sea anemones wrapped like living rubber bands around the ends of her long gleaming plaits. One lazily waved its tentacles. I'd never seen anything so astonishing and beautiful. Yet she felt strangely familiar. Who was she?

Call me Yeyemi, she said, without words. *You are safe. Here between worlds, at the parting of the veil, you may rest. But only for a time.*

Then I was back in the real world, lying woozy-headed in the car, and all that remained was a lingering sense of light and joy. I longed to return to that wonderful place.

Our birthday dawned bright and clear. Tall loudspeakers all over the courtyard boomed with Ebenezer Obey's latest release. People came and went, chatting, eating, drinking. All I could do was sit under the plumeria trees and watch. Two boys came to ask about my sling – probably children of Father's business partners in Ibadan. Bored, they soon wandered off. From when I could talk, Mother warned me never to let anyone get close enough to start asking questions. If we got asked to parties, Mother took Wura and said I was sick. People thought me a sickly child.

Years ago in primary school, I'd had a real friend and invited him home. Rashid was always alone, too, and so nervous he was practically mute, though I sensed the busyness of deep thoughts scurrying through his mind, just like mine. His tribal scarification marks, four across each cheek, made other kids meanly tease him. When Mother asked if he'd like some Fanta, he'd whispered, yes. She'd frowned.

In my room, he'd whispered, 'Let's play mommies and daddies. You lie down and I'll climb on top.'

'Now what?' I asked.

'We move like this.' He thrashed his arms and legs like a swimming frog. It wasn't much fun, but I was glad to have a friend.

'Now you're going to have a baby,' he said.

We'd rolled up a towel and shoved it under my T-shirt. I'd waddled around like I'd seen pregnant women do, holding my sides, groaning with great drama. Rashid laughed so hard, I got carried away and waddled past the window. Outside, Wura looked up and guffawed. Mother, unfortunately, was beside her. She'd been up in seconds, screaming, *Unnatural creature, son of disgrace*. Rashid trembled as if in a fit, then there'd been this dripping noise and he'd peed his pants.

Rashid stopped speaking altogether in school and ran off if he saw me. That hurt long after the welts from Mother's shoe faded from my back. I'd wanted to let him know it was okay. That I'd never tell anyone he peed himself. He didn't return after the holidays.

A girl blew a party horn near my ear then ran off laughing. It brought out a smile I didn't know I had inside me. Everyone was having such a good time, even Mother, radiant with smiles since Father arrived early morning from Lagos. He sat with the most important guests, wearing a gold lace *agbada*. He said something to Mother, who shouted for Emily the maid to bring more beer. She loved every second of shining beside him in her matching gold lace *iro* and *buba*, knowing how people envied her big round eyes, her brows arched like bird's wings, her smooth-as-camwood skin, the pillow-puff lips Wura and I had inherited (though she probably wished I hadn't) and her tall, handsome husband, smooth as okra soup. A couple of young women guests came to bend their knees before him in greeting, acting all shy and fluttery. Mother's hand latched on to his arm.

Roving praise singers stood nearby thumping out Father's importance on talking drums: '*Lustrous black jewel of immeasurable value. Majestic owner of palatial houses. Great hunter whose quiver is full of sons and daughters*.' Etc, etc. They somehow always knew to show up when there was a party.

Father rose, smiling smugly. Plastered naira notes to their sweaty foreheads. I'd once heard the gateman mutter how he's like the scorpion that can't help stinging to death the very frog on whose back it's crossing the river. I had to say, it described Father quite well. I'd heard the gossip about his biggest business competitor, who just upped and vanished. No one knew if he was dead. A journalist who insisted on investigating further was found floating face down in Ogunpa River after heavy rains, though people got early warning for once and fled before it overflowed.

To me, Father was as remote as Mars and twice as hostile. The year we turned five, he was leaving on one of his never-ending business travels and asked Wura what she wanted him to bring back. She asked for ribbons and a fairy-tale castle with a real princess inside that we'd seen advertised on an American TV cartoon series. Because I'd not fully understood I was barely to be seen and definitely not heard, I piped up that *I* wanted exactly the same. He looked at me like a person stares at the sole of his shoe after stepping in vomit. He never returned to live with us.

It took time for Wura to figure out I'd not literally driven him away as Mother ranted and, for a time, she resented me with all the pain her five-year-old heart could muster. It was the worst feeling. Mother locked me in my room for a whole week with only water and dry bread to eat. That was when I really began to draw. At first, it was to keep my mind off being hungry. Then I drew not to be afraid. Then I drew to stem the loneliness and the hurt. I covered whole notebooks. Again and again I practised eyes, then hands, then bodies, then movement. Feeling, tasting and testing the shape of life through my pencils and crayons, it was an intoxication to realize I *was* a creator. I could make exist whatever I wanted!

Afterwards, Mother told everyone Father had moved to Lagos because his business had grown too big to handle from Ibadan.

The rare times he visited and they talked privately, I'd put my ear to the door and listen because, according to my precious book of Yoruba proverbs, *it was because the kite had its ear on the wind that it didn't perish in the brushfire.* Mother, sobbing, asked once if he planned to leave her dangling for the rest of her life. Father icily replied, 'Forget it, Moji! I will not further besmirch the Akinro name by siring another monster.' I'd had to look up *siring* and *besmirch.* Monster, I'd understood just fine. Father loved using big words.

As the praise singers scooped up the last naira notes and moved on,

Emily, Mother's maid, emerged from the house hauling a large tub and handed out green bottles glistening with cold sweat. The men around Father nodded like agama lizards in agreement with whatever he was saying. Probably his tired old joke that if we'd had the 'sagacity' to be born in the dry season instead of September, we'd have saved him the yearly cost of renting canopies. They always laughed as if they'd never heard it before, knowing full well that Father could buy up every canopy in Ibadan with just his pocket change.

For sure the plentiful food would be talked about for months: *jollof* rice with golden fried slices of *dodo,* pounded yam with spinach and melon seed stew, *amala,* beaten until fluffy and served with bitterleaf soup and smoked fish. All prepared by the hired caterers fondly known as *olowo-sibi* – women born with cooking spoons in hand. The clanging of their giant cooking pots had woken us at dawn. The whiff of woodsmoke still lingered in the air.

It all smelled tasty, but struggling out of my chair was too painful. I was wondering if I'd practised so hard at being invisible that I'd actually vanished when Wura showed up with a plate of *jollof* rice, spicy chicken and Limca soda. She placed the tray on my lap and began cutting the meat into manageable pieces.

Her purple dress, hastily bought from a boutique in Bodija that morning, had nothing on the ruined one. A couple of friends tagged along, so I just let my eyes tell her how sorry I was, and how grateful that she'd brought me food. I wished she'd stay with me but there was pin-the-tail-on-the-donkey, a traditional puppet theatre and musical chairs. She blew a soft sweet puff of air on her forefinger, a bubble-kiss, pressed it against my cheek and flitted off like a butterfly. It was our own special way of saying, *I love you above and beyond.*

I was finishing my food when a silver Mercedes pulled up at the gate. Maami Akinro, Father's mother, emerged from the back seat, elegant from her headscarf – a towering blue *igele* with golden threads sparkling in the sun – to her blue shoes. She always arrived late from Ijebu and left with Father when the party was over.

Father went to meet her, removing his cap and prostrating to touch a finger to the ground. She laid a hand on his head, pulled him up. Embraced him. They talked for a bit before she went around greeting guests. As her path brought her closer to me, Mother appeared at my elbow, anxiously hovering. Then it was like being in a cage with two lionesses eyeing each other's throats. Without fail, after Maami Akinro visited, Mother would send for Mama Ondo, her own mother. They'd both pray loudly all night and sprinkle holy water from Mama Ondo's Seraphic Temple of Holy Fire all over the house. If Maami Akinro was headed out the front door, you could be certain Mama Ondo was headed in the back.

'What happened to your arm?'

I nearly looked around to see whose arm Maami Akinro meant. On her rare visits she hardly talked to us, though she always brought sweets. I supposed a broken arm was news. Then again, Father didn't ask.

'He was too excited about his party and rushed down the stairs and fell,' Mother said.

'I'm asking the child, *abi*? Can't he talk?' Maami's tone could freeze water.

Mother turned to me, brow raised.

'I fell, Maami, ma.'

'I see.' There was a long silence. 'Be more watchful in the future.'

'Yes, ma,' I whispered. *Watchful.* What an odd choice of word.

Then Maami Akinro's friend was tugging her away, saying she had to meet her new grandchild, and Mother said softly, 'Good boy. Well done.' Then she, too, was gone.

I struggled out of my chair.

On my way inside, I heard two women gossiping.

'Hmm, did you see the expensive lace Mama Sheri is wearing? Her business has just been booming recently!'

'I know! But guess what? Her neighbour's daughter suddenly died in her sleep last month!'

'*Ehen!* You saw where my mind was going. I'd long suspected she's a witch, a real airforce number one, flying out on deadly night missions to ruin lives and bring calamity! They say it was her coven that caused lightning to strike and kill her own sister.'

'I heard! And you should have seen how she cried crocodile tears at the funeral! People are so wicked!'

Feeling sorry for poor Mama Sheri, who for certain had merely commited the sin of prospering, I slipped into the living room to take my pain tablets. After we'd returned from the clinic, Mother had held out the bottle, telling me to take two every four hours. Flashing to that hand shooting out to push me, I'd shuddered. Something like shame crossed her face before she shrugged and sniffed, 'Stumbling and falling like a drunk when I barely touched you! *Mcheww!*'

I gingerly wedged myself against the wall behind the sofa with an *X-Men* comic. There was an action picture of Storm I'd planned to draw. It would have to wait till I could properly hold a pencil again.

Someone was urgently tapping my leg. I blinked up into eyes that looked just like mine.

'Wake up! Mommy wants us to cut the cake.'

'I'm sorry about your dress.'

'It wasn't you that tore it, o. How's your arm?'

'Painful.' I began to sit up and winced. Wura grasped my good arm to help.

'You know, Mommy's sorry even if she won't say so.'

I carefully straightened my crumpled-up comic. Wura would believe what she wanted.

'She said she was just urging you to move faster and next thing you tripped and it's her job to toughen you up as a boy or life will be worse for us.'

Whether Mother meant to or not, she *did* push me. And I'd never be the son she wanted.

Too late I realized I said the last part aloud. The pain medicine was definitely melting my brain.

'Why can't you see that nobody gets to choose? You could have died – and all because . . .' Wura's voice broke. 'I should never have let you wear my dress. Let's just go before she comes looking.'

I was suddenly flooded with the dizzying terror and loneliness she'd felt as she frantically called my soul back from wherever it was speeding while my body lay at the bottom of the stairs. Remorseful, I nudged her cheek with a finger. Pulled sorry eyes. As she tugged me towards the door, I promised myself once more that I'd never allow Mother's anger to separate us.

The cake, which Mother had got around to picking up in the morning, was covered in curly pink icing on one side and blue on the other. When we gathered around it for the family photo, I'd placed my hand atop Wura's. The photographer counted down to one and together we pushed down the knife, slicing a clean cut in between.

3

NOW

1991 (AGE 14)

I'm nervous. Excited. Worried. Unable to believe I'm really taking this first step towards the life I dream of having. Or that my mad, terrifying gamble somehow worked.

Mother is reading with painful slowness through my admission papers. Mr Driver unhurriedly pokes a toothpick about in his mouth. We're idling in a long line of cars snaking up the road towards tall, ornately decorated metal gates. Welded onto an arch above them is a shield engraved with two crossed pens and a globe of the world. Scrolling letters read, *International Secondary School: Courage, Truth and Excellence.*

I will my heart to climb down from where it's lodged halfway up my neck. My fingers miss the reassuring warmth of Wura's. Nearly every new experience, she's been beside me. Once, in a rare moment of chattiness, Emily described how ten-month-old Wura rose on wobbly legs, braced herself on the sofa, and stretched out her hand. I'd unhesitatingly grasped it and together, we took our first steps. We'd begged Emily to tell it again. She did, once. Mother's maid is the exact opposite of sentimental.

We turned fourteen this month. There was no birthday party. No one was celebrating. Still, during an awkward outing with Mother to buy my long list of boarding school items – four different kinds of shoes, a torchlight, padlocks, etc. – I spent my small savings on two identical wristwatches. Each round face held a tiny map of the world. Last night I drew a heart and wrote Wura's name on the inside strap of my watch, before fastening it on my wrist. She did the same with hers. I promised her that *nothing*, not time or space, can ever divide us. I reminded her that whatever Mother says, I'll never knowingly hurt her. Then we told 'remember when' stories till we fell asleep.

Today, she was too sad to come out to say goodbye, but sure enough when I looked up at her bedroom window as the car peeled out of our driveway, there she stood, hand plastered against the glass. I laid mine flat against the back windscreen in reply, and felt the ghosts of our fingers touching.

The gates open onto a long driveway lined with old flame trees. Their branches arch from stout trunks, touching in the middle to form a blazing orange tunnel. It's like a passageway to a new world. Hope flutters alive in my chest.

I chance another glance at Mother. Since the fateful phone call that cemented her terrified beliefs and set me free, she's only spoken to me to go over the rules. I must, 1) Never, *ever* take off my briefs unless I have *utter and complete* privacy. 2) Always shower with the door locked and a towel within arm's reach. 3) Immediately commit *harakiri* if I find myself in danger of disgracing the Akinro name. Okay, she didn't exactly put it that way, it's just Wura and I have been watching *Shogun* on TV ... She'd even called the school to demand a single room, but was firmly told they're reserved for prefects.

We slide behind a long line of cars inching towards a three-storey building vibrant with pink bougainvillea. Paths with neatly trimmed hedges wind into the distance, promising secret places to explore, should I find myself alone and friendless as always. Hidden sprinklers send a flurry of swallowtail butterflies dancing into the air. They flutter back down like happy children playing *bojuboju*. Beside the building, a marble fountain sits on a many-tiered platform. A flip-tailed fish on top rains sparkles of water into shell-like bowls. Yeyemi's unearthly smile flashes in my mind. I hope she can still reach through the veil to seek me. I decide it all adds up to a good sign. I'm meant to be here.

In the admin office, Mother scrawls her signature on the dotted lines almost as fast as the admin lady points to them. Clearly used to lingering parents needing reassurance, she smiles sympathetically and says I'll be well cared for at ISS. In reply, Mother snaps that she'll pay cash for the balance of my fees. While Mother counts the cash, the lady hands me a couple of keys with tags attached. Each has my name and a number, 312.

'One and a spare,' she says. 'Don't lose them. You'll be sharing with two others.'

My worries birth a million more. Who will my roommates be? Will they take one look at me and decide two plus two equals weird? Have I just jumped from frying pan into kerosene fire? The admin lady is explaining important things like rules and regulations and dorm life. I try to focus.

All too soon we're at the door and Mother is saying, 'Otolorin, behave yourself. Don't make me regret this.'

'Yes, Mother.' It's a sudden, surprising struggle not to beg her to take me home. She nods once and walks away fast. The edge of her long skirt disappears around the corner and the world tilts sideways and I'm sliding off and can't stop. My hand is raised towards her when someone bumps into me, says sorry with a wide apologetic smile and hurries on. I'm jolted back. All around me is life. An electric buzzing like a hive full of happy, purposeful bees.

Dragging my giant suitcase and bag, I merge into the crowd. As if drawn by magnets, my eyes fasten on a flock of girls chattering like weaverbirds. They look like they've stepped out of Wura's *Teen* magazine. She'd warned me that ISS is nicknamed Fashion Central. In my head, Lori steps up among them wearing an off-the-shoulder jean dress I'd drooled over. How warmly they smile! How eagerly they make space for her! In reality, one of the girls is pointing at me and they're laughing. I've been standing there staring, smiling like an idiot. *Goodbye, Lori,* I whisper. *For now.* From here on out

I will blend in. Be the best boy I can. Study like mad and earn that scholarship to America where they'll know what to do about my body before the worst happens and it's too late and I'm forever stuck the wrong way.

A long queue has formed outside the boys' dorm. Two men – probably teachers – are sitting at tables beside the door, marking names in big books before letting people in. There are tall boys, short ones, skinny ones and a few round ones for sure nicknamed *bọkọtọ*, who gamely take it in their stride. There are boys the gleaming black of *ọse dudu* soap, a smattering as pale as fresh milk *wara*, and everything in between. Voices high and voices low, each and every one of them someone's *real* son. Mother's earlier haste suddenly makes sense. It wasn't just to be rid of me. She must have felt like someone costumed in fake jewellery at a party where other guests wear priceless gems.

I want to turn and flee. To keep running till I'm past those wondrous gates and escaping to ... where exactly? There's nowhere I'm welcome. My only way out is through ISS.

I fall into line.

Ahead of me, a thin boy with hawkish features typical of Hausa northerners slings an arm over his friend's shoulder. 'Soji, my man!' he crows. 'I heard you totally rocked London this summer!'

Soji, tall and worryingly handsome, flashes a smug grin. 'You heard right! Remember Lola, that girl I met there last year? You'll never believe ...' They head inside, and I'll never know what happened with Lola while I stand here twitching like a lamb in ill-fitting wolves' clothing. Which are my roommates?

Behind me, an argument rages about whether *Kamaka from Hawaii absolutely killed it with last summer's luau* or not, and someone else insists he *can't blame Kole for skipping a whole week of school after that Blurb story.* They might as well be speaking Pig-Latin in Kanuri. What on earth is a *luau?* Or, for that matter, *Blurb?*

Children of rich, well-travelled, highly educated parents have graduated from ISS since 1963. Father, as far as I know, earned his education in the practical world of business, and Mother only finished primary school before helping Mama Ondo sell fabric. I've hardly left rustic, sleepy Ibadan except in my imagination. How will I ever fit in? Any minute now someone will point at me and shout, 'Imposter!'

My turn comes and I drag my bag and suitcase up the stairs. The admin lady said the dorm has five floors. First- and second-year boys share the first two floors, third and fourth years the next two, and final-year seniors have the top. At either end of each hallway are shared bathrooms with individual stalls. Except for dorm prefects, she said, it's against regulations for senior and junior students to loiter on each other's floors. It's meant to decrease bullying, which is deeply frowned upon at ISS. This sounds reassuring.

Too soon I'm standing at the door of 312 – third floor, room twelve, as marked on my key ring. I breathe, exhale, open. And step into light and air. Tall windows line one wall. Beds, closets and study desks neatly claim the others. A roommate is already there. We stare, startled, at each other.

'Hi, I'm Cornelius. Fourth year.' He has a long gentle face, long fingers, and the oddest air of not really being there.

'Oto. Third year and new. Nice to meet you.' It's tradition, the admin lady said, to introduce yourself with your name and year.

'Same here. That's your space.' He points to the only unmade bed. 'Our roommate is out and about somewhere. I'm off to piano practice. See you later.'

He leaves. My shoulders descend a notch from around my ears. He didn't seem to find anything about me odd. Still, he had such an absent manner it seems I might have had two heads and he'd not have noticed.

My roommates have already claimed the best spots, so my bed is nearest the door with my closet just beside it. I quickly realize it's perfect because when the closet door is open, it creates an enclosed area beside the wall where I can hide while changing. As for other boys' bits, the occasional eyeful is something I'll just have to deal with. Hopefully, no one makes a habit of strutting around naked. Cornelius certainly doesn't seem the type. But what of my other roommate?

Needing a distraction, I flip open my suitcase and hang my school uniforms (three sets of crisp dove-grey shirts and darker grey shorts) in the closet. Frantically stack socks and briefs into the drawers. Knock a bookend off the desk onto the floor where it takes vengeance on my toes. I hop around mouthing bad words for white-hot seconds till I catch sight of myself, foot in hand, in the wall mirror. A chuckle escapes. I stop. Stare into my own eyes and realize I'll live whole months without Mother's anger stalking me like a vulture impatient for its dinner to die. And I made it happen!

The dinner bell clangs. I've put away everything and no longer have reason to linger. I inch the door open. A pack of laughing, shoving boys rush past, rowdy as falling rocks. I shut the door fast and lean against it, heart hammering. On my roommate's desk sits a ridiculous eraser shaped like a yellow chicken. I remember Babalawo, his ancient, far-seeing eyes flashing a challenge. *All right, all right!* I mumble, take a deep breath, and step out.

4

BEFORE

1989 (AGE 12)

Had anyone asked me Babalawo's age, I'd have said Methuselah old, because his thin, wrinkled face never changed and his eyes held a whole universe. For as long as I could remember, I'd visited him every six months, usually just after my birthday. Mother said it wasn't any of my business to know why, and also, to keep my mouth shut about it or else. From which I'd understood that 'normal' children didn't typically visit an *Ifa* priest. She always dropped me off and picked me up an hour later, never stepping foot out of the car.

He was waiting outside his round, thatched-roofed hut when we arrived.

Mother rolled down the window, her face a tight mask.

'Do not return before sundown today. There is much to accomplish,' he said.

'What? I hadn't planned to return so late!'

'Your child is twelve and approaching manhood. The oracle says the time is auspicious for what must be done.' He had a voice to be obeyed.

Mother's mouth snapped into a grim line. Anyone else would by now be blistered raw by a rash of stinging words. One of the reasons her friends were few.

'Get out,' she hissed at me. 'I'll be back after six.'

*

Inside, earthy smells of herbs welcomed me. Here and there stood familiar wooden images, like friends I'd known all my life. I eyed the honeypot, trying not to drool, hoping it was one of those days he'd give me wild honey on the comb and I'd squeeze out every last drop of sweetness before spitting out the wax. I took my usual seat, cross-legged on a woven mat, and waited for him to begin the ritual of speaking incantations over me while dabbing my forehead and chest with white powder from his divination tray. That was pretty much what happened during our usual hour together. If there was time, he'd tell me a fable or myth, like how earth was actually a marketplace where the gods sent us to trade and learn proper conduct before returning to our true heavenly home. Or he'd share some particularly timely proverb. My favourite was: *the thief that stole the king's bugle – where will he blow it?* Such simple and deep truth! He'd given me my treasured book of Yoruba proverbs when I wouldn't stop pressing for more.

As always, I wished Wura was there but however much she begged and sulked, Mother refused. Annoyed at being excluded, she long ago stopped wanting to hear about my visits. *It's boring anyway,* she'd sniff. *Nothing new ever happens.*

Then it leapt out at me, just like those pop-up greeting cards. Etched among the images encircling the divination tray was a woman with a fish's tail and stars circling her head. Just like Yeyemi! I'd stopped seeing those over the years. Perhaps Babalawo might know something about her and that wondrous place I went! I turned to ask but he was rummaging in a wooden closet, looking unusually grim. I'd have to wait till he was in a more talkative mood.

Instead of sitting across from me, though, Babalawo handed me a white sheet and told me to undress completely then wrap it around me. He always wore the same, with one end thrown across his shoulder, like the Roman togas in my *Asterix* comics. Surprised, I stood, hoping he'd explain later, and not just say, 'When you're old enough, all shall be revealed.'

My sling was gone but I still winced removing my T-shirt.

'What happened to your arm, child?'

'I fell,' I mumbled. It wasn't easy to lie to those deep-seeing eyes.

He gently examined my shoulder, shaking his head, then smoothed on some mint-smelling ointment. It felt warm and tingly and immediately better.

'You must be more watchful,' he said, sounding eerily like Maami Akinro.

'Thank you, Baba.' I waited till he'd knotted the sheet behind my neck before removing my briefs. Though he knew our secret, Mother's words were branded into my brain. *No one's eyes should ever encounter what you have down there, or they'll run screaming.*

'Ready?' he said.

I nodded, suddenly nervous.

'Good. Hold on to this no matter what.' He held out an ordinary grey pebble. My palm closed around its cold smoothness. My heart started thumping.

'Follow me.' He picked up his horsetail divination staff and stepped out of the hut. I stared in confusion for a moment before rushing after him. We were quickly on a forest path bordered by thick vines hanging off tall trees. Birds shrilled to each other. Something rustled in the thick green bushes. Each minute felt weirder. Babalawo's long thin legs ate up the ground so fast it took all my breath to keep up.

We finally stopped at a clearing where a round thatch-roofed hut hugged the ground like a giant snail. Around it stood carved people, some tall, poking at the sky, faces dotted with white chalk; others crouched so low they were bumps on the ground. I heard the soft roar of fast-moving water. I'd never want to be here alone after dark. Babalawo pulled me inside.

An old man and a woman I'd never seen before sat very still on grass mats wearing white sheets like us. Tiny cowry shells woven into the woman's hair formed a delicate fringe that rippled like water when she turned her cool stare on me. The man, face stretched tight over sharp bones, looked as if he was on some grim mission. I wished they'd smile, or say welcome, or *something.*

'Sit down.' Babalawo pointed to a mat on the floor.

'But, Baba, what—'

'Hush and listen, child! At seven days old, your parents brought you and your sister to me for your *esentaye*: to establish your steps in this world and try to divine your *ori*, your destiny. The results were ambiguous. We're hoping, now you're older, the evidence will be plain and the oracle will speak more clearly.'

'My parents?' I gasped. Father and Mother were here with me and Wura?

Babalawo nodded. I was bursting with a torrent of questions but he held a finger to his lips as the woman came to kneel beside me, carrying a calabash half filled with water. Grey-green leaves floated on top. The other man came to sit beside her. My fingers twisted the hem of my white sheet.

'We are gathered today,' Babalawo said, 'to discern this child's unique *ori* and what interventions might be needed. When he was an infant, I did the casting of palm nuts. Though *Ifa* spoke in riddles, I understood that his destiny is uncommon and his path would be difficult, but his head is not cursed. Even so, his mother sank into heartbreak and denial.'

I stared. Wura had always insisted Mother was that way because her heart had broken but I'd never understood this before. I thought she simply hated me.

'The oracle instructed me to caution her that *a person who aims to drag another through a forest must first clear the path with his own back*. I'm afraid her bitterness has only grown. Over the years, I've held my peace for the child's sake but his life was recently put at risk. He said he fell. The oracle said otherwise. For both their sakes we must seek concrete answers. These steps are not undertaken lightly. Let us begin.'

Babalawo knelt behind me, swished his horsetail staff over my head.

It was more information than I'd learned in years. And did he just say he suspected Mother of harming me? What were they about to do? My clenched hands were sweat-damp. I dared not let go of my pebble though I had no idea why. I reminded myself that Babalawo had never hurt me.

The men started chanting by turns, one taking up where the other left off. They swished the air above my head with their horsetail staffs. Their chant was like the droning of gentle bees. The ground beneath my mat felt cool and hard. My breathing slowed despite myself.

Babalawo placed a hand on my good shoulder and firmly urged me backwards till I lay down. He was surprisingly strong for a man who looked so frail. I struggled to rise but a sharp twinge in my other shoulder reminded me it was still tender.

'What's happening? Baba, what are you—'

'Hush, child, be still!' It was that stern voice he'd used with Mother.

Wide-eyed, I watched the other man shift around, turning his back to me, still chanting. I looked pleadingly up at Babalawo but his eyes were shut. I remembered Rashid's face and was immediately sure I was about to be scarified. They'd surely hidden the razor blades.

There was a sudden wrongness of air as the woman flicked up my white sheet and parted my legs. Shock bolted me to the floor. Not scarification, then. But ... This couldn't be happening. There was, I thought hysterically, *barely anything* to circumcise.

She crouched forward, bony fingers searching briskly through fold and crevice. In my head I struggled. Did anything but lie there quaking, yet I couldn't move. Like those nightmares where something heavy sits on your chest.

'Please,' I croaked. 'Please don't cut me.' Warm liquid pooled uncontrollably under my thighs and somewhere, I died of shame. Now she'd know I didn't even pee from the tip of my tiny nubby part but from underneath.

'Be still, child,' Babalawo said. 'We're not here to do harm. Hush and be still!'

Tears slid from my eyes but I kept them wide open, watching now for the moment her face would twist with disgust, like when she found the opening I kept most secret, because Mother said its existence was proof of the devil at work. But she just carried on as if counting a newborn's toes to make sure all ten were present. Then she dipped her fingers in the calabash and sprinkled water over me, speaking incantations in deep *ijinle* Yoruba language. I heard *cauldron of life* and *daughter of clay.*

A moment later she covered me up, looked me in the eye for the first time and said, '*Pele,* my child. It's over. There's nothing to be ashamed of.'

Babalawo opened his eyes and stood. So did the other man. I sat up and scooted away from them till my back hit the wall. Clenched my ankles closed. If I shut my eyes tight enough, maybe I *would* disappear.

I sensed Babalawo's approach. A gentle hand wiped the tears from my face. I wrenched away.

'When you were an infant, we could not circumsize you as custom demanded, because things were unclear. We needed to see if the situation had changed as you approached adulthood. Apetebi is my wife and assistant. She examined you like a nurse or a mother. And Baba Alaba is an *onisegun* who specializes in herbs and medicines for healing. We seek to uncover the gods' intentions and resolve the riddle of your existence so as to guide you onto your true path. For it is ruin to pursue the wrong destiny.'

He could maybe have told me this earlier. Before they scared me witless. *And do they still mean to circumsise . . . ?* The thought had me quivering anew.

'Forgive the indignity. You would only have tortured yourself imagining worse had I told you what was ahead. Think of it like a visit to a doctor, except here we apply the ancient knowledge of our fore-fathers, *hein?'*

I opened my eyes and reluctantly nodded. The urgent question of circumcision burned on my lips but my voice seemed gone. He touched his divination chain to my forehead, then pried open my fingers and took the pebble. He joined the others at the opposite end of the big hut, where Apetebi talked for a long while in quiet whispers.

I knew I should be grateful someone cared enough to seek answers but I just wanted to be back home with an ordinary body no one needed to examine or cut. I pictured Wura laughing and jumping with her new green skipping rope. I'd been practising how to hop in with her. Timed just right, it worked like magic. The thought calmed me and took my mind off the wet patch on the bottom of my white sheet.

I heard the rattle of Babalawo casting his divination chain of eight linked half-shells on the ground. He rearranged and cast it again.

'She is quite a wonder,' he said.

What? Who? My eyes snapped wide.

'We have here a daughter whose *ori* made a most unusual selection in heaven before descending into the marketplace of life.'

Daughter?

'Obatala was hard at work in heaven, making human bodies from the clay of earth. It was a Sunday when the almighty, Odumare, expected to breathe life into the most beautiful creations, so he had to take extra care. Obatala was making a female body when his wife, the goddess Yemoja, brought him a cooling herbal drink to ease his labours. Unknown to them, *Esu*, the trickster god, had laced it with palm wine. Alcohol, as we know, is *ewo*, a thing forbidden to Obatala and his followers because it was while drunk at the beginning of creation that he made disabled bodies. It is his weakness. And so Odumare was disappointed with him when a finished body that looked neither fully male nor female arrived to be animated with life. But Yemoja, feeling guilty for her part in this blunder, offered to specially guide and protect this one as a female, if selected by her *ori*.'

'We have no need for my intervention then?' Baba Alaba asked my most pressing question.

'No. Apetebi confirmed what I couldn't when Oto was a baby. While she does embody aspects of the cosmic gourd enfolding both male and female facets of life, her stone whispered that the form which best favours her destiny in this lifetime is female. Yemoja shall be her guide but she must be taught also to avoid *ewo*, things forbidden to Obatala so as not to purchase trouble in the marketplace of life. That is the bargain of the gods. Those they will favour, first they burden.'

'*Ashé!*' Apetebi nodded and, for the first time, smiled at me.

I slumped with relief. My poor nubby part was safe from Baba Alaba's razor. And wait . . . the gods had pronounced me a girl! Every time Babalawo said the words *she* and *her*, he meant me! My heart did this funny little skip and my breath caught. It was almost too much an abundance of riches. Like ice cream with cake with icing on top.

'Perhaps, as protection from future harm, she could become an acolyte in this shrine.'

I cringed into the wall, every wondrous thing he'd said flying out of my head. What did he mean *acolyte*? That I'd forever live there at the *Ifa* grove? What about school at St Christopher's? Who would lend me comics? The encyclopedias I'd devoured from aardvark to zygote told about a huge world out there, with pyramids and waterfalls and northern lights. Worst of all, Mother would never let Wura visit. I'd lose her forever. And she was everything. My best friend, my light, my defender. She made me laugh and sang me songs and blew bubble-kisses when life was hard. And she needed me, too! I chased the spiders out of her room and ate half the beans she hated off her plate when Mother wasn't looking. We belonged together. I hid my rising sobs in my palms.

'Why so sad, child?' Babalawo was back beside me.

'I don't want to live apart from my sister.'

'No one will force you. We're just thinking of ways to keep you safe. I'll ask your mother to bring you monthly from now on. Is that better?'

'Yes.' I sagged with relief. 'And the . . . examination. I know I'm not normal and it was necessary but it felt horrible. Please, no more?'

'Never again. We got all the information we need. And, remember this, you're both normal and special.'

'So you all think I'm really a girl?' After years of being beaten for even hinting at this, it still seemed like a trick. Like he'd laugh and say, *April fool!* even though it was October.

'It's the choice your *ori* made.'

Joy blossomed in my chest. I hugged it close. Mother now had to agree, because Babalawo said so.

'Can we please go now?' I was desperate to take off the clinging wet sheet.

Babalawo nodded. I accepted the small gourd Apetebi handed me. The cool drink tasted fresh and green, like the scent of rain on long-dried earth.

'Come.' Babalawo held out his hand. The herbal drink was so soothing my feet seemed to plant themselves in the earth with each step only to get torn out again by the roots. In his hut, I lay on a straw mat and fell fast asleep.

Before Mother picked me up, Babalawo tied three strands of beads around my waist.

One was as transparent as water. Two gleamed all the colours of a peacock feather. 'These represent the deities your *ori* selected to guide you through life,' he said. 'Guard them close.' While I admired their sparkle against the bony hollows of my hips, he also tied a small, bell-shaped silver amulet on a leather strap onto my upper arm beneath my sleeve.

'Listen, Oto. These prophecies you must fold secure within your heart for when the time is right. First, *it is in the heat of the forest fire that the audacity of the dehinkorun plant is released.* Second, *if you remain fixated on where you fell, you will never figure out where you slipped.* Third, *only after your own self is claimed may your soul abide safely with you.*'

A thrilling, terrifying sense of power encircled me and I was swirled high in the air. Around me hovered a full suit of traditional armour like I'd seen on Benin warriors in my history book. It snapped – helmet, neck guard, wrist guard, chest plate, ankle bands – into place on my body and I knew in that shining moment that I could cross my arms and stop bullets mid-air like Wonder Woman. I'd never felt this before. Then it was gone and I was ordinary me again, standing wide-eyed in Babalawo's mud hut. Remember this also, he said, *the eagle raised as a chicken must one day recognize itself and choose to fly.*

Mother had been in such a hurry, horn honking outside, Mr Driver revving up before I'd shut the car door, that Babalawo barely had time to tell her to bring me monthly before we'd zoomed off as if escaping a raging fire. On the long drive home, I pretended to be asleep while thoughts chased around my head like harmattan leaves. How Mother used to wash Wura top to toe, armpit to armpit but always stopped at my waist and said, 'Wash down there.' How I'd thought it was just another thing mothers only did for girls till I understood she simply couldn't stand to be reminded of my difference. Yet Babalawo's wife had examined me and wasn't disgusted. She'd said there was nothing to be ashamed of, when shame was all I'd ever known. Most importantly, Babalawo finally had answers. Why else would Mother take me to him all these years if not to help us? I allowed myself the rare joy of my favourite daydream in which some miraculous event happened to make Mother become even half as loving to me as she was to Wura. For that, I'd endure almost anything.

The words tumbled out as soon as we were in the living room: how Babalawo said I was special, not cursed. How Obatala made me after Eshu tricked him with palm wine and Yemoja fought for me and my *ori* selected her to guide and protect me.

'See, Mother? I was right. They said I'm meant to be a girl!' I pulled off my T-shirt to show her my beautiful beads. My shiny silver armband.

Mother's teeth clenched on an indrawn hiss. Her hand flew at my face and I braced, flinching. The blow never landed. Terror flashed in her eyes but vanished so fast, I must have imagined it.

'Aiii! Jehovah!' she screamed. 'Get out and remove those disgusting fetish things and throw them in the dustbin. Now!' She was trembling, eyes wild. I edged around her towards the door, glad we were in the living room, *downstairs*.

'So this is their final plan to destroy me, eh?' she whispered as I fled.

That night, I couldn't sleep for thinking. Who were 'they', who were planning to destroy Mother? Why take me to Babalawo if it wasn't to help figure me out? What made her halt the hand she'd raised to hit me, looking as if she'd seen her own ghost? *Nothing* had ever stopped her before. I'd fetched my armband from its hiding place, slid it on, and felt a bit less heartbroken. It was as if Babalawo was there willing me to be an eagle, not a chicken. Telling me they'd investigated and concluded that I was special, not cursed. Clearly, he'd have a hard time convincing Mother. I could barely wait for a month to pass. Maybe hearing it from Babalawo himself would change things.

5

NOW

1991 (AGE 14)

The ISS cafe is open on three sides and brightly lit, filled with rows of tables and benches. As students pile their trays with food and swing familiarly into place beside their friends, it's quickly clear who's new. This obviously is the place to see and be seen, the beating heart of all things *gist*-worthy in ISS. The scandal-dissection centre. I join the serving line, trying to look as if I belong.

After filling my plate with macaroni and fish stew, I discover a new problem. All the new boys and girls are year ones, huddled separately at a pair of tables. I don't belong there. I spy one open spot at a table with boys of varying ages. Relieved, I head there. Then the boy sitting beside it turns around and I freeze. *Bayo!* I'd know that bush rat face anywhere! When he left my old school, I was simply relieved. I never thought to ask where he went. His eyes narrow in recognition and I immediately want to whisk myself elsewhere in a blink like they do on *Star Trek*. *Oh God, which room is he in?* Water spills out of my cup as my tray shakes. If I keep hovering, I'll attract attention. Which is the last thing I need. I'm dissolving into silent panic when someone taps my shoulder.

'Bit crowded over there, isn't it?' The boy tips his head towards the tables. He's also holding a tray with macaroni and fish stew.

I nod. My eyes are saucers. I can't help it. I know exactly how it looks because Wura's get the same when she's anxious.

'I'm Derin,' he says, smiling gravely, 'just arrived yesterday. You look new, too. Wanna go sit on the steps?'

I'm trying not to stare. His *dada* locks corkscrew every which way – a hairstyle that demands a certain level of audacity in Nigeria. On a half-*oyinbo* person, it's practically a declaration. Of what, I immediately want to know. I'm failing at not staring, riveted by warm greenish-brown eyes gleaming behind round glasses. They fill the world, crowding out everything and everyone else. Calm flows from him and blankets me. It's the strangest thing. My head nods, yes. I'll definitely follow him to the steps. I have the irrational feeling I'd follow him anywhere.

The steps lead down the side of the cafe towards a row of kiosks. A few students are dotted here and there. He's clearly already found the renegade corner.

Derin sets down his tray and picks a couple of flyers from a nearby pile. He hands me one to sit on. My breath whooshes out in pure relief.

His grin is sympathetic. 'Being new when you're not first year is the worst. I've just transferred from a school in Lagos.'

His startling honesty frees my voice. 'Thanks for the rescue.'

'No problem. You were looking how I felt yesterday – like you wanted the floor to open up.' His soft chuckle makes me smile.

'I'm Oto. Third year.'

'Akinro?'

'Yes! How did you know?'

'Snuck a look in the register yesterday while the admin lady talked to my dad. Pleased to meet you, roommate.'

'You're in 312?' I gasp.

'Yep. With Cornelius.'

'So pleased to meet you, too,' I say, not caring that my smile probably looks delirious. It makes sense they'd room us late-joiners – as people who transfer from elsewhere are called – together. Still, how am I this lucky?

The first weeks of term are a mad confusion of places to be and things to do. I worry I'll never get names right or remember which seniors are cool and which to steer clear of, which days cafe food is best avoided, which kiosks sell the best snacks. *Blurb!*, it turns out, is a wickedly brilliant satire magazine published monthly by a student committee. Here, they organize soirees (aren't those just parties?) and the theatre group performs popular plays to which families and local dignitaries are invited.

All students must pick an afternoon activity. Derin joins the chess club. He was junior champion at his former school. I shudder to see Bayo in charge of the football line-up and promptly sign up for mixed volleyball. He's bulked up so much he looks like he could fell a tree simply by running into it, and has apparently been nicknamed The Terminator for reasons I'm sure I don't want to know. So far, he's acted as if he doesn't know me. I'm mercifully too uncool or something for the tight group he hangs around with – mostly junior boys who seem only to ask how high whenever he says jump.

The art studio quickly becomes my second home. It's even more special because art is one of the few electives Derin and I share (since we room together, we're assigned to separate home classes). Mr Dickson, the art teacher, is a small, neat Ghanaian man with a trim moustache. He wears bifocals which he lowers, the better to glare at you, if he thinks you're not making full use of your potential in his class. Though he's unfailingly fair, everyone knows not to mess with him. He teaches all the levels and seems too knowledgeable for a secondary school, however exclusive. *Draw the idea of a fruit*, he might say. Then as he walks around, giving a nudge here, a correction there, *must an orange be round?* He's been known to sometimes quote poetry! I request extra homework, overjoyed to learn advanced techniques. One time I'm trying out a new method of adding highlights to a still life of periwin-kles in a glass of water when he stops by my easel and spends a good while thoughtfully rubbing a finger across his moustache. 'Superb work, Akinro,' he says. 'Superb work. Keep it up and you'll go far.'

If someone had turned off the cafe lights that evening, I know I'd have glowed in the dark.

I'm sketching away during evening prep when Derin, face half hidden behind his *dada* hair, peers at me sideways and asks if he can read me a few lines from a story he's working on to 'sound them out'. The Derin I'm getting to know is *never* hesitant. This clearly is something he doesn't share easily.

His mellow voice takes me into the world of a boy who must overcome his fear and, using an ancient map, travel to dangerous lands to seek the cure for a mysterious illness that's turning his mother transparent. Derin stops at the part where her hands are passing through everything and it takes all her will to hold his baby brother. I love it and ask for more. His ears flush red and he beams like it's the best thing he's ever heard.

Days later, I present him with a scene of the village in his story, as his words painted it in my head, down to the black and white goat chewing on a thorny bush outside the family hut. My stomach cramps as he stares at it for the longest time. I get why he was so nervous to read me his story. His opinion matters more than anyone else's, except maybe Mr Dickson's.

He finally looks up, catlike eyes aglow. 'You're amazing! That's exactly how I see it!'

'Well, thanks. *Your* story was inspiring.' My heart soars.

Missing Wura is like an itch I can't properly reach to scratch. Boarding students are permitted to use the phone box beside the admin lady's office for up to five minutes each week. It's better than nothing, but our time is always up too soon.

She asks if there's anyone I used to know. Only Bayo, I say, and some other girl whose name I can't remember. She goes silent.

'It's okay. He avoids me,' I quickly add.

'Mommy is a lot calmer,' Wura says during another brief chat. 'She has opened a lace fabric shop in the new shopping centre near our house. As long as no one mentions you or Daddy, you'd hardly recognize her!' Then, 'God, Oto, I'm sorry. I didn't even think!'

'It's okay, Wura. I'm just glad things are going well.'

Other than missing me, she's still having a great time in school, she says. I reach through the bond we've shared for as long as we've breathed, to sense how she *really* feels, and meet blankness. I'm flung back into the lonely terror of that first day in kindergarten when they tore her hand from mine, parting us into different classes as Mother demanded. The weeks we wailed miserably for each other. Now it's as if more than distance separates us. I blink away tears. It's for the best. Wura needs space to be herself and I must learn to stand on my own.

Finally doing great at keeping all things Lori locked down tight, I find myself surprised in moments of just being. I even dare, the occasional lunchtime Derin is off doing something chess-related, to sit with a mixed crowd at the cafe. It's all great until a girl makes some joke and it's a while before I realize the shockingly high-pitched giggle is coming from me. I quickly turn it into a cough and glance furtively around, feeling like someone caught with her left hand in the stew pot. The noisy table of boys nearby suddenly seem to find me more interesting than whatever they were discussing. I lower my head and focus on my food.

Next day I'm walking past some of the boys who stared at me in the cafe. They're whistling rudely at a second-year girl who, for some reason, already has enormous breasts hanging like pawpaw fruits from her thin chest, so she looks like she might topple over. Their eyes slide a challenge at me. *Join in. Do it and prove that you have balls.*

It's a look I understand. One that boys only ever direct at other boys. An assumption that my anatomy renders me susceptible to such dares, that I'd do anything to justify my possession of said body parts.

Nervously, hating myself, I squeak out a weak trill. She later points us out to her older brother who tells us to cut it out or he'll flatten every one of our faces.

Sodden with guilt, I drop an unsigned note addressed to the girl into the general mailbox. It says, *Sorry we whistled. You're all right just as you are.* I wish I had the courage to apologize to her face. Wura would. As would Derin. He'd never have whistled in the first place. I'm already like a dice trying to fit into a jar of marbles. With each shake-up, more bits of my true self get knocked away. If I don't watch it, soon I'll turn into Bayo.

6

BEFORE

1989 (AGE 12)

The magic of Babalawo's amulets must have gone to my head because days later, when Mother took us to the market to get new shoes, swearing our feet were growing by the minute, a wayward thought slid into my mind and took root. I trailed after her and Wura, lingering behind the woman hawking *moimoi* from a huge basin on her head. The second they were out of sight, I zipped to the best toy seller's stall and pretended I needed a gift for my sister. If they caught me, I'd shout, *Surprise!* Not that Wura would be fooled, and I could only afford this because she refused any pocket money unless I got the same. I'd rather that didn't change. I quickly rolled the slim box into my bulky sweater and hurried to catch up.

That night I jammed a chair under my door and took a long sniff of my new doll's sweet, shiny smell. Her fuschia dress made her dark skin glow. I named her Ebun, which meant gift, because she was my gift to myself, to Lori, whose *ori* had wisely selected the goddess Yemoja to guide her through life. I whispered secrets into Ebun's ear. In my imagination, she could go anywhere, be anyone she wanted. An air hostess. An astronaut. An artist.

A month slid by. I kept anxiously waiting for Mother to wake me early for a visit to Babalawo but dared not ask. One morning, Wura and I, still in our pyjamas, were playing Whot! in her room and enjoying the delicious breakfast smell wafting up from the kitchen. She was finally and gleefully winning when Mother opened the door and peeked through.

'I need you both to take some clothes to the driver's wife to mend.'

I glanced at Wura and knew inside she was rolling her eyes. Mother could stop using that tired old excuse anytime. It was like that trick played on children. An adult who wanted you out of her hair for a while sent you to another to fetch the *jenjoko* leaf and not return without it. The other adult made a big show of going to order the leaf. You waited and waited, because the *jenjoko* leaf didn't exist. We knew Maami Akinro was being kept waiting impatiently at the gate while the gateman checked 'to see if madam is around'. Mother likely suspected she was spying on us for Father.

Wura pretended not to hear. I was already on my feet.

'Wuraola! Get up and do as I say!'

'I don't want to go!'

Mother gave Wura a measured look which she returned with interest. 'You will go. No argument.'

'But I'm hungry!'

'You'll eat later. Get dressed and be downstairs in five minutes or else!' The door slammed behind her.

Wura stomped to her dresser and grabbed her favourite doll. I, too, picked a floppy one whose ropy hair would be fun to plait. I'd become quite expert since getting my Ebun.

'Put that back!' Wura hissed.

'Come on, Mrs Driver doesn't really watch us. We can play behind their shed.'

'No! Remember the last time? She looked at you funny for weeks. You're lucky she didn't tell Mommy!'

'But we can be more careful. We don't have to—'

Wura snatched the floppy doll and slammed it back on the dresser. 'I swear sometimes you're driving Mommy mad on purpose! She's only cruel when you pull this crazy stuff! People just can't handle it!' Her voice wobbled, thin and high.

'I'm trying, okay?' My knuckles rubbed into my eyeballs. She was right, I guess, to be terrified. Just before our birthday, I'd spent weeks practising football alone then plucked up the courage to stand in the St Christopher's school team line at break time. When I'd stepped forward, Bayo, a giant of an older boy with a face so like a bush rat's you could practically see those twitching whiskers, shoved me aside. He'd joined us from another school the year before.

'We only want strong, proper boys on our team,' he'd sneered. 'Maybe the girls will let you join their *suwe!*' The other boys had laughed. No one had challenged him. I'd burned with shame, reminded again that they bullied and ignored me not just because I seemed an easy target, but because something else about me disturbed them, despite my best efforts to act 'normal'. Was it the way I walked or talked? Or something more blurry – like loving singing lessons while most boys drove the teacher crazy with pranks? Bayo's voice had also been mean in a whole new grown-up way I'd never heard before.

'It's for your sake, too, can't you see?' Wura sighed. I once more considered telling her what Babalawo had said but then she'd insist on seeing my amulets and she was terrible at keeping secrets from Mother. Plus, I'd have to talk about the examination part, which was best forgotten.

As we turned to leave, she put her own doll back on the dresser.

Mother practically shoved us out but she was a little too late. As we trudged towards the short path leading to the boys' quarters where Mrs Driver lived, I heard the purring rev of Maami Akinro's Mercedes pulling through the gates. When I glanced back, the dark orbs of her sunglasses-shaded eyes followed me.

I was expecting Mama Ondo to arrive on the heels of Maami's visit as usual, but Aunty Abiye, Mother's cousin, came instead. She was a Temple of Holy Fire member, too. That night, their loud prayers filled the house till I fell asleep.

Something thumped against my window, startling me awake as harmattan wind rattled the house. It sounded like a bird. It was still deep night. Needing to pee, I tiptoed towards the bathroom at the end of the passageway. As I passed Mother's door I heard Aunty Abiye say, 'Mama Ondo told me a spiritual battle is upending your home, that you need help with your son. What's going on?'

Noiseless as air, I flowed down and put my ear to the gap between door and floor.

'Look, as I've told my mother repeatedly, my sorrows are mine to bear.'

'Really? She's getting old. Yet sick as she is, all her worry is for you. How long will you panic and send for her whenever your mother-in-law visits, eh? Are we not cousins? What burden can be so terrible you can't share it with me?'

Mother stayed silent.

'Tell me' – Aunty Abiye's voice softened – 'and I swear on my daughter's head it won't go beyond this room.'

If Aunty Abiye swore on her daughter's head, she meant it.

'It's a long and frightening story. Are you prepared?'

My nose tickled and I gulped down my breath, trying desperately not to sneeze.

'Would your mother have sent me if she didn't think I could help?'

'Then I'll tell you straight. Oto is abnormal down there. That child has the parts of a boy in front, but behind, God help me, he has a . . . a . . .'

'A *what*?'

'A vagina.'

'Holy Mother of God!'

I shivered. Put like that, I sounded hideous.

'That terrible day the prophetess Mama hired as a midwife pulled him out of me, she screamed. In a trance she said, "Mourn, mother! Mourn! For your true son from heaven was stolen from your womb by worshippers of Satan and replaced with an *emere* demon."'

'Jehovah have mercy!' Aunty Abiye's voice shook.

'She said he is an instrument fashioned to destroy me, however innocent he appears. That only Mama's prayers saved Wura from being turned, too. I was devastated. After nine hours of hard labour!

How could I love one and not the other, *hein*? See how they look alike! What was I supposed to do? Neglect him to death? For days I cared for them equally, hoping that somehow, this horror on his body would vanish. Mama spent nights in vigil at the Temple of Holy Fire, fasting and praying for Jehovah to convince me that the prophetess was right.'

I heard Mother sigh. A soft sob. Silence.

'Th ... then what happened?'

'Ah, Abiye, you won't believe this! The night before their naming ceremony, Wura woke up soiled and crying. I'd run out of nappies and the spare pile was in the guest bedroom, where Maami Akinro, who'd arrived that day, was staying. I tiptoed in, only to find her fast asleep on her back, legs crossed at the ankles, feet resting high against the wall. Her outspread arms lay still, fingers curled in like claws. On the pillow beside her was a small statue, the kind those fetishists make when one twin dies and the other still lives. Its bulging eyes, I swear, were staring right at me.'

'Holy Gabriel, Holy Raphael! Seraphim of light protect us!' Aunty Abiye stuttered.

'Everyone knows that's the position *osoronga* witches use to send their bird familiar out on a night mission to ruin someone's life. I fled back to my room, where I sat shaking like someone with epilepsy.'

'Oh, my poor Moji! She probably never heard you. When witches lie like that, their spirits are abroad but their bodies are empty.'

'I held Wura tight, ready to protect her with my life.' Mother sniffled. 'Oto stayed asleep, which was just as well. I couldn't bear to touch him. Who knew if his evil spirit was out flying too? I longed desperately to run to Laitan, who had taken to sleeping in another room, but how do you tell your husband his mother is a witch who planted a changeling in your womb? He'd have thrown me out!'

A loose feeling invaded my stomach. She really believed this of me!

'When I told Mama, she said had I listened to her and spent a week in the temple while pregnant, the prophets could have rooted out Maami Akinro's evil.'

'You made a terrible mistake!'

'Well, now I know! But soon after we met, Laitan banned me from the temple, calling it "a crude institution". You know how he likes to use big *oyinbo* words.'

I did. Words like *besmirch*.

'So that's why you went astray. It has troubled us so much.'

'Oh, how I've wept for my true son who never stood a chance before the marrow of life was sucked from his tiny bones! How my heart hardened against that thing they put in his place! Mama said the prophetess had a vision that we should quietly drop him at an orphanage before the naming, and just tell people he'd died in his sleep. Laitan refused. Better to hide him in plain sight, he said, because if his condition was ever traced back to us, the Akinro family name would be tainted with abnormality for generations.'

A roaring had started in my head, like wind before a terrible storm. Orphanage! They'd considered dumping me there. Like rubbish.

'At least you have a good daughter.' Aunty Abiye sighed.

'Wura is the joy of my life! Unfortunately she just won't accept that her brother's aim is her destruction. That he is being controlled by evil forces beyond her understanding. I do all I can to protect her from him but it is never enough.'

'And we all thought your life was a bed of roses!'

'Indeed! All those jealous women eyeing me sideways at the naming ceremony and all I could think was, *If only you knew!* By evening I was so worn with hiding grief and pretending happiness, I'd escaped with Mama and the babies to my bedroom, only to be followed by Maami Akinro and two elderly aunts from Laitan's village. I could smell Mama's terror of Maami Akinro stinking through her clothes like sweat. I cursed the tradition that gave her the right to stay in my house. *Give us our son,* one of the aunts said, *so we can wash him properly, as tradition demands.*'

'*Eh!* Those women would have gossiped up and down! What did you do?'

'I was too numb to even answer. Surprisingly, Maami Akinro said, *Our wife is tired, leave her be and return to your homes.*'

'But why?'

'Who knows her game? I just felt like a mouse toyed with by a snake that didn't need a meal just yet. It's been like that ever since. She's always showing up unannounced for no good reason. You see, when I met Laitan, it was rumoured no girl he dated lasted five minutes once Maami Akinro got involved. But our elders say it is reasonably expected during a fight that a ram must sometimes take backward steps to renew its charge. So I got pregnant.'

'*Ayiiee* Moji! Our elders also say when a leopard swaggers a dog does not swagger in response. It flees! You took on a bad enemy.'

'And all for nothing. Would you believe Laitan hasn't touched me since I gave birth? He said I must have done something to turn Oto like that. That I trapped him with my "inferior bloodline"!'

Mother started sobbing. Inside me, something broke.

'That is so bad. He visits, doesn't he?'

'For appearances' sake. He knows even if someone else wanted me, one hint of what I bore will send them running. So I have to obey him and act as if everything is fine. Can you believe he insists I take the boy to Babalawo?'

I gasped, forgetting to be silent. Then froze.

'A *juju* man? But why?'

'Who knows? Just take him there, he said, and your part is done. Last time the boy returned covered in demonic fetishes, and I'm telling you, my life flashed before my eyes! It was like the nightmare I kept having after seeing Maami with her feet on the wall. An *ere ibeji* wearing fetish amulets holding a red parrot feather. It just stared at me and didn't speak, but I knew one word from its mouth and I'd land in my grave!'

'*Oluwa o*! How have you endured this horror in silence?'

'I've not even told you the worst.'

'Worse? There's worse?' Aunty Abiye's voice rang with alarm.

'The day before their birthday, I caught Oto wearing Wura's dress. He began that disgusting behaviour when he was younger but I thought I'd beaten it out of him.'

'*Abomination!*'

'Can you imagine what people would say? Now you know why I call Mama all the time. I don't know what else to do.'

'This must end. There has to be a solution.'

'Find it, Abiye, and I won't hesitate.'

The scuff of slippers on the rug had me shooting into the bathroom, heart hammering. I needed Wura. Needed to hear her confirm the earth was still round. That someone calling it square didn't make it so. That I was just me. But I sensed her fast asleep. And I was suddenly terrified. She'd always been caught between us both. It seemed a crazy thought, but what if she took Mother's side? Because each time I'd done those 'Lori' things that threatened what was left of our family, I'd sensed her wavering.

Back in my bed, I lay trembling, pieces falling into place like a crazy jigsaw puzzle. Like why Mother sent us to Mrs Driver's house. I'd once asked Emily what happened after we left. She'd said Maami usually took a polite sip of the soft drink Mother offered then asked after me and Wura. Mother would lie that we were out with friends. After a bit of small talk, Maami would leave.

The few times Maami got to see us, Mother never took her eyes off the sweets she'd placed in our hands for a second. 'What do you say, children?' Mother would ask.

'Thank you, Maami Akinro,' we'd reply.

'Good. Put your sweets on the table. You can have some later. Off you go now.' The look in her eyes promised dire consequences otherwise.

By the time we returned, both sweets and Maami Akinro would be gone; which was annoying, because she always brought *goody-goody*. In all folk stories, a witch who wanted to convert a little girl gave her something to eat. Now I understood. Mother was desperate to protect Wura from being 'turned' by Maami.

Then there was the statue Mother said she saw on Maami's pillow. I'd once asked Babalawo about the statues in his hut and there'd been an *ere ibeji*, a wooden image representing a dead twin, which the mother fed and clothed like a real one, so the remaining twin could be persuaded to live. Why would Maami Akinro carry one about?

As for Father insisting I was taken to Babalawo, it made no sense when he couldn't even stand the sight of me, and scorned what he called 'primitive native religion'. His hypocrisy at least spared me the orphanage. I remembered watching the news when the state governor visited one to make an annual donation on International Children's Day. Thin screaming babies. Silent children in oversized clothes with sad, hollow eyes. Exactly how I'd look knowing no one loved me enough to keep me, and no one might ever come to take me home. I wouldn't even have known Wura existed. They'd have separated us forever! That rocketed me out of bed, desperate to go and just hear her breathe. I stopped and instead wedged a chair under the handle of my bedroom door, then fetched my treasure box from its hiding place under my bed.

It was calming to open it. Inside was my growing collection of things any reasonably fashionable girl doll should have. Clothes, hairclips, a pyjama set, teeny-tiny closed-toe shoes with high heels, all secretly bought. I remembered the joyful day I'd found an American Airlines stewardess outfit complete with tiny blue travel bag. I'd laughed along with the toy seller as she joked that a brother as generous as me deserved a discount. Now it seemed impossible that I'd ever laugh again.

I wedged my doll, Ebun, in my lap and began braiding her hair – section, over, under, loop – pushing away the picture of Mother huddled up with Aunty Abiye and Mama Ondo, all planning the perfect, permanent solution to her life-ruining problem.

7

NOW

1991 (AGE 14)

After that giggling incident in the cafe, I make sure to lower my voice. To not laugh out loud. It seems to work. Life carries on and I'm grateful for the easy rhythm of my days. One softly melding into the next, full of discoveries with Derin, whispered talks and simple delight in each other's presence. I've never known such peace.

I'm in the laundry room alone one evening, hurriedly dropping off my clothes before prep because I'd earlier forgotten. If I miss my assigned day, I'd have to wear dirty clothes all week. The laundry block faces away from everything and is farthest away in a lonely corner of the school compound, surrounded by thick bushy plants. No one comes here at night. They say *ogbanje* spirits often visit. That terrifying creatures hold monthly dances after dark, hopping about on one leg each, and whoever sees them will forever have to work harder to evade an early death.. I'm fourteen, I remind myself. Old enough to know the difference between fact and fiction. *Hahaha*, says the little voice in my mind. *Really?*

Someone dashes in and stops wide-eyed. His eyes are blank circles of distress and he's trembling. He's a year one boarding student on the first floor. I've seen him around but don't know him.

'Please, please … *shhh*,' is all he says, before diving under a pile of dirty sheets and keeping utterly still. I stare open-mouthed in confusion till a big, hulking boy strides in. This one I know, and immediately want to join that boy under the laundry.

'What are you doing here?' Bayo asks. Not just Bayo, *The Terminator*, my mind unhelpfully reminds me. So named, I eventually heard, for his relentless commitment to finding ways around ISS's no bullying rule.

Along with the sort of information carried by the wind, like not to even think of breaking bounds when a certain teacher is on duty, he's known for finding sly, shame-inducing ways to make people sorry they crossed him. Like flushing someone's head in a toilet after peeing in it. My barbed wire scars remind me I didn't even see him coming.

'I'm ... er ... bringing in my dirty clothes?' That should be obvious but I imagine it wouldn't be wise to point it out.

'Did you see anyone come in?' His eyes narrow.

'No.'

'Damn!' He mashes a fist into his palm. 'You're sure?'

'Erm ... actually, a boy ran past a minute ago.' I point left with a finger that only trembles slightly. 'He went that way.'

His eyes scan the room, then he smiles a slow, cold smile that makes me picture scales and a forked, slithering tongue. Everything in me wants to run.

He pockets his hands and saunters out, whistling.

I wait ten minutes. The pile of laundry stays motionless.

'I think he's gone. You can come out now.'

The boy climbs out. He's thin-faced, delicate-looking in a way that some people from the Delta are. Something about his mute, rabbit-like terror reminds me of Rashid. I long to ease that terrible look from his face.

'Are you okay?'

'Thank you,' he says. 'I must go.' He flees.

That's when I see the grass stain print of his shoes. They now lead out where they'd only led in.

I send up an earnest prayer to God and Yeyemi and the universe for trouble to stop finding me.

*

Either my amazing ISS luck continues to hold or my prayers have been answered, because after days of desperately glancing over my shoulders and getting so jumpy Derin starts looking at me with a question in his eyes, I realize Bayo seems to have vanished. Turns out he's been suspended for the rest of the term. No one knows exactly why since he's apparently always in trouble for one thing or another. I let out a breath I didn't know I'd been holding.

'Maybe this *oyinbo* can eat pepper, o!' Chidi, a third year boy, who fancies himself a real comedian, picks on Derin one afternoon. 'See his *jajajaga* head!'

He's mocking Derin's riotous head of reddish-brown *dada* locks, making a play on the joke that *oyinbo* people cannot eat pepper or they burn. Break is almost over, and we were walking back to our separate classes. Several students stop, scenting a good fight. I freeze, recognizing the bad feel of this.

Cool as coconut water, Derin says, 'Give me one good reason why that's your problem.'

Nonplussed, Chidi looks around for support. Instead, everyone awaits his reply to this clear-headed challenge.

'Because you look like *wẹrẹ-abugije*,' he finally counters. 'In fact, I heard there's a free room in Aro mental hospital!'

People burst out laughing. *Wẹrẹ-abugije* is an insulting name for a type of crazy person who roams the streets with reeking, fly-trapping dreads matted from years of neglect. Madness carries a terrible shame. Chidi is definitely looking for a fight. Unsurprising, since he's one of Bayo's gang.

'Who hates music here? Raise your hand!' Derin says, one hand in his pocket, the other casually raking through said hair.

They look at each other. *What?* is written on every face.

'Let me be specific. Who thinks Bob Marley was a madman?'

It's very in to love Bob Marley, deeply uncool to not. Most students have openly swayed to his music at some gathering or other.

'See, Chidi? Your logic is flawed. *Dada* hair rocks!' Derin's casual tone ices over as he adds, 'And if you think I owe you something, state it. Otherwise, don't mess with me.'

Derin walks off and I follow, awed. Checkmate! In a culture so riddled with nuance that 'good morning' can mean ten different things from an actual greeting to *may you die a painful death and be consumed by wild animals*, it's unwise to challenge a person who, in addition to pointing out the elephant in the room will bluntly state its scale and girth. Though people will surely shrug and say, *He's half oyinbo – what else do you expect?* Derin's outspokenness has earned him respect.

I glance back to see Chidi standing alone as people drift off to more entertaining things.

'You were amazing!' I say.

'Thanks.' Derin grins ruefully, looking for a moment far wearier than any fourteen-year-old should.

Longing to comfort him, I say, 'I get hassled too, all the time. Just because I'm quiet and well . . . different.'

Derin stops. Stares at the ground. 'Yeah. I always get the bullies who need to show the half-*oyinbo* he's nothing special.'

'Is that why you transferred here?'

'No. Dad wanted to give me a shot at passing the International Baccalaureate exams, and the schools cost more in Lagos.'

'I wish I had your courage.'

'I don't know . . . I just fake it. I'm not always brave. I used to go home in tears, as a kid. Then my dad gave me a book about an albino donkey the others bullied because he looked different. One day he caught sight of a zebra and became convinced life would be better if only he was one. So he painted on black stripes and the zebras welcomed him. Thing was, everyday he had to repaint his stripes in secret, and could never really play or roll around in the grass or do any of the fun things they did because he was scared they'd see who he really was. So he still wasn't happy. One day he got caught in a thunderstorm and the stripes washed off and his new zebra friends turned mean, too. But after the storm, he saw his own reflection in the still pool and how his coat shone and his pink eyes sparkled like gems. In the water his head bore a long, spiralling horn that glittered gold. He understood that neither the donkeys nor zebras could see his whole, amazing self because deep inside, he was a unicorn. He was unique. He decided from then on to just be himself. He went off and had many adventures and discovered a big world of animals who were different and doing just fine.'

'Wow!' It's like he just told my story. Out of nowhere comes the thought, *If there's anyone you can safely tell your secret, you've met him.* I shudder. Maybe later. I've only just found him.

'See, if you act like your uniqueness is a great thing and you couldn't care less about their opinion, they eventually give up. And that feels so good you do it again and again until you truly believe it. Sometimes I imagine I'm a planet, blazing and unique and determined to keep my own orbit no matter what.'

No one else would put it like that. I imagine myself a planet too, all soft greens and happy hazy blues, orbiting the sun, content and at peace. The face of the sun looks just like Derin's.

After that, we're wholly inseparable. Like partners in a three-legged race. Though he has classmates he's friendly with, it's me he hangs around with after class.

We never seem to run out of things talk about. Cornelius is always telling us to shut it at night so he can sleep. And the things Derin knows! After a literature assignment analyzing Amos Tutuola's literally out-of-this-world characters in *The Palm-Wine Drinkard*, Derin says he overheard his dad telling a fellow Unilag professor that had Tutuola not been in Nigeria, and had it not become recreational after his time, he'd suspect him of taking LSD. Derin had no idea what LSD was and says his dad declined, for once, to explain, so of course he went digging for information. We pretend to be tripping and fall all over the floor and each other in dramatic poses, laughing and talking nonsense. Cornelius sighs and pulls his pillow over his head, though I swear I heard him chortle.

It's as if our bookworm minds were created to delight each other. Aliens – for once here's someone who agrees with me that it's silly to think humans are the ultimate intelligent creatures in the universe. In him I find a fellow mourner of the great, vanished groundnut pyramids, smaller, edible echoes of the wonders in Egypt, which once dominated parts of the northern Nigerian skyline. Each was reputedly made of around fifteen thousand full-size sacks! All we've have left are pictures, some immortalized on naira notes.

During one of our many slow rambling walks back to the dorm after prep, I find myself exposing bizarre childhood oddities I've never shared with another soul. Not even Wura.

'Guess what? I once insisted in kindergarten that I knew what the colour pink tastes like – because I *did*. My teacher wasn't amused!'

Derin laughs, delighted. 'When I was six, I read about Icarus and became convinced not only could I fly, but I wouldn't make the stupid mistakes he did if I just got my calculations right. I created wings out of random things: plantain leaves, paper. Jumped off tables and cars and trees. Dad had to leash me till that idea passed!'

As we laugh, he slings an arm across my shoulders. I love just how right and natural it feels.

I miss him during Christmas break. Seeing Wura makes up for it, though it's much harder to live in my shell like I used to. I've missed her like I imagine people miss a limb they've learned to do without. As always, when we're together, it feels as if the world will always be whole. We spend days catching up on each other's stories. Her new best friend, how much she loves Home Economics, Agric Science and Physics but hates History. The cute older boys already asking her out. She's popular as ever. Any party she doesn't attend is apparently considered a fail. We sometimes end up fast asleep in one bed – which predictably drives Mother crazy. We dance to our precious collection of music videos, happy to touch hands and bump hips and laugh at our old jokes, bubbling over with the joy of being together again. There's unquestionably a part of my soul shaped only for her.

But how we've changed! I only have to look at Wura to see how my cheekbones have become sharper. How we're filling in around the hips, looking less like string beans with butts. 'We're getting matching curves!' I joke, and icy silence reigns for the rest of the day. I still feel sick with misery whenever she purposely shuts me out. I've been around Derin's forthrightness so much I'm forgetting myself.

Later, I'm rambling on about something or other when she snaps, '*Haba!* Derin this, Derin that. Keep it up and people will think you're his shadow or something.'

'You're just jealous!' I shoot back, surprised and hurt. *Or something? What does that even mean?*

She flounces out in a huff.

Do I really talk about him that much? Would others think it's abnormal?

Later, I offer to take out Wura's long braids, a tedious task she dislikes. It just isn't worth spending our precious time together angry. Her head rests against my knee as she sits half dozing on her bedroom carpet, while I rub coconut oil into her hair before gently unloosing each braid. She exhales a soft snore and I smile. Even drooling onto my lap, she's infinitely precious.

I read and paint, torn between longing to be back in ISS and gladness to be with Wura. My holiday art project is to create a perfect portrait of Yeyemi. I haven't given up trying, and I've learned new techniques. I fear that, like my sister, she's slipping further away from me as time goes by. I weep reading *Koku Baboni* by Kola Onadipe, about an unwanted twin who, after being left in the forest to die, is rescued, grows up, and goes in search of his mother, only to discover she'd loved him and never wanted to give him up.

When Mother isn't at the Temple of Holy Fire, she spends the day at her new fabric shop. I stay out of her way when she's home. Our silent agreement is clear. I keep up my end, she leaves me alone. She's even occasionally civil, usually after someone compliments her on having a son brilliant enough to be in ISS.

Wura rushes sobbing into my room one evening. She was out with Mother and I wasn't invited.

'What's wrong?'

'Daddy's wife gave birth to twin boys. We've had new siblings for weeks and didn't even know!'

My first thought is they must be healthy and perfect, if Father is sticking around.

'Every day I've missed him so,' Wura whispers, two big tears rolling down her cheeks. 'We've been replaced, haven't we?'

I wish I could turn into a lion and corner Father. Give him a piece of my mind while he shook with terror. Would it kill him to call Wura every now and then?

I pull her to the window seat where we now barely fit and tell her it's Father's loss if he wants to miss the joy in her cakes and the sweetness of her voice. Her beautiful face and smart brain.

Mother becomes a hurricane, crying and slamming things for two days straight, refusing to wash or eat. It's never before been this bad. Even as I can't help feeling sorry for her, I stay well out of her reach. When she throws herself on the ground and won't get up, Wura calls Mama Ondo, who is sick again and can't come. She calls Aunty Abiye next and an hour later, two prophetesses arrive and take Mother away. She spends three days at the temple, leaving us in Emily's care. When she returns, she's no longer raging. Just icily withdrawn. Her *sutana*'s sash hangs off the sharp bones of her hips.

At dinner, while I quietly eat, head down, Wura stubbornly refuses to take a bite unless Mother does. 'I'm already missing a father,' she angrily pleads. 'Must I lose you, too?'

As 1992 slips in, I mostly cease to exist for them both. They need each other and I'm just a reminder of everything that went wrong, though Wura would rather stab her own eye than say so. I count the minutes till I can return to ISS and sanity.

8

BEFORE

1989 (AGE 12)

St Christopher's school library was a closet. Each time I looked up, the walls had slunk closer. The magic combination of books, silence and dusty-ink smell normally eased my troubles but Gulliver's Flying Island of Laputa simply couldn't compete with the idea of a flying Maami Akinro. Or me as her evil apprentice. Rumours of witchcraft were one thing – every other person suspected their mother-in-law or the market-stall neighbour whose yams sold suspiciously better. It was entirely another thing to know Mother believed I was literally out flying on night missions trying to harm her and Wura.

Not long ago, Wura and I secretly recorded and watched that movie *The Omen*. We were so terrified we slept clutching each other, shaking like *akamu*. Now instead of the ambassador's wife, I saw Mother full of fear and hatred, convinced I was a changeling. Instead of Damien from *The Omen*, it was me the ambassador tried to sacrifice on a church altar, convinced he wasn't trying to murder a human child. Even after Mother shoved me down the stairs, I'd thought I was just a disappointment, and somehow, that could be overcome. But this? How did I fight this? A wet circle appeared on the pages of *Gulliver's Travels*, followed by another. I dashed the tears away. Aunty Abiye had left first thing, glaring a hole in the back of my head as I'd sat in front while Mr Driver took her first to the motor park before dropping us off at school. Wura had kept looking from me to her, sensing something was seriously off, but I'd kept my head down and my mouth shut and pretended I wasn't even in that car but in a rocket on its way to the moon.

I desperately needed the world to make sense. Mother's reasoning for my condition was a nightmare I couldn't seem to wake up from. Babalawo's was a myth I longed to believe; the way it used to sweeten my stomach to think sunshine on a rainy day meant somewhere, a leopard was giving birth. Or to picture a giant, bearded God thoughtfully taking photos of his creation when lightning struck. Except I learned from Nature Science class that lightning was an electric charge caused by frozen raindrops bumping into each other. If everything in existence had many stories, the real ones and the shadow ones and the fantastical ones, then what was my real story? Where could I find the story that would make Mother love me as she'd longed to when I was born? Or would at least make her stop hating me. Because I'd seen her happy, especially with Wura, and then the laughter bubbled out of her and she was everything warm and wonderful. If only I could make her see that I was just me . . .

Ready to jump clean out of my own mind, I shut the book. Let my feet carry me to the only person who could maybe quiet the buzzing in my head with a song and a bubble-kiss. I'd pull her aside. Tell her everything. I simply couldn't handle this alone.

The playground was noise and speed and laughter, everyone happily *doing* something. A mysterious foreign land to which I never got an invitation. From my very first day in kindergarten, it was as if there were giant rules written in the sky that everyone saw except me. Boys and girls automatically separated at break time but I sidled uncertainly from one group to the other, just wanting to play. With anyone. It started then and never stopped. I'd show up around a group of boys and it was like there was some unspoken signal because they'd all suddenly move elsewhere or talk and play around me as if I wasn't there. If I tried to butt in anyway, I'd get a swollen ankle from being slyly kicked or an 'accidental' elbow would hit my face. Sometimes, just to feel like I belonged, I'd sit under a tree near Wura's friends, reading a book. They called me her sweet, quiet brother and sometimes even smiled my way but I knew it stressed Wura, so I tried not to do it too often.

That afternoon, they'd set up a pretend *olowo-sibi* traditional kitchen and were cooking make-believe pepper soup for some imaginary feast. I grabbed hold of my courage and sat beside Wura. She said nothing, and I felt as welcome as a ghost at its own funeral party, but I was so very *tired*. I needed her right then to get up and take my hand and walk away with me. Unthinking, I picked up a spoon and stirred the mixture of water and brown chalk into which Wura had just added some plasticine 'meat'.

'Wura,' I whispered, 'Could you—'

She turned away, her blazing anger searing me alone. In the sudden silence, I realized what I was doing but couldn't seem to unglue my hand from the spoon. The other girls flickered rapid eye messages to each other. The ball rolled away from the boys but no one chased it. They were all staring at me. Boys, particularly twelve-year-old boys, did *not* join in girls' cooking games. Everyone knew this.

'Go away, Oto!' Wura whispered, the push from her mind so strong she might as well have shoved me. The spoon fell from my hand.

'Wura's brother is a sissy boy!' Bayo shouted. My ears tingled, hot with shame. He'd always been a bully but ever since the day I'd tried to join the football team, it was as if some new smell I personally gave off deeply offended his great ancestors.

'Haha! Wura's brother is a sissy boy!' Bayo yelled again, turning to his friends. Everyone looked from him to Wura, trying to decide who they could least afford to offend. Bayo wasn't much liked but was older and bigger and could be really mean.

My shouders hunched up to my ears. I was made of stupid! I should never have come here. Now all I'd done was drag Wura into trouble.

'Just go away before you make things worse,' Wura hissed quietly, eyes pooling with anger and calculation.

So fast he didn't see it coming, she dipped the spoon in the pot, flicked her wrist, and splatted a huge glob of brown on the back of Bayo's shorts.

'Look, everyone!' she cried. 'Bayo's soiled his pants. Just like a little boy!'

'Yuck!' said one girl.

'Ewww!' went another as they pointed and snickered at the brown goop dripping off his behind. Wura's aim was wickedly precise.

Bayo turned to glare at Wura and the boys behind him immediately howled with laughter. 'Sorry but it looks so real!' managed one boy between spurts that set the others off again.

'Stinky Bayo, smelly pants!' Wura chanted.

'Stinky Bayo, smelly pants!' the girls echoed.

Bayo grabbed his ball and stalked off.

It was clear who had won. Wura ruled in our year. She was the main reason I was mostly left in peace. As long as I stayed invisible.

I slid away, sick that I hadn't dared defend myself. That I wouldn't even know how, because the vulture of Mother's anger long ago pecked away my words and courage. Bayo's sissy boy taunt rang in my ears all the way back to my little corner in the library, where I sat and stared at neatly organized shelves till the books blurred. I never even got to tell Wura the reason our mother hated me.

I began roaming the outer reaches of the school grounds during break times, keeping to quiet places. The barbed wire rear fence was forbidden because it backed directly onto the railway line. Watching a train rumble past on its way to *somewhere that wasn't here* felt hopeful. Inside me was a shuddery pit that kept yawning wider ever since I heard Mother call me a thing. Since Wura also shut me out. And she could keep a grudge like nobody's business.

I skirted carefully around the rolls of barbed wire that lay at intervals on the grass. The groundskeeper must be planning some repairs. He mustn't catch me there or I'd get in trouble. A goods train chugged past, rumbling the ground underneath my feet. Some freight cars were piled with sacks of grain. Cows stuck their heads out the windows of another, horns and all, mooing at the passing school. I fought the silly desire to moo back or, better still, climb over the fence, jump on and ride away.

I heard rushing feet behind me. A hard shove to my back sent me flying straight onto a roll of wire. Landing felt like a million glass shards ripping into my abdomen and thigh. I pushed myself off, gasping with pain that just kept coming. My lower right side was on fire. By the time I sat up and looked around, my attacker was gone. I had a good idea who it was.

My uniform was a dirty, bloody mess. I struggled to stay silent, to not cry. The bell rang the end of break time and if I wasn't back in my seat in five minutes, I'd be in bigger trouble. If I went to the bathroom, washed up fast, and wore an oversize cardigan from the lost and found locker, maybe no one would notice. Then I saw blood had seeped down my leg to soak the edge of my white socks. I wanted to sit down right there and weep because how was I going to explain that? Instead I kept my head low and my eyes down as I ducked towards the square white building. I was rounding the corner when I ran smack into Mrs Goro, the assistant teacher.

'Otolorin Akinro, what on earth happened to you?'

'I fell, Mrs Goro, ma.'

She narrowed her eyes.

'I was running too fast and tripped on the gravel.' I hoped my ripped clothes weren't telling a different story.

She seemed unconvinced but grabbed my hand, hauling me towards the infirmary. 'That needs looking at. I'm surprised at you, Otolorin. You're not usually a troublesome one!'

It was pointless to protest. I just hoped no one connected my injuries with barbed wire and discovered I was loitering in a forbidden area. At the door, she handed me over to Sister Angelica, a nun from England, who was also the head nurse.

The nun helped me up onto a narrow table and told me to unbutton my shirt.

'Oh, and Oto, take off your shorts, too.' She was saying my name all wrong, with 'o' like in *oh*, instead of *or*. I tried not to whimper as she carefully examined the scratches.

'These aren't deep, just many and jagged. Gravel, hmm?' She quirked an eyebrow.

'Yes,' I whispered, fixing my gaze on the tiny spider making its slow way across the ceiling. From the corner of my eye I saw her shake her head. She'd probably heard tales taller than Cocoa House.

'Okay. I'll just clean them up then give you an injection in case of infection.'

I hated injections but figured I'd just flip over and the pain would be quick.

With gloved hands, she probed delicately at the edge of my briefs, eyeing a couple of long scratches that reached into my inner thigh. Surely she'd not . . .

'Take those off. We mustn't miss any of those scrapes.'

No! I shook my head. No way.

Her eyes glittered periwinkle blue like my crayon. She seemed amused. 'Little boy, there's nothing there I haven't seen before. I'm old enough to be your grandmother. Now stop being silly and take them off.'

'No, Sister. Sorry.' I was trying to be polite. To say I wasn't being rude or coy. Because she was dead wrong. There *was* something there she hadn't seen before.

'I have other things to do, child. You're wasting my time.'

'No. I can't,' I wailed.

'Then I will remove them for you!' She went to a side door and called out for Nurse Ade, a beefy man I'd have no chance of resisting. The second she turned her back, I grabbed my shorts, peeled out the front door, hit the back path, slid my shorts on and kept running. Straight through the school gate, right past the surprised gateman yelling, '*Stop! Stop!*' Out onto the road where a car swerved and horns screeched as I flew across and kept going. Cars braked. People's mouths moved as I flashed by them. A bleeding child wearing the blue checked uniform of my expensive Catholic school, running as if chased by death, attracted notice. My chest burned as hotly as my right side but I dared not stop.

9

NOW

1992 (AGE 14)

Back in ISS after Christmas break, I'm gratefully enveloped in Derin's solid, warm presence, even though things feel different again. Some older boys on our floor have begun to sprout tiny whorls of hair on their chests. When they talk, they sound like those bullfrogs croaking in the gutters behind the dorm at night. Twice now I've heard Cornelius groan in his sleep like he's dying, then quietly get up and towel-dry his bed in the cool moonlight. When he glances over to check if I've seen, I screw my eyes tight shut, cheeks burning, glad Derin sleeps like a rock. There's change going on all around me. Yet I seem to be growing softer around the edges, not pulling up lean and long like my dorm-mates.

While waiting for Derin to join me at lunchtime one afternoon, I drift over to the edge of a group listening to Hamza, the boy with the hawkish Hausa face. His father is a well-known oil baron millionaire. He's describing how he bumped into a famous boy band in a New York hotel lobby. Wura and I used to dance ourselves to the ground watching their videos. Rapt and envious, I stare at the movement of Hamza's curved lips. I've always thought he looks quite a bit like Jamal, the lead singer.

'Did you get a photo with Jamal? He's *sooo* cute!' coos a starry-eyed girl, as if she'd read my mind.

'He totally is!' pops out of my mouth. Silence follows. The kind where you'd hear a leaf hit the ground in the next town. I mumble something about liking Jamal's haircut and beat a speedy retreat towards the kiosks, stunned at my own stupidity. Since when did my brains turn to sap just because one good-looking boy is talking about other good-looking boys?

I see Derin heading towards me and am grateful he missed my brief slide into insanity. I think I might die if he ever decides I'm too weird for him.

'What's up?' He eyes my overly bright smile with suspicion.

'Nothing. Share a meat pie?' We've worked out a system where we sometimes split break snacks to help our pocket money stretch further on bad cafe food days.

He nods, throws an arm over my shoulder in that habit I've fast come to love and, as we walk away, tells me about a chess tournament he's hoping to qualify for. The next day, I go to the school barber and, though I hate to do it, get my hair shaved down to fuzz. Maybe I'll just stop talking to anyone but Derin.

Soon after, a late afternoon game of volleyball under a merciless sun has me chancing another quick shower though the dinner bell has rung. I'll just eat whatever is left before dashing to the art studio for prep. For once the water gushes down like September rain because I have the whole place to myself and there's no one else showering. Sheer luxury! If there's one scarce thing in a dorm, it's solitude.

There's a tune playing in my head. Deep down I know I shouldn't, but it's simply been too long. My hand flicks to the side, my fingers snap in rhythm . . . 1, 2, 3, 4! 'Ah ah ah ah ah ah . . .' My soapy loofah sponge becomes a microphone and then I'm hitting the high notes of 'La Isla Bonita'. It feels so good! Wura and I used to practise all the steps. I roll my hips, flick my imaginary flouncy red skirt, then throw the shower head a sultry stare that probably looks more squinty than anything else. I giggle at the thought, scrubbing and singing in rhythm.

'*La la. La la la la la* ...' I'm feeling like Madonna would definitely approve, when I hear footsteps and shut up. Everything stays quiet. I breathe out. Just my imagination.

I'm late for dinner anyway. I start rinsing off fast.

There's a soft click. The sound of the main bathroom door being gently shut. As if someone had stood there a while, just inside. Listening. A soft shudder crawls up my back.

Who was it? Have they left?

This time I definitely hear footsteps. Boat-sized feet with thick, hairy ankles appear below my shower door. I shrink closer to the far wall.

'Who's in there?' The deep voice sounds familiar.

'Oto.' I'm an idiot. Stupid! Stupid! What possessed me to sing?

'Yes! Akinro. I thought it might be you.'

It's Bayo.

'So, Oto with the honey voice,' Bayo says. 'You owe me for that lie you told in the laundry room. It messed up my plans and got me in big trouble. Maybe I'll forgive you if you keep singing.'

'Um ... no thanks. I don't know what you mean and I'm already late for dinner.' I turn off the shower. Since he returned at the beginning of term, I've tried to ignore his eyes on me. In the cafe. In the common room. On the sports field. I've watched some of his hangers-on turn into jumpy shadows of the eager, fresh-faced boys I stood in line with on my first day at ISS. Since that laundry room encounter, I've not seen the Delta boy with the terribly blank eyes and though I asked around, no one could tell me since I didn't know his name.

Bayo pushes the shower door. It rattles but stays locked. I'm trembling weak-kneed with relief when two meaty hands grip the top of the door and with a terrific crack rip it wide open.

I blink in pure shock, hand still outstretched for the towel hanging off it a second ago. The sight of Bayo's naked grown-up body, *with a standing up thing*, stuns me stupid a moment before I whip around to face the wall.

'Hey! Were you just staring at my *blokos*? Bad, bad boy! I know what you're thinking. Turn around.'

'No! Please leave me alone.' What does he want? I'm seeing images of being forced to eat my bar of soap.

'What's wrong with you, hiding like a girl? You even look like one. I'm surprised you found school shorts to fit that *yansh*!'

I feel his gaze on my bottom as he snickers and realize he's right. A boy wouldn't hide. Yet what else can I do?

'Go away, Bayo! I'm warning you . . .' I hiss, glaring at him sideways.

'Ooohh . . . or else what?' He widens his eyes and fake shivers. 'You'll knock me out with those tiny fists? Bewitch me with those big eyes?' His voice has turned teasing, almost friendly. I have a bad feeling I'm missing something fundamental.

His hand lands on my shoulder, spins me around. Mine fly to cover my front.

'Haha! Are you hiding precious jewels? Let's see what you think is so special!' With one tug, he effortlessly pulls my arms wide. I cross one leg over the other, hot shame flooding my eyes with tears. My chest rises in short sharp pants like a trapped rabbit.

'Nothing,' I wheeze, 'I've nothing special! Please let me go.'

I want to scream but can't. Only one thing could be worse – a dormfull of boys charging in. I look around wildly for a weapon. Even if I could free my arms, the soap dish is cemented into the wall. *Yeyemi, help me, help me, please!*

Bayo pins my wrists to the wall above my head. I go still as death. Mustn't struggle. Mustn't expose anything more.

Then he's laughing. So hard his eyes tear up.

'Hahaha . . . oh my God! *Hahahaha*! What is this tiny thing? How will you ever satisfy a woman?'

I stare at the white-tiled floor, not moving, barely breathing, light-headed with relief. He thinks I'm hiding out of shame that it's tiny. He can laugh all he wants about that. Gossip even. I don't care.

'You're really strange, Oto, do you know that? You look like an *iwin*. A mamiwater. Such a pretty face! I've always noticed. You need someone strong to take care of you, right?'

I shake my head furiously, no.

'Ha! I have to go now but we'll see. By the way, your shower door was stuck and I helped you break it so you could get out. That better be the story, okay?' He winks, drops my hands, turns towards the opposite shower stall. I make a mad dash for my towel.

He's pushing at the shower door when he stops. Turns around slowly with a puzzled frown. I know the exact second he figures something doesn't quite add up, and I bolt for the door. He kicks my legs from underneath and my face hits the white tiles and I see stars. He grabs one leg, flips me over, then stands there mouth agape, staring at the poor nub drooping over the folds above the place Mother calls an abomination. I want him dead. I want to die. Arching up, I punch his legs. 'Let me go, you bastard!' I scream, then panic because I screamed.

I'm struggling hard and he hauls me closer, bending over to get a better look and I've readied my fist to break his mouth the second he's close enough, when I hear footsteps.

'What are you doing? Let go of him!' Derin shouts. He's standing just inside the bathroom door, looking as if he can't believe what he's seeing.

Bayo drops my foot like it's white hot. I'm up in a flash, wrapping my towel tight around my waist, hands shaking so much I can't tuck in the edge and settle for just holding it in a death grip.

Derin reaches outside and grabs something by the door. He advances, brandishing the pointy end of a wooden mop at Bayo, looking like he means to crack his head open. 'What's going on here?'

I open my mouth but there's no sound. Shame, fear and anger close up my throat.

Bayo mockingly puts up his hands like a man under arrest. 'Hey, relax, man! I was just playing with him. What's your problem?'

'My problem, you bullying he-goat, is that that didn't look like playing.'

Bayo's humour vanishes. 'You better watch your stupid *oyinbo* mouth or I'll deal with you.'

'I'd like to see you try!' Derin's rage is calm. Not even Bayo's thick skull can withstand that broom handle.

I should do something, say something, but other than *Bayo saw and I'm finished,* my brain is empty.

Bayo's eyes flick from Derin to me. 'You room together, don't you?'

'So?'

'Have you had a good look at your friend? I think he's deformed.'

'He's not deformed. You're deranged! And I'd swear you were trying to molest him!'

'Molest *ke?* This freak?' Bayo snorts.

'I've heard about people like you. Better leave him alone or you'll regret it.'

'You idiots are not worth my time.' Bayo grabs his towel and stomps out.

I stand there feeling weak and stupid and scared. Rumours and suspicions can catch like wildfire in a dorm.

'Are you okay?'

'Yes. No.' I'm swallowing huge, shuddering sobs. Derin's hands are on my shoulders, gently rubbing, soothing. I stiffen, unable to accept the comfort, bracing for the unavoidable questions that will lead to him turning away. How much did he see?

'Bayo is a vicious bully. The worst kind. We had a couple like him at my old school. You can't let him win.'

I finally gather the courage to look into his eyes. They're amazingly gentle and understanding behind those round glasses.

'Thank you.' I hesitate. *How much did he see?*

'It's okay. You don't have to ask. I'll come with you to the duty master's office. We'll get that bastard kicked out!'

'*No!* Let's not report this, please?' He misunderstood my hesitation.

'Why? He was practically—'

'You arrived before he did anything. If this gets back to my parents, they'll pull me out of ISS, and I really don't want that. I'd rather deal with Bayo than them. I already crossed paths with him in my former school and survived. Just let it go, *please?*'

'They're that bad?' He looks bewildered. Unable to imagine such parents.

'Worse.' I'm gnawing my lip bloody, willing him to understand.

He draws a deep breath, shaking his head in disbelief. 'Okay. But if Bayo even looks at you the wrong away again, we'll take him down together, promise?' Derin holds up his palm. I flatten my fingers to his and we grip hands.

'Promise.'

'Still up for helping me with art homework?'

I nod.

Later, in the bright-lit art studio, when light slanting on paper makes it gleam like white tiles, slamming me back on my butt in that bathroom, my eyes go blurry and I'm gasping for air. Derin's hand on my shoulder brings me back. He says nothing but I look into his eyes and I can breathe again.

10

BEFORE

1989 (AGE 12)

The leg blocked my path out of nowhere. I landed on my stomach. There stood the gateman. He hefted me over his shoulder like a sack of rice and when I lifted my head so the world went back upright, I saw the St Christopher's school van parked by the road. He stuffed me inside, leapt in and held me down. My wounds rubbed on the seat and I cried out in pain. The driver merged into traffic, headed right back to school.

'Foolish boy!' the gateman ranted. 'You wan cost me my job! You *ajebutter* pikins no dey think. Just because of one small injection, you run comout like that! If motor hit you, na my trouble! Foolish boy!'

I wanted to say I was sorry, that I hadn't meant to get him in any trouble, but I was wheezing and shaking too hard.

He dumped me on the table in the infirmary where Sister Angelica was waiting, explaining where he found me. Her face was tomato red. The gleam in her eye now pure annoyance. She thanked him and he left.

I whimpered like a puppy. I couldn't stop. What was I going to do? Nurse Ade looked at me with gentle brown eyes. 'It's only an injection, you know. It will be over like that!' He snapped his fingers. Would those eyes stay gentle once he saw?

'Okay, child,' Sister Angelica said. 'We can go the easy route: I'll clean you up, give you an antibiotic injection and it will be over in minutes. Or Nurse Ade will hold you down, and it will take much longer and be a lot more fuss. Which will it be?'

Neither. 'Please can it be only you here, Sister? I'll take everything off without trouble. I promise.'

'Okay,' she said, softening a little. She probably thought I was both insanely shy and deathly scared of injections. 'Nurse Ade will be right outside, so no more silliness, all right?'

'Yes, Sister,' I said, as Nurse Ade stepped out and shut the door. I was gambling. Maybe *oyinbo* nuns didn't gossip. 'My mother said I shouldn't ever take off my undies.' It was all I had left.

'Well, your mother isn't here and we don't want you bleeding to death or getting an infection, so take them off.'

I prayed for something to stop this disaster. A flood, an earthquake. 'One . . . two . . .' she started counting.

A plague of locusts. Anything.

'Three. I'm calling Nurse Ade back on five. Four . . .'

I slid off my shorts. And my briefs. My weeping was silent. I could feel the pull of Wura's worried thoughts in my head. We always knew when one of us was sick or bodily hurt. She'd fly to my side the second she could. She'd have known sooner if she hadn't been giving me the silent treatment for days. Eyes shut tight, I tried to stem my terror. Breathe in. Breathe out.

Sister Angelica firmly pushed apart my clamped legs, lifting and bending the right one to the side. There was a long silence. I knew she was steeling herself. Struggling to do her duty despite the sight before her. I heard her putting together bottles and clangy metal things.

'I trained as a pediatric nurse, Oto. Do you know what that means?'

I shook my head. I didn't really care. I was doomed.

'It means I've seen many unusual things.'

I sneaked a peek from under my lids. Her face was calm.

She picked up some cotton wool with a long scissor-like thing, dipped it in antiseptic, and began cleaning the scratches from my inner thigh – one scratch nearly reached *that* place – to my hip. My teeth clenched as I hissed with pain, but I couldn't focus on that because why wasn't she at the very least crossing herself?

'I worked with an endocrinologist years ago, before I took my vows. That means someone who treats people with bodies like yours.'

I couldn't have heard right. She'd said *bodies*. Like mine!

'You most remind me of a couple of cases with whom I assisted the doctor. Both were instances of pseudohermaphroditism. Have you heard of it before?'

I shook my head, too overwhelmed to speak.

'What it means – deep breath, this will sting . . .' – she swabbed my cuts with purple iodine and I nearly leaped off the table – '. . . is that you appear to be somewhere along the spectrum and could be a girl or a boy.'

'I could be a girl?' Everything else faded away.

'Your parents never told you?'

'No. We don't . . . no one talks about it at home.'

'Hmm.'

I could have been rolled in barbed wire and dipped in a vat of iodine and hardly noticed. A *girl*! First Babalawo. Now Sister Angelica!

'So . . . you don't think I'm the devil's work? Like . . . like that Damien antichrist boy?' I had to know for sure.

'What, *who*?' She frowned. 'No, Oto. You're just a child. God created us all in his image and the devil does not create but destroy. This likely has to do with your hormones.'

'Hormones?'

She looked at me like she'd just remembered I was only twelve. 'It means your body started out one thing, got different instructions from your glands and changed its mind, but by then it was too late. Do you understand?'

'Yes,' I quickly lied, afraid she'd stop. It sounded almost like what Babalawo said, if you mixed gods and goddesses with textbook, science-y words.

'Turn on your side.'

She wiped a spot on my hip, tapped the syringe she was holding. I gritted my teeth against the stabbing pain. I'd endure ten injections to hear more.

'Sister,' I said, when I could breathe again, 'those other people like me, where are they? Are they doing well? Did they get to choose? I mean, boy or girl?'

'Well, that was years ago, in the fifties, but I think one of them was doing just fine once she commenced treatment. There have probably been advances in medicine since then. You are, rightly, filled with questions, but this is too complicated for a child. Why don't you ask your parents to come and see me so we can discuss . . .'

She stopped talking because I was shaking. Hard enough to rattle the bowl of clangy metal things beside my leg. The thought of Mother finding out someone else knew, and that they heard it from me, iced my blood.

'What's wrong?'

'If my mother finds out you know, she'll kill me for sure.'

'Oh. Was that why you ran away?'

'Yes. She's angry and ashamed I'm like this. I don't want to make it worse.' It went so much deeper than that, but how did I begin to explain to this Catholic *oyinbo* woman about flying grandmas and child witches and the things people here believed? Then again, she crossed herself before the statue of Mary with one foot on a snake that stood beside the infirmary. And Yeyemi had felt as solid to me as the table I lay on even though that magical place couldn't possibly exist. However confused I was about the real and the imaginary, I knew one thing for sure. If Sister Angelica talked to Mother, actual hell would break loose.

She covered me with a sheet and began putting things back into the medicine cabinet, her face all stiff. Was she angry?

'Sorry, Sister. It's kind of you to offer, but Mother fears everyone will gossip and Father already left us because of me. My sister misses him so. Please don't say anything to anyone.'

She slammed the cabinet door shut, winced at the noise, then faced me.

'It's not your fault. Don't apologize. Let's agree this stays between us.

I just find it incredible no doctor was consulted. Surely it was evident at the hospital when you were born?'

'I hardly get sick, and if I visit a doctor, Mother makes sure no one sees anything. Me and my twin sister were born at home.'

'I see. And does she have the same condition?'

'No.'

'That's highly unusual but Yoruba people do have some of the highest incidence of twins in the world. I suppose it would happen here if at all.'

Sister Angelica crossed her arms on her chest and fixed me with grave, curious eyes. 'So, in your heart, Oto, do you feel you're a boy or girl?'

She was asking *me*? For the first time since I crouched at Mother's door, the hole inside me shrank. The buzzing in my head stopped.

'A girl.' It unfurled from my mouth, soft and sure. 'But Mother says I have to be a boy, or else.'

'Goodness!' Sister Angelica looked troubled. 'Right then. I want you to remember two things. First, hormones in your body played a big part in how you developed. Second, your body is going to change as you grow older, and those changes can be unpredictable. To get changes that match how you feel, you might need medication. You don't want to get stuck the wrong way, you see?'

I nodded, getting why she'd rather be discussing this with a grown-up.

'I don't know what treatment might be available here. In England, the science is still young, and though I've not kept up with the journals, I understand they're making great strides in America. Your parents really should, at the very least, get a diagnosis . . .' She shook her head.

'Thank you, but I can't say anything. Could you please write down that word for me? The long one that starts with *studio*-something?'

A soft laugh tinkled out of her. 'Of course. And its pseudo; p-s-e-u-d-o. You know what? When you're older, find a doctor – someone you can trust – and show it to them. Don't wait too long, though. Things can change rapidly once you're a teenager.'

'Yes, Sister. Thank you so much.'

'Good. Now get dressed and hop along. Come back and see me anytime. Don't hesitate if you're in any trouble.'

I left the infirmary clutching a piece of paper with a word that looked like gibberish in her spidery, snagged-together writing; *Malepseudohermaphroditism?* I carefully folded and put it in my shorts pocket, feeling like the question mark at the end of the word.

Outside, Wura stood looking as if the world had ended, even though news of my escape and capture couldn't possibly have got out yet. I hobbled towards her.

'Are you okay? I've been so worried!' Her red-rimmed eyes betrayed that she'd been rubbing them hard. Unlike me, Wura didn't cry easily. She lifted the thin sheet Sister Angelica had draped over me and saw my torn, bloody clothes. I knew she felt guilty for being so cold to me for days.

'God, this looks terrible! What happened?'

'I fell on barbed wire. I'll be fine.' I didn't want her going after Bayo and getting into trouble for fighting in school.

Her arms gingerly encircled me. For long moments we breathed together, calming down. She'd become so distressed her class teacher had excused her to come and find me. They'd already called Mother. We went to sit in a quiet corner of the playground and wait for Mr Driver. Maybe I'd tell her about Sister Angelica and my piece of paper when I properly understood it all myself. Or maybe not. It was already enough that she constantly had to be on her guard defending me.

Mother called me a clumsy fool. An idiot. 'Is this the ridiculous rubbish they made me bring you home for? Why am I paying high fees for that school?' I'd shown her only the few scratches on my leg and though Wura's eyes widened at the lie, she stayed silent. I kept waiting for the blows. Normally, by now, I'd have at least a painfully twisted ear. I sent silent thanks to Babalawo. Considering what I now knew, owning something that seemed to stay the hand that shoved me down the stairs was like a magic wall suddenly appearing between you and an escaped tiger at the zoo. One you'd just discovered had been starving for ages. I wondered sadly if I'd ever see Babalawo again.

Life carried on like usual but nothing felt the same. *If you've been bitten by a snake,* my proverb book said, *every rope looks frightening at night.* The one good change was Wura got into baking after staying over at a friend's house. She kept bringing me the results of her efforts. The first time, it was orange biscuits. I sat there saying, 'Yum! Delicious!' till she bit into one and went, 'Aargh! Seriously, Oto, you're supposed to be my taster!' I laughed. Turned out she had mixed up the salt and sugar measurements. No one had ever baked in our house before and the delicious smells wafting in from the kitchen made those days feel special. Though I knew it was her way of dealing with things she sensed were not quite right, I was also glad she'd found something she enjoyed doing (apart from maths at which she was a wizard), like I enjoyed drawing and painting. I loved how she laughed when Emily and I fought over who got to lick the batter pan clean.

The purple iodine sealed my cuts, and they only needed redressing once. Wincing, I quietly did it myself. The wall of things I was keeping from Wura grew taller every day. I tried not to notice that she wasn't going out of her way to ask.

The phone now rang at six sharp every other day, setting my hairs on end. Before, Aunty Abiye used to call maybe once a month and Mother didn't use to glance at me before heading to her room to pick up on the extension. I couldn't eavesdrop on the living room phone – she'd know. Putting my ear to the door didn't work. For her, a phone remained a strange instrument that must be whispered or shouted into. Such little things reminded me that she'd never seen a real city till she met Father. Once time he'd teased her about how she'd stopped dead at her first sight of a skyscraper, looked up, then slumped against him with dizziness. Her laughter had sounded cracked at the edges. She'd grown up in a village in Ondo, and only went to primary school. She'd never learned, like I did in Nature Science class, the real cause of lightning. Or of raindrops splintering a sunny sky. Things really important to know because otherwise, a person could become lopsided in their mind from swallowing wholesale what they're told and never asking any more questions. I strained my ears anyway, and one time she shouted, 'I can't take him there, Abiye! You just don't know Laitan like I do!'

Take me where? Frightening images arose in my head. Nightly, I shot upright in a sweat dreaming I'd fallen asleep in my own bed but woken up in a dark box on a moving vehicle, knowing I'd never find my way back home. Always somewhere in the background Wura was crying but I couldn't see or reach her.

11

NOW

1991 (AGE 14)

Derin's friendship feels ever more like shelter since my peace was shattered in that bathroom. Bayo ignores me, though that might be more me being prepared to climb walls to avoid him. I try not to imagine him as something evil that's merely sleeping. All that stops him is that Derin saw and is unafraid to speak up. When I hear a rumour that Bayo is practically on his last strike as far as school transgressions go, I feel better. It means he has to watch himself if he ever wants to graduate.

Wishing I could have enjoyed blissful normalcy just a bit longer, I start searching the ISS library. But *Malepseudohermaphroditism* might as well be a ghost word. An alien word. Something that possibly exists but can't ever be found. Derin knows so much more about everything and is such a wizard at solving puzzles, yet I can't risk asking him.

'Any good?' Derin asks. It's just me and him alone in our room in that period of rest before the dinner bell rings. Cornelius is at piano practice.

'What?' I'm startled out of the book I was pretending to read.

Derin shakes his head. 'Open your eyes, Oto. ISS is only a passageway to other places. It's a tiny fenced school inside a small town, within a state, inside a country, within a continent, and we are not even to the galaxies yet. See what I mean? It will all just be a bad memory one day. Bayo is in his final year and will soon leave. Don't let him make you miserable meanwhile.'

'You're totally right.' I nod, grateful, suddenly needing to tell him what he's been patiently not asking. Why I'd endure Bayo over my own parents.

'My father mostly moved out when we were little. He hates me because ... well, because I'm not the kind of son he wants. I'm not ... you know ... tough and hard and all that.'

'But you're you. And you're okay. Better than that, you're great! Is your mom like that, too?'

Despite myself, I smile. This is Derin, unshy about saying what I mean to him. It's a way of being that I've never known, and the words tangle in my mouth when I try to say them back, so I give him things instead. A drawing of himself as Icarus with smarter wings, jokes he'd enjoy, a friendship bracelet I bought during the holidays that he's not taken off since.

'Yes. She even believes some real *Omen*-style horror movie stuff. That I'm some kind of evil *emere* changeling, planted in her womb by Maami, Father's Mother, to make him abandon us because she never wanted him to marry her.' It's only half the truth, but will do for now.

'Seriously? That's just ...' Derin shakes his head.

'I know.' I tell him all about Mother pushing me down the stairs, about her constant disappointment at every extra breath I draw. There's far more and way worse but I have to pick what to say that won't lead to questions I can't answer.

He screws his eyes tight shut for a moment, jaw clenched. 'I wish you never had to go back to her. I'd ask you home with me for the holidays if not for my stepmom.'

'Thanks,' I whisper, touched to the bone. 'I'd do the same if not for my mother.' We're quiet for a bit, and he's maybe, like me, thinking of holidays together, how much we'd enjoy exploring the other sides of each other's lives.

'Is your stepmom unkind? Does she beat you?'

'No. My dad doesn't think children should be beaten. She's not bad, but Dad's always trying to make up for my mom's absence, which sometimes annoys her. It's just, she's not *my* mom, you know? So I don't feel as free as my younger brother.'

'No one ever hit you? Even if you did something bad?'

'No. Dad makes me think about what I did and decide my punishment. If I pick wrong, then he gets to choose and it's always worse. Like when I was younger and I tore my neighbour's *Ghostbusters* cards because I was angry he wouldn't trade them. It was Christmas and Dad took me over to Gabriel's house and made me hand him my present, a Laser Tag game I'd only just taken out of the wrapping! I cried so hard. We ended up playing with it together anyway. Dad's a freethinker and says he hopes he's raising me to be one, too.'

'Freethinker?'

'It means deciding for yourself what to believe in, despite what others around you do, whether it's what to wear or if God exists. Dad says unless you're a sheep, you should think for yourself.'

'So are you a freethinker?' For so long I've been told what I'm supposed to believe, and here's Derin saying there's a choice.

'I don't really know. Our family is Catholic because here you have to answer to something but Dad believes "God" is actually the potential for good in every human being.'

'I like that! How come he's so ... um, open-minded?'

'I guess it comes from being a philosophy professor. You should hear the things they discuss when he gives dinner parties at our house! He sometime lets me hang around for a while.'

'You're so lucky,' I sigh, not wishing him any less but wistful for a home where I'm loved and taught important things.

'I know. What does your dad do?'

'He's a ridiculously rich businessman whose actual God is money, though he claims to be Baptist,' I grin.

Derin laughs.

'They don't treat your sister badly, though, right?'

'Mother adores the ground Wura walks on and Father seemed to care about her but who knows with him? God, I miss her.'

'She sounds amazing. Makes me wish I had a twin.'

'It's a joy.' My heart warms just thinking of her fierceness, her matter-of-fact love. 'I'd do anything for her, though we sometimes drive each other crazy. We're alike but different. You'll see when you meet her.'

'Well, I have you as my best friend. Next best thing.'

'The best!' It's the first time he's called me that, and I think I might melt into my pillow.

But the person Derin knows and likes isn't all of you, whispers that tiny voice in my head. *If your dreams ever came true, his best friend will one day become a girl named Lori.*

I tell it to shut up.

We all have the syllabus and knew this was coming. Most students hide behind their books. Some notoriously shy ones are absent. Even the class troublemakers are silent. Eating dirt would only be slightly worse that being called upon to answer a question.

The biology teacher has tacked a diagram of the human reproductive system to the board. Pointing with a ruler, she explains how babies' organs separate into male or female in the womb. She's so confident I wish I had the courage to ask, *what about when it doesn't happen that way? I'm sitting right here, existing! Where's the diagram of how I developed?*

'Monthly bleeding,' the teacher continues gravely, 'is a female reproductive signal of readiness for procreation. Today we'll discuss the biology. The practical aspects will be for a girls-only class. It's important that young ladies are well prepared for this milestone.'

It's like those trick pictures where the hidden thing suddenly pops out stark naked from where it's been lurking before your eyes all along. I *do* have a vagina. I knew women did something or other monthly but it's not like I didn't have enough other problems to worry about. I clench my knees tight. Will it run like a river? Pour out all of a sudden like an overturned bucket? How would I hide that from Derin? From a whole dormfull of boys? I can just imagine Bayo's reaction. He's kept his distance still, and I'd really like it to stay that way.

The teacher carries on about other reproductive methods, and I'm only half listening to how amoebas move using extensions called pseudopodia and reproduce asexually by dividing. It sounds vaguely familiar. I rub my eyes, longing to lay my achy head on the desk, catch the teacher's eye on me, and sit up straighter.

At dinner, I push my kedgeree around my plate. Derin glances worriedly at me so I eat a forkful. His upper lip sports a distinct fuzz. Some boys have been furtively darkening theirs with black crayon. He doesn't need to.

'Something wrong?' he says. 'Bad news from home? Life getting you down?' This last one makes me smile like he'd known it would. I mumble something about missing Wura. He tries not to let on that he doesn't buy it.

I swallow around the lump in my throat, desperate to spill all about how those hormones running amok in our bodies could any moment now capsize my life. He raises a skeptical brow and continues eating. I'll turn fifteen in a few months. What if I bleed *and* grow a moustache, too? Which, I guess, wouldn't be any sort of big deal in a world where that was okay, but that is not the world I am living in. I push my plate away.

I'm finally drifting into fitful sleep much later when it hits me. *Pseudo.* It's part of Sister Angelica's word! Have I been searching the wrong way all along? I toss and turn wide-eyed till morning.

I skip breakfast, so I'm alone in the library. Pull out every dictionary. I can't flip through the pages fast enough. First, I find pseudo: *pretended; false or spurious; sham, fake. Being apparently rather than actually as stated.* Then I find hermaphrodite: *a person, plant or animal that has both male and female parts.*

As I dig into thesauruses and old biology textbooks, hope leaches away page by page. I'd hoped so hard for so much. Surely I'm much more than a sham, fake person with both male and female parts!

I hear the bell and look up to see the librarian coming to kick me out for morning assembly. I can't face anyone. I'm feeling too wobbly inside.

I go to the school nurse and tell her I feel sick. Of course she can't find anything wrong, other than a slightly high temperature. I've been a model student, though, so she accepts that I have a terrible headache and gives me a dorm-rest pass, saying she'll check on me after lunch.

I pace my small room, trying not to cry. What will happen? Will I be in hiding for the rest of my life? Will parts of me seal shut and others keep growing? *How*, argues that small voice inside, *will you even be able to tell when you don't know what exactly you look like now?*

When I'm certain classes have started, I lock my room door, undress and squat above my small, square mirror, prepared for the worst. The whole situation feels weirdly indecent. It's no different, I remind myself, than looking at my ears or toes. Apetebi, Sister Angelica, even that dumb ox, Bayo, have seen as much.

I take a deep breath, look down. It's like my hands are trespassing, breaking some unspoken bounds. There's the small nub that looks neither like one thing or another, barely poking from under a hood. Bracketing it are labia (might as well use my shiny new biology words) that join together towards the back to form a slight swell right below my vagina, which I'm also calling by its proper name from now on. Everything behind looks the usual. Compared to what I've recently seen in textbooks, it's not so terrible. Just different.

The nubby part must have loomed large on my newborn self because, as Bayo scoffed, it's tiny. Barely the length and width of my littlest finger. Maybe it's an absurd thing to ask a fertility goddess, but I plead with every atom of my being to Yeyemi and the universe and whoever else is listening out there, *Please let me not bleed yet. Things are hard enough.*

I clean up, dress, crawl into bed, cuddle into my pillow and escape into *Evbu My Love*, a Pacesetters novel by Helen Ovbiagele that I've been saving for just the right time.

12

Somehow, Sister Angelica worked magic and no one mentioned my crazy escape, though for a while, to Wura's bafflement, the gateman glared at me.

I kept having nightmares about Bayo pushing me in front of the moving goods train and I went splat like a cartoon character. Only it hurt terribly and I woke up shaking.

I kept a constant watch over my shoulder. Who knew how deeply Bayo held a grudge? Especially since someone went and graffitied *Stinky Bayo Smelly Pants* on the boys' toilet wall.

The fading scars on my thigh reminded me it was best to stay safe in my library hideaway, where I worried about how one found a doctor who knew about hormones and glands before I was forever stuck the wrong way, and worried even more about what Mother was planning. Still, I thought I was coping pretty well until Mrs Goro's ruler lightly tapped my back one morning and I realized I'd dozed off from exhaustion. I'd never been so grateful to be ahead in class. Not that it would matter to Mother if I failed. Though my report card always said, *Otolorin continues to be academically precociously advanced*, she simply ignored it while praising Wura's every achievement like it was the moon landing.

Weeks later I stopped feeling that prickling on my scalp of being watched, and learned that Bayo had left St Christopher's. No one knew why. It was one less worry, and I was glad.

Wura woke up coughing and shivering with a fever one morning, and had to stay home.

After school, I rushed out of the car and hurried upstairs. All day long I'd felt her aches and pains like a faint echo in my bones.

I was halfway up when someone screamed. Followed by a loud crash from Mother's room. I raced in to find her leaning on her dressing table, breathing hard, doubled over as if from a terrible stomach pain. Her mirror lay in slivers on the floor. And there, to my great surprise, stood Father, wiping his face with a paper napkin. A broken jar on the floor behind him spilled cold cream on the green carpet. A small cut on his cheek leaked blood. Beside him was Maami Akinro, face tight, lips pressed into two rigid lines. My heart stopped.

'Where's Wura? What's wrong?' My words dropped like stones into the silence.

Mother stared at me, eyes streaming tears. She looked wildly around, picked up a shoe and flung it at my head. I dodged but stayed put.

'Control yourself, Mojisola.' Maami Akinro's voice was pure steel. 'Throwing things will not change matters.'

'I'll tell you what will change matters, you wicked, ungodly woman! Now you have finished gloating, why don't you throw a party and invite all your fellows to celebrate?'

'How dare you?' Father snarled. 'I raised you from the gutter. Gave you my name. Now you have the mouth to insult my mother! I'll show you who is wicked!' In a trice he'd crossed the room and landed Mother a slap that knocked her head sideways. Up went his hand again, but Maami Akinro's light touch froze it mid-air.

'Stop, Laitan! I didn't raise you to hit women and, dirty mouth aside, she has reason to be upset.'

I remained just inside the door, torn between staying put and going to find Wura. I could now feel her presence, sick, but nearby.

'Eh! Oyinlola Akinro, ever so generous!' Mother sneered, head raised high, tears blurring past Father's fingerprints on her face. 'God knows you've done enough. Why don't you just take that creature away and leave me and my child in peace?'

Her pointed finger found me and it seemed the rest of her would leap after it. I shrank back. She'd not only offered me up like furniture, but called Maami Akinro by her given name; rude to an elder, pure insolence to a mother-in-law. If she made the mistake of calling Maami Akinro a witch, Father would finish her. And Mother was the only thing keeping me and Wura together. The only home I had. I found myself praying under my breath to whomever was out there to help her keep her head.

'Go ahead!' she screamed. 'Take him!'

Father raised an eyebrow at Maami Akinro, acting, as usual, as if I didn't exist in any reality that included him. His eyes were like darkened windows, giving away nothing. A harshness tightened Maami Akinro's face. She gave one sharp shake of her head before staring in apparent sudden absorption at the framed wedding photo Mother had kept on her dresser, now lying shattered on the floor.

Relief left me weak-kneed. She cared only about Father. The rest of us could go jump in the Ogunpa River.

'And you, Laitan? Isn't he your son?' Mother taunted.

'That ... *creature* ... you thought you'd trapped me with is your responsibility, Moji. If you insist, I can make sure he's not your problem any more but I will divorce you and take Wura, too. And you'll never again see another *kobo* of my money. It's your choice.'

All relief fled. Make sure I was not her problem any more – exactly how? By disappearing me like he did other inconvenient people? *Please, Yeyemi*, I pleaded in my head, *if you're maybe real, and maybe listening, please help Mother think straight.*

Mother hugged her arms around her body as if holding herself together. 'All right, he stays. Two conditions. One, I will no longer pollute my life with your witch doctors and fetishists. If you want your son to go to Babalawo, take him there yourself. Two, send the driver with the usual amount every month and I'll not make trouble.'

'Make sure you don't, or what you think is misfortune now will look like paradise.' Father shrugged, seemingly unconcerned with Mother's conditions. I slumped against the wall, grateful and miserable.

Maami Akinro whipped around to face him, eyes narrowed even more. 'But, my son—'

Father raised his hand sharply and she shut up. Did she resent us getting even an allowance? A tiny drop in Father's vast ocean of wealth? As they communicated without words, it seemed only she had the key to wherever Father salted away his heart.

'Leave now, both of you,' Mother hissed. 'Don't let me see your faces here again.'

Father strode off without a backward glance, but Maami Akinro stopped where I stood petrified like an *Esie* statue. For one endless moment she paused, eyes shuttered, mouth twisted down on one side. The same look I saw on Father's face whenever he was unhappy and frustrated – pretty much anytime he was within sight or hearing of me or Mother. She was probably thinking what a mess I'd made of her son's life by being born. I directed my eyes to the floor. Soon, the front door slammed and all was silent.

When I looked up, Mother's shoulders were heaving. In her eyes shone a whole new world of hatred. I turned and ran, letting Wura's silent call guide my steps.

She was curled up on the window ledge in her bedroom, whispering to the doll clutched to her chest. 'Everything is fine. Mommy will never leave you.' Only last week she'd removed them all from her dresser and in their place laid out her growing collection of lotions and body sprays and hair decorations. Much like the growing contents of my treasure box, if I too could only display them for the world to see.

I slid in beside her.

'What is going on?'

'I was lying on the sofa downstairs when Daddy and Maami arrived, but he didn't even pat my head or call me his gold standard like usual. He just told Mommy they needed to talk so they both went straight up to her room. I wanted to show him I came first in maths class so he would be proud of me again so I went to get my report card and waited by the door. Then I heard Mommy screaming. She said ...' Wura's mouth trembled with trying not to sob. 'She said now that he's decided to marry one of the cheap *ashewos* he's been chasing all over Lagos, he and his mother couldn't wait to rub it in her face. Daddy told her to shut her dirty mouth before he shut it for her. Then there was a big crash and Maami Akinro rushed past me and ran in. Then they were all shouting at each other and my head was paining me. So I came here.'

A new wife! No wonder Mother had gone crazy. I gave double thanks that she'd kept her head, shuddering to imagine Wura a second-class citizen in some furious stepmother's house.

'He didn't even say *pele* that I'm sick!' Wura sniffled.

The pain in her eyes cut me open. I burned with shame that I didn't, and never would, have the courage to tell Father just what a cruel, selfish person he was. What did Wura ever do to deserve that?

I went to the bathroom and returned with a tissue. She let me hold it to her dripping nose and blew.

'To think we're suffering all this because of me.'

'Don't be silly. It's not your fault.'

And to think she didn't even know about the Flying Maami, or how Mother believes I'm like a real life Damien from *The Omen*, or Sister Angelica's warning that my body might anytime do unpredictable things! No way I could tell her any of that now.

When we were six, one of Father's young business partners picked me as pageboy for his wedding. He was marrying a woman from Abidjan and that flight was the longest we'd breathed the same air with Father since he'd moved out. I'd been mesmerised staring at my passport and dreaming of all the places I could go. Wura had refused to be parted from his side the whole three days. People said what a loving father he must be. He'd puffed up with self-satisfaction and lapped it up.

Mother had sent my measurements weeks in advance to the bride. I'd heard her on the phone discussing silver waistcoats and bowties. On the wedding morning, as other children in the bridal train got readied by the adults, I sat holding the lace-frilled silver pillow on which I would bear the ring to the waiting groom, telling myself I wasn't jealous of the flower girls because I'd been chosen for such an important task. A giggling three-year-old, naked as a gecko, suddenly flashed past, chased with a crisp white shirt by his adoring, exasperated mother. It was among those squirming, squealing, carefree children that it finally dawned how terribly something was wrong with me. Mother had taken no chances. Only I had arrived fully dressed.

On the flight back Wura stuck with Father, chattering like a squirrel till she fell asleep. Beside me, Mother buried her face in a fashion magazine. I could tell she was sore from Father now acting as if she was extra baggage, after displaying her like a prize in public. I stared out of the window as we took off. To my six-year-old eyes, the whole world looked like a giant Lego set I could play with if I stretched my arms down far enough. Later, when a kind-faced air hostess brought a notepad and crayons, I drew a picture of a woman holding hands with two little girls. In that picture, the air hostess was my real mother, and when the plane landed, she'd pluck me right out of that seat and take me and Wura to a sweet home where words and silence didn't cut like a double-edged razor. When I showed the air hostess what I'd drawn, she said I was smart and talented and my parents must be so proud. I glowed from the praise. Mother didn't even look up from her magazine.

When the plane landed, Mr Driver was waiting to take us back to Ibadan, and Father returned to his perfect life in Lagos.

Wura coughed, deep and racking. I lay a soft palm on her forehead and it was like she had a lit stove inside her. I gathered her close and rocked gently, humming 'Jonpe', one of our favourite songs; the dog that would not eat the leftovers, the stick that would not beat the dog, the fire that would not burn the stick, the water that would not quench the fire ... Wura's head nodded onto my shoulder.

'Will Daddy ever come back?' she whispered, her thumb finding its way to her mouth in a habit she gave up years ago. I hated to see my strong, fearless sister retreat into babyishness. I knew she'd hate herself for it later.

'Maybe,' I lied.

How she and Mother had both lived for his rare Sunday visits. Mother's steps would perk up and she'd take extra care with her appearance, making up her face and lining her big round eyes till she dazzled. He'd arrive just before the morning service at Ezra Baptist Church, where he insisted we went, where the rich and educated of Ibadan drove up in big fancy cars and dropped fistfuls of naira in the offering basket. Afterwards, we'd all go home together. I'd long understood he stopped by to keep up appearances with his business partners in Ibadan, but Wura acted as if he came just for her. The only time he ever paid me public attention, I'd tried to give my ice lolly to a beggar outside the church gate because he looked so sad and thirsty. One of his legs was swollen as a tree trunk, sagging with creased folds. Father had shouted at me to get away and into the car. It was a terrible shock, considering usually I could stand on my head and he'd not blink. And also, that he rarely raised his voice. I never saw that beggar again.

At home after church, he'd sit Wura on his lap and listen to her stories about life and school, his face a mix of love and regret. At that point, I usually found somewhere else to be. It wasn't that I begrudged Wura this one happiness. I just couldn't bear to stand there while he acted as if I was invisible.

He never stayed for lunch, though Mother prepared his favourite dishes. And, as the day wore on, it was like watching plucked *efo* leaves left out in the sun. She'd wilt slowly till he left. Sometimes, after those visits, Wura stayed in her room and wouldn't talk to anyone. Coaxing Wura out of her sadness seemed to rouse Mother out of hers, so it rarely took more than a day for Wura to perk up, and for Mother to revive. They'd known his affection and even love. For me, near or far, he'd never been anything but a painful absence. It felt as if doors were slamming shut. Father would marry a new wife and be forever unwelcome in Mother's sight. Maami Akinro would never again bring *goody-goody* we didn't even get to eat. I'd never see Babalawo again.

Wura sneezed, her shoulders hunched up. They looked way too small to bear such a heavy weight. She should be in bed. Under a blanket. She was always trying so hard to be strong for everyone, putting herself in harm's way to keep me safe; the brittle rope that kept us all from spiralling into total breakdown. I worried that one day she might break. I knew she remembered the day I'd asked for ribbons and a fairy-tale castle. I knew she struggled not to blame me.

'What if he gets new children?' she mumbled.

'We will always have each other. That's why we came to the world together, right?'

She nodded slowly, her forehead like a firebrand against my neck.

I tugged her off the window ledge and into bed. Then got some mentholatum to rub into her chest since Mother was clearly in no state to take care of such practical things. I climbed in and held her close, rocking her gently till she fell asleep, her breath smelling of cold and cough syrup. I hoped that Father would not fully abandon her.

13

NOW

1991 (AGE 14)

Mr Dickson brings a book of European classical paintings to art theory class. We're to pass it around and pick one each to discuss with a partner. I flip the pages and stop at a painting titled *Flaming June*. It's a woman with long red hair asleep on a couch with her red-orange dress spread out around her. Beside me, Derin goes still and tears well up in his eyes, then he blinks and they're gone so fast no one else saw.

In our room later, I ask him about it. His casual shrug tells me what he's about to say is anything but casual.

'She reminds me of my mom. After my Yoruba grandpa died, my Ibo grandma was afraid of the looming Biafran War so she sent Dad to Canada so he could study and remain safe. He married my mom there and they returned to Nigeria after the war. But grandma hated mom. I heard her say she'd saved his life and he repaid her by marrying some *oyinbo* woman that looks as if a bush is burning on her head.' He smiles grimly. 'Mom left when I was four.'

'That's so sad. Sorry.' All he'd say when I asked before was, *She doesn't live with us any more,* and Derin can clam up like, well … a clam, when he wants to. I had no idea he was hurting.

'I have a photo, but I rarely look at it. It's just too hard, you know?'

'Can I see?' It's so like him to create a space for that particular pain and firmly limit its power right there.

Derin grabs his wallet and pulls out a small photo. He stretches across the arm-span space between our beds to hand it to me. The woman in the photo has strong features like Derin's. Nothing about her face is small or delicate. Her reddish-brown eyebrows are thick as fox-tails; her red-gold hair blows about in large, wild curls. She's on a beach somewhere, her green eyes laughing into the camera as she tries to hold her dress down with one hand and shoo away a seagull with the other.

'Dad never talks about her, but I found this one day going through old boxes in our storage room.'

'You look like her.'

'I remember grabbing her hair when she was swinging me about and I wanted her to stop because I was dizzy. Even though I was laughing like crazy. She was fun.' Derin smiles. 'I always imagine what it would be like to live with my own mother.'

I've always imagined the opposite. 'Do you hear from her?'

'I get a card every birthday and Christmas, so I know where she is. She once called as a surprise on my tenth birthday. Ayo, my half-brother, picked up the phone and shouted, "Derin, it's your mommy!" I heard her say, "Hello, my Derin," and was so happy I could barely speak. Then Dad took over and told her never to call his house again.'

'At least you know she cares.'

'She left me behind.' His eyes are bleak with loss.

'Maybe she thought it was the best thing to do to protect you?' I long to take away his pain. Why do our parents bother to have us only to hurt us so?

'Maybe.'

'She's missing out on so much.' I return the photo and our fingers touch. I want to climb into his bed and hold him tight. Kiss his face everywhere. I squelch that thought like it's fire ablaze on my bedclothes. Where did *that* idea come from? He's my best friend. Nothing more. I can't ever think that way again.

'Guess what?' Derin says brightly, and I know he's done talking about his mom. 'My favourite uncle, Dad's half-brother, was born with six toes and fingers on each foot and hand. People whisper that he's an occultist and a grand wizard among other things, so he wears rings on his smallest fingers just to drive them crazy. You should see people cringe when they have to shake his hand. We have a good laugh afterwards!

'I mean,' he continues, arms under his head, gaze fixed to the ceiling, 'I mean, take Chick Webb, for example.'

'Whozzat?'

'An American jazz drummer. Dad plays his records. Unless he sat on a platform, you could barely see him behind the drums – he was tiny with a big hunchback, you know? He was first to hire Ella Fitzgerald . . .'

I never really got what having an 'old soul' meant till I met Derin. Going on about Ella Fitzgerald and some jazz drummer or discovering obscure groups while everyone else is obsessed with the current top ten hits. Is he hinting it's my turn to open up? I don't think he saw anything the day Bayo attacked me. I'd whipped my towel on fast. Having six toes or a hunchback is one thing. What I saw in my little mirror shatters our fundamental human sorting system.

But Derin is not just anyone, argues the little voice in my head. *If he's all right with the real you, how amazing would that be?*

Year three ends and I'm dreading the longest time I'll spend with Mother since I escaped to ISS, as only fourth years and above can remain in school for summer camp. But then, there's Wura! Dying to see her, I rush into the living room, hug her close, then back away. She smells different. Not bad, just weirdly metallic. Her old dewy scent was always comforting. I probe the usual warm space that binds us and it's closed down tight. Mother hovers nearby, looking anxious. I greet her and she side-mouths a reply. Worried, I grab Wura's hand, ignoring her reluctance, and tug her up to my room.

Up there, the mirror reflects her wire-taut, arms-folded body. Stiff and concave as though if she tried hard enough, she could back all the way out of it. On her chest are two slight bumps, just like I've noticed on some girls in my class. My fear is huge and nameless. She's *my* person. In this whole wide world she's half of me. The silence stretches. It's almost absurd how alike we remain: taller, slimmer, my jaw a shade squarer.

Our necks are longer, our collarbones delicate bridges. Amazing that hair and clothes and attitude make people see on one side a girl, on the other a boy. That Mother can look at us and believe I'm some devilish spirit inhabiting her real child. Wura's eyes won't meet mine.

'What's going on?' Has Mother finally succeeded in turning her against me?

'Nothing.'

'You're lying.'

'Okay, nosey parker! It's just something girls get. You know ... periods?' That particular arch to her eyebrow used to be reserved for other people being irritating pests. Never me.

I sit hard on the bed. 'How does it feel?' Wura is really doing this new thing that changes your smell and makes you act strange and lets you have babies.

'Well ... my stomach ached for a while and I felt sick, but that was the first few times and now, well, it's just there.' Wura twists the beaded bracelet on her wrist.

'It's been going on all term and you didn't tell me? We've always shared everything.' *Liar*, whispers the voice in my head.

'Unless you plan on bleeding, it's not exactly any of your business?'

Ouch! 'What if I do?'

Wura's eyes widen almost comically. 'But you can't! You don't really have a real ... I mean, a real ...'

'Don't I? Should I show you?' Who can blame her when even I couldn't face that reality till it ambushed me in biology class?

'No. *You* can't have periods. That's just too much.'

'Really? Thanks for the support!' It came out harsh. What's happening to us? I take a calming breath. 'Look, Wura, I don't want to fight. But maybe if it happens, Mother will finally admit she's wrong.'

'And maybe if I flap my arms and pretend I'm a turkey, I'll finally lay eggs! Do you remember which mother we're talking about? Use your brains! How would you explain periods at that school where you're so happy, eh? And what would your friends say? Just ... stop wishing for things that only bring trouble.'

'But what if it happens?' We've no idea what is going on inside of me and there's no one else I can turn to.

'Then you hide it, same as you hide everything else. Otherwise we're screwed. What good will it do to advertise your differences now? This past year has been good for everyone. Can't you try and keep it that way?'

Her words sting like pepper finding that cut on your finger you'd forgotten about. It isn't that Wura doesn't see. She just doesn't see *any other way*. She thinks the sooner I accept the 'reality' of spending my whole life in hiding, the sooner we'll be safe, because look how disastrous it's been already. It's pointless to remind her Father caused all this. He hurt us all, not me. He had the power to keep us safe but didn't.

Wura paces, twitchy, longing to be anywhere but here. I want to reset the day and come home to a sister who doesn't sound so alarming. We should be breathless by now with the joy of being together, swapping stories, laughing non-stop. I fear I'm losing her. She even talks differently. When did she start saying *screwed*? There'll be plenty of time to worry later. First, I must deal with practical things.

'So, does it run like water? Like a tap?' I'd planned to eavesdrop on the practical class the girls got from the biology teacher but the way boys avoided even passing by that classroom, you'd think they were carrying out castrations in there. I know I'll just kill myself if one day in the cafe I suddenly start spouting blood in full view of everyone.

'No. Just little drips.' Wura frowns.

'How do you stop it getting everywhere?'

'Why are you asking?'

'Just in case! Why are *you* being so difficult?' Tears well up despite myself.

'Sanitary pads. They're soft with some sort of netting on top and you peel off the paper at the back and stick it in your undies, okay?' She looks embarrassed, but I have to push on.

'Do you have extras?' There's no earthly excuse for asking a girl at school, and I can't be seen buying any; I've lived with boys long enough to know they'd rather be chased by mad dogs.

'Mommy gave me five packs. You can have one, but for God's sake, don't let anyone see it, and *don't* let her find out.'

'Thanks.' Mother. Of course she gets periods, too. Those are the days she's barred from the Temple of Holy Fire for being impure. I start to understand why Wura is being so wary. Monthly blood is supposed to make powerful *juju*. A 'witch' could use it to all sorts of 'evil' ends, including making someone barren or turning her into a fellow witch. Mother thinks I'm in league with Maami Akinro, and believes Maami Akinro is out to get Wura. I can't stop the tears spilling over. It's not that Wura thinks I'll knowingly hurt her, but that Mother's influence is worsening.

'Look, it's just . . . I'm sorry. Mommy has been so different since you left, and I've never known you so happy, either.'

I'm suddenly awash with Wura's feelings. Her constant petrified worry for me. How worn out she feels jerked like a stick between dogs by her love for me and Mother. How glad she's been to set this burden down for a year. How deeply she's longed for a normal family.

That night, I dream I'm on a dissecting table in biology lab and Bayo is holding a scalpel and everyone crowds around, poking at my open insides, except I'm a toad. Bayo says it's quite clear I'm neither *Bufo bufo* nor *Bufo regularis*, but *Bufo freak*. I wake clutching my stomach. At least, come exam time, I'll remember the Latin names of the common toad.

In the following weeks I check my underwear every chance I get and spin into silent panic when I get a stomach ache. A desperate consultation of my proverb book yields, *It is foolishness to stop sleeping for fear of bad dreams*. Until it happens, if it happens, I'll just carry on as best as I can.

As days pass, Wura and I tiptoe our way back to being close. Together we hang, above her bed, a pen and ink portrait I made by way of saying sorry. *Sorry I'm different. Sorry you lost your father because of it. Sorry it's driven our mother crazy*. It's copied from the photograph I carry in my wallet. I've added a twining border of roses and thorns. If you make a line in the middle where our cheeks touch and fold both halves in, our faces are a mirror match. No matter what, we'll always find our way back to each other. We're one soul in two bodies.

I'm watching a documentary about the Afro-beat musician Fela Kuti when Mother comes into the living room. She recently rose in temple ranks to Grand Senior Prophetess, and never leaves her head uncovered any more.

She's soon complaining loudly on the phone to Aunty Abiye, while cutting her eyes meaningfully at me, about a prophecy that her fabric shop would flourish but for her ongoing battle with evil. Considering she practically lives in the temple and spends non-stop on offerings, I doubt evil has anything to do with it. If Father ever stops sending money, we'll be in trouble. Not for the first time, I wonder about her soundness of mind. Though maybe, as Wura said, she's a different person when I'm not around.

Mother hangs up the phone. Sits down. I consider leaving but I really wanted to see this.

'Oshi!' She hisses in disgust, shifting as if the sofa she's sitting on has turned into a runaway camel.

I sigh. Why she still bothers watching TV I don't know, since it only seems to confirm her opinion that everyone else is headed toward hellfire and damnation.

Onscreen, Fela sits in tight red briefs, puffing at possibly the most gigantic roll of ganja ever to see the light of day, talking about his philosophy of life. It's fascinating to watch this man who dares to be exactly who he wants. He married his queens (twenty-seven of them on the same day!) to silence people who called them prostitutes just because they were his backstage dancers. They were free, he said, to leave anytime they chose. Some scenes show them making up their faces. One queen has carefully sketched a curving pattern of white chalk dots – delicate as lace – on her forehead and around her prominent cheekbones. Her big eyes are darkened with kohl, her lips painted near-black plum. Her gorgeous face brings back memories, a stab of loss. I now only glimpse Yeyemi in my dreams. Those dreams where I'm Lori.

If I saw her again, I'd have so many questions – will I be okay? Will I get periods? Will Sister Angelica's word ever mean more than I found in the dictionary? I'm doing well at ISS, and she's only ever appeared when I was desperate or endangered. She once said something about the cost of rending the veil between worlds and how it must always be paid for.

Beside Fela, two of his wives gaze steadily, defiantly into the camera. A third sits on a chair nearby, smoke curling about her face.

'Ha!' Mother huffs, wagging a finger at the TV as if those in it can see her. 'Children of disgrace! Sitting there like common harlots, shamelessly smoking weed before the whole of Nigeria! One can only wonder who cursed their parents! *Mchew!*'

Things unsaid float in the air like an unacknowledged fart.

I tell myself her words don't hurt any more. Whatever anyone thinks, Fela's queens at least have the courage to dance, literally, to the beat of their own drummer. Maybe it's the only way.

14

BEFORE

1989 (AGE 12)

Father wasted no time. Two weeks later, *NaijaMoves*, one of Mother's favourite society fashion magazines, featured him on the front page. He sat smugly smiling, his new bride kneeling before him, his Rolex glinting as he stuffed her handbag with fistfuls of dollars and pounds and naira to show – as was customary at a traditional Nigerian wedding – that he'd always provide for her. *Plastics Millionaire Weds Lagos Beauty!* crowed the headline.

Mother shut herself in her room, sobbing, till Mama Ondo arrived. She kept saying over and over like a broken wind-up toy, 'He did it, Mama. Married someone else and left me alone to mind his mess. All these years hoping he'd return! Yet he did it!'

Mama Ondo only stayed a week. She was awaiting an important delivery for her fabric shop. I was glad to see her go. The air felt heavier to breathe when she was around.

Tense, miserable days passed during which we tiptoed around and Mother wore mourning black. Sunday morning, she woke us up at 6 a.m., picked out a white dress for Wura to wear and the best she could find for me, a cream shirt and trousers. She'd not picked out our clothes since we were toddlers. Outside, we waited for Mr Driver to bring the car round. Ezra Baptist Church service didn't start till ten. Where were we going? I shivered despite my long-sleeved shirt. The harmattan haze clouding the air hadn't yet lifted and a watery finger of sunlight barely poked through. It brought back those mellow mornings we'd set off first thing for Babalawo's hut. I felt sore with loss. He never had a chance to tell me the meaning of the oracle's messages. Or what steps to take and which forbidden *ewo* to avoid, so my *ori* would not buy trouble in the marketplace of life.

In the car, Wura sat sullenly silent. She hated waking up early and, on a weekend, it was added injury. I was wide awake because the newly determined look on Mother's clean-scrubbed face was worrisome.

We pulled into the car park of a white building that looked like it could house a small plane. On a spire at the top stood a giant gold angel. Six outspread wings sprouted from its back, three on each side. A long paved path led to the entrance. Mother told us to take off our shoes. Wura's eyes were huge reflections of mine. Our hands fumbled close and clutched tight as we stepped through massive purple-painted wooden doors, into the Seraphic Temple of Holy Fire.

From the doors, a long purple rug lined a path to the pulpit. On it knelt three men in long white robes and purple sashes with gold fringes on the ends. Tall sconces holding burning candles blazed behind them. Waves of people wearing long white robes and sashes of different colours filled the aisles on either side, the women's heads covered in tight scarves with no hair peeping out. Few wore normal clothes like us, though Mother's white *iro* and *buba* were modest, and her cotton headscarf was nothing like her usual elaborately tied, towering brocade *igeles*. We were all barefoot.

We sat beside one of the windows lining the inside wall. The giant doors boomed shut.

'Let us arise and pray,' said one man in front, who Mother whispered was Woli Omolaja, the most senior Woli prophet. He prayed so long my legs got tired. Then everyone began to sway and sing, '*mimo, mimo, mimo*,' which meant 'holy'. Soon the temple was brimful of incense smoke, as though a grey cloud had descended from the sky. I longed to go outside and breathe fresh air but knew I'd better stay put.

The choir began to sing. There were drums and cymbals. People danced with abandon, taking turns to sway and spin while others stamped and clapped so hard their hands must ache for days afterwards. One woman started spinning wildly on her heels, faster and faster like a top, till I was dizzy. The senior Woli shouted, 'Hallelujah, the angel has visited our prophetess!'

Four women urged her to the front, where she collapsed. All of a sudden she arched up, strained and vibrating. For seconds, only her heels and clenched fists and the back of her head touched the ground, then she deflated like an empty sack. The women carried her out through a side door. I finally remembered to shut my mouth, the corners of my eyes seeking Wura's. She too looked as though if the temple had flies, she'd just swallowed a few.

From my seat by the window, I watched them lay the prophetess in a square space. It was filled with white sand and enclosed by a low cement wall but open to the sky on top. A covered well sat nearby. She looked as if she'd fallen asleep on a tiny beach. The Woli began preaching the sermon, but my eyes remained fixed on that window. This was nothing like Ezra Baptist Church, where people wore their Sunday best and sang softly from hymnals.

The women stuck seven lit candles in the sand around the prophetess. I hoped she wouldn't flail around and catch her long white dress on fire. She lay still for ages, then suddenly got up and walked jerkily inside like a zombie, followed by her assistants. She wrote something in a big book with a purple cover lying on a gold-fringed cushion beside the altar, before lurching back to her seat.

When the preaching ended, the Woli picked up the purple book. He called out some names and said the Holy Angel had a specific message for those people. A tall thin woman and a younger one who looked like her stepped out to the front. The Woli announced that the Holy Angel declared during the prophetess's trance that the mother's failing business and health were a result of her daughter's upcoming wedding to a man the Temple disapproved of. He ordered the woman to break off her daughter's engagement if she wanted to prosper or be well, then told the daughter she would be the cause of her mother's death if she persisted. The daughter sobbed as though she would die right there and then. Her mother loudly thanked Jehovah for revealing the solution to all her problems.

·When, four hours later, the purple doors opened and we stepped out of the hazy temple, I blinked into the sunlight, surprised a normal world still existed.

I never got used to it, Sunday after Sunday. Mother also went alone two evenings a week and returned smelling like a stick of incense.

At every service, the 'purifying angel of fire' sent a general message to the temple, and sometimes to a specific person. When the *Terrible Book of Unending Doom* (as Wura and I now called it) came out, it was like court TV. Misfortune was almost always an inside job: sibling, relative, in-law, business partner, friend, husband, wife. The whole world (outside of the Seraphic Temple of Holy Fire) was out to get you. Often, a wife who had been desperate to have children came forward to display her 'miracle baby', after spending nights at the temple under the altar cloth. The senior Woli always looked especially pleased, as if he'd waved a magic wand and created the baby himself.

Still, it all left Mother ecstatic and, as long as I sang and clapped along, she let me be. The worst thing was the fasting every third Sunday. To take my mind off my unhappy stomach, I thought about good things, like honey on the comb (which took me back to Babalawo's calm, herby-smelling hut) or Yeyemi's long, gleaming plaits swirling in sun-sparkled azure blue water (I'd given up wishing she would appear again, figuring if I had to be at death's door or something for it to happen, maybe it was just as well) or me and Wura laughing till our sides were sore, watching TV repeats of *Village Headmaster*. (Once I giggled aloud remembering Chief Eleyinmi dismissing someone's arguments as 'nonsense and ingredients!' just when the Woli paused preaching. Mother's look could have turned me into stone.)

*

After a few weeks, Mother woke us early as usual but poured some oil that smelled like dead flowers on our heads. She gave us floor-length white robes, mine square-necked, theirs round.

'God, that oil stinks! And why do I have to wear this thing?' Wura looked ready to hurl it on the ground.

'It's not a thing – it's a *sutana*, as you well know. We're wearing them because our period of probation is over and we're true Temple members now.' Mother's face glowed like she was about to walk down the temple aisle and marry an angel.

'But I want to keep wearing my own clothes!' I knew she was desperately hoping to not run into anyone from school wearing a *sutana*. It was decidedly *razz*, definitely uncool. She'd started spending break times with a new group of girls. I'd longingly spied on them trying on pink lipstick behind the playground, though they wiped it off before returning to class. Mother had stopped wearing any make-up as per Temple rules, which also included no alcohol. Mr Driver had happily relieved Emily on her way to throw out all the alcoholic drinks in our house.

'Wura, don't annoy me. This is an honour for us!'

As we walked down the temple path, the long, wide *sutana* sleeves dangling to my palms, I was tempted to flap my arms and pretend to fly away. Wura subtly fluttered one hand and caught my eye. We kept smothering laughter till I got hiccups.

Beside the door, I saw a metal cage against the far corner wall. Huddled inside was what looked like a small dog. Then we got closer and it moved and all laughter left me. A girl, about seven, crouched in there, not even able to fully sit up. She stared dully out from between the bars, wearing a brown robe that was rough and scratchy-looking like sack cloth. Her matted hair was dirty and she was so painfully thin her knuckles stuck out like sharp knobs where her fingers tightly grasped the bars. She pulled faces as her lips moved in soundless conversation with no one.

'Devil-possessed,' Mother muttered in response to Wura's wide-eyed shock as she hurried us past.

After the service ended, we walked past the caged girl who was silently weeping, face turned to the wall, shoulders trembling. Though she was in the shade, the heat must have been terrible. I couldn't stop thinking about her.

The next Sunday, while the Woli preached, I pretended a stomach ache and whispered to Mother that I needed to use the bathroom. She glared at me and shook her head. We were discouraged from going out mid-service as toilets were considered unclean and were built apart, furthest from the temple. 'But I have a running stomach feeling. I must go now!'

Mother's look said I'd pay for this. She gestured to an usher who quickly came to let me out of a side door.

I tiptoed around to the cage. No windows looked out on this side. The girl watched me with solemn eyes. I put my finger to my lips, *shhh*, then held a tube of Smarties I'd hidden in my robe pocket through the bars. She took it, eyes suspicious. I mimed opening it and putting one in my mouth. She did so. A huge grin split her face. She popped in five more.

'Are you okay?' I whispered.

She tipped her head to one side, scrunched her face and her mouth moved but made no sound. She was probably deaf-mute or mentally handicapped. I wished I could break the padlock and set her free. Instead, I put my hand through the bars and she trustingy placed hers in it.

'I wish I knew your name. If you can understand me, please don't believe the bad things they say. You're not a devil or a demon or anything like that, okay?'

Her dark eyes softened, her face grew serious and still. I touched my hand to my chest, then to hers, trying to say what words could not express. She slowly nodded. I left her eating Smarties and snuck back in. My stomach really did feel sick. Worse things were going on than I knew.

The next week she was gone. And I was in trouble. The Wolis had traced her chocolate-smeared mouth back to me. Those Smarties I fed her, they said, had allowed the devil back in, just when they'd nearly succeeded in starving him out.

Nightmares haunted me like never before. In one I was a heap of mouldering sack cloth and bones, long-forgotten in a cage in the temple's storage room. While Mother's anger was familiar, these Wolis were a whole different beast. I was terrified to seek help from any grown-up because who knew what they believed? Like my proverb book said, *all lizards lie on their stomachs, therefore we can't tell which one has a belly ache*. There was only one solution and even if it felt like frying pans and fires, I had no other choice.

'Otolorin Akinro! Are there ants in your pants?' my teacher snapped. I was normally so quiet, she called me her brainy class mouse, but today I'd been jumpier than a bagful of gnats. First clang of the lunch bell, I shot out of my seat.

Halfway to the infirmary, though, worry slowed my steps. All morning I'd nursed the tender, crazy hope that together, Sister Angelica and I would come up with some grand plan to tell Mother about glands and hormones. But what if she'd changed her mind about helping me?

Nurse Ade opened the door.

'Can I please see Sister Angelica?'

'She's in Sierra Leone.'

'But . . . but I saw her just this morning!' There was no mistaking that straight-backed stride. She'd been on the path leading to the convent, which was forbidden to students.

'Ah! You probably saw Sister Eunice, her replacement. They do look alike. It was supposed to be temporary but well . . . we'll miss her.'

I stared stupidly at the toes of my shoes. Why did I not come earlier?

'Is something wrong?' Nurse Ade sounded kind, worried. He was a nurse, too. For a moment I was tempted but who knew if, so to say, he was a lizard with a belly ache or not?

'No. Thank you.' I slinked past the teeming playground and its happy-sounding normal children, and found my silent corner of the library.

All I had now was my piece of paper with the magical word Sister Angelica had written. I'd sealed it in an envelope marked, *Otolorin, aka Lori: who she is in plain scientific fact?* It was carefully taped to the back of my precious *Doobees Practice: Drawing Art and Animation* book. The safest place I could think of. Though my tongue kept tripping, I'd also memorized the word: *Malepseudohermaphroditism.*

I stared miserably at the silent rows of books. Just me and a whole lot of . . . words. Maybe I could find something that would rip the web of lies the Wolis and prophetesses wove around Mother. Show her in plain scientific fact that I wasn't some devil spawn, just her child. I'd searched indexes and titles and references. I'd found nothing.

15

NOW

1992 (AGE 15)

Year four at ISS feels like coming home. I'm delirious to be back, standing in line with my luggage, chatting away with Derin about books and movies and games and anything. It feels ridiculously good to be together again. Derin excitedly describes his strategy to write a regular feature for *Blurb!* It's ambitious for a new-joiner but he's as driven to succeed as I am. We both ended year three coming first in our respective classes. As we put away our things in our new room, number 414 on the fourth floor, I battle a familiar worry. Cornelius, now fifth-year, has moved up to a two-person room, and our new roommate, a third-year student transferring from another day school like we did, hasn't yet arrived.

Days later, he shows up but leaves after one awkward night of muffled sobs. Turns out he's extremely homesick. This continues for three weeks till he finally doesn't come back at all. Room fees are paid in advance for a year and apparently his parents are too rich to bother finding a replacement, which leaves just Derin and me. Marvelling at my luck, I settle in like a cat on a sun-warmed stone.

That is, until I see Bayo's hulking form at assembly and learn he failed to graduate and will attend some remedial classes as a day student. At least he'll no longer live in the dorm. It's a small blessing. I know to count those.

I'm moving to block a spike one afternoon during volleyball practice when I find myself lying on the court with no memory of falling.
I slowly remember I skipped lunch after just getting over a cold. Soji,
the team captain, is immediately beside me.

'Someone get the glucose!' he shouts. There's always an emergency
kit nearby. Soji upends four heaping spoons of white powder into a
bottle of water then holds it to my lips while supporting me with one
strong arm. Within minutes, my head clears, the threatening headache
is gone, and I'm lying there staring up into his eyes and wondering why
I'd never before noticed they're so honey-dark.

Now each time he looks my way, my stomach does a funny dance
and my heart hammers like rain on a tin roof. It gets ridiculous. He's
playing shirtless and I miss a simple pass because I've been dreaming of
painting stars all over that sweat-gleamed back that looks like a perfect
night into which a girl could happily vanish. Sometimes, he'll smile as
if he knows the riot he's causing inside me, but it's all in my head. I'm
just a boy on his team suddenly afflicted with a mysterious clumsiness.

One time, when he pauses to correct my underhand serve, Soji's
long thigh touches mine, his warm breath puffs against my neck, I
inhale a heady mix of clean sweat and deodorant and the ball slips from
my nerveless fingers. While I heeded Sister Angelica's warning about
glands and hormones and random changes happening to my body
once I became a teenager, I certainly didn't consider my mind might
go awry as well. Mortified, I glance around to see if anyone noticed and
there's Bayo standing at the edge of the football field, which borders our
court, eyes glued on me. Day students often stay over for games. His
arm is casually draped over the shoulder of Chidi, the boy who tried to
embarass Derin about his *dada* hair. Chidi kicks the ball and they take
off after it. I start wondering if I should quit volleyball.

One evening, I pull out an atlas in the library and find a stack of novels
hidden behind it. They're old and dusty but in perfect shape. I smuggle them out and instantly discover an obsessive, new guilty pleasure.
Romance novels. I can't get enough. They're like sweets – zero nutrition

but oh, so delicious! Silently thanking whoever hid and forgot them there, I ignore the alarm bells ringing in my head, along with advice from my old proverb book that *a person who sells eggs should not start a fight in the market*. Reading romance novels in a boys' dorm isn't just starting a fight, it's setting the market ablaze. But I simply can't help myself.

I'm methodically exploring the library on a quest for more hidden novels when a flyer tucked in a book catches my attention. I've ignored them on various noticeboards but this one seems like a sign. *The theatre group is recruiting!*, it states in bold red letters. Still unnerved by Bayo's stare, I reason that if I give up volleyball, I'll need another afternoon activity so I might as well try this. Maybe I'll fit right in. Theatre, after all, is about dressing up and acting like someone you aren't. Fairy queen Titania's costume from last year's play was to die for. Not that I'd ever be allowed to wear anything like it. This year's play is *Wedlock of the Gods* by Zulu Sofola, which is somewhat like *Romeo and Juliet* set in old, traditional Nigeria.

On audition day I show up bright and eager at the large building where the group rehearses. It used to be the gym before some wealthy parent donated money for a new one because it wasn't up to the standards expected for his son. It's filled with fascinating props and old sets. Beside a witch's hat and a papier-mâché *igbo* mask, a fabulous, shimmery pair of gold high heels immediately catch my eye. I tell myself to keep moving right on.

Moments later, I'm standing deflated before the theatre committee, mortified to discover the chickens in the coop at home can probably act better than me. A senior on the selection committee kindly offers me the position of general assistant. It means I'll fetch water, paper, props, etc., as needed. I accept because I already know I want to be part of this cheerful place with its collection of odd, quiet and popular types. They've come together for this one thing, like rivers that normally flow their separate ways briefly forming a tributary (it's been an intense term with a new geography teacher!). I soon fit like a foot in a shoe and wish I'd joined sooner. Then again, maybe I wasn't ready. Being around

Derin has certainly raised my confidence. He simply took one look at the bustle and noise of the set, wished me luck and stayed away.

I'm doodling the pictures the actor's words create in my head during rehearsals when that same senior peeks over my shoulder. 'That looks really good,' she says. 'You should submit an entry for set design.'

My entry makes it to finalist and ends up being chosen. Derin looks at me like, *well, of course it would!* Then grabs and swings me about in celebration. My heart just about swells to bursting. I wrestle and protest for him to put me down, only partly faking. He's recently been feeling too cool about shooting up four inches taller and takes every opportunity to display his newfound superiority. I'm afraid he'll feel my heart thumping too hard against his chest, my stomach fluttering like mad touching his.

I'm suddenly the most popular person in theatre group, which somehow spills outside as well. Shouts of *Hey, Oto, well done!* and *Best set design ever!* follow me everywhere. Mr Dickson, who is close friends with the theatre mentor, our literature teacher, even pops in to see what the to-do is about. He studies it for a full five minutes before nodding at me approvingly and leaving. It all goes to my head for a bit before panic sets in. I once saw a documentary about how catfish are lured out of the safe peaceful depths by spotlights in which they swim enthralled, right till the moment they're hauled out and clubbed to death.

Derin teasingly calls me the Fresh Prince of ISS, but stops when he realizes I'm truly terrified. Being noticed has never brought me anything but grief. 'Live a little, Oto,' he says, 'you've earned this. I'm seriously proud of you.'

My sudden celebrity also has me turning down invitations to popular parties – who knew there were so many? Worse, there are suddenly *girls* making mushy eyes at me. I'm praying no one actually makes any moves because what on earth am I supposed to do?

I'm applying a brown wash to a thatched roof hut on the huge canvas that will be the stage background when my hand slips and a green section of forest turns muddy.

'Here.' Tiwa, an imposingly pretty girl with perfect hair and a voice like a flute, is holding up exactly what I need – a wet rag to remove the smear before it dries.

'Thanks.' I smile, glad I won't have to redo that bit.

'It's looking good.'

'Thanks.' I try to hide my discomfort as she watches. She's part of the opening chorus, and a day student in a different class. I've seen her around but don't know her. Now every time I turn around, there she is.

'I don't have a lot to do between rehearsals, so I help with the set,' she tells me and so she stands there chatting about this or that, not seem- ing to notice I barely talk or that my body is giving huge *not interested* signals. Still, I laugh when she imitates our theatre mentor, calling her an old wet hen, which is increasingly how she frets and fusses, looking more harried and ruffled when someone flubs a line or stands in the wrong place. We all adore her and, since rumour is they're both single, think she and Mr Dickson would make a perfect couple.

Tiwa thankfully doesn't seem inclined to make sappy eyes at me. There's less of that in general as I stop being flavour of the day. We argue about which *Abiku* poem is better, John Pepper Clark's or Wole Soyinka's. *Abiku* are children whose friends in the spirit world always lure them back, creating a cycle where the poor mother gives birth only for the baby to die and then reenter her womb to be reborn. I prefer the poem where the *Abiku* defies, even threatens, those who would shackle her. The first line always takes me back to that unbelievable deed that freed me from Mother. Other parts of it, though, make me shudder. I tell Tiwa I like it because the imagery is so powerful.

'I prefer the one where the mother asks the *Abiku* to stay put or stay dead,' she says, eyes twinkling. 'It's what I'd tell that child, and not so nicely either!' Her words, so unlike the poem's solemn plea, make me laugh. She can be wittily, wickedly funny. By end of term, we've not only agreed they're equally brilliant poems, she's barrelled past my walls and moved into a place in my life. She's that girl with whom I'd have sleepovers and crucial talks about shoes and make-up and boys, in a world where such a thing was possible.

16

BEFORE

1990 (AGE 13)

Feet bare, we stepped gingerly onto the hot cement path leading into the temple.

I hunched down small and quiet. A trancing prophetess was soon carried out to 'sacred land'. When the preaching began, I disappeared into the drawing of Yeyemi I'd been working on, lines and curves of colour merging and unspooling within my mind, the thunder and sweetness in her eyes impossible to capture, like trying to draw air on paper. I was layering several browns for depth when Wura elbowed me. Woli Omolaja was staring right at me. In his hand, the *Terrible Book of Unending Doom*. I shrank deeper into my seat. Wura's hand gripped mine.

'The almighty has spoken to our prophetess. It is his will that a young soul in this temple be set free today from the clutches of the devil.'

Dread stole my breath.

'The enemy who seeks your downfall is often the person closest to you. This child not only caused trouble for the temple by undoing all our good work on a devil-possessed child, he has all his life wrought destruction upon his mother's life. The enemy must not prevail. Otolorin, step forward.'

'Get up!' Mother hissed.

My knees refused to unlock.

She pushed me into the aisle, breaking Wura's hold. 'You can walk or be dragged, but you're going up there!'

Two ushers siezed my arms. Too many white-robed bodies stood between me and the giant doors. My feet faltered forwards. I felt their eyes stab at me from all sides like accusing fingers. What had Mother told the Woli about me? Did they really believe I'd harm my mother and sister? That I went flying like a bird at night?

They stood me among seven candles burning on tall metal sconces, and Wura's frantic worry beat at the tight cage of my chest. Mother must practically be sitting on her. Her fierce strength, the mad swirl of her outraged anger, kept me upright. People started singing. It sounded like a funeral wail. One Woli circled me, his swinging censer billowing smoke so thick and strong my head lightened and swelled like an overblown balloon.

Woli Omolaja gripped the sides of my face.

'Holy Michael! Angel Gabriel!' he shouted. '*Malaikas* of heaven! Cut the hands of the devil holding on to this boy!'

He squeezed so hard my jaw popped open. Dizzy, I scrabbled at his hands.

'*Ramsalaramballa!*' he shouted, wetting my eyes with spit. His breath stank of eggs gone several days bad. My breakfast of ekọ and bean cakes roiled to life in my stomach. My knees buckled. Slippery like slugs, his lips touched my ear. 'Out evil spirit!' he screamed.

Sour saliva filled my mouth. I tried to say, *I'm feeling sick,* but my breakfast heaved up all at once and I was gasping and I couldn't breathe and the candles, the white robes, the Wolis all slowly tilted sideways and faded away.

She caught me in her outstretched arms, looking every inch a goddess in a shawl of green and gold seaweed that floated around her as if it was alive. It wrapped itself around us. In that embrace, I breathed easy.

'I'm so glad you're back!' I cried, drinking Yeyemi in with my eyes, holding tight so she'd never let go.

I'll always come when I can. The veil between worlds is not easily rent.

Time bought must be paid for. Nevertheless, rest a while, sweet weary one. Rest now.

I rested and rested.

From far away I heard my name. It came again like a tug on a line hooked into my heart.

You must go.

'But I want to stay with you.'

It is not permitted. Half your soul is on the outside. You must go.

Yeyemi opened her arms. I floated out and up. Silver sea stars and glowing jelly fish danced a spiral around my swirling long plaits. It was the sweetest goodbye.

'When will I see you again?' I cried wordless, but there was no answer.

Something wet plopped on my cheek. I opened my eyes, saw Wura's desperate face above mine.

I realized I was no longer at the front altar but lying on a bench at the back of the temple. People were still singing. My teeth chattered. I felt so cold. '*Sorry, sorry, sorry,*' Wura kept whispering as she stroked my brow. Nearby, a prophetess was sponging something – vomit, going by the rank smell – off Woli Omolaja's white robe as he talked softly to Mother. He glanced my way. His smile was smug.

'Be assured, Sister Mojisola,' he said, 'that the removal of the demon inhabiting this body and the restoration of your true son is only the beginning of Jehovah's miracles. Soon, your husband shall wrench himself from the arms of that Jezebel and return to his rightful home with you.'

Mother's eyes brimmed with tears as a smile lit her face so radiant, I stared. Then, wonder to end all wonders, gentle arms scooped me up. Mother pressed me close as she carried me, heavy as I must have been, out of the temple. She lay me down in the back of the car then climbed in. She lifted my head onto her lap. Asked if I was thirsty. Too stunned to speak, I nodded. Such kindnesses had only ever been reserved for Wura, who sat up front with Mr Driver, eyes fixed on the rear-view mirror to keep me in sight. Mother held a bottle of water to my lips and cautioned me to sip gently.

Back home, she tucked me into bed and returned with a bowl of corn *ogi* made just the way I liked it with plenty of milk and sugar. I'd surely woken up in a different dimension, like in my comic book where Wonder Woman fell through a time warp and met her double on a duplicate earth. Because this couldn't be happening. As I relished the custardy sweetness, her hand lit on my brow, warm and soft. She looked at me like someone she could maybe love. Joy stabbed me so sharp it hurt.

Later, Wura told me how, when she'd sensed me choking, she'd pushed Mother aside and raced towards me. Then I'd coughed and a slew of vomit had hit the Woli.

'It's all good, though, isn't it? See how different Mommy is now!'

'Yes,' I smiled, and allowed the hope for a happy home that had always fluttered desperately in Wura's heart to settle into mine.

Will this be enough for ever, though? asked that little voice in my head. *What about glands and hormones?*

I told it to be quiet. According to my proverb book, *it is the greedy hunter who, carrying home a load of game meat on his head, stops also to dig crickets out of holes with his big toe.*

Peaceful months slid by. I sang, prayed, fasted. Choked down the acid-tasting 'holy water' the Woli gave Mother to dose me with, determined to keep this version of Mother who'd always longed, deep down, to love me. It was worth it just to see Wura happy. Mother would put her hand in fire if the Wolis asked, so if they said I was cured of whatever, then I must be. It had to be enough. It was more than I'd ever dreamed. And though Mama Ondo's eyes narrowed at Mother's kindness to me during her visits, surely the Wolis' assurances were enough for her, too? One time she'd been airing her head as she sometimes did when she had some moments alone on the verandah and I was sent to call her in for dinner. She snatched up her wig and crossed herself the moment she opened her eyes and saw me. I asked Wura if she knew what was up with the wig, and she said Mother once told her she was an only child because Mama Ondo's first two babies died as newborns. The grief of losing them, Mother said, had made Mama Ondo pull out her own hair. She'd only stopped after Mother survived babyhood. By then the hairs had stopped growing back. It was such a sad story, I decided to try and think more kindly towards her, even though it was hard.

The school year ended and I unsurprisingly passed with top marks, since I usually finished most assigned books by the middle of term. Wura did well, too. She was probably smarter than me, but had an actual life. Normally, her slightest success was cause for rejoicing while my report card got tossed aside with a shrug and *at least you're not entirely useless.* This time, though, Mother laid a hand on each of our shoulders and said she was proud of us! Wura moved closer and laid her head on Mother's chest. Then she grabbed my hand and pulled me in with her. Fuzzy with happiness, I rested my head on Mother's other side and heard her heart beat – *thump, thump, thump* – against my ear like the best lullaby. Wura looked into my eyes and then her mouth wobbled, then she just gave up and sobbed with joy, and Mother asked what was she being a crybaby about? And then we were all laughing.

To celebrate, Mother took us to Ibadan's best superstore. I'd only been once before and it still smelled as if the air itself should cost something to breathe. Wura chose gleaming stick-on earrings in thirty different shapes and colours. One for every day of the month, the pack said. All her popular new friends had some.

'What about you, Oto?' Mother smiled.

I desperately wanted the rainbow loom. The picture on the pink box made it look like painting, only with thread. But that picture was of a happy little girl, busily weaving. An unfamiliar anger swelled in my chest as I picked the ping-pong bat set instead. It would be fun to play with Wura but, as always, it wasn't what I wanted. Mother nodded in approval. I pretended not to hear Wura's relieved sigh.

Alone in my room that night I opened the brand-new pack of girls' undies. They were crisp and white, each with a beautiful flower embroidered on the front. Mother had bought them for Wura and they'd both searched high and low after we returned from shopping before concluding they likely fell out of the shopping bag on our way to the car. It was an impulsive theft I'd immediately half regretted, but it was too late now. I slipped on the pair with tulips and felt instantly better. I'd only wear this one, just this once, I promised myself.

17

NOW

1992 (AGE 15)

'This is delicious!' Derin cuts himself another slice of cake. It's the beginning of term, and of course I came back with cake.

'Wura baked it.' It's the fruity kind I love.

'Wow! I'd better put in my application early!' Derin jokes.

'Haha! Join the long line.' My laughter rings hollow in my ears. Way back when Derin first saw a photo of Wura, he'd been struck both by her beauty and how alike we looked. I'd caught myself smiling, thinking it meant Derin thought *me* beautiful. I'd wondered then where that ridiculous thought came from. I still don't want to know. Neither do I want to know why the thought of sharing him with Wura, even as a friend, makes me want to light things on fire. That, I suppose, is how she's always felt about what's hers.

I immediately get busy putting away my clothes. When, for heaven's sake, did I start thinking of Derin as mine?

With discipline lax on the first day of term, Derin and I sneak up the fire escape stairs after lights out to lie on the forbidden dorm roof and watch the night sky. I've missed him so much it's hard to not just stare at him non-stop. But it's more than that. He went home ordinary Derin and came back ... magnetic. I glance yet again at his profile, and he catches my eyes. His smile, which always bubbles up so easily for me, stops my heart mid-beat, after which it seems determined to pound all my blood into my hot face.

Tell him who you really are! that small voice in my head says. *It will be okay.* It sounds just like that voice that once urged me to try on Mama Ondo's wig. To wear Wura's dress. The one that said it was okay to sing in the shower. And look where all that got me.

Derin points out a squiggly collection of stars. 'That's the constellation called Orion. If you mixed that into Yoruba mythology, it would be called *Ode*, the hunter. If you draw an imaginary line between those bright ones, it resembles a man with a bow and arrow.'

I follow his finger and it does indeed come together like a join-the-dots picture.

'So, Derin,' I say in my best investigative reporter tone, 'are you sure your dad told you the truth? You're not in actual fact the adopted outcome of a union between a dictionary and an encyclopedia?'

'Haha, very funny!' Derin pokes me in the side and I try not to squeal out loud. 'I just love reading Dad's books and magazines. When I was younger, he'd read them to me and show me the pictures. Then, as I grew up and could read them for myself, it all started to make sense; like putting on my glasses for the first time and really seeing. These days he suggests books he thinks I should read so we can discuss them after. Those are the best times. There's such a great big world out there, so many different types of people, so many ways to live and be, you realize there's no one right or wrong way.'

My heart starts pounding loud enough to deafen me. *There's no one right or wrong way to be.* Maybe I can do this slantwise 'So ... did your dad ever tell you any Yoruba creation myths?'

'Yes. I love those! It's kind of uncanny how cultures worldwide have similar myths about a watery earth where everything must be newly formed by gods who quarrel among each other just like humans, but with superpowers. My favourite from the Yoruba cosmology is about Obatala. Wanna hear it?'

A shiver runs down my back as I nod. What were the chances?

'Odumare, the supreme god, put Obatala in charge of making

human bodies. He was good at his job, except when he got drunk on palm wine. He'd fall asleep afterwards then wake up to realize he's made a batch of imperfect people. Some with one arm or leg shorter than the other, some with no eyes, some with twisted bodies. And that's the explanation for basically anyone who doesn't look the norm. You know, like albinos and dwarves and so on.'

'So that would include people like your twelve-fingered uncle, and that hunchbacked American drummer you told me about?'

'Exactly. It's all make-believe, of course, but Dad says our own stories and myths are what make us eternal because that's how we learn from past mistakes and pass on the lessons and wisdom of our ancestors.'

'That sounds right.' I'm thinking of Babalawo, but unwilling to mention I used to see him. Not that Derin would judge but I've learned to not reveal things that lead to questions I can't answer. I sometimes wonder if Babalawo accepted and declared that I'm a girl without so much as a blink because he's a kind and good man who truly sees people for who they are, or because *Ifa* and the Yoruba cosmology have provided answers for so many centuries to so many people's life issues, that to him my condition was just another 'riddle of the gods' as he put it, for him to solve. I was just another person for him to unite with her life's purpose, a creation of Obatala whose *ori* had given him instructions on who I wanted to be.

'Dad always says, *By all means take your pinch of Thackeray, but with a bushel of Thiong'o.*' Derin's voice brings me back from my musings.

'I know Thiong'o, but who's Thackeray?'

'Some old English writer who wrote this huge book called *Vanity Fair* that's one of Dad's favourites. So which deity do you like best?'

'Yemoja,' I say, remembering the lost joys of visiting Yeyemi's realm. 'She is the divine mother who birthed the other gods and goddesses. She is so beautiful!'

'Ah! Dad once took me to an artist's studio in Badagry. He had a stunning painting titled *Yemoja*. She wore a crown of stars.'

'Sometimes the stars shine on her fingernails,' I dreamily add.

'Oh yeah? And how do you know that?' Derin's grin is teasing.

'Because sometimes . . . okay, this sounds really strange but . . . she appears to me? Or, well, used to.'

'In your dreams?' Derin's eyebrows are clearing the rim of his glasses. Are his eyes more guarded? I hear a faint noise in the stairwell and perk my ears. Things stay silent. It also gives me a moment to think about how to answer Derin.

'Yes. I mean *no*! I don't really know. When things got really bad at home, she'd kind of appear and I'd feel better . . .' That wasn't even what I'd planned to say.

'Like an imaginary friend?'

'Yes.' My arms fold around my chest. The damp night has slid under my skin. 'We should go in.'

Derin nods, bumps my head sideways with his to show we're all right.

What sane fifteen-year-old still sees imaginary people?

Though the dorm is forbidden during class hours, I dodge Kokumo, the newly elected and somewhat over-efficient dorm prefect, and his deputy, Fayemi, and slip in during breaktime. Tiwa lent me a book belonging to Fatima, a friend of hers, who needs it for an upcoming test. I was recently startled to receive a joint invitation with Tiwa to attend an off-campus party I've no intention of sneaking out for. I've ignored it and she hasn't mentioned it. People seem to think we're dating. As long as we both know it's not true, it doesn't matter. Tiwa probably laughs herself silly at the idea. It's strange to find myself in this small circle of friendship but I'm enjoying it. Especially since it's kind of widened to include Derin and all four of us sometimes spend lunch breaks together. Still, I'm glad they're day students and after class still belongs to Derin and me.

I unlock my closet door and have the weirdest feeling things aren't as I left them, though nothing is missing. On the floor of my closet, my suitcase, which I've stupidly left unlocked, seems undisturbed. No one else has a key to my closet padlock, not even Derin. I have to run back to class, so I shrug off any disquiet. Later that day, I sign up for the dorm handyman to replace my closet hasp with a heavy duty one. It takes forever for him to get round to requests, but he always eventually does.

February half-term break soon rolls around. As a fourth year, I'm allowed to remain in the dorm. I've been waiting for this forever. I've heard half-term breaks are bliss. There are usually no more than twenty to thirty boys left in school and, for once, fourth and fifth years band together to have fun. With no compulsory organized activities, the days are filled with games and the nights with storytelling. Or you can just loaf around till all hours. The gateman even turns a blind eye when the designated student sneaks out to buy *suya* roast meat and chicken from a nearby clubhouse. I've heard tell that older boys smuggle in beer and even whisky, though everyone obeys the unspoken rule that only fifth-year boys can indulge – which is absolutely fine by me. Few girls stay. I guess once parents hear how lax discipline becomes, unsupervised teenage boys on the loose around their daughters doesn't sound so good.

I'll miss Derin – his dad wants him home every holiday – but it will also be great to relax, be less vigilant, even sleep naked! Not that I would, but the *idea*! I'll also be looking after our latest prized possession. A month ago, during a school trip to the local fisheries, we bought a small tank full of colourful guppies with fantails like mermaids. They flash every jewel colour: emerald, quartz, ruby and more. We've cared for them together, Derin doing the morning feed and me the evening. I love having these beautiful creatures in our room, belonging to us both. They nudge back memories that grow more deeply buried inside me as time passes at ISS, memories of a being as beautiful and incredibly perfect in every detail. I remind myself Yeyemi knows I'm happy, and so she lets me be.

By lunchtime on the day the half-term break begins, almost every student who isn't staying has left. I overindulged in a classmate's breakfast birthday goodies and I'm not hungry. Besides, I've been dying for some quality time alone with my favourite activity.

Outside, the wind picks up, howling as if it wants to beat its way in. My room feels extra cozy. I wait to be certain Derin is gone, then lock the door. I slide a hand under my mattress, unable to resist the fresh stash of romance novels hidden there. I've been buying them from the bookstore in town, hands clammy with nervous sweat, pretending they're a gift for my girlfriend. I recently discovered that shyer girls hide and secretly pass them around in their dorms in illicit enjoyment, I guess, of what they aren't yet bold enough or, in my case, *wouldn't dare* to experience. I wish more of them had covers with people that look like me and was delighted to find a couple, but however the hero is pictured or described in the book, his eyes, in my mind, are always an intense, catlike greenish-amber, or a knowing, half-lidded honey-brown, his body somewhere between tawny copper and deep midnight. Either gets me all warm and bothered under the bedclothes.

In case Derin comes back unannounced, though, I've wrapped each book cover in newspaper. I plan, every night, to read myself to sleep and dream of the handsome man who'd one day sweep me off my feet while declaring his undying love.

I lie back and crack open the first page with a happy sigh. Life is sweet!

I hear a key in the lock. The door opens. I think I'm hallucinating when I see Bayo. He shuts it, turns the lock and pockets the key. My feet hit the floor before my brain says to move, my whole body stretched taut. The ground is a long way down if I jump from the fourth-floor window. I'm probably alone in the dorm. Even if I scream, the few remaining boys are in the cafe. Why, dear goddess, am I not there with them?

Smiling a skull's smile, Bayo moves fast, plants his giant hand like the flat of a spade on my chest. Shoves hard. I fall back on the bed, my head bouncing off the wall, stunned stupid.

He brackets my knees with his legs, picks up my book.

'So what are you reading?' He sounds almost gentle. Ice crawls up my spine.

'Nothing. Just go away.' *Think. Think.*

'Go away?' he jeers. 'Not till I get what I'm after.' He opens my book. Snickers. Reads aloud. *'I will love you as long as there are stars in the sky. All I ask, sweetheart, is that you wait for me.'* His mockery makes it even more condemning.

If I can just grab my heavy wooden chair ... I slide slowly sideways.

'By the way, my sister keeps your same kind of Kotex in our bathroom at home. These poor innocent boys have no idea what a freak they're living with. A boy that bleeds!'

My world shatters. I feel cold all over, remembering those times, three or more, I'd found things placed ever so slightly wrong. The feeling that I was missing something but unable to figure out what. I wasn't imagining things that day I signed up for my lock to be fixed. Because he no longer lived in the dorm and I had Derin as witness of his past attack, I'd thought myself safe. Now I know why he's nick-named The Terminator. He won't stop till he gets what he wants, however long it takes.

'There's obviously something terribly abnormal about you, but I've not told anyone. *Yet.*'

'There's nothing wrong with me!' I hiss through clenched teeth.

'Right. Anyway, I'm offering you a deal. You cooperate, I stay silent. Isn't that fair? Everyone is in the cafe filling their faces with fried rice, and I watched your *oyinbo* boyfriend leave. No one will disturb us. This room must get very busy after lights out, eh?' He gestures crudely and my stomach heaves. His mind smears dirt on every good thing. He flings aside my novel and it glides under Derin's bed. He slides his hand down my arm, his rasping breath smelling like the chemical used to preserve specimens in the lab. Whatever he's been drinking, it's awful.

'Look, I'm graduating soon. I won't reveal what I know and in return, I get to do what I want because you'll quietly open those nice legs and let me, okay?' He grins, his pupils all swallowed in black. His trousers strain against his fly. I'll sooner jump out of the window. I no longer care it's on the fourth floor.

'No.' My head shakes from side to side. 'No. No you don't.' No one ever again gets to do anything to my body that I didn't agree to.

Bayo grabs my shorts. Rips them open. I punch him and he laughs. I go for his eyes with clawed hands. He dodges, knocks over my bedside table. My lamp and the fish tank crash to the floor with a mighty crack. There's a faint *flop, flop, flop* of fish dying on vinyl tiles. I fight him with all the anger I've ever felt. With nails and knees and feet. In my head I hear Mother's voice telling me I'm evil and evil will always find me. I hear *demon, emere, unnatural creature*. He catches my wrists in one hand, fumbles with his belt buckle with the other. What if he makes me pregnant?

'No! Stop, Bayo! Let me go!' I'm screaming despite myself. *Stay silent. Stay silent.* I must save those poor fish. Put them back in water. He stuffs my mouth with a corner of my sheet and I can't breathe right. The room vanishes and I see water, I see fish, I see a big, ugly hook. I see Yeyemi swimming along in all her glory and then that giant hook gets her, and she fights and fights and it's up to me to save her and the water froths in a rage and my shoulder catches on the sheet and it falls out and I can breathe and I free one hand and go for his throat. My nails gouge red from chin to shoulder. He snarls and I knee his stomach. Somewhere in the art supply case next to my bed is an X-Acto knife. I need to reach it. Only minutes ago I was so happy. My head is pounding so loud. Then I realize it isn't my head.

The door bursts open, and there like a superhero stands Kokumo, the dorm prefect, his bunch of room keys dangling from his hand. Behind him is his deputy, Fayemi. And the dorm handyman. Their eyes are bugging out at the sight of us. Bayo jumps off me. He stands there opening and closing his mouth like a landed fish. I realize my face is wet with tears, my throat raw with screaming. I rise, trembling, holding my ripped shorts closed. Kokumo turns to the handyman.

'This is a dorm matter. We'll handle it. If we need you later, I'll let you know.'

The man walks away shaking his head. He's just saved me from being raped or becoming a murderer. He picked the best possible time to fix my closet lock. All I can think is, *thank you!*

'What, exactly, is going on here?' Kokumo's tone is icy.

Two boys caught, one partially undressed, in a locked room at ISS is a whole other kind of bad place to be. Father will kill me unless Mother gets me first. I must find my voice.

'B-Bayo was trying to undress me. I was f-fighting him and telling him to stop. He wanted to . . . to . . .' I can't say the word. It's too grown-up. Too dirty. I'm suddenly shivering.

'You lying freak! I just wanted to make certain before I told everyone your privates look diseased.'

'Really? And how do you know that?' Kokumo says, still in that cool voice.

Bayo opens his mouth. Shuts it. I can't hear any more flopping on the floor. My knees wobble. I lock them stiff.

'Bayo broke into my bathroom stall last year and started grabbing me. I was lucky Derin came in and stopped him.'

'Is that true?' Kokumo stares at Bayo like a cockroach he's just found in his stew.

'So what? I only wanted to expose whatever he's hiding. His privates look deformed! What if he has something infectious?'

Kokumo's eyebrows rise. His eyes fix on me and I want to slide under the bed.

'Anyway,' Bayo sneers, 'you can't believe what his roommate says. *Oyinbo* people lack morals like ours. I'm telling you all sorts have been going on in this room!'

'Okay,' Kokumo says, 'let me get this straight. You developed a random suspicion about another student's private body parts. Therefore you broke in while he was showering to investigate. And though no one has meanwhile caught any terrible infectious disease, since your results at the time were unsatisfactory, you decided to investigate further?'

'*Abeg*, Koks, stop talking like a dictionary. I'm telling you he's not what he seems.'

Kokumo's nostrils flare. 'Only my friends may call me Koks. And you've not answered the question.'

'Aren't you supposed to keep this dorm safe? Why don't you look for yourself?'

Kokumo shakes his head and turns to Fayemi. 'I'm taking Bayo to the duty master's office. Bring Oto there once he's decent.'

All the way down the hall, Bayo loudly protests that the duty master will support him once he hears what I've been hiding in my closet.

I fall on my knees, trembling so hard I can barely pick up each tiny dead fish. Fayemi joins in to help. Under the bed, on a wet shard of glass, two are still twitching. I slide them into a bit of water left in the broken tank. I swallow repeatedly, fighting the urge to throw up. *And you thought*, taunts Mother's voice in my head, *you could amount to anything? Hiding among people who would only run if they knew?*

'Ready to go?'

I nod. 'I just need to change my shorts.'

'Okay.' Fayemi leans against the wall. I wish I could know what he's thinking. Behind my closet door, I change shorts. What if the duty master believes Bayo? What possible explanation can I give for having sanitary pads in my suitcase? A student only gets searched if he's suspected of stealing, or hiding contraband items. Sanitary pads aren't contraband. *If you're a girl.*

18

BEFORE

1990 (AGE 13)

The morning Mama Ondo was to arrive for yet another visit, Mother's ear-piercing yell of '*EMILY!*' catapulted me, heart thudding, from sleep. I got to the guest room at the same time as Emily, whose eyes widened in dismay. The overflowing bathroom tub had soaked the guest room carpet, leaving a smelly, soggy mess.

'*Ehen!* After all these years of trying to drum sense into your head, you act like a village girl who doesn't know how to close a tap?'

'Sorry, madam, I was sleepy by the time I finished cleaning yesterday night and never remembered to close the tap.'

'You will be sorry, you ignorant cow. As if you haven't lived in a modern house long enough. Maybe we should just dig a well for you in the backyard!'

I felt sorry for Emily. Mother loved mocking her 'village' upbringing as if hers was any different.

Immovable as usual, Emily simply said, 'Sorry, madam. I will start to dry it.'

It was a puzzle how Mother's behaviour rolled off her like so much water off a duck's back. As if she had some secret power that made her not care. More likely she knew that Mother knew she was irreplaceable. She was hired before we were born, and was intimately aware of the great and terrible Akinro family secret, aka *me*. I was certain she'd never told a soul and wondered sometimes what kept her so loyal despite Mother's attitude.

Wura ambled up in her favourite blue pyjamas with little red lady-birds, rubbing sleep from her eyes. She flashed me a look of *What's up with Mommy now?* I shrugged.

'Wura,' Mother said, 'Mama Ondo will have to stay in your room.'

'No way. It will smell of Holy Fire perfume for months!' She scowled, chin raised, ready for a fight.

'I don't have time for this, she'll be here any moment,' Mother snapped, turning to me. I immediately nodded. That I couldn't afford Wura's antics was a sharp reminder that we'd never be equal in Mother's eyes, but Mother affectionately rubbed my head and that thought passed. Ever since the Woli 'delivered' me of demons, she's only once slapped me lightly on the arm. I was playing dangerously with a lit candle, trying to create a sculpture from the dripping wax.

I'd barely packed a few clothes before Mama Ondo was in my room with her suitcase and holy incense and candles. At least I'd get to sleep over with Wura, something Mother normally discouraged.

I was watching *Short Circuit* the next evening when Mother shouted my name. I hated to stop, because Number Five being alive was just as funny the third time around. Wura raised an eyebrow. I hadn't done anything wrong I could think of. I headed upstairs.

'Get in here, Otolorin Akinro!'

Arms crossed, she and Mama Ondo stood by my bed like twin pillars of stone. Confused, I looked from one to the other. Then I saw it. Lying open on my bed. My shoebox. My treasures surrounding it like mismatched bargains at a market stall. I clutched the sides of my T-shirt to stop myself from snatching up Ebun. I felt the tremble begin from the centre of my head and spread to my feet. *She's mine!* I was trapped between terror and rage. Too old to play dress-up, I'd found something else I loved doing. On secret late nights, I'd taught myself to hand-sew. The gown she was wearing came from an old pink lace top Mother had thrown out. Next to her tiny, lovingly created wardrobe was my colourful hair bauble collection, a lipstick tube with a gold-trimmed cap and an empty perfume bottle with a top shaped like a bird.

It was all bad enough till I caught sight of the pack of flowery undies, three pairs rolled inside their transparent box. My heart sank. There was no way out of this. None.

'*Oya*, Oto! What's all this?' Mother glared off to the side as if she wanted to know even less than I wanted to tell.

My mouth opened and shut as I desperately sought words to help me keep the mother who said 'bless you' when I sneezed. Downstairs, Wura's heartbeat synced in frenzied thumps with mine. *Today has a bad smell*, was the first thing she'd said when we woke up. I'd rolled my eyes, sniffed and joked it was probably just me. We'd laughed and forgotten all about it.

Mama Ondo's foot tapped rapidly on the floor. '*Hein*, Moji? Did I not tell you? See what always happens when you don't listen to me? Remember Jehovah's words. *When an unclean spirit has gone out of a person, it passes through waterless places seeking rest, but finds none. Then it says, "I will return to my house from which I came." And when it finds the house empty, swept and put in order, it goes and brings with it seven other spirits more evil than itself, and they enter and dwell there, and the last state of that person is worse than the first.* That boy is hiding girls' *pata*! And you claimed your troubles are ending! You better open your eyes before you lose another precious thing in your life.'

I wanted the magic power to seal Mama Ondo's mouth shut forever. Mother glared at her then looked away, chewing at the side of her lip. All I could think was, *Please be okay. Life has been so good. Please let things be okay.*

I heard the faintest squeak. The tenth stair made that noise when you were sneaking back up after a late night snack. Or when you were eavesdropping. Wura brushed right past me, picked up the shoebox. Began putting everything back inside. Her hand paused only for a faint second on the pack of undies.

'Wura, what are you doing?' Mother snapped.

'Getting the things I kept in Oto's room.' *What does it look like?* her tone implied.

I marvelled at her sheer nerve.

'Since when did you do that? Are you now turning into a liar? Because, God help me, I will beat that nonsense out of you!' Only once did Mother ever beat Wura like she meant business. Wura had slyly slipped a *goody-goody* sweet Maami gave us into her pocket and was later unwrapping it to share with me when Mother caught us.

'What? I kept them here because I don't have enough space!'

'Wuraola,' Mama Ondo said, 'Jehovah hates lying little girls. They will burn in hellfire.'

'They're *mine*, Mama Ondo! Anyway, why were you snooping about under Oto's bed like an old *amebo*?'

I gasped. She'd gone too far.

Mother rounded on Wura, grabbed her arm. 'You will not talk to your grandmother that way! Apologize right now!'

'Sorry, Mama Ondo,' Wura mumbled, stubbing the carpet hard with her foot.

'Louder!'

'Sorry, Mama Ondo!' she shouted, sounding anything but.

I dared not look at her. The abject gratitude written all over my face would betray us both.

Mother snatched away my treasure box.

'For your rudeness, I'm throwing these things out. I'm sure some street urchins with better manners will enjoy finding them. You can also peel all the potatoes for dinner tonight.' She marched Wura away.

Shaking her head as if wondering what the world had come to, Mama Ondo stood aside to let them pass. As I left, I let Mama Ondo see what I thought of her busybody malice and was glad she looked away first. In Wura's room, I collapsed on the camping bed Mother had set up for me, feeling as if the earth just quaked but left me alive. Wura's sideways glower as she'd left told me, had she known about my secret hoard, she'd have burned it all.

Later, she informed me to keep my sticky, ugly hands off her belongings in the future, then coldly ignored me. Sharing her room lost all its joy. On the third night of silent treatment, I began mournfully singing about how nobody loved me and I'd just go into the garden and eat worms. She started giggling and we were soon nearly okay again. I thanked her over and over for saving me and promised I'd never try to steal another thing of hers again. I couldn't believe my narrow escape.

When Mama Ondo finally left, it was if the air cleared of something dankly poisonous that made each breath a risk. Though Mother was cooler towards me, it was nothing like the old days. Given time, I was sure all would be well again.

Inside, the space where my treasures had allowed me to be me yawned empty and aching. I told myself I was getting too old for them anyway.

I was belly down on my bedroom floor, days later, history textbook open, copying a drawing of the warrior Queen Amina of Zaria astride a black stallion. She wore a red royal turban. Her ears winked with emerald-green earrings. Like Yeyemi, she looked brave and strong and beautiful, holding a long, deadly spear. Someone who wasn't scared to take on the world. Who wouldn't let anyone take what was rightfully hers without a fight. Just how I'd be, if I only knew how.

I'd left the door and windows wide open, so the lingering stink of Mama Ondo's holy incense could finally disappear.

Wura's sudden cry hit my ears. 'No, Mommy! You can't do this!' My body registered her distress. Quick as thought, I was at her door.

She vibrated with rage, watching some of her beloved dresses, neck-laces, shoes disappear into a plastic bag into which Mother was fiercely cramming anything with the slightest hint of red. For certain this was some new Temple ban. Or else Mother had fully lost her mind.

She dug deeper in Wura's wardrobe, pulling out a faded pink T-shirt with a cuddly bear in a tiara that said 'Papa's Princess' in red letters. Wura's lower lip vanished under the top one. 'Daddy gave that to me!' she howled.

'Years ago. It's too small for you now anyway.' She mashed it into the bag.

Wura yanked it back out. Mother slowly straightened. Her fists came to rest on her hips. Wura looked her dead in the eye, planted her fists on her hips, T-shirt clutched in one hand, a mirror-image of steely determination.

Mother heaved a sigh. Suddenly, unexpectedly, she sagged. 'All right. Keep it but never wear it. Understood?'

Wura nodded. Sniffed. Tears spiked her lashes like dew on a spider web. Into the open channel of our connection dropped one quickly smothered thought: *This wouldn't be happening had Daddy stayed.*

I tiptoed back to my room.

Mother soon charged in, threw open my closet and started jamming things in the bag. My mind tried to race one step ahead as her eyes darted around, hungrily seeking more things. I didn't care about my clothes. My beads and amulet lay buried under a corner of the carpet, books permanently piled on top to hide the slight bump. What would have happened had Mama Ondo found them?

I was stealthily using my foot to flip the cover of my schoolbag over my Queen Amina drawing when she sighted my open case of colour pencils, all 150 arranged neatly in their slots by shade. We dove for it at the same time. She held it high in the air.

'Please, Mother, not those!' They were costly, my prize for coming first in class. They'd given me unimaginable freedom to draw and blend and shade. What would I do without my twenty red-toned ones?

'Shut up about your drawings. Woli Omolaja said this house must be rid of the devil's colours!'

'They're pencils,' I cried. 'Pencils! Not the devil's anything!'

'See this boy, o? Since when did you grow a mouth to shout at me? Is it because I have been treading softly with you these past months?'

Unthinking, I lunged, desperate to reclaim the one thing I'd earned that was truly mine. My art was my soul. I simply couldn't lose them. Especially not to that stinking Woli's ignorance.

Mother's arm went higher, her face incredulous that I dared fight back. In my head I knew I should stop. *Reconsider.* But I couldn't. I jumped up and grabbed her arm. She tried to shake me off, pummelling me left and right.

Then Wura was through the door and flying at us like a small whirlwind screaming, '*Mommy, enough!*' just as Mother viciously thrust me away. I slammed smack into Wura. She pitched backwards, flailing, then crumpled and lay perfectly still, blood dripping from where her head had bounced off the dresser's edge. For a moment I froze, then I was on my knees desperately calling her name.

Mother snatched Wura up as if she weighed nothing and ran downstairs shouting for Emily to get Mr Driver.

I followed, barely breathing.

When the car screeched to a stop, Mother lay Wura in the back. I climbed in front but she came around and dragged me out. 'Get away!' She screamed. 'See what you did? Mama warned me. Oh God, she warned me!'

I watched the car peel off, sobs ripping out of me as I collapsed onto the driveway. *My sister! My sister!*

Emily pulled me up, walked me upstairs to my room. She looked at me a long moment as if weighing her words, gently patted my shoulder and left shaking her head. Coloured pencils lay scattered like accusations all over the carpet. I climbed into the window seat and imagined Wura curled next to me. I closed my eyes. Willed life into her with all of mine. We'd made all sorts of plans for our upcoming fourteenth birthday. She *had* to be here so we could do all those things. Or I had to not be here. There was no here without her.

It was dark, a narrow place. A tube. Red everywhere and a *boom, boom, boom*, regular as a ticking clock, and in there I sank. Down, down and tears seeped out and ran down the walls and they echoed with ancient sobs. It was the saddest place in existence and its gloom steeped my heart in my body like a living thing in hot water. The pain! There was no bearing this pain. But then I was flushed out and carried like a piece of flotsam and washed up and up and up and then I knew where I was.

Hope glowed in the distance, a small, still point of silver-blue light. I swam eagerly forward to meet it. Yeyemi's palace was spun gold walls and shimmering silk floors. I floated up to her throne and there was Wura eating a luscious-looking guava and hanging out with several young girls all dazzling with fully grown jewelled tails and diamonds in their hair. She was looking extremely pleased to be there and deep in discussion about calculating the mathematical ratio of glimmer to matte in a perfect eyeshadow. As she gestured, I saw that scales had already begun to shimmer on the backs of her hands. They were so beautiful! I was half compelled to pick up a guava and join in too, especially when I caught a glimpse of my reflection and saw I wore the most beautiful shell bra and waistbeads of all.

I drew closer to Yeyemi and she smiled kindly as if she already knew what I'd ask.

But I couldn't talk. All I could do was shake my head in mute pleading and let my eyes say, *Please, please, not her. Not yet.* I couldn't be alive and out there and she was here.

One boon you have in one lifetime, beloved. To use for yourself or another. Are you certain? For there is no taking it back and there shall be no other.

I smiled with all my heart and nodded.

19

NOW

1992 (AGE 15)

Mr Dickson sits at his desk, his expression the same mild as usual. He's called me his best art student, ever. What will he call me after today? At one side of his desk stand Kokumo and Bayo. Fayemi nudges me to stand opposite.

'Otolorin, tell me what happened,' Mr Dickson says.

I do, ashamed to say what Bayo wanted, how he'd ripped open my shorts, which now lie on Mr Dickson's desk, brought along by Fayemi.

Kokumo describes how, since he and Fayemi have to stay till tomorrow, they decided to get the last of the students' requests fixed. They both have master keys and must sign the handyman into any room. Fayemi thought he'd heard a loud crash and screaming so after knocking with no reply, they unlocked the door and entered.

'So the door was locked but you gained access with your master key?'

'Yes, sir.'

Fayemi agrees with Kokumo's story. Then it's Bayo's turn. Mr Dickson's eyebrows rise when Bayo describes me as a flirtatious, immoral, deformed and diseased freak whose presence in the dorm threatens the safety of innocent boys. My mouth gapes at this re-arrangement of facts. Mr Dickson asks about the bleeding scratches on Bayo's neck. Notes the dark stains under my nails. He asks Bayo to empty his pockets.

I'm confused.

Looking equally puzzled, Bayo slides his hands into his pockets then freezes. His eyes blink rapidly and he starts as if to run. Kokumo steps in his path. Fayemi blocks the doorway.

'Go on,' Mr Dickson says. 'What have you got in there?'

Bayo seems petrified, so Mr Dickson asks Kokumo to search him. From Bayo's pocket, Kokumo pulls out a set of keys. The nametag reads: *Otolorin A. Room #414.*

Mr Dickson is either God or a mind reader.

'Bayo, it appears you stole a student's spare key, then locked him in his room with the intention of assaulting him at a time when you calculated the dorm would be empty. By your own admission, you previously broke into his shower stall, ostensibly to investigate your unfounded suspicions, but with the actual intention of bodily assault.'

'No! I was only trying to prove there's something abnormal about him!'

'You have broken multiple rules. As a remedial day student, you weren't even allowed in the dorms. Since your arrival, you've been an elusive but persistent danger to the younger boys. That's finally over. You're suspended pending the principal's investigation.'

'You're wrong!' Bayo growls. 'He was trying to be unnatural with me. He must have heard something and started pretending to fight just before the door opened. What kind of boy walks like that, eh? You should see how he sometimes looks at other boys, especially that *oyinbo*! I even saw them kissing on the rooftop. I'm telling you, I was only trying to expose him for what he is!'

Anger, hot and alien, bubbles up like lava in my stomach. 'You're lying. We never did, you liar! Liar!' I'm screaming. If Bayo turns this into something else, implicating Derin, expulsion would be the least of our problems. ISS's court of social opinion judges hard and never forgets.

'It's okay, Oto. Calm down. I believe you.' Mr Dickson's words are a bandage, water in a desert, sanity. Was Bayo watching? Listening that night Derin and I were on the rooftop? I nearly told Derin my secret!

'But I searched his things,' Bayo shouts. 'Found sanitary pads—'

'It was a joke,' I feebly protest, and to my shame, start sobbing. 'Just a joke played on me by my twin sister!' I hate lying but what else can I do?

Mr Dickson shoots up so fast books thump to the floor. His open palm slams hard on his desk. The rest of him is deadly still.

'Bayo, listen carefully. Even if Oto possessed contraband items, it's the prefect's duty to find them, not yours. You're already neck-deep in trouble. I'd advise you to stop digging. This isn't your first incident here, and you're old enough now for prison.'

Bayo's lips twist in a sneer. 'Prison? You and whose army? Remember "Ghana Must Go"? You don't even belong here.'

Shock ripples through the office. No one talks like that to a teacher!

'I'll add that comment to the incident report.' Mr Dickson's words are quiet but hard. 'Prefects, escort Bayo to the security guard and tell him I sent you. He'll know what to do.'

Bayo glares at him, then me, eyes so blank with hatred I'm trying to back right through the wall. Those eyes say I've made an enemy for life. I don't breathe till Kokumo and Fayemi hustle him away.

Strange how the floor is trembling, I think.

'Sit down.' Mr Dickson points to a chair across from his desk.

I sit.

'Do you need to see the school nurse?'

'No, sir.'

'Anything else you want to tell me?'

Like what? That Bayo may be a twisted lying bully but in truth I've been wondering what it would feel like to kiss my best friend? That I'm not entirely what I seem?

'No, sir.' I've never found it easy to lie.

He shuffles through a box filled with small cards arranged by alphabet, pulls one out. 'Okay. The emergency number here is your mother, correct? She'll need to sign off on the incident report and decide whether to take you home. You can talk to her as long as you want.' Mr Dickson picks up the phone.

In my head I've leapt across the table and snatched it from his hand. Snapped the cord out of the wall. In reality I'm helpless. Is this how people feel when they know they're dying? Is there no way to stop this?

A gurgling fills the office and I gladly welcome the wave that crashes over my head. If Yeyemi has come to take me away right now, I'll happily go. Except it recedes, leaving me stunned wide awake. *Ask him. You must learn to ask for what you need.*

I blink and I'm still in Mr Dickson's office and he's holding a ringing phone to his ear. In a second, Mother will pick up.

'Stop!' I shout.

'*What?*' Mr Dickson jumps, holding the phone away.

'Please hang up, sir. Now. I'm begging you.'

Mr Dickson immediately hangs up then stares at me like he's considering making another call. This time to the mental hospital.

'Sorry, sir. It's just if you call, Mother won't care that it wasn't my fault. She'll punish me and remove me from ISS and I really, really don't want to leave. Please let me tell my parents my own way? I'll take the report home to be signed. God, I just want all this to go away . . .' What am I saying? Things like this don't simply go away.

Mr Dickson sighs. Takes off his glasses and rubs at his eyes. He's silent for a long while. I stare at the scarred leg of his desk. He has no idea he holds my life in his hands. That his decision could harm me worse than Bayo did.

'Okay. But it must go on record that you insisted on informing your parents yourself. Will you remain at home for the rest of the break?'

'No. I'll just tell them and come right back.'

'As long as we get the signed report back in your file it should be fine. We'll only need to bring in your parents if Bayo's parents contest his expulsion and want a formal hearing – though I doubt it, since for once he was caught literally red-handed by reliable witnesses.' Mr Dickson pauses, shakes his head. 'Finally! That boy just kept confounding justice whenever he showed up here like a bad penny.'

'Thank you, sir.'

'And you can relax. The security guard won't let Bayo out of his sight till he's gone, and the dorm caretaker will keep a permanent lookout for him. I'll tell you something else, though. Boys like him are systematic about who they pick on. I've watched you in my class, and your gentle nature is one of the things that attract bullies like him.'

I'm staring at the floor, not about to admit knowing what he means by my 'gentle nature'. Never mind it being only *one of the things*.

'You could learn self-defence. It builds confidence. Have you ever thought of karate?'

'No.'

'I'd like you to consider joining the karate club. Good for body and mind.'

I picture people beating each other bloody. 'I don't like fighting, sir.'

'Karate is different. It's a series of choreographed movements. Like a dance. Do you like dancing?'

'Yes.'

'Why don't you come to the dojo beside the senior rec room tomorrow evening? I teach the advanced class, but I'll introduce you to the beginner's class teacher. We hold practice sessions during the half-term break. Try two. If you hate it, you don't have to do any more.'

What I'm hearing is that Bayo is only one species of snake in an already over-infested forest. That there'll always be people whose reality and sense of balance is so threatened by the existence of someone like me, they'll do anything, however drastic, to fix it. So *they* can feel better. It's not exactly news. It just hits home to hear him say it. This *will* keep coming at me.

'Okay.'

Mr Dickson's eyes say he knows there are elephant-sized things I'm not telling him. In a minute, I'll be a sobbing mess.

'Good. I'm just glad those prefects stopped this incident from being something worse. Try to not let it define you, Oto. It will be okay. And I'm here if you need anything.'

He hands me a day pass, because even during half-term, we're expected to remain in school. I thank him, then I'm running once I clear the door. The school rings with a hollowness that echoes in my gut. There are barely thirty of us left in a place usually ringing with the voices of hundreds, and I've never been so alone.

Other than the broken fish tank, the room doesn't look as if something so terribly violent just happened. I fill a large bowl with water and slip the surviving two fish inside. They swim round and round in their new confinement. Derin's bed is stripped. For a brief moment I allow myself to curl up around his pillow. It still smells of him, Lux soap and boy. *It will be okay*, Mr Dickson said, but he doesn't know Mojisola and Laitan Akinro. Should Bayo's parents arrive loudly protesting their son's innocence and my parents are called in, nothing will ever be okay again.

20

BEFORE

1991 (AGE 13)

Long, miserable hours later they returned, Wura's neck stiff in a brace.
Beneath a row of neat stitches, a shaved patch above her temple swelled,
like someone had slid a smooth lump of rock under the slit skin.
Though my heart still felt like a sinkhole endlessly refilled with sorrow,
I knew with a fierce joy that Wura would live. She would be okay.

Mother carried her into her own room. Guarded her like a hawk.
Watched me like something dangerous. Somewhere in her head, whatever evil controlled me had been overcome, and she'd let herself care.
Now she was stuck on what Mama Ondo said about a cast-out devil
only going to bring seven more.

When Wura finally emerged, she calmly insisted it wasn't my fault,
but barely talked otherwise. It was as if hitting her head had knocked
the fight right out of her. Like a brave, fierce dragon whose flames had
been doused. She wouldn't even let me hug or help her. No colour
pencils were worth this. Why did it have to be Wura that got hurt?

The next Temple service came a week later, a night one. Wura was
much better but not well enough to attend. It wasn't as if I could refuse
to go. And I'd do almost anything for Wura's tears to flow from happiness again, not grief.

All evening, I trembled with nerves, certain it was only a matter of

time till the *Terrible Book of Unending Doom* turned my way. But then
the last prayers were said and my thoughts turned squarely to food and
bed. Glad to finally be free, I raced to the car, white robe billowing in
the evening wind. Mother soon caught up. With her were two Wolis.

'Oto, Woli Omolaja wants you to stay behind for a purification and
baptism vigil. We're lucky he's set aside this time for you.'

My heart sank so fast my chest felt sucked in. I wanted none of this
'special time'. Yet I felt my head nodding. Anything to keep the peace.
And for certain I wasn't being asked so much as told.

'Good boy. I'll go home to check on Wura and return later.'

What? She wasn't even staying? What if something went wrong?

Yet, as far as Mother was concerned, things went right the last time.
Where Wura saw me choking, Mother saw me delivered from demons.
If it worked then, it will work again, I reasoned. After all, what did the
Woli do other than scream into my ear and make me sick with his
incense and smelly breath? As for the baptism, they'd throw a bucket
of holy water over me and be done. I tried not to think of cages. The
little girl was probably home doing just fine.

Everyone was gone. Outside the temple, we halted before a small shed-
like place built into the walls. I'd always thought of it as a storage room.
Woli Omolaja reached into the folds of his robe, drew out a long metal
key and unlocked the door. My body half turned to run before my
mind caught up to the fact that the others were standing right there. He
pushed me inside. The walls were brown, the cement floor bare except
for a wooden box covered with a thick pile of palm fronds, and two lit
candles on stands in the corners. He prodded my shoulder, pointed to
the ground. I knelt, shaking. I swallowed and it sounded terribly loud.

'Otolorin, we heard how the devil is using you to endanger the life
of your sister. Begin now to meditate upon your sins and beg Jehovah's
forgiveness.' Woli Omolaja stepped out and the lock clicked.

Shadows flickered in the gloomy candlelight. I reminded myself that
Mother said she'd be back to get me. Plus, pissy or not, if I wasn't home
by morning, Wura would tear down the house. That thought comforted

me. Underneath the incense the air smelled of sickness and tasted of sadness. *Probably people retching from being in such closed quarters with Woli Omolaja*, I thought, to divert myself.

My leg began to cramp. It had been probably an hour. Rubbing out the sharp tingle of pins and needles, I decided to sit. I wished they'd return and get on with it already. My stomach cramped thinking of the palm-oil yam pottage with smoked shrimp Emily had started cooking before we'd left. I was practically ready to eat the palm fronds. The candle flames merged and came apart in a sluggish glide.

The door crashed open.

'Get back on your knees!' Woli Omolaja shouted. 'You're here for purification, not to sit around! This is no joking matter. Tonight you shall part ways with your demons.'

I scrambled into position, the stench of incense and bad breath that always hung around him like an *obuko* goat making me gag. I wondered if no one ever taught him to brush his teeth properly. The other Wolis slid silently in. Each picked up a palm branch. I imagined they were for swishing over my head, like the feathery softness of Babalawo's horsetail staff on my brow as he'd blessed me with incantations.

Woli Omolaja began praying as if he had only seconds left on his personal phone line to Jehovah. 'Holy Gabriel! Holy Uriel! Holy Metatron, king of angels! Sever this child from the bonds of evil!'

I stifled a nervous giggle. Who knew there was an angel called *Metatron*? It sounded like a villain the G-Force fought in *Battle of the Planets*. Wura wouldn't believe it.

A palm frond thwacked on my legs, lightly stinging.

'Otolorin, confess your sins! Renounce your spirit companions!'

I crossed my arms, seamed my lips tight and glared at the Woli. The fronds hit harder, ends flicking the tender backs of my knees, my earlobes, stinging like tiny hornets. I bit hard on my lip to not give them the satisfaction of crying. I tasted blood. Dust from the fronds filled my nose. A sneeze blew its way out, *achoo!* all over the Woli's *sutana*. Bloody specks peppered the white. It brought a surprising surge of satisfaction.

'His demons are now fighting us with blood,' Woli Omolaja hissed, breathing hard. 'Last time it was vomit. We must take stronger action.'

He opened the wooden box. Seized something long and thin and looped. I was already on my feet when the horsewhip licked into my back like liquid fire. My mouth opened soundless. The other Wolis pulled my arms wide and forced me back down. The whip landed again and again and I was screaming, begging them to stop, promising I'd give up evil companions and demons. That I'd never sin again.

If I lay perfectly still on the white sands of sacred land, the grains didn't dig into the burning lines on my back and thighs. Through incense clouds wafting from the censer Woli Omolaja held above my head, stars twinkled in the sky like any other night. Tears slid into my ears. Why did Yeyemi not come? Did I renounce her? Was she evil? No, it was the people who whipped me till I fainted that were evil.

Mother knelt beside me, her face blocking the moon. *Did she know they were going to do this?*

'I want to go home,' I whispered.

'Not yet. You must first be baptized in holy water.'

'My back is burning. Please take me home.'

Mother blinked away the sudden glaze in her eyes. 'You think this is a party for me? I should be at home with a loving husband and blameless children, not here battling for your soul.'

'Hellfire will burn worse than your back if you die unbaptized,' Woli Omolaja sneered.

They lifted me out of sacred land and, as Mother steadied my trembling body, her arm grazed my welts. I hissed in pain. I'd run but they'd catch me in two seconds. *They'll douse you with water from their holy well,* my pain-scrambled mind bargained, *then you'll go home. Then you'll figure out how to make sure this can't ever happen again.*

'The stream will help it feel better,' Mother offered.

I gaped at her. What stream?

Woli Omolaja was already headed towards a narrow path behind the temple, his lamp barely piercing the deep night. The other two Wolis gripped my arms and marched me forward. Mother followed, carrying a candle in a tall glass jar. I looked back to see her lips moving fast and silent, bargaining with Jehovah.

The night shivered with nameless sounds. Stray dogs howled. We trekked a while before reaching a stream hidden behind tall bushes, flowing sluggishly, dark like the oil Mr Driver drained from the engine of Mother's car. Nothing like the silvery stuff of light in Yeyemi's world. My heels scraped lines in the earth as Woli Omolaja dragged me in. The water closed in, silently slurping. I'd never swum before – not in real life. *Don't panic, don't panic,* I breathed, as my *sutana* rose to my chest. Something brushed against my ankle. I quickly told myself it was just weeds. He gripped my shoulder. Raised his other hand skywards. I forced my shivering body rigid. He'd pour water from his cupped hand onto my head, like John the Baptist in my picture bible, then I'd go home and Wura would sing 'Jonpe' for me and the world would finally stop breaking.

His hand slammed down to clamp the back of my neck.

'Holy Michael!' he howled, eyes burning, 'wash the filth of darkness from this sinner!'

And in those eyes I understood I wasn't meant to survive this. Not intact. I saw the girl in the cage as she was before he got hold of her. Too bright, too bold, too strong-willed. And so her stepmother claimed she was devil-posessed and Woli Omolaja dimmed her light till she'd stopped talking at all.

'Yeyemi, save me!' I screamed seconds before he slammed me face down. My feet churned. I couldn't breathe. The hand on my neck pressed harder. I swallowed water, flailed, grabbed onto his *sutana*. The water glugged as he struggled to stay upright. From the corner of my vision, something swept fast towards us. A slinky shape. Darker than the dark. Woli Omolaja screamed and dropped on me like a felled tree. We sank down, down, down.

I was lying on my back. Water slid from my mouth, down my cheek. I couldn't cough out any more. Enormous stars twinkled down. There were too many of them to be entirely real. I was here yet not here. I remembered in patches. Struggling with the Woli. Then Yeyemi came. Then I somehow dragged myself onto the bank before I collapsed. My body was alive with pain. *Everything* hurt. I heard a soft sob and turned my head. Mother sat alone nearby.

'Can you move?' she said.

I slowly sat up, glad for each breath though it felt like inhaling thorns.

'The Wolis left. They said your evil demons redoubled in power instead of fleeing. Something bit Woli Omolaja! That never happened before in this holy stream!'

'But Yeyemi's not evil! She's . . .' I snapped my mouth shut. What *was* she? I shivered with awe, remembering how she'd flipped out of the depths and smiled, bubbling with pure life but armed with death, like a snapped live electric wire I once saw crackling on the roadside after a rainstorm. Her eyes were twin flames, her teeth all pointy and sharp, her hair big as if the moon went dark and circled her head, just like Diana Ross! She'd picked that thought right out of my mind and laughed. I'd laughed too, gone forward to meet her, frolicking like a fish in the waves, finding I could swim after all and the water now sparkled silver-blue. She'd let me stay a while. In that in-between world, time worked differently. But . . . did Mother just say something *bit* the Woli?

'This must end,' Mother mused as if she were alone. In the dim lamplight, tears gleamed down her cheeks. Her white scarf slid down one side of her head. 'Mama thinks he's beyond redemption. Yet why would Jehovah not restore what was stolen from me?' Then like a wish from her deepest soul, she whispered, 'I would have been satisfied with one child. Better a dead baby than a living horror.'

The pain rose and rose inside me, sharp, shredding, spinning. Ten times worse than the night I'd heard her call me a *thing*. How I'd hoarded her rare smiles. Treasured the scarce hugs. This must end, she said. But how? My eyes closed I was so weary.

A hazy image arose before me. A body on a slab. It was far away. Surrounded by swirling mist. I strained to see better. The face was blurry. The pillow-puff lips were closed and I knew at once they were forever silenced. A sickly cloying scent filled my nose, like that time a mouse died trapped inside our kitchen wall.

Wura gently dabbed antiseptic cream into the raw welts on my back and legs. I lay on my stomach, clenched my teeth against another wave of pain. Something plopped onto my back. Then another. Wura sniffled. I wanted to joke that tears didn't heal raw wounds except in fairy tales, so she'd laugh and stop crying. Instead I fixed my dry eyes on her bangles, which tinkled softly as she reached for more cream, glinting a subtle hint of red depending on the light. Their sparkle somehow made life seem less sad.

'I'm not talking to Mommy right now. This madness went too far.' Wura stopped, chewed her lip. 'She's losing her mind with heartbreak and suffering. Yet she just wants . . .'

'What? To get me killed? Father is obviously never coming back and I'm never going to be anyone's perfect son or brother!'

Wura's hands went still. The bed gave as she rose. I closed my eyes and turned to face the wall. Heard the door click as she left. I wasn't sure why I was angry at her. Inside and out, I hurt.

Mother ranted that the Woli's bite wound wasn't healing. That his entire arm remained swollen despite days of overnight prayer vigils in sacred land. I still didn't remember what exactly happened, though there *was* a brief dull ache in my jaw, as if I'd clamped down hard on something. Like wood . . . or bone.

I imagined his fingers fatly sticking from his palm like sausage rolls. Maybe a long stay in hospital would help him reconsider his favourite pastime of torturing children. Wura was now always out visiting some friend or another from daybreak till sundown. When Mother complained she screamed right back that it was school holidays and she was now fourteen years old and not a baby, and she could do whatever she wanted. Our birthday had come and gone silently as they fought non-stop. Though Mother ignored me, worry gnawed a hole in my stomach. The tension caging her body, stick-like from fasting, told me this wasn't over.

It was up to me to save us all from ourselves but the plan forming in my head was so audaciously crazy, I'd never have the courage to carry it out. Mother feared only one thing. If I failed, there'd be no mercy.

21

NOW

1992 (AGE 15)

I have to use the day pass so it gets stamped by the gateman and it looks as if I went home to get the report signed. All I actually do is roam around the shopping centre, not really seeing anything.

Back in my room, armed with the duplicate of a vaccination consent card Mother signed long ago, I practise her simple scrawl, MAA in linked letters, over and over till it's perfect enough to forge onto the incident report. On all the questions – do my parents want to be contacted about the incident, see the principal, take further specific action? – I tick no. Feeling like a criminal, I go and slide it into Mr Dickson's private mailbox, scared if I go in, he'll somehow know exactly what I did.

It's gone past dinnertime and everyone will be huddled around the traditional bonfire on the sports field, where they'll tell stories past midnight. I've been looking forward to it. Instead I find myself in the laundry room, not knowing why I'm drawn there. I might be the only student not terrified of it after dark. All is silent and still. Outside, the stars twinkle. I slide down, hug my knees to my aching chest and cry. I am so very tired.

Hiding in my room imagining the worst won't get me through the half-term break. Nervous but determined, I drag myself to the karate dojo the day after. Then it's a new kind of magic to see boys and girls my size easily take down people two times bigger. Mr Dickson was right. I vow then to take every precaution to stop being an easy target for the Bayos of this world. I'd once have laughed to find the proverb in my book that says, *Trust God but tie up your donkey.*

Afterwards there's a cooking class where we make a steaming vat of coconut rice over an open fire. I sit there staring into the flames till someone thrusts a plate in my hands. I eat. Days pass in a strange unreality where life seems paper-thin, and the coming hurricane could pull it down whole or rip it to shreds. Mostly we sit around or play games. Someone dares me to try my first sip of beer, which I promptly spit out, only to be laughed at. It will taste better next time, they assure me.

It's when I'm alone that the nightmares come. I stab Bayo in the throat again and again with my X-Acto knife but he just laughs and keeps coming as his neck gapes and his blood splatters on my white *sutana,* and Woli Omolaja rattles the purple *Book of Unending Doom,* screaming that I'll never stop attracting evil.

The night before school resumes I curl up around Derin's pillow and try to breathe. Anxiety writhes like a tangle of salted worms in my chest. Tomorrow I'll know my fate. If I survive this, in addition to guarding myself, I must now watch out for Derin so no one sees what isn't allowed to be there.

22

BEFORE

1991 (Age 14)

I stepped out of the house to see Emily and Mr Driver, supervised by Mother, busily loading the car with stacks of yams, coconuts, candles and incense. It was part of the 'penance' Mother was paying because I'd 'polluted' the holy stream. She'd earlier ordered me to get into my *sutana* and get downstairs. Mostly, she'd addressed the wall to my right.

Ever since Woli Omolaja expressly commanded my return for a 'deliverance of fire', Wura had threatened all sorts of self-harm if she was separated from me – a reassuring sign that my real sister was still in there somewhere. Now she stood by the car mutinously white-robed, arms folded, every line of her body screaming defiance. Her eyebrows flew up to see me still in shorts and T-shirt. *What are you doing?* she fired in silent warning. *Go back and change before she sees you!*

I shrugged, masking my own thoughts. Though Emily had washed it the best she could, seeing the faint rusty marks where my back had bled only swelled the storm brewing inside me. I couldn't bear that *sutana* to touch my body. Not ever again. Or drink holy stinky water. Or be left by my own mother to the tender mercies of holy torturers. Suddenly I was gulping air. Tides of panic rose in me and crashed into Wura. She was instantly by my side.

'I won't leave you,' she whispered, taking my hand. 'Not for one second.'

It wasn't enough, though. She hadn't seen the cunning and viciousness living in Woli Omolaja's eyes. And his crusade against me and the demons of his imagination were now personal.

If I got in that car, those huge temple doors would shut behind me, maybe for the last time. Because Mother would never stop trying. And Wura could never truly understand.

A strange scent entered my nose, like ozone after a thunderstorm. Though the late noon sun was low, already half gone, I saw every dust mote dancing in the air. Everything was sharply outlined, trees jaggedly etched against the light. Up ahead, a flock of *lekeleke* smeared the sky silver-white. If you fluttered your hands and sang the right song to them, like Wura and I used to do when we were little, they'd gift you a feathery white spot on your fingernail. Everywhere, life called to me. The car shimmered and vanished and then I was in a passageway made up of millions of kind faces peering at me, with no beginning and no end. They were whispering among themselves, the sound like dry brush on a windy day. *Isn't she something! She's so brave! Such a wonder! A truly good person!* Out of the swirling mist stepped Babalawo. *Eagle or chicken?* he whispered. Beside him, shockingly, emerged Sister Angelica. *You must live in order to find the word.* Queen Amina sat perfectly balanced on her horse. *When the spear sees battle, it rejoices. Use your weapon.* And then Yeyemi arose, flame-eyed, in a big roil of silver-blue water and they were all gone and I was looking across into Mother's furious face. I *would* end it.

'Please, Wura,' I whispered. 'Stay here. Don't follow me no matter what.' I spun around and ran back inside.

Mother strode into my room, hands fisted on her hips. Through the plain white sheet pulled over my head, I saw her *sutana*-ed outline bearing down on me like an avenging ghost.

'Get up or I'll call the gateman to tie you up and carry you outside!' she snapped. 'Woli Omolaja is only doing what must be done to save our family. You'd better come peacefully.'

It was as if two voices were coming out of her mouth at once, and the other was saying *Woli Omolaja will only rid this family of your god-forsaken presence.* I yanked the sheet off my face. Mother's gaze was unflinching, her face cement hard. That old switch in her head had flipped all the way beyond *worst.*

I sat up and, filling my eyes with Yeyemi's fire, flicked the sheet completely aside.

Her jaw dropped. Her eyes skipped to the armband tied to my fore-arm, slid to my left hand clutching the dried bone of a chicken leg, claws curled and stiff, crudely tied with black rope to a red feather. Her face went slack with terror. I surged from the bed to halt before her at my full height. She reared back, stumbled against the wall near the door.

'Enough!' I hissed. 'It's time we're honest with one another. I flew with Maami Akinro late last night. She gave me this *juju* spell after whispering your name into it.'

'Ah, Jehovah!' Mother gasped.

'Yes. You force me back into that miserable temple and your legs will go dry as bone and wither like matchsticks and we will turn you into a cripple. Woli Omolaja's rotting hand is your warning. Know also that we can convert Wura anytime I want, and turn her against you.' Above my Y-fronts, my waist-beads glinted icily in the fading light. I stepped right into Mother's face, pointing my fetish of feather and bone at her legs. 'Now, Mojisola Alake Akinro, will you let me be?'

Shuddering, Mother planted her palms flat on the wall as if to steady herself. She looked so destroyed, so terrified, I nearly blurted out that my only 'evil' powers were eavesdropping and an active imagination. Even then I longed to reach out and say, *Mommy, it's just me, your child. If only you'll look from your heart.* I clenched my jaw. This was no time to be weak. If I'd ever doubted that she truly believed her stories about me and Maami, here was proof.

'I curse the day you entered my womb,' Mother whispered, spun around and left. My legs gave way and I sagged right onto the floor, shaking. Then I made myself get up and watch with grim satisfaction as she drove off with Wura, whose face was turned up to my bedroom window till the car vanished out of sight. I lay my forehead against the cool glass and thought of nothing.

I was woken from dreams of drowning when Wura came in and perched, as was her habit, on the edge of my bed. For once she was guarded, wary. Morning light picked out the raised circular patterns on my bedroom curtains. They must have returned late from the temple.

'So what happened?'

Unsurprisingly, Mother didn't tell her what I did. It would raise questions about Maami Akinro she'd rather not answer. As for me, the time for telling Wura passed that long-ago day on the playground. It was the moment, though I didn't know it then, that our bond had changed. The moment I'd understood that, because she needed both me and Mother, I must spare her some things. Otherwise she'd have to choose. And even if she chose me, she'd come to resent it. Mother loved her with the ferocity of a hundred lionesses. I couldn't take that from her. God knows how I'd craved it and how my brief taste, even of the watered-down version, was like every good thing in the world wrapped into one constant, necessary gift.

'I'm leaving,' I said instead.

'*What?* For where?'

'Boarding school. In ISS.'

'But . . . but we resume at St Christopher's in a week!' Wura gasped.

'*You* were going to resume in a week. I was going to rot away in some godforsaken Temple torture chamber.' Mother would simply have told the school I was sick while her Wolis set about breaking my mind and body. What would have remained when they were done?

Years ago, after coming second state-wide in the common entrance, I'd had several choices of secondary school but Mother decided we'd just move across the road to St Christopher's, run by the same nuns as our primary school. It never occurred to me to question or refuse. I had no voice.

'No . . .' Wura shook her head as if doing so would make my words go away.

'I called to find out and they have an open spot left. They were so impressed with my high scores they agreed to hold it for me. The acceptance form arrived by post today and I've already filled it in.' I'd barely slept after I spoke to the admissions officer, telling her in my most grown-up voice that my mother would be in touch to finalize arrangements.

Inside, I was terrified. A boarding school meant people you couldn't get away from. Lots of them. Day and night. Given my history, it seemed the last place I should be.

'International Secondary School, no less! And you arranged it all yourself,' Wura whispered, awed. 'And Mommy agreed?'

'She'd better.' My eyes narrowed with resolve.

'Wow! Who are you and what did you do with my brother?' Wura's voice quavered, spoiling her attempt at humour. Tears sprang to her eyes.

'Yeah, well, it's amazing how seeing your sister's head cracked like an egg, then getting whipped and half drowned can open your eyes.' The scar above her temple was already hidden by the hair growing back but I'd never unhear the sound of her skull hitting that dresser.

She sighed miserably. 'I can't even come with you. My scores aren't as good and if they ony have one spot . . .'

'It will be okay. And, once I'm gone, you can live freely instead of worrying all the time.' She'd never stopped being reigning queen of her cool friends.

'Are you implying I should somehow be secretly happy about this?'

'No! We will see each other during the holidays.'

'It won't be the same. And for your information, Mr "I'm suddenly too tough to need my sister", I'll never stop worrying about you.'

'Okay. But instead you can do it from a safe distance, hmm?' I feebly joked.

One of the few world-class international schools in Nigeria, ISS offered courses and exams that could guide the brightest students to placement in an American university. That possibility hung before me like the kind of glistening dream that vanished the second you opened your eyes. If I kept studying hard, I could one day get a whole *other country* away from Mother, to a place where doctors could help my body make changes that matched how I felt. I kept that part to myself. It would just make Wura sadder.

We fell silent as an unfamiliar new space opened up between us. There'd be no more talking late into the night – mostly me listening to who did what to whom during her friendship-and-drama-filled days; no more games of Whot!, which I let her win. No more dancing like crazed creatures (when Mother was out) to music videos we bought together to learn all the latest dance moves. They were marked *Property of Oto and Wura*. I'd once heard Mother say Wura wouldn't sleep when we were babies unless we were touching. Perhaps she'd been worrying about me even then.

I looked into clear brown eyes I'd adored all my life and for the first time in days, the stone that was my heart softened. Tears slipped down my face. 'I will miss you *so* much.'

'I don't know how I'll do without you.' Wura's grin was watery with snot. 'Who will I tell when Linda is being an idiot and copying my hairstyle again or that stupid Akim starts calling me his wife?'

She'd picked the silliest reasons. I pulled the long sleeve of my pyjamas into my fist and scrubbed her nose with it. She rolled her eyes but let me. I spread my arm and she curled into my side. Our heads tilted to touch as we'd done a million times before. Not counting the handful of times Wura had stayed over at a friend's house, we'd never been apart.

Yet, from the depths of her sadness, something unfolded and stretched towards the light.

Mother returned from the market early afternoon. I found her in the living room, where Emily was helping her hang up fresh curtains. Figuring she'd seen and heard it all, I launched into my arguments.

ISS, I told Mother, was the second most selective boarding school in Nigeria, and was far enough so we'd be well rid of each other, but close enough that Mr Driver could come and get me for holidays.

'You think I'll just set you loose out there to go and bring calamity?' Mother sneered. 'Forget it.'

Forget it? She'd silenced me all my life, and now I'd made her fears real, she was sure to pull some game-ending tactic. Auntie Abiye and Mama Ondo were probably doing the live version of rolling in their graves. Who knew what they were now planning? Mother had once threatened to lock me outside for child traffickers to steal. Would I awake one day to find myself bound hand and foot, a stranger's property?

'ISS was so impressed with my scores they offered me a spot at the last minute. Do you know what an honour that is?'

'I DON'T CARE about your scores!'

'They only take the best. Everyone will envy you having a son there.'

She was suddenly paying attention. Now I just had to ease her terror that I'd expose my privates or something, and bring the world crashing down on our heads. I reminded her that there'd be fences and gates and rules and strict teachers. How no one in school ever saw a thing – well, except Sister Angelica, but she needn't know that. I added details she'd rather not think about, like how I timed bathroom breaks for when it was almost certainly empty, which made the Y-fronts she bought me a joke, since what I had didn't work for peeing through the gap.

I painted a blissful picture of peaceful years with me gone, while she got to boast of a son in ISS, even hinting that being around so many boys might turn me into a proper one.

Underneath it all lay the soft, unspoken threat, *I'm in league with your worst enemy.*

'And who will pay for it? Your father will never agree.'

'Why don't you ask him right now?'

She eyed me with a sneer of disbelief.

'If you don't, I will.'

The sneer vanished as she understood the nature of my game. If I called Father, his wrath would fall on her head, since it was her responsibility to keep all evidence of my existence from his sight and hearing. ISS fees were, as she well knew, nothing to him.

Her hand trembled as she dialled. I raised my chin. Even grew the nerve to press the speakerphone button.

A soft, sing-song voice at the other end said, 'Akinro residence!'

Mother went stone-faced. I waited for the phone to hit the wall and shatter into a thousand pieces. Instead, she said through gritted teeth, 'I want to speak to Laitan.'

'Yes? And who are you? This is Mrs Akinro, his wife.' No softness there as she reacted to the venom in Mother's voice.

'This is Mrs Akinro, his *first* wife.'

There was dead silence. It lasted and lasted till my stomach was clenched like a fist.

Then Father said, 'Yes, Moji, what do you want?'

Mother curtly explained. The ice in their voices could freeze the whole world twice over. Father was silent so long I feared he'd simply hung up. Then, in that gentle tone that boded no good, he said, 'The one responsibility I gave you for that abnormal creature you're passing off as my son is to keep him from disgracing my name. Yet even that is too much for you? You want to pack him off to some boarding school where who knows what can happen? You're perilously testing my benevolence. You'd better keep him where you can watch him, understood?'

Mother nodded. Then remembered to whisper, 'Yes.' She was looking at me and I knew we were both thinking of Wura. How Father threatened to take her away from Mother and leave Mother homeless and penniless. My teeth gritted with the effort to stay silent. I'd find a way. I just needed to think. I'd find a way that didn't bring harm to Wura.

'Good,' Father snapped. 'And if you ever upset my wife again, you'll regret it. Her condition is delicate. If you must speak to me, call my office.' He hung up.

Everyone knew what a delicate condition meant. Soon, I'd have a half-brother or sister. Mother's hand lowered to her side, still holding the beeping phone. For long moments, it was as if the real her had decamped and left a staring shell. I stood torn between anger and deflation. I wanted to snatch that phone back and tell Father what a sad and sorry excuse he was for a human being. I'd been so certain he wouldn't care. Except he was even more anxious that my 'deformity' never get exposed because of the ancient Yoruba custom of *iwadi*. This practice of systematically digging up everything about a prospective marriage partner's lineage for taboos (mental illness, 'abnormality', suicides, etc.) remained alive and well. I could taint his soon-to-be child's future.

'So much for your big words and big plans.' Mother was laughing, a wild sound terrible to hear. 'Since you're so powerful, maybe you can fly to your witch of a grandmother and use your godless *juju* to change his mind. Just know, if you cause him to take Wura away, she will suffer at the hands of his new wife and it will be on your head and she will never forgive you.'

'What did he say?' Wura asked later.

'He refused.'

'What will you do now?'

'I don't know.' I had no second plan.

'I'll help keep you safe. You shouldn't have to run away from home!'

I thought of things staying the same, maybe getting worse, and knew I couldn't bear it. In my heart I cried out to Yeyemi.

The next morning during breakfast, the phone shrilled.

Emily picked up, said Father was on the line for Mother.

I heard Mother saying, 'Yes.' Then, 'Okay.'

She returned to the dining table. Edged past me like she was wearing lace and I was a thorny bush.

'Your father said you can go on one condition.'

My spoon clattered into my cornflakes. Wura's expression would be the stuff of comics if I weren't sure I looked just as stunned.

'That you remember whose name you bear and don't bring him shame.'

In her strained, hushed voice I heard fear. Cold and stark.

I had no idea what changed Father's mind but Mother had clearly drawn her own conclusions and they were scaring her stupid. Even Wura seemed freaked out.

I simply gave silent, heartfelt thanks and vowed to never do anything to destroy this chance that I'd been given. A week later, we drove past the gates and under the archway of flame trees, and I became a year three late-joiner student at ISS, with warnings ringing in my ears and hope lit in my heart.

PART TWO

The mouse is a bringer of disaster to the home of the innocent. Snakes do not eat corn.

23

NOW

1992 (AGE 15)

The principal sends for me first thing. Being summoned to his office normally means high honour or terrible calamity. I've never been in there before. I take one last look around my room with its tall airy windows. Derin's books are neatly arranged next to mine on our bookshelf. The two remaining fish forlornly circle their bowl.

The secretary tells me to go straight in. I knock and enter, trembling from head to foot. Principal Akiolu is standing behind his desk.

'Come in, come in,' he booms energetically, as if welcoming me to a loud party. 'So you're the one at the centre of this brouhaha!'

Terrified and unsure how to respond, I jerkily nod.

He's short and stocky with cheeks shiny from good living. The end of his tie dangles off the precarious slope of his rounded stomach. Some student long ago nicknamed him Shortput. Only the boldest ever speak it among themselves. He's rumoured to have ears everywhere. All over the walls are photos of him awarding students with medals and trophies or shaking hands with important people like the state governor. A huge, framed certificate shows he graduated with honours from a university in America.

Across from him, Mr Dickson sits, hands clenched, face neutral. My stomach drops even further.

'According to this' – Principal Akiolu waves the paper on which I'd so carefully faked Mother's signature – 'your parents have chosen to take no further action?'

'Yes, sir.'

'Good! Smart decision! Bayo's parents have removed him from ISS. I believe that should settle the whole unfortunate matter?'

My mouth hangs open. *Settle the matter?*

'Not so?' Principal Akiolu is still smiling. It's as if everything has receded save for his gleaming teeth.

'Y ... yes, sir.' Maybe my ears aren't working well. Is he really saying ... ?

'Now run along and don't make a commotion about this. We prefer our school free of scandal-mongering.'

I turn in utter shock to Mr Dickson, who looks as if he's eaten an *orogbo* bitternut and sucked on a lemon at the same time.

'Oto,' he says, 'are you quite certain that's what you want?'

'Yes, please.' I beg him with my eyes to let it go. In a different world, my parents would hold Bayo accountable for his wrongdoings, and Principal Akiolu wouldn't be treating attempted rape as an 'unfortunate matter', but my proverb book says, *it is the foolish fly that follows a dead body into the grave.* Bayo is gone. I'm still here. That has to be enough.

'Dickson, the boy has spoken. No need to make a mountain out of an anthill, correct? Unless there's something else you want?' The principal turns to me, still smiling but only with his mouth.

'No, sir.' I shake my head rapidly. 'Thank you, sir.'

I walk out into dazzling daylight.

Everywhere students spill out of cars, mill around, shout to each other. I can't believe I'm still here. The sun comes out from behind the clouds and every single bougainvillea on the admin building wall seems lit from within. I breathe out, feeling like a grinding stone has been lifted off my chest.

Back in my room, I swiftly bundle my romance novels into a plastic bag and dump them in the outside rubbish bin because the next time I open one, all I'd feel is danger and all I'd hear is Bayo's mocking voice. I tell myself it's just as well anyway. Between theatre group and new friends and more peace than I've ever had, I made the mistake of thinking I could relax. I ignored how, lately, Lori fights to look out of my eyes at the beautiful boys around, to take over the swing of my hips. Romance novels seemed a safe way to keep her sated, but then they also encouraged her.

Any moment now Derin will be back. The thought of anyone hearing or believing Bayo's insinuations and what it would do to Derin makes me want to stop existing. I especially have to hide those bomb-like words from Derin himself. Because then he'd start noticing things. Like how I look at him, though mostly when he's not looking. How I make excuses to touch him. How I ask him for bedtime stories he's equally eager to tell, because the sound of his voice is the best music in the world. Then there are all the impossible things I've finally admitted to myself I want. Things that would destroy our friendship. Things Bayo made sound disgusting, which is how the world would see it. I only have to remember Wura saying, *Derin this, Derin that*, in that hurtful tone so tight with worry that I'd once again imperil us all.

'I mistakenly knocked over my table,' I say, fighting tears, when a devastated Derin asks about the fish tank.

'It's okay.' He pats my back and I allow myself to lean into him for one brief, sweet second. 'We can get another one.'

That evening as we walk to the cafe Derin slings an arm around my neck. My whole body goes stiff as dried glue, though it's something friends do all the time. I don't realize I've shrugged him off till I catch the hurt look on his face. Then it's too late to do anything but walk on as if nothing happened. Still, I sit that bit further from him in the cafe, knowing it's for his own sake. My head says I should find some excuse to change rooms. My heart argues no, it would be a terrible thing to do to us, an overreaction, like burning down the forest when I only needed to raze the weeds. Perhaps it's selfish, but I can't imagine being with anyone else. And he's still the best keeper of the secret he doesn't know I have.

*

There's whispering and gossip when Bayo doesn't return. There are rumours he's finally been expelled, though no one is certain. They make guesses at which past misdeed finally caught up with him. He's apparently been suspended in the past only to return weeks later acting like nothing happened. The more stories surface about him, the more the boys who hung around him keep a low profile. Bayo once boasted that he could spit in a junior boy's food right in front of him, and make him eat it! The boy did it tearfully, without complaint. He never lived down the shame and disappeared from school not long after.

All things considered, I've been extremely lucky. Kokumo asks how I'm doing one morning in the cafe. I tell him I'm fine, and that's that. I watch to see if he and Fayemi are paying closer attention to me, or to me and Derin, but they aren't and I'm grateful. I wonder what they've come to know of Bayo since he arrived at ISS.

Though something haunts my eyes when I look in the mirror, I throw myself into living normally, burying the horror of Bayo in the same place I buried the Wolis. Except Derin knows me too well. He's been adding two and two and is anything but stupid. He keeps asking what's wrong.

'You'd tell me if things got really bad at home, wouldn't you? Maybe my dad can help?'

'Yes.' Better to let him think the trouble lies at home.

He stops asking after the hundredth time I've replied *nothing*.

One morning I wake up feverish. The nurse gives me some aspirin, points me to the crisp dispensary bed and leaves with a cheery, 'I'll check up on you later.'

There's a soft puff of wind on my face, like a bubble-kiss made of air. The window was shut, I'm sure of it. She comes through it anyway, a flowing starry mist. Silver-blue covers the floor, shimmering, rising, lifting the bed and then it's not the dispensary any more, but her palace underwater. And there she sits on a throne of shells, knitting with needles made of the sun and her skein is filaments of light. She beckons me forward, her smile grave, her eyes banked with fire and love. With each step, I'm made buoyant till, flowing, I arrow through the water. Little jewels swim alongside and when I turn to look, they're my fish and they aren't dead after all! I laugh with joy to see them and in the manner of this place where words are spoken silently, they tell me they're here now. Here in the great hall where Yeyemi welcomes all, those that were and few that are. There is neither greatest nor least. I sit naked in her lap and she dresses me in the garment she has woven, then holds me close, and so returns me back to myself.

24

1992 (AGE 15)

Intrigued, Derin checks out the karate dojo, too. Turns out he's a natural, calmly executing his kicks and turns with precision. He soon advances faster than me but I don't mind. It means we get to practise together. He also snaps up the chance to write a regular column for *Blurb!* I'm thrilled when he invites me to do the comic strips and illustrations. Both activities provide a safe space between our old closeness and the wall I'm daily raising to hide what my heart seems determined to broadcast in neon.

As two of the top ten students in our year, we're allowed an early first attempt at the International Baccalaureate exams. It's everything I defied Mother with waist beads and a feather for, and I'll do whatever it takes to ace it. I quit volleyball, unable to keep up with everything else *and* theatre group.

Knowing the term will be nose to grindstone, study-wise, Derin and I sign up for a school trip to Olumo Rock in Abeokuta. *Dopemu* jokes fly around the bus.

'Dopemu comes home from his first day in school. "What did you learn?" his mother asks. "Not enough," Dopemu says. "They want me to come back tomorrow!"'

Derin knows many jokes and keeps everyone in stitches. It's this whole playful side he doesn't show very often. It's hard to not look at him too much. Or laugh too loud. Or breathe. Or anything. Because every time my eyes meet his, my breath catches and I imagine things. Like what his hand would feel like stroking my cheek. Or how his lips would taste.

'Tell us a joke, Oto!'

God! Even the way he says my name ... *What is wrong with me?*

'I don't know any,' I mumble.

He turns away. His quiet acceptance of the distance I've created between us hurts, though it's what I want. He's always respected my space. Never questioning why I dress and undress under my robe with my back turned like a nun or why he sometimes finds our room door locked with the key left in. He just knocks and waits. We're both silent for the rest of the journey.

The trip isn't all play. Derin plans to write an article for *Blurb!* about how Olumo Rock in the city of Abeokuta, which means 'under the rock', provided ancient settlers with shelter and a vantage point for sighting enemies. My assignment is to take photos for the article.

I'm snapping away at the scenery when I look up and see Derin, bathed in sunlight on the summit of Olumo Rock, light bouncing off his wild hair as he punches his fists in the air, looking like a young god. A delicious shock starts from my toes, tingles its way up between my thighs and spreads through my body till every hair shivers with pleasure. Lori is wide awake. Hours of karate have turned Derin's baby fat into sleek muscle. I'm tall for a girl, but he's a head taller. He's sixteen and utterly beautiful. When our eyes meet, he smiles. I click the shutter.

Like a speck of dust on a bead of water, life seems suspended the following term. It's study, *Blurb!*, karate, study, *Blurb!*, karate. Afternoons are taken up with extra classes. I simply can't keep up, so I drop out of theatre group, much to Tiwa's annoyance. There's another reason. I was running late for the last planning committee meeting and was just about to step in when I heard someone teasingly ask where her boyfriend, Oto, was. She laughed this twinkly shy laugh and said, 'I don't know. He's probably on his way.' I froze and considered not going in but someone was right behind me. Now when she complains that she never sees me any more I just tell her it's the exams. It's more like guilt that I've no idea what to do with this new situation.

Then Tiwa's friend, Fatima, suddenly seems to need Derin's help and advice on every last subject. She's taking the IB exams early too and though she's a day student, she's been staying behind for afternoon prep. I'm shamelessly glad that outside of school, her strict Hausa Muslim parents rarely let her out. Still, Derin and I spend many hours helping and encouraging each other. The two weeks during which we take the IB exams are a haze of brainwork, after which I collapse and sleep for a full twenty-four hours.

The results arrive just before summer holidays. Many students did well. I'm stunned to find I've scored seven in five subjects, six in one plus a bonus three for my painting of Yeyemi, titled *Goddess of Rivers and Seas*. The highest ever for an ISS year four! Derin has a top score of seven in five subjects and five in one, plus a bonus three for his written essay. We grab each other and shout and swing around like wild things.

During the special presentation ceremony to which friends and family of successful IB exam students were invited, Mr Dickson beams and presents me with a gift from the school – an expensive set of paints and sable brushes. Derin receives a massive pile of books presented by the literature teacher. My heart has never held so much happiness at a time. Despite everything, my dreams will happen! I just have to do equally well in next year's GCEs and ISS will facilitate and pay for my applications to top American universities with scholarships. Derin seems to be headed that way, too. Though we've hardly talked about life after ISS, I can't imagine a world where I don't see him every day.

'Your twin has incredible talent!' Mr Dickson says to Wura afterwards. She beams shyly at him. He's enjoying a large slice of the cake she brought, topped with a candle shaped like a graduate's cap. Her showing up was the best surprise ever. I called to tell her about my results and the ceremony but never dreamed she'd come. I accepted that I'd never have family at school events like other students.

Wura lied to Mother that the cake was for a friend's birthday, and got permission for Mr Driver (who's sworn to secrecy and, like everyone else, has a special soft spot for Wura) to bring her. She can only stay a short while. When she hugs me tight and says, 'You've done so well!

I'm proud of you!' I feel as if I've already graduated, though there's still the local GCEs and ISS graduating exams to go.

Derin's dad, whom I only see from a distance, is busy making the rounds (a reluctant Derin in tow) proud as can be, talking to practically every teacher. I'd have loved to meet this man who raised the miracle that is Derin, but the school registrar whisks him away to his office. The single wrong note to the day is the look on Derin's face when he briefly breaks away from his dad to join me, and sees Wura. He stares as if he's been hit on the head. He is also completely lost for words – which never happens. Jealousy pierces my heart, stinging like a vexed scorpion. In a right and proper universe, it's me he'd be looking at like that.

She's all slim curves from chest to hips in a lavender dress and keeps turning heads, and quite a few boys suddenly want to come and chat as I walk her back to the car. She's barely been around three hours and is already turning my world upside down. I'm glad she came and, I shamefully admit to myself, glad she's leaving.

We're nearly at the car when Bayo sidles up. Dark glasses cover his eyes. My heart starts pounding and my head feels light. What's he doing here? No one seems to be paying any attention. I guess he's not forbidden from attending events open to the public. Maybe one of his friends is celebrating. My courage flows from pure anger. He should not be here. He will not spoil this day.

'Ignore him,' I whisper to Wura.

He doesn't take the hint and blocks our path.

'Go away, Bayo.' I stand between them. I'll karate chop his head off if he tries to touch her.

He spares me one long, icy look that's full of hatred. 'I'm allowed here, so shut up. Hey, Wura, remember me?'

'Yes, old smelly pants. How could I forget?' She doesn't miss a beat.

'Good. Make sure you don't.' Bayo kicks a stone into a nearby tree trunk and stalks off.

Wura rolls her eyes and gets into the car. She hasn't seen him in years but no doubt his face will still look as bush-ratty when he's ninety. As if she'd forget the boy who, I'm certain she's always suspected, tried to rip me open on barbed wire. And she doesn't even know the worst. She doesn't need to. He can't touch us now.

Mr Driver turns on the engine, and I lean in through the open window to blow a bubble-kiss on Wura's cheek. She laughs, surprised and delighted. It's been too long since either of us did that. It feels healing. Like everything is going to be all right.

Summer camp is uneventful in the best possible way. I join in the bonfire night and take my turn telling a scary tale and eat the delicious roasted, spicy *suya* meat we've all contributed to buy. Karate, craft workshops, movie nights and lots of free time to do absolutely nothing rounds off three perfect weeks. I miss Derin and I'm glad Fatima lives in Ibadan and can't dig her claws in over the holidays. She's become nauseatingly persistent and I can't tell how Derin feels because the wall between us is no longer one-sided.

By the end of summer camp, I'm curious to meet the new boyfriend Wura raves about every time I call. She met him, she said, just after my celebratory lunch at ISS. She received a special invite to a party organized by some popular university student. Apparently he'd seen her at another party and wanted to meet her. He's at the University of Ibadan, no less! Her friends just about died of jealousy. It's quite the coup for a secondary school girl.

'He's eighteen,' Wura says. 'I don't remember seeing him before, but then, there were so many parties this term! He's named like the prophet. I don't know, though,' she adds, giggling, 'if the prophet was hot as spiced sin. Because Elijah is!'

I laugh. I'm also thinking, we're only fifteen, eighteen sounds a bit old. Then again, we'll turn sixteen soon.

25

1992 (AGE 15)

Mr Driver arrives to ferry me home. The city streets are jammed. He shouts and pounds on the horn in vain. Throngs of people have brought traffic to a standstill for the *Oloolu* masquerade. Once a year, *Oloolu* emerges carrying a human skull in a calabash, and afterwards visits the homes of Ibadan chiefs. He then takes the calabash to a secret location at midnight, where rituals are performed to prevent natural disasters from happening in the year to come. Girls who stayed in school for summer camp already left the day before because, according to tradition, any female who sees *Oloolu's* face will shrivel up and die.

Young men rush about flicking whips and canes. A horde of them suddenly take off in hot pursuit of a woman who's darted out of a slow-moving bus and dashed towards a shop. She slips in and the owner shuts the door just in time.

Through a space in the crowd, I glimpse the beaded edge of *Oloolu's* swirling, multi-panelled robe and instinctively duck down. When I look up again, *Oloolu* has been swallowed up by the crowd, and Mr Driver is looking most dubiously at me. Feeling stupid, I pretend to have dropped something and busily root around in my schoolbag.

Yeyemi once asked what I want most in my human life. Sitting in her ample soft-scaled lap while tiny jewel-tone crabs plaited her long hair with ruby pincers, I told her I wanted to be an artist, but above all, I wanted to be a girl, to perhaps be someone's wife someday, maybe a mother. She smiled and said sometimes we ask for what we already have.

Perhaps I should step out of the car and find out once and for all, what am I? Do male pseudohermaphrodites also shrivel to death? I'll likely just get a good whipping and no answers, and I've had enough of that for a lifetime.

'Foolish women!' Mr Driver mutters. 'Running like chickens! As if the radio did not warn them that *Oloolu* is coming out today.'

We emerge from the throng and he floors the pedal. Soon I'll see Wura! Soon, too, I'll see Mother.

The first time I meet Elijah, I can't stop staring. His hair gleams dense and dark, neatly cut in that square-top, low-sides look with precise sideburns, inviting touch. He looks like some magazine model. He reminds me so much of Soji, who's long since graduated. All I have left is a photo of him in the volleyball team. Then Elijah smiles and the illusion breaks. Where Soji looked endearing, Elijah looks almost feral. It makes me shudder in a good and bad way all at the same time. He's the original bad boy, and I've watched those leave a trail of broken hearts in ISS.

Elijah stares right back, open-mouthed. 'Wow! It's true. You really look just like Wura!' Then, 'No offence, man!'

I feel that stare all the way to my toes, which curl up with pleasure inside my shoes.

Elijah spends almost as much time with me as he does with Wura whenever he comes around. He played some volleyball once, though his favourite game is football. We set up a makeshift net in the court-yard. Wura yells encouragement from the side and sometimes brings snacks and cool drinks. The court-side service is usually prompted by Mother popping around to ask Wura if 'those boys are not getting too hot out there in the sun.' As far as Mother is concerned, Elijah – the son of a prominent chief – can't come over too often. For once she seems pleased I'm playing my part.

One afternoon, Elijah tries to block me and we fall in a tangled heap. His fingers linger a moment too long on my chest as I move to get up. I look at him in confusion and dazed longing before we both laugh and continue the game. I tell myself nothing happened. It was all in my head. But the way he's making me feel is new, foreign. I'm hyper-aware of every inch of my skin, under which I've surely grown live wires in place of veins. Some days I detest myself. Others I feel as though I could bring down the moon if I jump high enough. Lori flutters to rebellious life whenever Elijah favours me with me one of his sidelong glances. I'd swear he's doing it on purpose and yet, years ago, I thought the same with Soji and was wrong, so it's obviously not real. Plus, he belongs to Wura, which makes my thoughts a hundred reasons wrong. What sort of hypocrite am I anyway, thinking these thoughts while feeling how I do about Derin? It's as if I have two brains and they're doing a tug of war. I hate being such a mess.

With one last holiday week to endure, I'm in the living room watching the credits roll at the end of a sad, perfect movie about forbidden love. A tangy waft of hairspray announces Wura's arrival. She's just returned from the hairdresser and her hair is done up in the sleek Sade Adu style, highlighting her beautiful forehead. She glows with that special joy of being in love; a dreamy look I've seen on many faces in school as people pair up and take moonlit walks and steal kisses by the fountain at night. She's going on a special date with Elijah for our birthday. 'It's my sweet sixteen,' she said, when I complained. 'Go find yourself a girlfriend!' I try not to be sad that she remains so wilfully blind about me. Life would indeed be easier if it's a girl that trips my feet like Elijah does.

Wura sits beside me on the small sofa and peers intently at my face. I have the sickest sensation she's read my disgusting mind. The smile I give in return feels stretched. She reaches across and with gentle fingers, rubs icing off my cheek. During the movie, I'd eaten one of her delicious cupcakes.

I wake up from a dream I've had many times before, thankful it's my last day at home. It's always exactly the same. *I'm a huge bird, flying unburdened through the night sky. My big black wings press down the air and I push upwards, tilting with the wind. Finally, I land in a big tree in front of a house. Light spills through the windows and it looks cozy within. I'm happy, though, to be outside, safe in my tree and able to fly away, though my senses tell me I belong inside that house. I'm too content to have the whole wide world to fly in, so I settle for the night in my tree, tuck my head in my wing and go to sleep.*

In the old days, I'd have told Wura I had the black bird dream again, but not any more. I brush away the lingering sadness, glad I'm going back to school and, best of all, back to Derin. That dream has always felt like a premonition, urging me to escape.

26

1992 (AGE 16)

'So, these two fleas have just stepped out of the cinema, right?' Derin begins.

I'm unpacking my suitcase. Derin arrived a day earlier, and is already settled into our new two-person room. He's been talking as if the reservoir of things he's stored to share with me is spilling over. It seems amazing we've made it this far. Fifth year! Not that Derin is acting like it at the moment. He's now, most painfully, been quoting from some book of truly awful jokes unearthed from his dad's library.

'*Riiight.*' I roll my eyes.

'Quit batting those lashes and listen!'

'Sure.' I flutter my eyelids like a pair of frenzied moths then clap a hand to my mouth. It's even harder these days to control the high-pitched laugh that escapes when I find something really funny. My voice, like my body, has foundered on some in-between island, while everyone else sails smoothly left or right.

'I'm trying to tell a joke!' Derin rumbles, eyes narrowed in a mock glare, and his new bass voice hits all the right notes in my heart.

'Okay, okay. I'm listening.'

'What did the guy flea say to the girl flea?'

'Umm ... I wish movies would stop portraying fleas so negatively?'

'*No!* You're not even trying!'

'But I am!' My mouth aches from trying not to laugh. 'Okay. What did he say?'

'He said . . .' Derin starts laughing so hard he has to catch his breath and try again. 'He said, hey, babe, shall we walk or shall we take a dog?'

I smile.

'Well?' Derin's eyes are so wide they seem about to overtake the lens on his glasses.

'Uh, it was funny. Really . . . *umm* . . . funny.'

Derin grabs his pillow and tries to whap me. I dodge, grab mine and land him a good one. I rule at pillow fights – something Wura long ago conceded. Derin knows my weakness, though. He throws aside his pillow and tickles me till I beg for mercy and promise to laugh at every single joke he'll ever make. Then it's like someone sucked all the air from the room as his lips hover inches above mine. They're plummy red as if he's rubbed them with those little flowers kids use as pretend lipstick. His breath tickles my top lip and I tremble. Something flickers in those cat eyes. His heart speeds up against mine. His lips part as he draws closer . . . closer, then suddenly jerks away, grabs his pillow and flops back onto his bed.

For long seconds I'm still, breathing in panicky jerks. My body is liquid and wide awake and thrumming even as my stomach swirls with panic. The dinner bell shatters the silence. As we walk to the cafe, planning what to write and draw for that week's issue of *Blurb!*, Derin is exactly his normal self. I must have imagined that brief moment I saw desire, fear and utter confusion cascade through his eyes. Anything else makes me feel as if the earth would skid to a halt, flinging me into dark, lonely orbit.

Exactly one week later, Fatima walks into the cafe at lunch break and I have to rub my eyes to believe what I'm seeing. She's wearing Derin's prized red jacket with 'Man U' stitched in yellow on the front. The one his dad bought him for the English football team they both crazily support. Something dark twists in the base of my stomach and I kill it fast. I've no right to those feelings.

From then on, it's understood that they're officially a couple. A new, hollow silence fills our room, as Fatima becomes *the thing Derin won't talk about.* Just like when I wouldn't talk about what happened that half-term break our fish died. I'm desperate to know how he really feels about her. When I mock tease him about it, he clams up and changes the subject. Maybe because my soft teasing hides sharp needles.

At least they can't get up to much, I console myself. Fatima is a Muslim Hausa girl and must stay pure till marriage. I'm not proud of myself for being glad about this. I'd also get on better with her if she didn't suddenly move herself into every spare moment of Derin's life. Always needing help with this project or that assignment, her hand touching him, stroking his cheek, clutching his arm like some greedy little pet.

'Didn't Fatima look cute in Derin's jacket?' Tiwa says shortly after this terrible development. 'I'd love something of yours to wear, too.'

What? 'Erm ... I don't really have anything?'

'Yes, you do!' She looks meaningfully at me. I want to cry.

After prep that afternoon, I walk into the library art alcove, *our* place, and there's Fatima holding hands with Derin under the table, gazing into his eyes. It's like I am swelling into a living cyclone of pure rage. I want to rise up in a wave that will destroy the books and library and the entire school and sweep me and Derin away and drop us safe on a shore where there's no Fatima and I'm Lori and it's my hand he's holding.

Feeling sick and lost, I turn right round and head to the dorm. I don't know if they saw me and I'm too miserable to care. From my closet, I grab my tie-dye Bob Marley T-shirt and wrap it up. Tiwa will be happy, and all her friends, including Fatima, will hear about it. I'll officially seal my fate.

Between heated dreams of Elijah, daydreams of Derin, and the girlfriend I suddenly seem to have acquired, I feel like a ripped flag, flapping three ways in a gale. As if that isn't enough, the once flat nubs on my chest have started looking distinctly puffy around the edges. I see bare male chests all the time, and some are puffy too. I tell myself it doesn't matter that unlike those boys, I haven't a spare ounce of fat. As for my hips, baggy trousers are, thankfully, in. I just have to make it through this year.

*

'I finished this yesterday. What do you think?' Tiwa asks, holding out pages covered in her tidy writing. We're sitting at the base of the fountain, while she waits to be picked up by her older brother. As I read, I get a bad feeling.

'Is this some literature assignment I forgot about?'

'No, silly! It's for *Blurb!*'

She's spent a week putting together a story for the next issue, complete with ideas for what I'd draw. Something smells off about her sudden discovery of a creative writing side.

'This is nice, but me and Derin already have this month's story. In fact, we've pretty much got the whole term covered.'

Tiwa goes from disappointed to livid in one second flat. I don't even have time to feel bad.

'Sometimes I don't understand you. People have noticed you'd rather spend time with Derin than me. I know you've always been best friends but it *is* getting embarrassing. What sort of boy prefers his friend to his girlfriend?'

A boy who isn't really one, I bitterly think. A *male pseudohermaphrodite*. We started out as friends, why can't things just stay that way?

'Fatima said she hardly gets any private time with her boyfriend because you're always there. It'd be great if you and me do more together, you know. Give them some space?' She says 'space' with her fingers up in air quotes. Something in me snaps.

'Look, me and Derin do that *Blurb!* section together and that's how it will stay, okay?'

Her lips purse tight. She curls her fingers, frowns down at her painted nails. 'Perhaps Derin won't mind. Maybe you're the one with a problem.'

And she has no idea how big of a problem. 'Think whatever you like, but here's some free advice for the future. Never mess with an old friendship.' I get up.

'Hey! Where are you going? I can't even talk to you any more?'

I keep walking, terrified I'll break down weeping. Tiwa's words summoned the ghost of Bayo's insinutions, though I'm sure she didn't mean it that way. Halfway up the dorm stairs, the truth slams into me like a *danfo* bus. Tiwa and Fatima are Derin's best protection from me.

After three days of apologising to Tiwa and being coldly ignored (during which Fatima seems to have grafted herself onto Derin's side) I get an exit pass. At the shopping centre, I find a T-shirt that says *This Chick Rocks* spelled out in sparkly sequins above a fluffy yellow chick wearing sunglasses. I can't resist buying one in my size, too. It isn't dangerous like the pack of sanitary pads now locked in a small box inside my locked suitcase, and I can always say it's a gift for Wura. I give Tiwa's nicely wrapped gift to a classmate to pass on to her. Inside is a card saying, 'I'm sorry. Let's be friends again?'

Tiwa comes to sit beside me at lunch and slips her arm around my waist. This is new. As I do the same, I feel terribly fake, but relieved. Her only fault is that what she wants, she has no idea I can't give.

The night ISS turns thirty is a big deal. Feverish preparations for the student party have been going on for weeks. Girls flitting back and forth in the cafe, giggling and squealing about this perfect dress or that killer pair of shoes, misery in the dorm when boys got turned down as dates. Derin and I have never been part of the party scene, as Derin hates parties (though when he chooses to dance, he moves like a dream) and I've always kept a low profile. Tiwa and Fatima, though, were determined their 'guys' would do them proud – something we all knew was mostly lost on Derin, who has no time for anything apart from books, writing, chess, karate and music. (I refuse to include Fatima in my list.)

A loud crackle splits the air. The DJ taps his microphone, booms, 'Good evening, Great ISS-ites! Welcome to the ISS thirtieth birthday Black and White Party. Here to open up the dance floor are this year's finest, Mr and Miss ISS!'

The gorgeous fifth-form pair step onto the dance floor. She's wearing a beautiful white dress, and he's in a white shirt and black trousers that hug his slim thighs. Fairy lights slowly twinkle on and everyone claps. The events committee has done a fabulous job, from the black and white ribbons twined around the cafe pillars to the balloons floating above our heads. The DJ starts off with a popular hit. I decide tonight I'll try and be happy.

Tiwa arrives fashionably late. She's clearly taken time to look extra special. Her silver top and short skirt show off her midriff. Her hair is done in a side plait with sprayed-on streaks of gold. Her black pumps have cute white bows, per the rule that everyone wears something black and white. She looks amazing, and I say so. She giggles and shyly dips her head.

My stonewashed jeans, black and white Converse high-tops and Izod shirt make me one of the best dressed and most miserable people there. Derin is nowhere to be seen. Lately, that's how it's been.

'Thanks.' Tiwa slides her hand into mine. Her lips shimmer rosy pink. At some point, I'm expected to kiss her. As she tugs me onto the dance floor, her chest grazes my arm.

The music changes to the slow dances, starting with an old hit about friends you can always count on. In the shadowy light, I see Derin walk onto the dance floor with Fatima. He's wearing black jeans and a body-hugging long-sleeved white top and I try to pick my jaw up from the floor. He still wears those thick 'Coke-bottle' glasses, without which he's half blind. When he takes them off, though, you just have to stare at those greenish-brown cat eyes. It's been my secret pleasure forever – that moment he takes off his glasses at bedtime. I'll sometimes ask some random question just to make him lean closer and blink owlishly at me. I hate to think of Fatima getting to see that, too. The tiered flounces of her red satin dress curl about his thighs as he pulls her close. She slides her hand into the back pocket of his jeans. Derin sees me and grins. I might have grinned back.

The lights go dimmer and I turn my face from the sight of Fatima clinging to Derin as if she's drowning. Tiwa somehow takes it as a move to kiss her and obligingly tilts her face. I peck her cheek and gently press her head onto my shoulder, like Wura and I used to do if one of us needed comforting after a scare. Tiwa sighs and clings tight. I feel sick. Hate myself. Hate Fatima. What would her strict father think of his daughter's hand down a boy's jeans? For sure she borrowed that strapless red number she's wearing and told some big old lie so she can be here. I'm churning with ugly thoughts. So much for a happy night.

I fast-forward my thoughts to tomorrow evening. Me and Derin sitting together at one desk in our room, composing a comic strip for *Blurb!* It will be a satire about the party, with mean teachers as alien gatecrashers, and Mr and Miss ISS as superheroes who fly in and save the day. I close my eyes and draw sketches in my head. Derin always comes up with great dialogue.

When I open my eyes, the shiny red of Fatima's dress is gone and Tiwa has danced us towards a shadowed part of the cafe wall, against which several couples are plastered. If the boys grind-danced the girls any harder, they'd go right through like Wile E. Coyote, leaving a body-shaped gap. I know I'm just bitterly jealous. I take Tiwa's arm and guide us instead towards the steps. Out in the soft, warm night, she smiles sweetly. My feet grind to a halt. She's assumed we're headed somewhere more intimate.

'You're so pretty, Tiwa.' She deserves better. Many dateless boys would give an arm to be in my place.

'And what are you going to do about it?' She peeks at me from under mascaraed lashes. Tiwa has no qualms about stating what she wants. How hard can one kiss be? Impossible, I'm finding. I like her very much, but I also very much do not want to kiss her. Plus, I've never kissed anyone before. Tiwa snuggles close. She'll go however far I want, and I'm expected to want a whole lot. Which means Fatima is giving Derin a similar free pass, short of doing the actual deed. They'll almost certainly compare notes later. I have to do something. I take a deep breath; slant my closed mouth over hers. She presses up against me. She feels all wrong, like a woollen sweater on a sweltering day. I fight the urge to immediately peel her off. Instead with a show of reluctance, I lift my head and say, 'Tiwa, how about we just dance tonight? You're too special to just crush up against some wall.'

She looks at me with shining eyes. 'You're so sweet!'

Kissing her forehead, I decide we must 'break up' no matter what. This is just wrong, and unfair to her. Not tonight, though, because then everyone will know she got dumped on Black and White Night and she'll be humiliated and hate me more. Christmas vacation will give us time apart, then I'll do it at the beginning of term. Derin's reputation should be safe. No one can miss the way Fatima has been plastered all over him.

After Tiwa's brother picks her up at midnight, I'm glad to head to the dorm, take off my stupid trousers and shirt, and close my eyes and ears to the world. I've no idea what time Derin returns.

27

1993 (AGE 16)

Dawn is just breaking. Near the henhouse, our cock crows loudly to establish who's boss. Half awake, I feel flush with nerve-tingling warmth. The faces behind my closed eyelids keep changing, first Elijah's, then Derin's. I force Derin's away. I've made a strict rule not to think that way about him. Elijah is just as wrong, but it isn't as if those thoughts will ever happen, or harm anyone. I slide a hand down my pyjama bottoms. Not long after that day I studied myself in the mirror, I borrowed an encyclopedia of world flowers from the school library as part of a class project. My breath caught when I saw the Cymbidium orchid, because the heart of that flower was recreated on my body, with delicate petals enfolding a nub of a pistil. As if nature was saying, *look, nothing I've made is ugly.*

Lately, I can't seem to get enough of playing with what I've ignored for so long, and as memories of words from the pages of my long-discarded romance novels paint steamy scenes in my mind, I try hard to stay silent as my body goes crazy, all the air wanting out of my lungs at once. When my back touches the bed again and my brain reassembles, I wonder, it feels so good alone, how will it be with a boy I love?

As I drift up and out of my daze, I see once more the chipped iroko wood of my bedposts. The plain blue sheet that covered my body lies roped and rippled from all my thrashing. It's New Year's Day, and the noise outside means the cooking women are here again. And family, friends and neighbours will go from house to house, eating and drinking together, congratulating each other on living to see another year. Mother will have rice and *moi-moi*, fried meat and *dodo* ready for anyone who drops by to visit and wish us well – usually Temple members or her customers.

As one loud cooking woman's voice tinkles up through my open back window, asking another to fetch her some *maggi* cubes, I'm glad I was quiet earlier. I lean over the windowsill to watch them come and go, carting pots and firewood from their bus to the backyard, as choreographed as ants after years of working together. Their *iro* are tied knee-high in preparation for a long morning of cooking in huge *agbari ojukwu* pots on massive wood fires. I giggle like a two-year-old. The idea of a pot named after the bald, shiny dome of the legendary Biafran War leader never fails to set me off.

Wura pads in on silent feet. Even fresh out of bed, my sister is pretty. No girl in ISS can compare with her.

'Are you laughing at Ojukwu's head again?' She comes to stand beside me.

Our bond might no longer be as tight but some things never change. 'It *is* funny! What are you doing up so early?'

'Can't sleep. I woke up feeling afraid, you know. Today has the smell of a bad day.'

I remember Wura saying something similar, the day Mama Ondo discovered my treasure box. She's visiting again and the house feels booby-trapped everywhere. I make a silent vow to keep to my room as much as I can.

'Elijah is back from his grandfather's village. He's coming over today. I can't wait to see him.'

'That's nice.' I, too, want a handsome boyfriend who would come over to visit me. I veil my disgusting envy by focusing on a woman outside, wrestling a live catfish from a bucket of water onto a slab of wood, preparatory to slaughter. I wish Wura would talk about anything but Elijah. It's all she ever does nowadays, and I know way too much about him, from his favourite foods to his dislikes to how much he loves partying. Was this how ridiculously I carried on about Derin when I first met him?

'I wonder what to get him for Valentine's Day.' She dreamily strokes the curtain beside her.

With the flash of intuition that now rarely arcs between us, I know they've not yet gone beyond kisses. She's crazy about him but something is stopping her. It's partly Mother hassling her with Temple of Holy Fire rules about staying pure – especially since she believes having me was her own punishment for breaking those rules. Partly she's scared. We've, after all, only recently turned sixteen. She's thinking maybe Valentine's Day would be perfect. My stomach rolls like a cement mixer.

'Off to shower!' I say, and escape, hoping to be saner by the time I'm done. As the warm water slides down my skin, I find myself wondering what a first time with Elijah would be like. That feral smile. Those wicked eyes. *What on earth is wrong with me?*

When Elijah arrives that evening, he looks terribly grown-up in his damask *agbada* over a long-sleeved *buba*. He's brought along a friend: a spotty, lanky but cute boy called Udo, who seems deeply under-whelmed to be here. Making the holiday rounds can get tiresome, especially while playing third wheel to a newly reunited couple. After we say our hellos and make idle chat for a bit, Udo takes himself off to a corner to work on the mountain of rice and meat and *moi-moi* he's piled on his plate. He's clearly not up for conversation. I don't blame him. Wura is eyeing Elijah like Udo was eyeing the food. And I need to stop sneaking glances at him. I slip away, knowing no one will miss me.

In my room, I pop in a CD by Osmium Cookies, a little-known band with the sweetest poetic lyrics. It's a Christmas present from Derin and one of the precious few CDs I own, since they're so expensive. A wave of sadness washes over me – for missing Derin, for being so stupidly in love with him, for my crazy lustful thoughts about Elijah, for my mind getting as mixed up as my body. Longing for a switch to turn off all this thinking and feeling, I shut my eyes and merge into the song, letting its lyrics sweep me away.

'In a world of hurt, heartbreak is a flower that blooms red and dies and leaves only a scent but the flower was there, to live, to be, to change. The

field. Nothing more, nothing less. Not wasted, not wasted. Meant to be a flower. Meant to leave a scent.'

'Hey! That sounds different. What are you listening to?'

Startled, I swing around to see Elijah, his *agbada* discarded, wearing just his *buba* over his trousers.

'Erm … Osmium Cookies.' What's he doing here?

'Will you dub it for me?'

'Yes.' I'd never have thought he'd like this, but then people can surprise you. His aftershave smells delicious and lemony. I'm trying to remember why it's a good idea for me to leave immediately. I'm like driftwood cast ashore, with no power to move on my own.

'Udo is only interested in pigging out, and Wura is helping your mother with some guests. Am I disturbing you?'

Oh yes! 'Not at all.'

He grins and the tiny, enticing gap between his front teeth just holds me rooted. Each glance into those thick-lashed eyes is churning me up inside. The song ends and I nearly trip over my own feet racing across the room to play another CD, just to have something to do.

'Guess what? I brought contraband!' There's boyish mischief written all over Elijah's face. He whisks two beer bottles out of a brown paper bag like a magician producing rabbits from a hat. My eyes widen. I grin with guilty delight because Mother would go berserk if she knew there was the devil's poison, aka alcohol, under her roof! Elijah cracks them open and holds one out, his stare a challenge.

I begin to shake my head. For one thing, I made the unhappy discovery in summer camp that beer tastes like I imagine dirty laundry water would; for another, returning downstairs reeking like Mr Driver on his day off will only get me into trouble. Randomly, I remember Babalawo saying it is *ewọ* – taboo – for the handiworks of Obatala to get drunk.

And yet, here is Elijah, acting like I'm one of his cool university friends. For once I want to be normal. Shed my constant burden of watchfulness that's only tripled since Mama Ondo arrived. It's just one beer. What's the worst that could happen?

My hand closes around the cool bottle. I begin gulping it fast to avoid the taste. Elijah shakes his head, eyes mildly mocking. 'Hey! Slow down or you'll miss the best part!' From his trouser pocket, he fishes out a small bottle, steadies my hand, then tips the contents into my beer. 'You, Otolorin Akinro, are about to receive an education!'

I dubiously eye the bottle. I've already swallowed half the beer and the room is beginning to feel too warm yet deliciously cosy. It feels like he's inviting me to partake in some secret rite of initiation into real adulthood. I take a sip. It's strange, syrupy. Like something else, but I can't remember what. I drink it all down. Everything goes blissfully quiet inside my head. I lift my arms, sway gently to the music, my hips moving as if oiled, feeling so, so fluid and free.

'Congratulations. You've just met the 'meister.' Elijah is studying me like an ant under a thing . . . a bottle . . . a lens! Yes. That's what it's called.

'Meis . . . shter, who?' My tongue feels clumsy. I sit on my bed, suddenly unable to stay upright.

'Jäger. Latest and baddest booze in town. Courtesy of my cousin's father's booze cabinet.'

Something sounds off in his voice. Before I can dwell on it, my chest hitches and I croak up a most undignified burp, which makes me giggle. Then I can't stop giggling.

Elijah rolls the empty bottles under my bed and I'm thinking, *Smart move!* I congratulate myself on playing my role so well. Palling around with my sister's boyfriend like a normal brother. Mother would approve. Minus the devil's poison, of course! I laugh at my own amazing wit. I'm liquid and flowing, and the world is a marvellous, shiny place. I lean back on my elbows, and the bulbs on the ceiling light switch pleasantly between glowing and blurring together. It's so hilarious I cross my eyes to make them even blurrier. So this is what drunk feels like! I totally get why people do it.

Elijah drops belly down beside me on the bed. Faraway some alarm goes off that it's maybe not the best idea but then he's holding the *Blurb!* magazine I'd earlier tossed there, saying, 'This is really good!'

I shiver with delight at his praise. On the cover is my drawing of Mr and Miss ISS. He's looking at my cartoon of girl-shaped holes in the cafe wall on Black and White Night. Derin loved the idea and made me add a scandalized-looking Road Runner whose face looks remarkably like the girls' dorm caretaker's, looking down from the cafe roof, going, *Tut! Tut!* instead of *Meep! Meep!* But I don't want to think about Derin right now. 'I d . . . drewsh . . . it.'

'They didn't say you're so talented.' His compliment makes me buzz but he's looking at me like I'm a really beautiful . . . spider. Or something. Being drunk is making me see things! Our bodies are nearly touching and my skin is electric everywhere and I need to move away but can't seem to do so. Dimly, I wonder who *they* are. Wura's friends? His friends? But thinking is too much effort so I give up. 'I need to lie down,' I mumble, then remember I already am.

The room sways ever so gently as I slide fully onto my back. Elijah must have moved too, because I stop wondering about anything and I'm back in a place I vaguely remember being before. That moment with Derin on my bed in school. Only this time it's like a surreal dream where Elijah mashes his mouth to mine. Shocking and unbidden, an image flicks into my head. A memory of Wura, sick and shivering, that day Father finally left us. When I held her as she cried herself to sleep, her breath smelling of cough syrup. Cough syrup! *That's what this meister drink reminds me of!*

But Elijah's lips are moving and I'm drowning and my thoughts keep skittering away like dropped marbles . . . *No!* This is wrong. The room has to stop spinning. Elijah needs to stop.

'Gerr . . . rof me. Stop,' I mumble. Elijah shoves his tongue in my mouth like wet meat. Imagining this was one thing but in reality, it's ugly. A terrible, terrible thing we're doing.

'Please. No. Think of Wura!' I wrench my head aside. His hands palm my chest.

His body is suffocating me. In my head I'm struggling hard, but my muscles are slack, and I can't seem to get coordinated. I didn't imagine the looks. Those touches playing volleyball weren't accidental. I am the most naive person alive. Lacking social cues a person my age should have. Any clued-up teenager would have known.

'Let's see if you're truly some kind of half-girl *ashewo* freak!'

'What?' *He's just called me a prostitute freak!* I'm suddenly saner, pushing him, shouting, 'No! Stop. GET OFF ME!'

There's a soft scuffling outside the door. A sound any eavesdropper would recognize. Then the shuffling away of slippered feet on carpet. Who was it? What did they hear?

'Get off me! Someone might come in!'

'That's the bloody idea!'

He's crazy! Wura has been dating a madman and I've been flirting with him! There's a soft *tap tap tap* on the door.

Elijah suddenly whips me around so I'm above him, just as the door swings open.

Everything slows into a blur as Wura stands there, slack-jawed, with Udo behind her. The tray she's holding crashes onto the floor. Elijah flings me off, slamming my head hard into the wall. Stars spin before my eyes. He punches my mouth. *Pervert!* he shouts. Smack. *I was just admiring his drawings when he jumped on me!* Smack. *Do I look like a girl?* Smack! It's like bricks landing on my face, my stomach. I double up, retching. Udo, looking as if *he* will throw up, pulls him off. 'Don't kill him, Eli. That bastard isn't worth the trouble. Come on, let's get out of here.'

Elijah leans close and whispers, 'That was for my cousin, Bayo. And don't think it's over.'

One of my eyes won't open. The other is part shut. Wura is wringing her hands, shaking her head. I want to say, *He's lying,* but there's no Fayemi or Kokumo to save me this time. No Derin as witness. No one would believe me. Especially not Wura. Because she's always known about my 'hidden' desire for Elijah. She communicates this clear as day. She's used to me wanting what's hers. She just never imagined I'd go this low. Elijah storms out, Udo behind him. Wura follows, sobbing, *I'm sorry, Eli. Oh my God, I'm so sorry.*

I try to go after them but the world dips and the floor rises and I fall over, heaving. Whatever he drugged me with has left me boneless.

I want to tell my sister, *Get away from him!* But my swollen mouth won't work right. A proverb slides out of the pain-choked recesses of my brain. For the first time ever it sounds like an accusation – *the mouse is a bringer of disaster to the home of the innocent. Snakes do not eat corn.* I look around and none of it seems real. What have I done?

Mother rushes in, swearing she's finally going to kill me and nobody better stand in her way. I curl into a corner of the wall and wait to die.

'Moji, no,' Mama Ondo says. 'Don't touch him. It's the excuse your enemy needs to harm you. We have guests. You must keep this quiet! Come away now. We can deal with that creature later!'

Then I'm alone in a silence I wish would last forever.

I drag myself up, lock the door. Mother might come back to finish me off, which is no more than I deserve, but I can't die without warning Wura about Elijah. Who is, of all things, Bayo's cousin. Then I remember I never told Wura about Bayo's attack. Why would she believe me? She was so excited about that special invite to the party where she met Elijah shortly after my celebration at ISS. Was that when Bayo got the idea for the perfect trap to get his revenge on us? Why would Elijah stick his neck this far out for Bayo, cousins or not? Yet, I've played into their hands like a fool. And Wura is paying for it. My karate skills never even mattered. It's like we learned in literature class, studying world mythology. They're Greece and they sent in a Trojan Horse.

Something sticks out of the *Blurb!* magazine Elijah was looking at. I limp closer and open it. It's a patch of paper stamped crudely with a skull beneath two smoking guns. Underneath is written, *Forgiveness is a sin.* Even I know a confraternity insignia when I see one. It's a warning. Just in case I have any ideas about seeking justice. I thought this couldn't get any worse and I'm dead wrong. For a long time in school, rumoured whispers about university confraternity cults sent chills up our collective spines after the older brother of one student was left paralyzed. That event consumed the newspapers and we read all about their symbols and insignias and cruelty. How they consider themselves 'brothers' and an attack on one is an attack on all. How they stalk and beat you bloody for things like chatting up a girl they consider theirs. Bayo and Elijah aren't just evil. They're dangerous. They've destroyed what little home I had and broken Wura's heart. *And don't think it's over*, he said. *Oh sweet goddess, what have I done?*

Later, someone bangs on the door. I creep out of bed and throw up in my rubbish bin, feeling like something dead and rotten that somehow still breathes. It hurts everywhere, but worst of all in my heart. First thing in the morning, I'll beg Wura to listen to me. Even if she can't forgive me, she must stay away from Elijah.

Dear Yeyemi, please help Wura. Please let me sleep and wake up yesterday so I can go back and change everything. It seems such a childish plea but it's all I can think and ask, over and over. When sleep eventually comes, I toss and turn in nightmares but she stays away. Maybe this time it's too real, and I've broken something beyond repair. There's no such thing as going back in time.

28

1993 (AGE 16)

The dorm caretaker lets me in, though I'm two whole days early. 'Na ya wife beat you?' he jokes, staring at my swollen, battered face. I manage a weak smile, which hurts, and say he should see the other guy. He shakes his head as though to say boys will be boys. As he helps carry my luggage to the fifth floor, I wonder what he'd do if he knew the truth. That I let my sister's boyfriend lead me on till, together, we broke her heart and spirit.

Mother had pounded on the door that morning, threatening to slash it with an axe. When I opened up, she'd gagged at the smell of vomit and told me to get packed and get out. While she banged pots and pans in the kitchen in time with her rage, I knocked on Wura's door. Called her name. No answer. I turned the knob. She'd locked me out. I laid my forehead on the door, placed a palm flat on the smooth wood, imagined her doing the same on the other side. I begged her just to hear me out. Mother screamed at me to leave her daughter alone and get my disgusting self out of her house. When I walked past the guest room, the door was open. Mama Ondo stood just inside. Her face barely moved but I could have sworn she was smiling.

Surrounded by my hastily packed luggage in the driveway, I looked up and there stood Wura, arms crossed. 'I'm sorry,' I shouted, though her window was shut. 'Please stay away from Elijah. He's a vicious person.'

'Liar! I hate you. I hope you die!' I read her lips as clearly as if she'd screamed at me. She cracked the window open, flung something at me and vanished. It was her watch, face smashed in. Out on the street, I eventually found a taxi willing to take me all the way back to ISS for a big chunk of my pocket money.

I've since called home twice, but they simply hang up when they hear my voice. I can't afford another taxi ride back. I can only hope once Wura calms down, I can convince her to stay away from that snake and beg her forgiveness.

My best companion becomes the large bottle of Panadol painkillers I stole from the medicine cabinet at home. Every bit of my body hurts. Heartache is no longer some vague notion in a sad song. It's physical, like when a plane dips low, sliding your stomach into your throat. Sometimes, my face is wet long before I realize I'm crying. I can't eat, which is just as well because the cafe isn't yet open, though I can buy snacks from the kiosks. I have a spare key to the art studio, where painting keeps me from falling completely into that lost place where I keep hearing Wura's sobs, her acid grief scorching away what's left of our once tight bond. *Forgive me, Wura,* I whisper. *Please forgive me.* Maybe Mother is right and I'm cursed.

29

1993 (AGE 16)

I've never looked forward to anything so much as seeing Derin. I'm desperate for his calm presence to blanket and reassure me that I'm not the worst human being that's ever lived. Tiwa arrives first. She hugs me then draws back to examine my face. 'Did a wall quarrel with you?'

'You should see the wall! Anyway, how was your holiday?'

She launches into a story about her sister's party and it's comfortingly normal to hear her usual witty take. Then I remember I'm supposed to 'break up' with her first thing. I open my mouth but can't bear to cause yet more pain. It can wait till later. She might even be over it already.

I'm as tightly slung as a catapult by the time Derin walks into our room.

'Did your mother do that?' His eyes fill with such angry sympathy, I have to look away. It would be so easy to say yes. She's done worse. Yet I've never outright answered him with a lie. Not while he's standing there looking as if he wants to bodily tear apart whoever hurt me. Yet if I reveal even a tiny bit of the truth, it will invite questions. And Derin after answers is like a heat-seeking missile unless he chooses to let it go.

'No. Just some crazy boy who picked on me.'

'Who? Because I really need to practise my roundhouse kick.'

'Some local troublemaker back home.' I shrug dismissively and try to smile but my face goes all wobbly. The giant wall is back between us.

'Well, I hope you gave him a good decking.' Derin raises an eyebrow.

'So what's that?' I point to the small black box on the floor that looks like a vanity case, trying not to think how I never had a chance to deck

Elijah at all, and still don't know what he gave me to drink. How, had I been sober and wiser, Elijah should have been collecting his teeth from my bedroom floor that night, seconds after I told him no.

'Just wait and see!' Derin picks it up.

I let myself be swept up in his excitement as he places it on our reading table and pops open the latch. Inside is a portable electric typewriter with gleaming silver keys. Derin strokes them and beams like he's just found love.

'My present for doing so well in the IB exams. Isn't she gorgeous?'

'Yes, it … she's beautiful!' I suddenly envy the relative uncomplicatedness of his life.

'Dad said he might get me a computer someday soon!'

'Really?' The only computers in ISS are a pair of huge, square things in the freezingly air-conditioned 'tech room' near the admin office. Most students eye them dubiously. The staff who use them are protective as parents with newborns.

'Well then, what will you name her?' I tease.

'Name? Seriously? You choose.'

'I think Morenike is a good one. You know, *I've found someone to cherish*? Mori-baby for short.'

'Oto! It *is* a typewriter.' Derin rolls his eyes but he's smiling.

'Settled. Mori-baby it is.' I laugh. Then hate myself for being able to laugh. Because I don't deserve to.

'How about we type up the next story for *Blurb!* after dinner?'

'Yes, let's!' I want to freeze time. How utterly low and stupid my itch for Elijah was! Now I've wreaked destruction as surely as hacking at the wrong pillar will bring a house down on innocent people's heads.

That evening, as we walk to the cafe, Derin slings an arm over my shoulder. He's missed me, senses I'm covering up some pain, and wants to let me know he's there for me. I let him, shutting down the part of me that rears up in shrill warning. Longing still for the right to wind my arm around his waist while wearing his Man U jacket. Knowing I do not deserve even this much.

In the cafe, some people stop eating and stare at us. It's probably just our matching Casper the Friendly Ghost glow-in-the-dark T-shirts that say 'Chilling Together' on the back, my Christmas gift to Derin. I must stop imagining things.

That night five-year-old Wura holds a hand to her chest. Blood soaks her hibiscus-yellow dress, her white socks, her white sandals. She slowly tilts open the hand to show me the empty hole behind. *I loved you so,* she says. *Why would you do this?* I wake up trembling.

30

1993 (AGE 16)

The next morning, Gamba, my second favourite sparring partner at the dojo, takes off like he's practising for the Olympics when I approach him. I shrug. Keep walking. He's probably just late for something.

People seem to avoid meeting my eye and suddenly have somewhere else to be if I'm nearby. I tell myself to stop imagining things, keep my head down and will the day to go faster.

At lunchtime, I go and sit on the steps. I wait and wait but Derin doesn't come. We don't share any classes today. He probably has a lunchbreak meeting with his chess club. I guess he forgot to mention it.

On my way back to class, I pass by Chidi. He whispers something into his companion's ear. They both glare at me. My heart stutters so hard I grab my chest. It's suddenly like I'm tied down on railway crossing tracks, hearing the whistled warning, feeling the thundering through my bones, with no idea which direction the train is coming from or when it will hit.

I'm still hoping I'm wrong. That this is just something else. I've no idea what is being said. I could confront someone, but I'm terrified to know.

I skip karate practice, though I'll be marked down for missing my afternoon activity, and then dinner. Not that I could eat. All I want now is a chance to talk to Derin in private. To find out what he's heard. I try not to think the worst. I don't know how you prepare for your life to end.

*

It's almost lights out when Derin walks in. He sits across from me on his bed, stares at his clasped fingers, then says, in a tight whisper, 'Did you do what they're saying you did?'

I sit up. Finally! 'What are they saying I did?' It's hard to keep my voice steady.

'That you tried to kiss your sister's boyfriend so he beat you up.' The words hiss through his clenched teeth.

So that's the story they're being fed. Almost certainly by Chidi.

'I didn't! He came up to my room and gave me beer with something in it then suddenly grabbed me. I told him to stop but he wouldn't. Then Wura and his friend Udo walked in and saw us. He said I'd been flirting with him then went crazy punching me.'

'Right!' Derin is on his feet. 'Wura knows you'd never do that. So she can just come here and say he's lying. It will be the three of us against that bastard.' He looks ready to go get Wura immediately.

'She won't,' I whisper, knowing in my heart that this is where I lose him. 'Because I ... kind of ... flirted with Elijah.'

'You *kind of* what?' he says in flat disbelief.

'I didn't know what Elijah was up to.' God, I sound disgusting. And pathetic.

'What *he* was up to? How could you do that to your sister?' Derin's fingers push behind his glasses to rub his eyes. They're shaking.

'I don't know. She hates me and I hate myself. But I didn't mean to. It's just ...'

'You know what else? You lied to me.' His eyes are molten with anger. And tears. I've only seen that once before. This is more than betrayal. This is his heart breaking. I reach out my hands, willing him to see me, hear me.

'I was afraid. Please just let me expl—'

I jump as the door slams shut.

Lying awake, I play our talk over and over, holding each word, examining it from all sides and beginning again, like prayer beads on a rosary, till I find my scrap of salvation. Derin never once called me perverted or disgusting. He's angry that I lied to him. That I betrayed Wura. He can't imagine doing something so low to someone he loves. And those tears told me how deeply he cares. I sob his name into my pillow, my heart bleeding endless pain.

31

1993 (AGE 16)

For the entire next day, I only see Derin during the two classes we share, and he sits as far away as possible. He doesn't return to our room and things disappear from his closet. He must be making do with a mattress on someone's floor, which is against the rules. I didn't know that a heart could break and break and keep on breaking while leaving you alive. Not even at the worst times with Mother. Yet I cling on to hope. He always said it's important to weigh situations for yourself and not just follow the herd. Sooner or later, he'll hear me out.

Two days pass before I finally corner Derin between morning classes. It's as though he's developed a new ability to vanish whenever I'm within ten feet of him.

'Won't you even give me a chance to explain?'

Nearby, a group of students silently gather.

'Look' – Derin keeps his voice low – 'right now I'm seriously confused. Even if, for whatever messed-up reason, you pursued your own sister's boyfriend, I was thinking, okay, some people have issues. Maybe you just need help, right?'

I knew it! He's never anything but fair.

'Then I hear about a half-term break incident you forgot to mention. And that my name was brought up in a school disciplinary report. I *knew* something was wrong. I asked you so many times, but you just lied! If my dad hears about this ...' Derin stops, jaw wobbling.

'Derin ...'

'I remember us agreeing to deal with Bayo together. I trusted you.

Maybe I'm just the world's biggest fool. Right now, we're screwed. People are saying Bayo got unfairly expelled because he caught us . . . erm . . . doing things with each other and tried to report you after you came on to him, too.' Derin's ears have turned a dull red. 'I don't understand you any more. Just leave me alone, okay?' He pushes past.

The watching students disperse, glaring at me. Some girls hiss. I miserably watch as Derin heads towards Fatima. He says something, touches her arm. She slaps his hand away and storms off.

I stand helpless. As I'd feared, the ISS court of public opinion, with its tendency for guilt by association, is judging hard. Our legendary closeness, our two-person room, our stupid matching Casper T-shirts. I feel as if someone has shoved a plastic tube down my throat like they do in hospital dramas.

I must help him. Students normally settle our problems among ourselves but I'm now scared for him. I should go to someone. Kokumo and Fayemi have long since graduated. Would Mr Dickson believe me yet again with Udo and my own sister as ready witnesses? And Wura angry is like Mother times two.

Why did I forget, like Maami Akinro and Babalawo warned all those years ago, to stay watchful? Eshu, the trickster god, gave Obatala alcohol so he would fail at his most important task. His chosen are never supposed to get drunk. It's only a myth. But myths exist, as Babalawo once said, to help us learn to avoid buying trouble in the marketplace of life. Only I've failed to learn. And everyone I love is paying the cost. Wura slams the phone down each time I call. It's killing me inside that I can't make her see what Elijah is.

The next evening at prep, I sit alone at a table in the cafe pretending to study, trying to ignore the whispering and the feeling of eyes boring into me from all directions, working up the courage to do what I must to save Derin. I'll just tell people Bayo was right. That I'm not normal. That I've been deceiving Derin and he's innocent. Maybe I'll wait till lunchtime when the cafe will be fullest, when day students and boarders eat together. It seems like a sensible plan. My head aches. I'm reading the same sentence over and over. Nothing makes sense, so I lay my head on my arms, trying to decide whether to take some more Panadol from the bottle I've taken to carrying in my book bag.

Someone bangs so hard on the table, I jump. Tiwa and her friends stand there looking like they mean to depart with pieces of me. Day students should be long gone. Why are they still here? The entire cafe goes as silent as chickens sensing a circling hawk.

'What do you want?' It's been all avoidance and nasty looks. She turned against me so fast she must have whiplash. Not that I blame her.

'I'm disgusted I wasted my time on you!' Tiwa snaps. 'I'm no longer your friend, never mind girlfriend.'

Fatima purses her lips. Issues a long, insulting hiss.

'Look, Tiwa, we don't need all this drama. I'm sorry, okay? I was even voted off *Blurb!* yesterday. Just . . . please leave me alone.'

'You know this isn't about the magazine. *Abi* you thought I wouldn't hear about your little holiday adventure? How you tried to be unnatural with your sister's boyfriend? No wonder you won't touch me! Thank God, because now I couldn't bear the thought. I should have known something was wrong with you but not in my wildest dreams could I have imagined *that*! You're so disgusting I can't even look at you.'

'Then don't look at me,' I shout. She's trying to save face. Fair enough. In fact, I should just make my announcement now. These girls will make sure it spreads like headlice.

'Just so you know, Derin is gone,' Fatima says, voice tight with hurt. '*What! Where?*'

'He's left the school, you filthy animal! And if you think you can make a fool of . . .' Tiwa launches into another rant and all I can think is, *Derin can't be gone. My life was supposed to be derailed, not his. He did nothing wrong.*

'Answer me!' Tiwa shouts.

'Look, Tiwa, why don't you just piss off and leave me alone?' I'm not even aware I spoke.

'*Oloshi buruku!*' she hisses.

'Depraved he-goat! Pursuing boys like a girl!' Fatima goes one better. If looks could kill, there'd not even be my body left to bury.

'You know what God did to those immoral men of Sodom and Gomorrah in the bible? God will punish you. Just wait and see,' adds some girl whose name I don't even know.

I grab my things and walk away, jeers and insults following me from all over the cafe, ringing in my head along with the words *Derin* and *gone*. They'll be glad to know 'God' started punishing me before I knew my own name and clearly isn't done yet.

Derin probably decided to go home till things settle down. Though angry and distant in the last few days, he's never been cruel. Perhaps he left me a note! I hurry towards the dorm. All the way up the stairs, I feel eyes watching me, hear voices whispering. *Depraved! Demon! Disgusting! Freak!* Soon I'll be one of those crazy people roaming naked in the streets, hair matted with dirt and lice, eating from rubbish bins and yelling nonsense at passers-by.

Our room door is slightly open, a triangle of light piercing out. I nearly weep with relief. Fatima lied. Derin isn't gone after all! I take a moment to gather my courage, then step silently inside.

A young boy removes one of the few shirts still hanging in Derin's closet and stuffs it into the suitcase lying open on his bed. I recognize him from Derin's photos. Beside him, packing Derin's books into a box, is his dad. My breath catches. They both look up.

'Where's Derin?' I realize, too late, it would have been polite to greet them first.

'Hi! I'm Ayo, his brother. Derin has—'

'Ayo, shut up and pack! We don't have time to chit-chat!' Derin's dad snaps. 'And you, young man, don't you have somewhere else you should be?'

I shake my head. Nowhere as important as right where I'm standing. 'Sir, my name is Oto. I'm Derin's roommate. Please, where is he? When will he be back?'

He sags as if the whole world fell on his back. 'Ayo, go to the car and wait there for me.'

Ayo hesitates but his father's glare has him dropping Derin's karate belt and scurrying out. I remember the day he earned that blue belt. How proudly I watched him perform each move with swift, elegant strength. How I wrote his name inside it in fancy script. How he later talked me through my nerves at taking my own test, his cat eyes warm with encouragement and unwavering faith.

Derin's dad sits heavily on his bed. 'Sit down.'

I sink onto my own bed facing him, because however terrified I feel of this unhappy man, I have to know what's happening.

'Derin ...' he begins, and then stops, swallows hard, causing his throat to bob up and down. His mouth twists and he drops his head down into his hands. When he looks up, his eyes are moist. This is going to be bad. Grown men never cry in public unless someone died. In my mind I'm begging Yeyemi for help. Begging that angry God to do anything to me but spare Derin.

'You said your name is Oto?'

I nod, unable to speak.

'I like to think I'm a civilized man, which is why you're still alive right now.' He stares at me with murder in his eyes. 'I received a phone call yesterday from the girl my son is dating. Apparently some boy was unfairly expelled for trying to expose your habit of ... *preying* ... on innocent boys. None of that would concern me, except somehow my son was implicated as your accomplice. After she told me some people were planning to seriously harm him, it was clear I had to remove him immediately. I raised Derin to find the best in people. That naivety made him vulnerable to a creature like you. He still maintains that what he saw was an attack on you, but he can be too generous for his own good. I've cleared my son's name with the principal, and can only hope that other poor, innocent boy will be able to salvage his education, too.'

I almost laugh out of sheer hysteria. Bayo, a poor, innocent boy. Me, the terrible predator!

'I'll only tell you once. Stay away from my son. He wants nothing to do with you. If you ever try to contact him, you'll regret being born. That's all I have to say. Now get out and never let me see your face again.'

I'm frozen, blood whooshing in my ears. He was supposed to be open-minded. A freethinker! To listen to all sides! I want to explain to him why I already regret being born. How I'd sooner not exist than harm a single *dada* lock on his son's head.

'Get out of my sight!' he roars.

Somehow, I'm on my feet blindly walking.

Just outside the dorm is a group of boys. I hear footsteps behind me, unsubtly following. I break into a run, dodge behind the giant baobab near the sports field. I hear them arguing about which direction I went. One voice is definitely Chidi's. Alone, I could handle him, but three boys are too many. I suppose I could just let them beat me to death but I have vital things to say to Wura first. Their footsteps sound closer and closer and I bolt from my hiding place, running full tilt till I find myself in the empty laundry room where I collapse on my knees in the dark then slide under a pile of laundry, panting. It's the one place no one comes after dark, yet I hear them pelting towards the door. I stay as still as I can.

He must be in here ... I can't wait to land him one good hot slap ... Just one? His own mother won't recognize him after I'm done! Their voices carry nearer and nearer.

Any moment now they'll find me. Any moment now ...

One of them screams. Shrill as a five-year-old.

Did you see that? ... See what? ... Chineke God! I think we should go ... yes, we can get him later ... They tear off. The silence is sudden. Whatever their imaginations conjured up from the laundry room ghost and *ogbanje* stories must be terrifying to scatter them so.

I wait a while before sliding out. Moonlight leaches through the laundry windows, lending an eerie glow to the piles of white sheets. I close my eyes as the tears leak out. The laundry room feels suddenly very cold though the night is warm. All is completely still and silent. My watch shows half past nine. I kept Wura's cracked one. They're good, forever watches, but I had no business making promises I couldn't keep.

I'd have once been fearful to miss roll call before lights out. Now that seems like another life lived by someone fortunate enough to have such worries. Principal Akiolu is probably planning a disciplinary hearing. He must be furious he believed me the last time. They'll kick me out of ISS and it's goodbye to distinctions, good references, and my application to an American university.

Right now I should be preparing for bed, looking forward to Derin's deep voice telling some ridiculous joke or spellbinding story as I fall asleep. I'll never hear that again. His gentle snores will never again comfort me when I startle awake from a nightmare. I desperately hope he'll be happy wherever he goes, and the day might come when he doesn't think too badly of me. His dad will keep him safe. Fatima will only be too happy to spread the word that he was just my innocent victim. She loved Derin, too. I can admit that now. *She* knew to save him by calling his dad. I didn't. Because in my world, a dad is not who you run to when you're in trouble, it's who you run *away* from. Most importantly, he's safe. Now I just want Wura to be, too.

I pull out my notepad and torchlight and begin writing a letter. *My darling, beloved twin* ... This way she'll have no choice but to finally hear me.

In it, I tell her everything. Beg her forgiveness. Ask her to not ever feel bad and to know I'll finally be at peace. That my dearest wish is for her to be happy. I fold it over, seal it with tape and write, *For Wura Akinro's Eyes Only,* then carefully place it on my book bag after pulling out my bottle of Panadol and a pack of Actifed pills left over from when I had a cold. In the ghostly moonlight I find a small bowl and fill it with water from the sink. My hands move all by themselves like a slow-motion dream. First a gulp of water, then the cold pills. Then two Panadol, then more water to wash away the salty taste at the back of my throat, then three pills. Then more. When the bottle is empty, I pull the pile of sheets over my head and close my eyes. I do not wish to be found. I think of the boy who dived under dirty laundry to escape Bayo. Lying to save him drew Bayo's attention to me like a snake distracted by new prey. Yet I remember his wide, terrified eyes and know I'd do it again.

My heart starts punching my chest like furious fists, my blood rushing hot. My skin is too tight and I'm dizzily burning up and don't know any more where I am. For a hazy moment someone else is right there with me, the gentle Delta boy and, as my eyelids weigh heavier and heavier, I hear his soft whisper: *Thank you . . . I must go.*

Then there's nothing.

32

1993 (AGE 16)

Blue. Aqua, azure, turquoise, teal. These are the colours of my world.
I tried so often to paint this new world when I was in the old one and
failed, because how do you capture beings of light, living in light?

When I first arrive, she tells me without words that she understands. That I'm forgiven. That temptation makes fools of the
best of us.

'I want to stay with you forever,' I say. 'I'll never forgive myself in
that old world.'

'You will, daughter,' she replies, 'in time. For now . . .' She stretches
out her arms and cups my face in her hands, tilting my head so I look
right into her eyes. In them lie all the wisdom and knowledge and
fathomless beauty of life, the oneness of all souls that ever were and
ever will be. Light invades my being and I gasp with the pleasure of
understanding that when the candle flame of one life burns out, it
becomes a part of the energy that lights up another. That no life is
purposeless, though some might go askew.

And so I become light and forget everything but the joy of living
in palaces made of water that hold their shape like marble, rippling
with a radiance that gathers and fades like shoals of tiny fish. I'm at
peace here. Love flows from Yeyemi through all of us, her children,
and connects us as a whole, so our joys are one another's joys and
when one laughs, we all laugh also. I am my true self. I am content.
This is where I've always belonged.

*

I hear beeping. A steady *beep, beep, beep*. I open my eyes and everything is white: the ceiling, the walls. The sheet covering my body. The sound changes; the beeps speed up. I look to the side and see a machine. My hand hurts. I lift it and see a needle stuck into my skin, attached to a long transparent tube leading to a bag of fluid. I'm in hospital. I recall, clearly, what I did. Actifed and Panadol, dizziness, fading out then half-waking to vomit as though I'd never stop. Passing out again with relief that it was finally all over.

Helplessness and rage swim through my body along with whatever is dripping into me, keeping me alive. I want to return to that place the hospital pulled me from. I want it all back: the happiness, the heady knowledge of being in the water world where I truly belong, with Yeyemi, surrounded by millions just like me. There was no pain, no misery, no sorrow. There was no hunger, no hurt, no lack. I want back into that bliss. Who cheated me out of my happiness and brought me back to a white world of beeping machines?

The door opens and a nurse comes in, her starched white uniform crackling with her air of efficiency.

'Ah! You're finally awake,' she says with a smile. 'For a moment there, we thought we'd lost you. Can you hear me? Can you speak?'

I try to say *I wish you'd lost me*, but all that comes out is a dry croak. My lips won't obey me, and my tongue feels as though I chewed a dry lump of bread days ago and forgot to swallow. My throat is a freshly tarred, fiery highway burning down to my stomach. The nurse bustles away and returns with a cup of water, which she holds to my lips.

'Drink,' she says. 'You've been out for two days. You had us worried. You just wouldn't wake up though all your vitals were fine. Your throat might feel painful. We put in a tube to pump your stomach.'

I manage a couple of sips and water runs down the side of my mouth. She wipes it with a paper napkin. 'I'll go and get the doctor.'

A minute later, a stout man with eyebrows fat as beetles arching over square glasses comes in. He unhooks a stack of paper from the foot of my bed, spends some time studying it, then sits in the chair beside me. He doesn't smile.

'I'm Doctor Akpan. You're extremely lucky to have been found so soon after you swallowed those pills. You barely escaped liver damage, but I'm glad to say you've made a perfect recovery.' Something about his manner makes me suppress the impulse to tell him I don't consider myself lucky.

'Who found me?' I whisper.

'A teacher from your school. I'd like to talk to your parents but I understand your teacher contacted your mother and she still hasn't shown up since you were rushed into ICU. He said she just asked if you were dead or not. In twenty years of practice, I've never heard anything so callous!' He pulls a handkerchief from his pocket and wipes his glasses, peering at me with eyes that look both half blind and appalled.

'You've seen what I am. She was probably hoping to hear I'd died.' She'd have been terrified to be seen and pointed at. The mother of the monster in the ward. Because in the eyes of the world, only monsters birth monsters.

He sighs. Appears at a loss. 'Listen, you're young and I understand you've had some troubles. Yes, your body is unusual, even in medical circles, but that is no reason to kill yourself! We may not have the most modern facilities here, but there are specialists who can help. And great advances have been made abroad.'

Really? Can they fix broken hearts, too? Because nothing matters any more. The school will never let me back to take my remaining exams or give me good references. I've lost my twin sister and my best friend and wrecked the lives of everyone that matters. I've no home to go to. I have puffy nipples that are beginning to poke out in tiny mounds so I've been wearing two of my baggiest T-shirts at a time. Who knows if I'll soon grow a matching beard? All my striving was for nothing. My hopes and dreams are dead. I should be, too.

'Thank you, sir.' It's not as if he had a choice about saving my life. He was only doing his job.

Doctor Akpan sighs. He glances at his watch. Shakes his head. Surely he has other patients to see, normal people with problems he's trained to deal with. Who aren't teenagers with inexplicable bodies and incomprehensible families.

'Erm, maybe your teacher can help you decide where to go after we discharge you? You're really lucky to be alive and well.'

He leaves and moments later, Mr Dickson walks in. Of course it's him. I want to face the wall and ignore him, but I owe him better than that. He sits down and looks calmly at me. The silence stretches till I get nervous, then angry.

'You should have let me go.'

He shakes his head. Continues to stare at me with those wise eyes that see too much.

'I'll just try harder next time. Now you know Bayo was right and I'm a freak, why are you still here?'

'First of all, Oto, you will not take that tone of voice with me. I'm your elder and teacher. Secondly, you're not – and I detest that slang word – a freak. Nature has seen fit to give you a little extra of everything, and one day I'll introduce you to the Greek myth of Hermaphroditus. Thirdly, I've heard the stories going around, but I'm confident you have an explanation. As for wanting to die, I hope I can persuade you that few things are worth dying for, and youthful mistakes mostly don't fall in that category.'

I've not said a word in my defence and Mr Dickson is already on my side. Why? And he said Hermaphroditus! How does he know that word? I twist my hands in my lap, unsure what to say. I don't want to care any more. Not about him or anyone or anything. I don't want to feel. I'm supposed to be dead!

'You're lucky I found you so soon after you took those pills. Remember Gamba, your sparring partner at the dojo? He said a boy came to tell him he saw you run into the laundry room to escape a mob intending to beat you up.'

I nod. So Gamba still has a conscience, even though he abandoned me just like everyone else.

'The boy insisted Gamba come directly to tell me, though Gamba can't seem to remember who he was.'

Mr Dickson pauses. Fixes me with a hard stare.

'The doctor said you'd barely eaten for two days and those pills would have taken out your liver in another few hours. It took Gamba a while to find me. Let me tell you something about Panadol: it doesn't kill immediately, but slowly. First it dissolves your stomach lining, then it dissolves your liver, and then you die a slow painful death that might take months.'

As those grim words sink in, tears well up in my eyes and seep into my ears. Mr Dickson comes to stand by the bed, takes a white handkerchief from his pocket and wipes my face. His kindness only makes me cry harder, till I'm sobbing as if I'll break in two. What did I ever do to deserve it? He pats my shoulder, saying, 'It's okay, it's okay now, let it all out. You've had a hard life. It can be better from here on.'

How can anything ever be better?

'Your mother said if you're conscious, to call a taxi and have it drop you at home. Between her attitude and what the doctor told me about your body, certain things seem clearer. I wondered why you spent so much of your holidays in school. You can tell me about your father when we leave the hospital.'

I nod. I guess he means to drop me at home himself. It's the kind of thing he'd do. I've no idea what Mother has in store if I even last a night under her roof. Or Wura, who can be vengeful as a nest of hornets. A pants-wetting kind of dread pools in my stomach. Oh, why am I not still with Yeyemi? Somewhere in the medicine cabinet at home, there must be stronger pills that won't fail.

'So. Correct me if I'm wrong but it seems home is not a safe place for you right now. Would you like to stay with me till you figure out where to go?'

'Would I like to stay with you?' I parrot, totally unable to grasp what he's saying.

'I'm a bachelor, so you'll find things very basic, but I do have a young woman who comes in to clean and cook every other weekday, so you'll be well fed.' Mr Dickson smiles, knowing full well that's not top of my concerns.

'You'd let *me* come and stay with you?'

He nods patiently. 'Yes, Oto. I'm worried for your safety. Unless there's somewhere else you want me to take you?'

'No. I've nowhere else to go.' A sharp pain reminds me there's a needle stuck in one of the hands I'm wringing. I can't not warn him. 'Mr Dickson, you've been wonderful to me and I'm truly grateful, but the way bad luck seems to follow me . . . I don't want to bring you any trouble.'

'Pah!' He makes an impatient gesture as if he's flicking a fly over his shoulder. 'You leave that whole mess alone for now. I can take care of myself. All I ask is for you to focus on getting better and figure out what you want to do with your life.'

Which life? The one I've just failed to get rid of?

The door swings open, and Doctor Akpan comes in. He peers into my eyes with a light, makes me cough and say *aaaahhh* while I flinch from the cold stethoscope, then removes the needle in my hand.

'Well, Oto, it seems you're in the clear and there should be no after-effects of your ill-thought suicide attempt. In future, child, seek other solutions to your problems!' His manner is brusque, but there's concern underneath. He turns to Mr Dickson.

'You may take young Oto home. As long as he rests, he'll be fine. Just make sure he drinks plenty of fluids. Any pain or bleeding, bring him right back. And keep an eye on him as we discussed.'

33

1993 (AGE 16)

I stare out of the window as we drive towards Onireke, a respectable, though not wealthy part of Ibadan. It's thankfully far from our house in Bodija. We pass some children teasing a sturdy little goat with blunt, stubby horns. I crane my neck to look. The goat charges, headbutting a child's bottom and flipping him over its back. He gets up, screaming with laughter. Goat and kids all seem to be having a great time. It's the sort of thing I'd never see in refined Bodija, nor Derin in posh Ikoyi. How he would laugh. I'll never get to tell him.

I must have made some sound because Mr Dickson glances at me then switches on the radio. It's playing *Agborandun*, a sort of people's court, where disputes are resolved by audience participation. A man is claiming he has a right to keep his wife's lands after divorcing her because she kept giving birth to *abiku* babies who died anyway, after he'd spent a fortune on doctors and healers. I think about Maami Akinro and Mother. About the *Terrible Book of Unending Doom* at the Temple of Holy Fire. About Bayo and Elijah. And how people build their own little stronghold of reality, lock the doors, throw away the keys and then position themselves on top like snipers, shooting down whoever doesn't conform.

I think of how Babalawo's amulets bought me years of peace and joy and opened the door to my future. How I've slammed shut that door because of a stupid crush and dumb fear. How badly I've hurt those I love most. And here I am in Mr Dickson's car not knowing what lies ahead, or why I'm still breathing. I lean my head against the door.

Close my eyes. Mr Dickson changes the channel to something with local music.

Mr Dickson's house is a small, unpretentious white bungalow but growing in the front yard is a showstopping rainbow riot of flowers. There are roses and violets and hibiscus and cowpeas. I gape in amazement.

He smiles. 'I love gardening. It's relaxing.'

He certainly is unique. It wasn't unusual in ISS to walk into his office and receive an impromptu lecture on early Benin sculpture or medieval art. He's been known to spout spontaneous poetry on some unsuspecting fellow teacher. After he shuts the gates, he helps me out of the car. My legs are shaky and I lean on him as we head inside.

In the middle of the of the living room stands a round wooden table covered with books and art magazines. A couple of chairs and matching two-seater sofa with plump blue cushions surround it. Beyond a square brown rug, black and white linoleum tiles shine bright and clean.

'Come on. I'll show you your room.'

My room! I'll have to go back to ISS and pack up. Oh God, my letter to Wura. There are things in it no one else should ever see! As we walk down a short passageway, I feel like throwing up the little water in my stomach.

Mr Dickson opens a door. In one corner of the plain room sit my suitcase, travel bag and a couple of boxes. On my book bag lies the letter, my writing undisturbed across the the taped edge saying *For Wura Akinro's Eyes Only!* I turn to Mr Dickson but find no adequate words.

'I thought you'd like that back. It's private, eh? Go on and settle in. I'll be in the living room when you're done.' He pats my shoulder and leaves.

I sit on the single bed and look around. The walls are soft green. White curtains with yellow flowers hang from the windows. The bare closet is open. I miss my room in ISS with a fierceness so sudden and dizzying I bite my clenched knuckles to suppress the sob. Even my room at home would have been familiar. I don't belong here, but for Mr Dickson's kindness.

I need to lie down. Just for a minute. Under my breath I'm humming 'Jonpe' as my head touches the cool pillow, and I'm imagining it's Wura's lap and she's singing to me in her sweet, soft voice about the dog that refused to eat the child's leftovers, the stick that refused to beat the dog, the fire that wouldn't burn the stick, the water that wouldn't douse . . .

When I open my eyes, it's dark outside, and a light sheet covers me.

I try a couple of doors before I hit on the one leading to the bathroom, where I wash my face and brush my teeth. I follow the smell of food wafting in from somewhere beyond the living room. Mr Dickson is in his kitchen, laying placemats, cups and cutlery on the small table.

'Ah! Here you are!' he says with a big smile.

'Sorry. I didn't mean to fall asleep.' My face arranges itself to smile back.

'That's okay. You need rest to get your strength back. Dinner is ready. I'm having rice and stew but Dr Akpan said your stomach will be tender, so I made *ogi* for you. Do you like it with milk and sugar?'

'Yes, thank you. What can I help with?'

'Nothing, nothing.' Mr Dickson waves his hand airily. 'Make yourself comfortable. In future, I'll expect a healthy appetite at my table. Tinuke cooks a delicious beef stew. She just left a while ago. I don't know what I'd do without that girl.'

I wonder why Mr Dickson isn't married. He's at least forty years old. He puts a bowl of hot *ogi*, a can of Peak milk and a box of sugar cubes in front of me, serves himself and sits.

'Eat, eat,' he says, and digs in.

I do, surprised how good the *ogi* tastes and how fast I inhale it.

For a while, the only sound is the occasional tap of spoon and fork against our plates. Then Mr Dickson sits back and says, 'Tell me what happened.'

I twirl my spoon around my empty bowl.

'Look, Oto, whatever you say won't go beyond this room. I just want to understand the source of your problems so I can better help you.'

'Did you see what I am?'

'No. But the doctor asked if I knew you were of indeterminable gender. The word he used was hermaphrodite. I've read somewhere that's not a biologically appropriate term to apply to humans. Anyway, many things about you fell into place.'

'Do you think he'll tell anyone?' Not that it matters any more. This is a stop-gap. Mr Dickson will, at some point, send me back home and then I'll kill myself properly if Mother doesn't get me first.

'Doctors are not allowed to gossip about their patients. It would be unprofessional. And he's probably seen it all before.'

'Really?' Where are all these other people like me? I wish with all my heart to meet just one. To talk to someone who speaks the language of what I feel every day.

'I'm almost certain of it. Now, why don't you tell me your story?'

He's taken the day off work tomorrow, which is just as well if he really wants to know everything.

'It might take all night.' I get up and start clearing the table.

'That's okay. Leave the plates in the sink for now. Let's go and sit in the living room.' He opens the fridge, brings out a cold Coke for himself and hands me a small bottle of Lucozade. 'That should help settle your stomach.'

I don't know where to begin.

'Start from wherever you're comfortable.'

I stare at the brown rug and wonder if mind-reading is his bonus superpower.

'When I was little, Mother told me I was a monster that should never have been born . . .' Once the words start, I can't stop. To have a willing grown-up listen to me without judgement is like lancing a ripe boil. The relief far outweighs the pain. I tell him I know deep inside I'm a girl. About Babalawo and my amulets. Sister Angelica and her warning. The Seraphic Temple of Holy Fire and their whip-happy Wolis. About Maami Akinro and how Mother believes she's a witch who implanted me in her womb, about Mama Ondo and my treasure box, and everything else that has ever happened. It's a long time before I get to now.

'So I went up to my room that New Year's Day and Elijah came in. He brought some beer. Put something called jaggermister in it. It made me drunk and dizzy, really fast.'

Mr Dickson shakes his head.

'He kissed me and I . . . well, the truth is, I'd kind of . . . maybe flirted with him a bit before. But I told him to stop. I swear, I did!' I peek up at Mr Dickson. He'll hate me now.

He only nods.

'Wura and Udo, Elijah's friend, came in and saw us. I don't know how I could have been so stupid. And now she hates me.' A tear tickles the edge of my nose. I brush it off. 'In school, the rumours began about Elijah, and then people started whispering about me and Derin. But we're just friends. I swear nothing ever happened, even if maybe I wanted it to. He was just my best friend.'

'Did Derin know about your body?'

'No. I was always careful, though we were roommates every year.'

By the time I run dry, NEPA has struck with one of their frequent electricity blackouts and we're talking by the flickering light of hurricane lamps.

'Oto, no child is ever responsible for the circumstances of his or her birth. Your parents' behaviour is abusive. Nothing justifies or excuses it, but you've striven hard and endeavoured to prevail. That's highly admirable. I know you think all is lost, that it's time to give up, but you're still around for a reason, and you will find your way. All I ask is that you stay alive.'

That night I sleep like the dead.

34

1993 (AGE 16)

I put away my things, lingering on those that hold special memories: my art portfolio, my IB certificate, treasured books. Wura's broken watch. There's the Osmium Cookies CD, Derin's final gift to me. I refuse to think of what happened when I last played it. I'm sad to find my precious *Doobees Practice: Drawing Art and Animation* book is missing. Sister Angelica's word is still tucked inside. It must still be at home since I left in such a hurry. Not that any of it matters any more.

Mr Dickson says his first name is Victor but unless aiming to be rude, a Yoruba person never calls an elder by just his first name, so I call him Mr D, which suits us both fine. He'll head off to ISS in the morning and, by unspoken agreement, bring no news of the aftermath of my disappearance, which I understand Principal Akiolu has played down considerably. Bayo has, apparently, been allowed back to redo his final year. Given the rumours circulating, should I protest, I would only be found guilty of Bayo's accusations which are still in the school incident report that got him kicked out in the first place.

'Bayo's parents will do any underhanded thing to bail him out of the consequences of his misdeeds. I've come up against them before, and Principal Akiolu just keeps bending over backwards,' Mr D says.

'They can't do this! How does he keep getting away with it?' I want to go to the principal's office and break every last picture of him honouring students as if he himself is any sort of honourable person. He'd rather spare ISS any scandal and keep the rich parents generous than see justice done. Rage leaves my head feeling dry and empty. It's the first true thing I've felt since I woke up in hospital.

'You have a choice here, Oto, and I won't tell you what to do, but to have any chance at the bright future you've worked so hard for, you mustn't give him reason to formally expel you from ISS.' Though Mr D's voice is calm, his hands clench till the veins stand out.

What future? 'They've set it up so I can't win, haven't they?' While I'm certain Bayo isn't sure exactly what he saw that day in the bathroom, it's fifty-fifty as to which ISS and the world will judge worse: a boy who loves boys or, as Elijah put it, a half-female freak. For someone so lacking in intelligence, Bayo's cunning is almost genius. With Udo and my own vengeful sister as witnesses, I have no chance. And that's not even counting Father's threats to Mother if my 'condition' ever became public. Like a chameleon that nature made slow and half blind then omitted to give a weapon of self-defence, once my cover is blown, I'm easy pickings. The cafe must be buzzing with all the juicy *gist*. Even if I could go back, the other students will make my life hell.

I've been part of the problem. If I'd said something about what Bayo did to me that got him quietly removed – but not expelled – from ISS, he too would at least be facing the ISS court of public opinion upon his return, but I didn't. I kept silent. Because I had too much to hide. This was how he picked his victims – those for whom speaking out would cost more than exposing him. And here I was, still keeping silent. After he cost me my sister's love, my best friend's devotion (not to mention ruining his plans and I don't even know where he is or what is happening to him), my home, and my dreams.

'Ah, but winning rarely wears a recognizable face in the worst moments of life. Many great people in history at some point faced the choice of losing a battle in order to win the war. Someday that boy will get his due. Right now it's more important to preserve your future, and I have some ideas about how we'll do that, going forward. I'll need you to cooperate with me. You must live, Oto! Or he will, indeed, have won.' Mr D's eyes, fierce behind his glasses, stare straight into mine, willing me to hear him with my soul, not just my ears. I'm trying.

With Mr D's help, I write a letter formalizing my withdrawal from ISS due to ill health – my records show I was rushed to hospital in gastric distress but there are, thankfully, no further details. This way, I can't then be expelled. Writing each word is how I imagine it must be to chew broken glass.

Afterwards I call home, and my heart lifts to hear Wura's soft voice say hello. When I say hello back, she hangs up. I later emerge from my room with swollen red eyes. The thought of Wura defending Elijah makes me want to break the new lock on Mr D's medicine cabinet.

'There's nothing you can do if she won't listen,' he says.

'But she doesn't even know what a snake Elijah is!'

'Your sister seems smart. Maybe she just doesn't want to know. Often people only hear what they need to when they're ready.'

I just want to sink into a well of despair, but Mr D insists there'll be no slacking off from my studies. 'You've made it this far. You just have to keep taking one step at a time till you see your way clear.'

Mr D sets me tough assignments: books to read and essays to write. He endlessly feeds my mind and I let him, because that stops me thinking about more effective methods than Panadol. I study every art style and period. His favourite is Nok art dating back to the sixth century BC.

'Note their skill and stylistic excellence,' Mr D says. 'Africans have been making elegant art for centuries.'

The more I get to know him, the more I feel as if I'm finally getting a glimpse of what having a good parent is like. His study room is filled with everything from encyclopedias, art books and philosophy texts to great literary works. He returns, he said, to his mother's house in Ghana every other year during school holidays to devote himself to his true passion – sculpting intricate bas relief panels into which he incorporates figures from world myths and folktales. She sells them for him. I run my fingers over a scene of people dancing on a moonlit night, the only work of his displayed on the study wall. They look startlingly alive and inspire a flash of pure joy I'd forgotten I could feel. His collection of *Asante Akua'ba* figures, carved from dark wood, speak comfort to me with their gently rounded faces and soft eyes.

Most evenings pass with Mr D at his desk marking papers, making notes and occasionally murmuring to himself, while I sit in the corner chair, reading or studying. He says I'm one of the most restful people he's ever been around – something I didn't know about myself before. I wonder what other good things I don't know about myself. He grows fruits and vegetables behind his house. There are tomatoes, peppers and okras. He teaches me to identify the varieties of spinach – *tete, amunututu, shoko*. I've eaten cashews before, but never picked one from the tree. The pouchy pale fruits are attached directly to the branch and, stuck below each like a fat green comma, is the case hiding the nut. I'm watching for the fruits to turn an exact shade of flaming red-orange, because they're acidic and give you horrible cramps if you eat them too early, but ridiculously delicious if you pick them at exactly the right time. Too late, and they smell like old dish rags.

Several birds watch with greater interest. One afternoon, after calling Wura as I've faithfully done once weekly only to get hung up on as soon as whoever picks up hears my voice, I'm slumped miserably under the tree when something goes *splat!* on my head. A black, long-beaked bird bursts into song that sounds suspiciously like raucous laughter. Muttering angry threats about catapults and sharp stones, I stomp to the hose and turn cold water full force on my head. Then find myself smiling as I watch it launch gracefully into the sky. Mr D's garden, along with pooping birds and stinging ants and dirt-crusted nails, offers a new kind of peace.

In his library I find that book he brought to art class with the *Flaming June* painting. I remember Derin trusting me, sharing his pain about missing his mother. What wouldn't I give now for those things I took for granted? The tender light in his cat eyes when they lit on me, his laughter, the curly baby hairs at the base of his neck when he packed his *dada* locks up in a rubberband so they wouldn't get in his eyes during karate practice. His long fingers tapping away at Mori-baby, his treasured typewriter, in the peaceful privacy of our room. I sob so hard I lose my voice. Mr D makes me a soothing honey and hibiscus drink. 'You may think you wronged Derin, and perhaps the situation would be different if you'd trusted him with your secret, but that horse has well and truly bolted, and you must now focus on taking care of yourself. I'm sure he'll be fine. Things will get better.'

I do hear him. I just don't see how.

As I regain my strength, we practise karate. Mr D is incredibly patient. I can't take any formal belt tests, but when Mr D puts me through my paces some days later, he reckons I'd merit a blue.

I find a large book titled *Treasures of the Louvre* left out on the desk in Mr D's study one morning. I flip through, thinking, *what an amazing place! How I'd love to go there one day!* I turn another page and see something that doesn't seem quite ... My jaw simply drops. A reclining marble figure. An unmistakable curve of breast lies under the woman's upraised arm but lower down, there's ... well ... the complete serving of *ogẹdẹ* and *agbalumo* fruits, as the cruder boys in the dorm might put it. I sink into the nearest chair and read that it's a photo of the *Borghese Hermaphroditus*, which was made in the second century BC. She looks quite different from me down below but I'm dazzled to finally hold proof that bodies like mine have always existed, not just everywhere but for *centuries*!

I read the short article on the Greek myth of the son of Hermes and Aphrodite. A water nymph found Hermaphroditus irresistible. He refused her advances, but she ambushed him in a pool while he was bathing and the gods granted her wish for them to be eternally united by melding them into a man and woman in one body. Hermaphroditus, distraught, also got his wish that anyone else who swam in that pool would suffer the same fate. Which apparently explains every future 'hermaphrodite' born thereafter. In Greece, anyway.

This business of making up stories about why people like me exist has been going on for a really long time. Surely there's more to it than besotted nymphs and drunken gods. Still, it stirs something in me. For the first time since life went to hell, I pick up my pencil and start drawing. It's soon skimming the paper like my hand has wings.

Mr D comes in to find me finishing the pencil sketch.

'Ah, good. I thought you'd find that interesting.'

'I can't quite believe it. Do you know more about hermaphrodites?' It's strange to finally say that word out loud.

'Unfortunately, no, but many cultures worldwide have a representation. I do believe somewhere I have a book of African sculpture that includes the *Nommo*, ancestral spirits of the Dogon people of Mali. They appear with a human torso and a fish-like tail.'

'Oh, I'd love to see that.' To think Yeyemi appears in the imagination of people in another culture!

Mr D smiles. 'I'll find it for you. You know, if only humans embraced each other in all the glorious permutations nature presents, there would be less pain in the world.'

He sounds ... wistful. Sad. I set aside my own troubles, really look at him.

'I'm about to tell you something for your ears alone.'

I nod solemnly.

'When I was a boy of about thirteen, my parents brought a distant cousin from my father's village to live with us in Accra. They thought a companion, someone to roughhouse with and look up to, would enliven their quiet only child who did nothing but read books and draw pictures. I was so badly bullied I'd come home bleeding. They'd just switched me to yet another new school.

'His name was Justin. His parents had recently passed away and his family was glad to let my parents take over the expense of raising him. He was a year older than me. We took to each other like duck and water. My parents were glad. He was the fearless older brother I'd always longed for, who led the way into parts of town I'd never dared on my own. He showed me how facing down bullies is all about attitude and, believe me, bullies don't go away, they just grow older. In return,

I brought him into my world of books and art. We shared a room and would talk late into the night. He dreamed of becoming a drummer in a band.'

Mr D pauses. Takes a deep breath even as I hold mine, knowing my heart is about to break for him.

'One night Justin slipped into my bed, curled up behind me and went to sleep. I was surprised and pleased. It felt right. After that, we slept in the same bed every night. My father walked in on us early one morning. It had been a sweltering night and all we wore was underwear. He threw Justin out. It didn't matter what I said, he was convinced Justin was corrupting his innocent son.

'I fell ill for a long time, I was so heartbroken. This only convinced my father that Justin must have used some sort of *juju* magic to ensnare me, and my illness was a result of the spell wearing off.'

'Just like my mother!' I gasp.

'Yes, Oto. It's a universally occurring mindset. People just give it different labels. Justin's name was never spoken in our house again. Till my father died ten years later, he watched me as though I might, if he took his eyes off for a minute, grow a second head.'

Mr D has been staring at the floor all this while. He looks up. Smiles.

'Shortly after I got better, my mother introduced me to a karate teacher who bought bread from her bakery. She told me the same thing I told you. Try it and if you don't like it, you don't have to keep going, but you need something to give you the strength to believe in yourself. It saved me.'

I force myself not to blink till my tears are gone.

'Have you seen Justin since?'

'No. No one would tell me where he went and by the time I was old enough to search, it was as if he'd vanished from the earth. He was probably shipped off to live with another relative, maybe outside Ghana. My mother swears she has no idea. I hope whoever it was took good care of him. He must have been devastated.'

This explains a lot about Mr D. He couldn't save Justin, but he's trying to save me. 'I'm so sorry.'

'Thank you, Oto. See, the trick to living is knowing which challenges to engage – sometimes just by buckling down and hanging tight till you push through – and which to rise above. And to never lose sight of what makes life meaningful for you. I discovered that opening young people's eyes to art brings me the greatest fulfillment, because creativity is the branch upon which human intellect blooms.'

I nod. It sounds noble, but terribly lonely. I wonder how many stranded young souls he's rescued over the years. I'd hug him but for the odd formality he preserves around himself.

Days later, after dinner, Mr D begins pacing the length of the study, rubbing his moustache with his forefinger. I put down my book and wait.

'Khalil Gibran was an artist. He was also one of the greatest poets that ever lived. He said, *Knowledge of the self is the mother of all knowledge. So it is incumbent on me to know my self, to know it completely, to know its minutiae, its characteristics, its subtleties, and its very atoms.*'

I seize a pen and some paper. I've begun keeping a journal at Mr D's insistence. Writing out your feelings, he said, is like cleaning a wound with antiseptic. Things fester otherwise.

'I have a copy of *The Philosophy of Logic* somewhere in my bedroom. I'll dig it up for you later.' Mr D takes off his bifocals and starts cleaning them with one of the immaculately pressed handkerchiefs he always carries. 'It was irresponsible of your parents to not seek medical advice. I took the liberty of going back to see Dr Akpan.'

I sit up.

'He's a general practitioner, but he has recommended a urologist who'll examine you at no charge and in strict confidence, as a part of her research. Your name won't be mentioned. You'll likely be referred to as Patient X or similar. She can't treat you, but she can offer some clarity and perhaps a diagnosis?'

I almost rub my ears to make certain I heard right. It's as if he's just said his personal space shuttle is waiting outside to fly us to the moon. Those words smell like hope. And hope is expensive. It's asking me to deal beyond here and now. To imagine that there are still dreams worth pursuing. I have, for example, decided not to notice that underneath my nipples, it's now puffed up like tiny doughnuts, because noticing implies that I have a future. Yet here's Mr D offering what I so badly longed for once upon a time.

'But ... *what's the point?*' It's a wail of anguish I can't control. I'd meant to thank him. To say thanks but no thanks. Nothing matters any more.

'The point is, you already made an almost fatal choice. How can you make the right choices without being informed? If you're still remotely thinking of ending your one, precious life, shouldn't you at least go knowing who you are?'

'Sorry. I'm sorry. I know you're only trying to help me.'

He pats my shoulder. 'I understand. You're done caring and yet here I am poking your sore spots. It's so much easier to give up, eh? I've been there, remember? Sleep on it. Let me know in the morning. Whatever you decide won't change the fact that you're my best and most beloved art student!'

I don't sleep a wink. If I do this, I could get answers. Am I male? Female? Somewhere in between? Will the bumps on my chest get bigger? Will I menstruate? Grow a beard? Can I have babies? And, if I finally know, will it leave me wanting even less to live?

35

1993 (AGE 16)

The urologist is a slender, soft-spoken woman with a brisk manner. Mr D is nearby in the waiting room, which is reassuring. It takes two visits, during which my body is prodded and probed and clamped open in ways I'd never known was possible, with medical photos taken (my face covered) and everything measured, including my teeth. The urologist asks questions about my comfort but is neither warm nor motherly. She's professional. I feel like a particularly interesting specimen. With legs spread open in stirrups on that examination table I flash to lying on my back, Bayo leaning over me, finger poised to discover if what he was seeing was real, and remind myself this is a small price to pay. Unlike so long ago when Babalawo's wife was trying to ascertain the mind of the gods, I'm clear about being examined so I can understand myself. What Babalawo began with his *Odu-Ifa* divination, she will hopefully expand upon with her urology degree.

When she has her results, I ask Mr D to be there for what feels like a court verdict.

'Well, Oto,' the urologist says, 'you test as XY. Usually, that would indicate a male phenotype, but your external presentation lies somewhere between clitoromegaly and a micro-penis. You also present with partially scrotalized, posterior labial fusion. All of which create an indeterminate appearance.

'Your ultrasound showed no uterus. You do, however, have budding breasts, which will develop as your delayed puberty advances. My best conclusion is that your body is partially insensitive to androgens, a condition known as incomplete testicular feminization. It used to be called male pseudohermaphroditism. The terminology keeps changing and might already be different. Ambiguous genitalia is not my speciality – it's just incidental to my current research.'

The urologist opens a folder and places a piece of paper on the table before us. It's headlined *Genital Virilization Staging Scheme*. It's covered with diagrams of what look like groups of brackets and squiggles and lines, but are quite clearly reproductive organs. They're numbered zero to six.

'I'd place you at about a stage two,' she says, tapping the third diagram, which looks somewhat like what I have. 'As you can see, stage six has the appearance of a fully virilized male, and stage zero a fully unambiguous female. Going by that, you should ideally have had a female sex of rearing. This, if I understood right, is your preference?'

I nod dumbly. I have budding breasts that will keep growing. I should have been raised female. Mother was dead wrong. I'm not a changeling. Or any sort of demon. Or cursed. I'm Lori. I've always been. And an *expert*, a medical researcher, just said so. It matters. Despite everything, it matters very much right now to hear this. I want to climb on her table and shout, *I am Lori! I am Lori Akinro!*

I look at Mr D. He smiles. *It is incumbent on me to know my self.*

'Now, I'm sure you have questions,' the urologist says.

I try to think, to ask intelligent things.

'My twin sister got … um … periods a while ago. Are you saying I'll never have any?'

'If I'm correct – and keep in mind there's a margin of error since we couldn't perform the expensive karyotyping or hormonal assays – you don't have female internal reproductive organs, therefore you won't menstruate or bear children. However …' The urologist glances at Mr D, brows raised. I nod. It's perfectly okay for the man I've started thinking of as a father to know everything about me.

'You have a close-to-adequate vaginal introitus, though it ends blindly with no cervix. A gynaecologist will be able to give you more details. Keep in mind that you might have gonads – internal testes – that sometimes turn cancerous unless removed. They will likely not virilize you any further.'

'So I could die from cancer?' I don't even have time to be embarassed about the words vagina and introitus and what they imply. I've only heard whispered things about cancer, that it kills people horribly.

'Well, it's just recommended that the gonads are removed at some point. It is a costly operation with a long recovery period. Afterwards, you'd need to take synthetic hormones for life, which is also expensive. There's also the option of corrective cosmetic surgery. American surgeons have achieved some excellent results.'

'What corrective surgery?' Mr D asks.

'For Oto, it would be genitoplasty where the where the clitoris is cut down to a more typical size or removed altogether, and the partially fused labia separated to give a more normal feminine-looking appearance.'

My knees snap closed. The thought of someone taking a knife to my poor nubby part is even more excruciating than it was during Apetebi's long-ago examination. Yet, the words *normal* and *typical* carry such alluring possibility. If I'd been born 'normal', I'd be the beloved child of Chief and Mrs Akinro, pampered in a prosperous home with my siblings. Normal means looking like any other girl, a gift those surgeons in America can apparently bestow. Which is like my birthday cake arriving after the guests have left and the decorations came down. Because I'm obviously not going anywhere.

'Are those necessary for Oto's health?' Mr. D asks.

'Not unless discomfort arises. They just normalize the body for easier social integration.'

'Do you know of any means of getting Oto's true gender recognized?' He's asking all the important questions, just like a proper parent should. And I'm grateful.

'Well, I know of one instance. A note from someone like me or a reputable gynaecologist stating that Oto is female could theoretically be taken, along with her birth certificate, to court by her parents to swear an affidavit to effect the necessary change, which could then be reflected in her passport and all other identity papers.'

My Parents. Well, all the cows in Nigeria will sprout wings and fly before they'll do such a thing.

'Feel free to contact me with any questions, and if you get further information about your family medical history, it will be helpful for my research.' She picks up her files and we know it's time to leave.

'I will. Thank you so much.' She had questions about my extended family when she examined me, few of which I had answers to. Had there been others born like me? None that I knew of.

We drive back to Mr D's house in silence. Inside me it's like sunshine and rainclouds all at the same time. I'm a girl! A *girl*. I have girl parts as labelled in biology textbooks, just differently assembled. Somewhere inside, I might have gonads that could cause cancer. I'll never have my own babies because I'm a girl with XY boy chromosomes. I bury that last thought deep inside and decide to concentrate on the good part. The *being a girl* part. As Mr D is teaching me, the art of cultivating a desire to live includes knowing how to temporarily look away from things that might wipe out your ability to see at all.

A strange energy seizes me in the days that follow. I don't quite know what to do with it. Like there's a motor engine revved to life inside me but there's also a heavy foot firmly on the brake. I mope around, picking things up and putting them down. Sighing. Unable to settle. Longing to do something but not knowing what. Watching me stew, Mr D gets this look on his face as if he knows a secret. I feel inexplicably annoyed at him but he only grins when I frown.

I'm leaning forward to grab my towel one morning when, in the bathroom mirror, I see an unmistakable silhouette under my out-stretched arm. The urologist did say this could happen gradually or fast. It's as if some internal pump keeps filling them up. Soon, the edge of my T-shirt sticks three inches out. I bind them flat with cut-up pieces of cloth. I still have to, *want* to, live with Mr D. I won't attract attention and get him in trouble.

Restless as the edge of a thunderstorm, I finally decide to venture out one Saturday. Mr D delightedly hands me some naira and tells me to enjoy myself. I don't know Onireke at all but he's described the general area that serves as town centre. I wander aimlessly about, glad I'm unlikely to run into anyone who knows me. It's only when I find myself standing before one of several 'ready made' dress and fashion boutiques that I realize my wily mind, or perhaps Lori's, was meandering with an agenda. I glance inside, and the owner looks up and smiles, waving at me to come in. I wave back, want and dread equally ripping my stomach, then scuttle away sideways like a startled crab. I take the bus back home, too unsettled to do any more adventuring.

Like a river shaping angles into curves, Lori's presence flows strong. It's as if the urologist broke the dam and I can no more stop her coming out than I could turn the earth around. It's a relief. It could, if only I was free to feel it, be a vast joy. Like drilling through and finding the well of water you've always known existed underground, after years of suffering drought.

I find myself back at the boutique, nervously purchasing the thing that draws me most – a make-up kit I pretend is for my girlfriend, though it's not like I've anything left to lose. The owner recommends, in addition, the *tiiro* sold in little metal canisters imported from Hausa merchants up north, saying it gives a silkier line than eye pencils. She throws in a small disc of face powder for half price.

Back home, I practise lining my eyelids, then swiping on lipstick, then daintily patting powder onto my forehead and nose, one thing at a time, gingerly, awkwardly. It's as if I'm doing something furtive that will get me killed, until I realize that's Mother's voice in my head and promply banish it to the outer realms of darkness, wherever that might be.

When my face is fully made up, I stare at the stranger in the mirror, astonished how all my life I've longed to meet her, and now here she is. High-arched brows, bronzed cheekbones with the proud slant of a Yoruba sculpture, soft coral lips. 'Hello, Lori,' I whisper, then have to widen my eyes so the tears won't fall and ruin my mascara. I wave, blow myself a kiss, then giggle, feeling silly. I know I want to see her every day. I want to be her for the rest of my life.

If Mr D knows what I've been up to, he doesn't comment. Just shows me where he keeps what he calls 'excess household funds' – as if he can really afford any excess – and tells me to help myself within reason. I try to be prudent, though I thought I'd died and gone to heaven when I walked into yet another boutique and the *shoes*! I couldn't try them on, of course, but I'd measured my feet and knew my size. It was just a question of pretending, as usual, that they were for my girlfriend. When I added a bra, the lady's eyes seemed knowing, and I became afraid, but she also smiled, which made me wonder if maybe some people out there are okay. More confident now, I bargained down the price of a gold-trimmed blue *boubou* with matching *igele*, identical to one Wura used to have that I'd always adored, foolishly wishing she could share and rejoice in my transformation, picturing us happy together, identically dressed, twin sisters in every way.

Later at home when I slide on the *boubou*, it fits just right over the gentle upswell of my bra. I tie on the *igele* in a simple style around my head and nearly jump back from the mirror because right there is Wura, staring back at me. In that moment, I miss her with an ache that is bottomless.

36

1993 (AGE 16)

'Pack up your IB certificate, your best artwork and evidence of your school extracurricular activities,' Mr D says one morning. 'We have a trip to make.'

He drives us to a place on the outskirts of Ibadan that I've never been. A sign outside says, *Education USA Advising Center*. My heart starts doing triple beats. He hums softly to himself as I stare wide-eyed at him, a million questions storming my mind as the lift takes us to the top floor.

Mr D pays the fee that gives us access for a few minutes' talk to a counsellor, Mrs Ladipo, an elegant, American-sounding woman who looks delighted when she sees my IB certificate, then nods and smiles her way through my art portfolio. She's saying miraculous words like *high-achiever* and *scholarship* and *university* and *America*. I sit there in a sort of daze while they talk at length and come to the stunning conclusion that under her guidance, I could get good enough marks to swing an admission and hopefully a scholarship to a university in the United States! As comprehension dawns, though I'm shaking my head in disbelief, my grin must be visible from outer space.

Then she says how much the membership fee for the US Center facilities and her services would be, including personal assistance with finding and applying to the right colleges, and I'm in a different kind of shock. When she piles on the added costs of taking the required exams, my armpits break into sweat though the room is air-conditioned.

'I'd figured about that much.' Mr D digs into the beaten-up leather case I'd wondered why he was carrying and heaves the giant pile of naira onto the table. I don't know how much a school teacher is paid, but it's certainly not this much, even in a month. He can't afford this. I've seen how carefully he budgets and how sparingly he lives. 'But you can't . . . I mean, it's too much. I . . .' I don't know what to say.

'Oto, I invested some money years ago in the ISS teachers' co-operative, hoping it would mature and become available when it was most needed. That happened two days ago, and I can't think of a better use for it.'

I'm weak with gratitude. Shame out of nowhere swamps me for every thought of killing myself. This amazing man has steadfastly believed in me even when I lost what little belief I had in myself. I simply absorb him with my eyes as he signs and enters his contact information as my guardian, looking as if he's just solved one of humanity's most pressing issues. I try not to think about how Father spends the same amount on any one weekend imperiously 'spraying' people at parties.

I follow Mr D outside in a living dream, clutching tight the photo ID card that gives me full access to the US Center. In tears I thank him and thank him and vow I'll one day pay it all back.

'Just make it worth my while by succeeding,' he says, patting my shoulder. We celebrate with lunch at a nearby bukateria before heading to his home, now my home and the most peaceful place I've ever lived. Mine for as long as I need. Mine till I leave for America. Because I intend to do everything to make that happen.

Mrs Ladipo said I needed to start straightaway to meet deadlines for the next batch of admissions, so I'm back at the US Center first thing the next morning. She's from a place called New Orleans, and came to Nigeria as an exchange student but stayed and married a Yoruba man. She said in her country, she'd be called African-American, and so would I. It's one of the first things I learn. She's kind and encouraging. 'I'm happy to help such a talented student,' she says in her drawly voice. 'You can come to me for help about anything.'

Under her coaching I study for the TOEFL and SAT exams,

spending practically every daylight hour there. I write essays and personal statements. Mrs Ladipo says *Blurb!*, karate, the theatre group, my art portfolio, even volleyball, make me a well-rounded and desirable candidate. Who knew? If I score high enough in my exams, she'll send my application to a few carefully selected top universities – we can just about afford the application fees – and also apply for scholarships and grants. It blows my mind all over again. How amazing would it have been to grow up with someone like Mr D? I've only read about adoption in books but I wonder if one day he could really become my father. No question about it, he hung every last star in the sky.

Time flies and life settles into a rhythm. Studying in the garden, I eye that same bird I'm sure was the one that pooped on my head, and wonder if it's back to do it again for luck. As I laugh, it occurs to me to change my name to Lazarus not Lori. Because I truly feel like I am back from the dead.

37

1993 (AGE 16)

Mr D comes home one evening with an unmarked envelope and hands it to me.

'You might want to go and open that in private,' he says, in reponse to my puzzled look.

In my room, I open it to find another envelope – blue and finely wrinkled like it has travelled a great distance over a long time. My shaking hand rises to my lips. It can't be! That familiar writing. Each letter scrawling left against its neighbour, the 't's crossed with a flourish. Wavy postmarks ride across a stamp showing a tiny replica of an American flag. It's addressed to Mr D at ISS. Memories flood in. His smile. His subtle scent. Sunlight glinting on wild *dada* hair. His hand reaching across the space between our narrow single beds to offer up some treasure found just for me. The fierce pride in his cat eyes the day we got our IB results. I wipe my eyes with the edge of my sheet. I have to open it. I'm terrified to open it. I lift the taped-down flap to find another envelope that says, *For the exclusive attention of Otolorin Akinro.*

Only he dots the 'i's in my name that way, rounded like a circle. I open it and out flutters a single sheet of paper.

```
Writer/Journalist    Seeks    Talented    Artist    to
Collaborate in New Comic Book Venture.
If interested, please contact Derin Adenola, 255
Avenue B, NY, 10009.
```

```
Phone number 718 001 0001
Your response is urgently awaited.
```

Derin. *In America.* How is he there? Why now? No one else would write a letter like this. It's *so* him. Putting things in a way that says just enough to me and nothing at all to anyone else. Mailing it to the one person he knows would likely get it safe into my hands. I'm laughing with joy, hand over my mouth and crying. I read it again and again till the words and numbers are imprinted on my mind.

Then reality hits. What if he's still angry? He can't be, and write such a letter, right? But what if I'm wrong? Or if he's changed his mind since sending the letter? I'll need some time to think this over. I'm no longer the person he used to know. I couldn't bear it if he rejected me all over again. Besides, his father said he'd make me sorry if I contacted him. I don't need any more problems right now. My focus should be on my SAT and TOEFL exams, not on the boy whose life I upended and nearly destroyed just because he'd had the courage to befriend me. Truth is, I'm simply terrified. Tucking the letter away, I resolutely open my textbook.

Days later, I take my exams and crawl home to collapse into an exhausted sleep.

In my dream I'm minuscule, ant-sized, running all over the surface of a world globe that keeps spinning and tilting, threatening to fling me off, but none of the countries stretched under my feet hold Derin's scent because I've waited too long to search and now I'll never find him again. I awake panicked and fly to the living room.

Then I'm holding the phone in a death grip, my heart walking a tightrope with no safety net.

'Hello?'

His voice is deeper, smoother but very much the same.

A golden feeling envelops my body, steals into my bones, leaves me breathless.

'Um . . . Derin, this is Oto. I just wanted to say I got your letter and would love to accept the position – that is, if it's still open as I'm sure by now you must have other friends who . . .' My nonsensical words spill out in a rush then I shut up.

There's silence. Then the loud music in the background turns off.

'Oto?' Derin's voice is full of wonder. I used to know every nuance of that voice. When it was happy and when it was sad. When it was wistful and when it held hope. 'I waited and waited and thought you'd never call. I'd given up. I thought maybe you couldn't forgive me.'

Direct to the heart of the matter. That hasn't changed. 'Forgive you? Am I not the one who needs forgiving?'

'No. I thought long and hard and realized I never gave you a chance. I was so scared, I panicked. I'm so sorry, Oto. I dropped the ball and I want to set that right. I can't tell you how much. Please forgive me?'

For long moments I can't speak.

'I . . . Thank you, Derin. But I've never blamed you at all. You reacted like anyone would in that situation.'

'I wasn't anyone. I was your best friend, and I should have stood by you no matter what. I've really missed you. How are you? Where are you?'

'Fine. I'm living with Mr D – I mean, Mr Dickson – in Ibadan. I just took my TOEFL and SATS. I'm hoping to come to the US – that is, if a university accepts me and if I get a scholarship.' His loud whoop makes me hold the phone from my ear, smiling.

'Oh, Oto, that is amazing! I really hope you get in. I'm in New York. To have you so close. God, that will be awesome!' His voice is radiant with unfeigned joy and I let myself bask in it, let myself feel this shining moment as if it's all a real possibility.

I need details. What's it like? Does he have friends? Is he happy? But all too soon, the international phone card Mr D normally uses for calling his mother in Ghana gives a warning beep. It's running out and I have to say goodbye. I give him Mr D's number and he promises to call the very next day. I hang up and stare dumbly at the wall, feeling as if I've just lived a whole lifetime in the course of a few minutes. Then I get up and let the joy lift my feet off the ground till I'm dancing right there in Mr D's living room.

Derin calls as promised. He's in a prep school while he waits to start at New York University and study Journalism and Creative Writing, just as he's always wanted. His dad straightaway packed him off to his mother, who'd recently moved to New York. He was so depressed at the sudden change in his life, she wasted no time getting him into school. It was the only way they figured he'd be okay, and his excellent grades meant he was sought after.

We talk as often as possible, catching up on our lives, our hopes, and just like that our old magic is back. I tell him most of what has passed, glossing over details that can only ever be said in person, like swallowing a bottle of Panadol. I simply say I'm at Mr D's because Mother doesn't want me back. His shiny new American curse words do not bear repeating.

He tells me how cold winter was in New York, and about all the friends he's made, how it was such a shock to be in ISS one day, and America with his mom the next, how he still sometimes struggles with the strangeness of it all and the sheer burden of figuring out where in American society he belongs. He tells me how his mom can't do enough to make up for all the years they've lost. He also tells me how badly he's missed me. 'Having you here is the one thing that would make this place feel most like home. I've wished it with all my heart, even when it seemed an impossible wish,' he says, which makes me cry. I don't hesitate to tell him how I've missed him, too. I also don't add that I'm fairly certain wherever he is will always be home.

His voice at the end of the phone keeps me going through the nail-biting wait for my results. I hear so much about his unconventional young New York writer friends that I'm desperate to meet them. His awe at suddenly being surrounded by people who are not only different but revel in it. At rubbing brains with people like himself, who aren't afraid of the stark truth. People who believe that everyone has the right to be exactly who they are, including a couple who refuse to answer to boy or

girl and insist they're simply themselves, which sounds so liberating it
blows my mind! I hope he's saying what I think he's saying, because this
time I mean to tell him. I just can't think how. Our calls are expensive
and I'll have to be brief. How do I reveal something so huge thousands
of miles apart, on a staticky phone line?

'I'm different from other people.' It just comes out. Right in the middle
of a conversation about contemporary American writers that Derin
can't wait to share with me.

'I know.'

'You do?' A leaf would have knocked me on my butt.

'I ... um ... found a book among the things Dad packed from our
room. He assumed it was mine. I still have it. It's titled *Doobees Practice:
Drawing Art and Animation?*'

I gasp. Page 20. I wrote Sister Angelica's word a lifetime ago!

'I looked up that word after I got here, and so much immediately
made sense because, before that, I'd also found a ... um ... romance
novel under my bed in our room? It was after that half-term break
when you were acting weird and I didn't know why. I remember it was
titled ... *cough cough* ... *Her Passionate Desire.*'

'Oh!' I feel hot all over. It was the book Bayo caught me reading. In the
turmoil that followed, I forgot all about it, thinking I'd got rid of it along
with the others. The sweet, teasing grin I hear in Derin's voice, though,
wipes away in an instant any lingering torment from Bayo's cruel taunts.

'I was just hoping you'd eventually tell me what was up with you,'
Derin says. 'I sort of didn't want to make assumptions? You kept things
so private. Then I ... well, I felt all confused because after that time
Wura came for our IB celebration I couldn't stop seeing you how I'd
always really seen you and ... Does that make any sense?'

'Oh! *Oh!* Yes.' He'd just felt confused ...

'And I also, um ... I'm sorry, I didn't want to embarrass you. But ...'

'But?' I whisper, my heart tripping into my throat.

'But I saw ... um ... that day in the bathroom. I'm not sure. I ... I'm
sorry. I just put it out of my mind straightaway.'

I breathe out. He did see. He didn't want to believe what he saw. Also, it was too private. And now we both know. And he's still on the phone. In fact, he's sought me out when he needed never contact me again. I sniffle; a tear has slid into my nose.

'Then things went crazy after those rumours at ISS and I felt so scared and hurt and ... um ... jealous? Though I certainly had no right. Then Dad swept in and whisked me off without warning and next thing I knew I was in New York with Mom. I've so wanted a chance to say it's okay. You're wonderful however you are and I ... er ... really like you and, um ... yeah.'

I'm sitting on the floor. My legs gave and I simply slid down the wall while he talked.

'Please say something?' His voice is husky.

'I. Okay. Thanks.' *Jealous*, is all I hear. Though other things crowd right behind that word in my mind's current traffic jam, like, *Sweet goddess, he saw me properly naked*. And, *He knows what I truly, intimately look like*, and, *I'm in love with him* and *He might be with me too ...*

'That's it?' There's relieved laughter in his voice.

'You like me?'

'A bit insanely, yes.'

'Um, me too.'

'We have so much to catch up on.'

'Yes, we do.'

38

1993 (AGE 16)

I can't wipe the happy smile off my face as I head out of the US Center, thinking of Mr D's reaction when I tell him the good news. Of the joy that is sure to shimmer Derin's voice. I passed with top marks and Mrs Ladipo has sent out my applications straightaway, saying that even though I'm late, I will still get consideration because I am a straight-A student. Mr D will take care of my ISS references, which isn't a problem since I was never expelled. All that exists on my records are unproven allegations from a fundamentally untrustworthy source.

It feels like an impossible hurdle I've crossed. True, I must still be accepted with a full scholarship, which apparently carries less chance than winning a lottery. But I've come this far and, as my proverb book says, *If you will eat the honey in the rock, you cannot sit there worrying about the sharpness of your axe.* You get on with it. After all, I got myself into ISS. One thing at a time.

I'm starry-eyed looking down at the paper with my high TOEFL and SAT scores and the list of three American universities I might one day attend, when before me appear two giant sneakered feet. Even before I look up, I know. Standing there is my worst nightmare. My body coils like a spring. I step back, trembling. Shove my results into my book bag. What business could Bayo possibly have here?

'Planning on going somewhere?' He stalks me step for step.

'Get out of my way.' My heart is slamming against my chest. How did he know I'd be here?

He's even bigger and his eyes are hard and red. There's a healed scar jagging across his jaw that didn't used to be there, bisecting his goatee. Like he needed to look any more sinister. Fear twitches under my skin like an itch I refuse to heed.

'I can't do that. I want something from you. I'm thinking I don't need to remind you what happens to you and your sister when I don't get my way.'

'Haven't you done enough? Just leave Wura alone, or I swear—'

'You'll what? I know all about your plans. America, eh? Just wait till they get hold of your ISS records.'

'My records say I left school because I wasn't well. Unlike you, I've commited no actual crimes.'

'Haha! Believe me, that could change. Look, I was all set to attend this easy little college in London. My annoying father wants the grand prize of a son with an MBA, however rubbish, and won't let me rest. Which is fine, don't get me wrong – more partying in London for me. Except that Ghanaian is once more determined to be a pain in my arse.'

Fury wipes out my fear. 'You are the pain in everyone's arse. And for the record, you're not fit to clean Mr Dickson's shoes!' An MBA indeed! For certain all the British pounds his parents have won't save Bayo from speedily becoming Her Majesty's guest at Thameside Prison which, I've heard as a joke in ISS, contains so many criminal Nigerians, they serve *amala* and *pọmọ* for dinner. Because that is his nature.

'Whatever. Consider this a friendly warning. Principal Akiolu not only likes his job, he needs to cover his own *yansh*. Cross me and what he'll put in your ISS records will shame a ten-naira *ashewo*.'

'He's the principal. Not a criminal like you!'

He laughs. 'You're defending Akiolu? My father owns that man. Look, it's easy. All you have to do is keep your mouth shut about what happened at ISS and deny whatever anyone says about me – especially Dickson – and all this will go away. In fact, Akiolu himself will write you a shining reference and give you that badge of merit you so nearly earned if you hadn't ... ahem ... lusted after my cousin.' He grins. 'God, your sister was so gullible!'

'Not gullible. Just trusting. Something you'll never understand.'

'Whatever. Just do as I say or I promise it will hurt. And don't think for one second that your sister is safe. You mess up and she'll pay. As for Dickson, he'll soon be packing his Ghana-Must-Go bag.' Bayo chuckles darkly at his own joke.

I'm queasy with horror. Is he stalking Wura? How? The only time I cornered Emily for two seconds on the phone she assured me that she'd neither seen nor heard of Elijah since that New Year's Day. That Wura was too ashamed to contact him. Which doesn't mean if he comes calling now, pretending he's forgiven me and wants her back, she'd say no. Then who knows what they'd do?

Bayo calmly watches the worries flick over my face. It's maddening. 'If anything happens to Wura or Mr Dickson, I promise *you* won't be safe anywhere in this world.' Though my voice is a shaky squeak, I mean every word.

Bayo gasps, shudders. His eyes suddenly darken. He glances quickly around, slides his finger along my jaw. Licks his lips. 'I love it when you fight. How is it you just keep getting finer, hmm? We have unfinished business, remember? I'll be better than your half-oyinbo. Pity he disappeared and left you to face the music alone.'

My breath escapes in a hiss, my book bag hits the floor and I'm whirling away preparatory to planting my foot deep in his solar plexus when there's a flurry of wings and a black bird swoops out of nowhere straight into my face and I trip and I'm sitting on the floor, winded.

Bayo laughs, though he eyes the bird a bit uncertainly. He turns and strides away. By the time I gather myself to follow, he's past the gate and getting into a red Jeep. As he drives off, he folds his fingers to form a cocked gun, holds it to his temple and his lips say, *Pow!*

I lean, trembling, against the wall. On top of the flagpole from which the US Center's American flag waves, the bird sits cleaning its feathers, one dark eye on me. A lone fluffy black feather flutters down to rest on a wooden signboard I read on my first day and have ignored many times since. The one that lays out the US Center rules in huge letters, including, *fighting and other unruly behaviour will go on your record and get you permanently barred from the US Center.* The bird caws, wheels round once in the sky and flies away.

My thoughts whirl urgently. What does Mr D know that he hasn't told me? I've been so busy with my studies, then wrapped around the joy of Derin that I've hardly paid attention to much else. Like how he's been looking somewhat drawn and sad in recent weeks. I've been putting it down to work stress. Now I wonder and walk even faster to the bus stop, desperate to get home and, *please goddess*, find him safe. Every other red car makes my heart thud and every tall, bulky boy in a black T-shirt turns into Bayo. But first I must warn Wura. She *has to* hear me.

In the taxi to Mother's house, I reason that if I can talk to both of them, all the better. Wura might not listen but Mother never takes her daughter's safety lightly.

It's a shock when, with saddened eyes, the gateman says he's not allowed to let me in, ever. He's known me since I was knee-high. I ask if he'll give Wura a message from me and he says Wura herself would ask Mother to fire him for doing that. Desperate, I eye the walls. He shakes his head gently. I could possibly karate my way through him, but he's got a hand on his truncheon and might not hesitate to use it. My shoulders are shaking with trying not to scream or jump and knock him down. I open my hands in a silent plea, look in his eyes.

'She no dey home,' he finally says. 'She done go stay with her friend for two weeks. Das all I can say.' His face closes up.

'Please, which friend?'

'*Walahi*, make you dey go now!' He glances nervously towards the house. Mother must be home.

I turn around and leave, for now.

Light-headed with worry, I wear a rut in the living room rug, waiting for Mr D to return from work. If he's not back at the usual time, I don't know what I'll do. He's not rich and doesn't know any powerful government people. He's involved in my troubles only because he has the biggest and kindest heart in the world. When the door opens and he steps in all in one piece, I fly into his arms, nearly weeping with relief.

'Oof! Steady on,' he says. 'What's the matter?'

I explain how Bayo cornered me and threatened us all.

'I should have foreseen this,' he sighs. 'After enrolling you at the US Center, I gave the ISS registrar the address to forward your transcript and references. Principal Akiolu must have found those records, which is almost certainly how Bayo knew where to find you.'

'But what else is going on? Bayo said if I deny you, he'll leave Wura alone. I just knew I'd bring you trouble.'

'No, no. This predates you. Bayo was once implicated in the abuse of a young boy named Godwin, who begged to be withdrawn from the boarding house. He was later found dead on train tracks not far from where he lived. It was ruled an accident, though I believe he simply took his own life – something his parents deny because suicide carries such a terrible stigma in Nigeria.'

I'm dumbfounded. 'Why didn't you tell me this before?'

'It was all I could do to persuade you to live. You needed to heal and thrive, not be terrorized all over again. It haunts me that I couldn't save Godwin then nearly lost you too. The boy was just beginning to trust me when something – probably a threat from Bayo – made him clam up and flee. When I pushed for answers, Bayo's parents complained to Principal Akiolu that I was targeting their son for no reason. After Godwin died, his parents were devastated but uncooperative. I had to let it go.'

'So they're now cooperating? That's why Bayo is after us?'

'No. Another boy who was Godwin's friend has finally found the courage to step up with a similar story. He's been having nightmares and has apparently convinced himself he's being haunted by Godwin's spirit to tell the truth. His parents reached out to me a couple of months ago, which is why Akiolu is trying to shut me up by threatening my reputation. All of a sudden I'm suspect – an unmarried forty-two-year-old man with an "unhealthy" interest in the boys under his care. None of it is true or can be proved, but I've watched Akiolu increasingly turn into their submissive guard dog. Whatever Bayo's parents have on him must be big. I'd give a lot to know what it is and put an end to this terror.'

'They've been threatening you for *months*?' It hits me like the sky fell on my chest. Despite the danger that having me in his home has put him in, he's not said a word. Because he knew I had nowhere safe to go.

'Yes, and this time they're really going for the big guns. The boy that came forward helps build my case but it's not enough. I've also secretly rallied a few other teachers to my side but we have no hard evidence.'

'I'll leave.'

'To go where?'

'I don't know.'

'I will not let you put yourself in danger again just to satisfy those criminals. Like I said, I couldn't save Godwin but I won't lose you, too. Unless you really want to go home, you stay right here.'

A sudden, horrifying thought drops clean into my mind.

'When did Godwin leave school?'

'You joined as a third year, right? I think that would be in your first term?'

There's a sick, creeping feeling in my stomach.

'Describe Godwin?' I ask, dreading the answer.

Mr D does till, clear as a portrait, I see in my mind the exact picture of his delicate Delta features. The boy from the laundry room. I was so glad I saved him that day. But I only delayed whatever horror was waiting to befall him. I can only imagine how much worse Mr D feels.

I remember now how in my haze, while I lay there slowly dying, he'd seemed to join me under that pile of sheets. I remember hearing again that softly whispered, *Thank you . . . I must go*. How nobody could properly remember or find the boy who alerted Gamba from the dojo that I was in danger in the laundry room. Every hair on my body stands on end. His name was Godwin. And he is dead.

39

1993 (AGE 16)

The very next day I knock on the gate of Mother's house again.

Derin taught me chess, or at least he tried. I sometimes managed a decent game. I hear his bass voice as if he's beside me saying, *a swindle is a clever, unexpected move that creates confusion in order to rescue a hopeless position. Chess is like war, and swindling is a crucial skill for any serious player.*

This time, I will get inside.

The gateman cracks it open.

'*Sannu*, Wura! Welcome! You return early?' He gives me a huge smile. Everyone adores my sister.

'*Sannu*, Mr Tanko,' I reply in Hausa, his language. 'Yes, my friend got sick.' And just like that, I'm in.

At the door, I press the bell.

Emily opens it. My blue *boubou* trails the edge of my high-heeled shoes. My matching scarf is tied into an elaborate *igele*. My *tiiro* has turned my eyes dark-rimmed and secretive. My lips glisten pink.

'*Kaaro*, Emily.'

'Welcome back, Wu ...' The word never ends as her eyes widen. She's cared for us since we were babies. Her eyes drop to my chest, then slide sideways back up to my face. Her head gives a quick shake.

'*Ta ni yi?*' she asks in Yoruba. *Who is this?*

'It's me, Otolorin.' I'm creating confusion all right.

'Ah!' She clasps her hands to her chest. Then to her head. 'If your mother ... if madam ... Ah! Please, for your own sake ...'

'It's okay, Emily. Just let me in.' I didn't mean to reduce her to a babbling wreck. 'Has Wura called?'

'Yes, just this morning.'

I breathe properly for the first time in days.

'Oto …' Emily whispers, then stops, a scared look crossing her face.

'What?'

'Nothing. Just … *shora*. Wait in the sitting room. Madam won't be back for a while.'

What is it with everyone telling me to be watchful?

Emily heads outside to do some chore and I'm alone. Every corner, every little thing reminds me of Wura. I hear the echo of our voices everywhere, like a movie with ghost children in a haunted house. Worry and loneliness threaten to swallow me whole. It feels as if the very walls are just watching and waiting. I pace. Open and shut cabinets. Fight tears to see a videotape marked *Property of Wura and Oto Only!* in Wura's squiggly scrawl. God, we were so young!

I need more of her. Of us. I go up to my old room. It's starkly empty. Everything I owned is gone. Books, games, treasured gifts. Mother threw them out. I'm glad I took what mattered most with me to ISS. I even look under my bed. All that's left is a dusty marble that rolled there during some long-ago game of *Jenje*. It stings like acid on someone who has already been macheted. I make sure to add this raw pain to the long list of things Bayo and Elijah will pay for. One way or another. Whatever it takes.

Desperate for anything that will bring my sister back from being an absence and an echo, I tiptoe into her room. She'd hate me for being here, for doing this. Feeling like the worst sort of intruder, I open her closet. When I raise her clothes to my face, the sweet, hot-pepper scent of Amarige, her favourite perfume, drops me in an illusion of her embrace. I swallow again and again past the spike that seems lodged in my throat. Mother will return any moment. I can't afford tears. I can't afford weakness.

Mr Driver's typical gunned-pedal roar sounds on the driveway and I hurry downstairs.

Mother enters the living room, freezes, sways, then draws a hand across her face as if she's just walked into a tangle of cobwebs. My hand lights on the amulet on a string under my *boubou*. Years ago the brass shell was tied to my arm.

'What . . .' she gasps, one trembling finger pointed at me, 'are *you* doing here dressed like *that*? Have you lost your mind? What in heaven's name is that on your chest?'

'I'm quite sane, thank you. And these are breasts. I'm simply the girl I've always told you I am.'

'Woli Omolaja prophesied this!' Mother's nose flares as if something stinks, her whole body turns away from the sight of me. 'When he said that old witch would launch a new attack, I imagined horrors, but growing breasts? If you think this will break me, you're both mistaken. Now get out of my house! Return to that Ghanaian teacher of yours. Who knows what unholiness ties you together?'

'No. You have to listen.' No point getting angry. She'll never see anything but vileness where I'm concerned.

'Not to you. Get out before I—'

'Wura is away, right?'

Mother hisses. 'Why are you asking? So you can go and attack her next boyfriend? Is that your plan? *Ọmọ eshu!*'

'Look, I don't have time to explain but for your own safety, you need to keep Elijah and his cousin Bayo away from her.'

'Which cousin? Why? What have you done now, you abomination?' Mother shrieks.

'You've heard of confraternities?'

It's the one thing I know will get her attention. She goes very still. Eyes widening to round coins of fright. Everyone has heard the stories and seen the news headlines. The maimings and murders. Rape and assault. Blackmail of professors for grades. And many are children of the powerful, and therefore untouchable. The sort of vicious company a son who would make Father proud might keep. The first confraternity was founded in the fifties by Professor Wole Soyinka to be something like the American fraternities, and nurture Nigerian intellectuals regardless of background. They've since mutated, via the military government and as those in power grew more corrupt, into something more like the American mafia in movies I've seen. Spawning ever more violent new cults, operating like the deadly shadow underneath everyday life that one prays never to have the misfortune of tripping across.

'Elijah and his cousin belong to them. They're threatening to harm Wura if I say anything about their attack on me.'

'Attack? *Shio!* You mean your disgusting behaviour. See what you caused?! *Hein?*'

'I won't waste time discussing who caused what. We should be turning to Father for help, but he'll probably give them the guns to shoot us. Just, please keep Wura safe while I sort this out.'

'I don't believe you.'

'Please, Mother, I'm begging you. These are really angry and dangerous young men. Please go and get Wura and keep her safe. That's all I care about.'

She finally sees that I'm deadly serious. 'So you'll keep your mouth shut for your sister's sake?'

'I'll do whatever it takes to protect her.'

'*Mchew!*' she hisses, though her voice is not so steady. 'As if you didn't cause all this *wahala* in the first place. You think you're now some local hero, *abi?*'

'I don't just think it. I *know*. And by the way, don't punish the gateman for letting me in. He thought I was Wura. Anybody with eyes can see that we're sisters, whether you accept it or not. Goodbye.'

My high heels *click-clack* all the way to the door, as I hear her urgently telling Emily, who's been standing there practically blended to the wall all the while, to fetch Mr Driver.

I call and update Derin on the madness of the past couple of days. First he congratulates me on my results, which I've practically forgotten. Then, 'We need a plan,' he says, all business once he gets over first being shocked, then furious. 'We can't let those bastards win a second time.'

As we strategize, I'm grateful to have that brilliant brain on my side doing what it does best. It feels as if together, we can do anything, so long as there's trust. Just as he said so long ago, when I should have had the courage to follow my heart.

By the time we're done, I'm raring for battle. It's like that sweep of being armoured I experienced when Babalawo sent me forth with amulets. Only now I can add Derin's boldness and strategy. Bayo used Elijah like a Trojan Horse to destroy our lives. We'll also be coming at him from an angle he'll never have anticipated. Fighting fire with fire might burn down the town but when you're left with no choice, it just might smoke out the enemy.

40

1993 (AGE 16)

It takes me a few investigative visits to several places, lurking in the shadows with a cap pulled low over my head, but I eventually find out which is Elijah's favourite watering hole and when he tends to be there. Stallion Club is the latest trendy spot catering to the children of Ibadan's wealthiest. The entryway is meant to scream class and money, with a pair of rearing white horses lit from within, touching hooves high above. If the idea of unearned money had a sound and a smell, this would be it. The mix of heavy perfume and aftershave, the spice of expensive meats roasting, the pop of corks and bubbling over of golden liquid into clinking glasses, laughter deep and tinkling, labels representing designers who probably couldn't locate Ibadan on a world map. I keep in my mind's eye the image of that Delta boy, Godwin. I think of him flinging his small eleven-year-old body in front of a train. I think of Bayo and Elijah enjoying this opulent life while he's dead. It fills me with rage. And rage gives me strength. My proverb book says, *one should cultivate one's own madness as you might need it when the time comes to confront the madness of others*. Today is do or die. I plan to live.

I've been sitting cross-legged on the tall barstool for half an hour, trying not to look as twitchy and shattered on the outside as I feel inside. I don't know how well it's working because though I've attracted some sidelong glances, no one has approached me yet. Or maybe it's something else. I worry this won't work. Do I look right? Am I a bit off? Can anyone tell? The music is loud. Pounding. Some new band that has just sprung up. Another young hopeful climbing his way to stardom,

Nigerian-style. Onstage with him three dancers shake their butts in short, tight glittery skirts. The singer is sweating, springing all over the place like a leashed tiger. People are dancing, the girls on point to the last fingernail, like I've tried to be. I'm grateful for dim club lighting. At least people won't suddenly see double were my twin to walk in. Ever since I called and Emily told me Mother had already left for Ondo with Wura, the thing that had gripped my neck since seeing Bayo again has loosened a little.

Dry-throated, I signal one of the uniformed staff for a drink. The old guilt arises to remind me that at least Obatala spiked Eshu's drink in secret. Elijah did it before my very eyes and still I fell for that age-old trick. I'm sticking to Coke and taking no chances. I watch the server's hands as the bottle is opened right in front of me. He charges five times what it should cost. I'm still wincing at the price of admission. In another life, in a different body, would I be here spending Father's money just as carelessly? I take a sip, worrying about my make-up, even though the lady in the boutique told me it was designed to be sweat-proof. Thinking about buying make-up stops me from thinking how crazy this is. I move to rub my damp palms on my thighs then remember that silk shows stains. I didn't anticipate how unnerved I'd feel, out in public as a girl for the very first time. As if there's a spotlight on me, following me. I remind myself that I just have to play it cool. Look relaxed. Like I'm enjoying myself. Not a mouse twitching in a snake's domain.

It's not long before he strolls casually in, looking as handsome as ever. I hate him. I've never had this feeling twist my stomach so hard. I feel again the wet press of his lips against mine, the shock of his fist exploding into my jaw. He goes around greeting people as if they're his loyal subjects. They welcome their local celebrity like he's a mini god. His friends are everywhere. My knee is jittering and I press it hard against the barstool to make it stop.

Elijah pauses midstride. Our eyes meet. In his, startled recognition. I'm imploring Yeyemi under my breath. *Let the illusion hold. Let him see what I want him to see.* How Wura would hate me if she could see me right now. The body-hugging silk lavender dress was one of her favourites. I hunted the markets and stores till I found an almost exact copy, since I lacked the nerve to go to a tailor and have it made. My wig is the same centre-parted, tucked-behind-her-ears style she sometimes wore fresh from the hairdresser. I've copied her dark-eyed, precisely lined pink lips style of make-up.

He lopes towards me with that confident, predatory walk. Girls eat him up with their eyes. I pretend not to notice his approach.

'Wura? Wura Akinro! What are you doing here?'

'Oh, hi, Eli! What were the chances?' It's Wura's voice. The loving voice I've heard from the first time we could make sounds. I hope I'm not talking too much, or too fast. I remind myself that Wura does talk fast – and a lot. I stay seated. I'm barely two inches taller than Wura, but he's been close enough to us both that it might give me away. I make a big show of crossing my legs, so the slit in the side of my dress displays my high heels and more besides. It took hours of practice to be able to walk in them. I've even added, with a brown marker, the tiny moon-shaped scar Wura got on her right knee from falling off a swing when we were little.

'I'm surprised. This isn't your usual scene.'

'My cousin dragged me along. He's somewhere probably chatting up some poor girl. Anyway, how are you? It's so good to see you again,' I coo, hating myself.

'Really?' He looks pleased and suspicious at the same time.

'Of course.' I do my best sad face. 'Life has been miserable without you.'

'Wait. Your freak of a brother isn't here too, is he?' Elijah looks nervously around.

'Aww now, don't be like that. Anyway, who knows or cares where he is? That cheater.' I pout, curving my lips into a plump pink bow.

I lean forward, flick an imaginary speck of dust from his collar. Amarige, Wura's signature scent, wafts around us. 'I've missed you so much.' The dress has a low front. Wura used to wear a camisole. I'm wearing a push-up bra instead. His eyes wander down. If there are any doubts in his mind, that should settle them.

'All right then. How about a drink or dinner sometime?' he says softly, his eyes darting furtively around. I know he has a girlfriend. I've seen her on my scouting missions.

'Oh, I don't know . . .' I peek out from under my lashes.

'Come on, for old time's sake?'

'Okay. How about the Central Garden's Motel restaurant? I know how much you love *isi-ewu* pepper soup. Theirs is amazing!' As part of my plan, I'd gathered information on the best spots for that pepper soup. I'm now glad for how Wura used to obsess over every detail of him and talk about it non-stop.

'Ah, you know me so well. Anything for *isi-ewu* and your beautiful face. Saturday at eight and afterwards I'll show you how much I've missed you, hmm?' He winks.

'Bad boy! Is that all you'll show me? See you there.' I smooth my hair and smile. I've seen Wura tease him like this. I'm also wishing I hadn't bothered with dinner because my stomach really doesn't agree with what I'm doing. I tell it to shut up and bat my lashes. I didn't realize till now how many of my sister's characteristics are steeped in my very cells. I fight the terrible sensation of betraying Wura all over again. I'm not. I'm saving us all.

'Yes.' Eli's lips curl in that feral grin. Then he looks up and suddenly steps away from me. I follow his gaze. At the door stands a girl, arms crossed at her chest, glaring and looking every inch the pissed-off girlfriend. Eli mutters a hasty, 'See you soon', and takes off towards her.

Grateful for the easy out – I was going to pretend my cousin wanted to leave early – I totter towards the door. Outside I slump against the wall for a moment, stunned how readily I was Wura but also very much me.

Derin's breath whooshes out with relief when I call to say I'm safely home. He's not eaten or slept, his stomach was so knotted with worry – which pleases me and takes away some of the horror of the night, the bad taste at the back of my mouth. We're still here, our voices pulsing warm to each other, even if this is only the shallow end of a deep plunge and we can't see see what lies at the bottom.

41

Eight p.m. on Saturday night my nerves are fried. I've never been so terrified. I touch the amulet on my necklace and in my mind's eye arises an image of Yemoja that I found in one of Mr D's art books. In one hand she held a peacock feather fan. In the other a glintingly sharp machete. She looked fierce and beautiful and powerful, like she could flirt with you or kill you and it was all the same to her depending on her mood and what you deserved.

Elijah shows up, all confidence, and the bartender points to where I'm sitting at a table in a shadowed corner. How could he think my sister would want him after he dumped her? Yet, the last memory of him from that terrible New Year's Eve was Wura apologizing for my existence. It's probably what he remembers, too.

I rise as he strolls towards me. My tight black jeans and top are designed to make a guy's thoughts whirl hopelessly in one direction. It's working. Elijah's eyes seem to struggle with climbing any higher. Good. The less of my face he focuses on, the better. Under my wig, my head itches but I can't scratch. It's a bad time to remember how, when I auditioned for a role in the ISS school play, they said I couldn't act to save my life. Except I now know Wura's every twitch is embedded in my body's memory.

'No need to sit. I already ordered us room service.' I smile as he strokes my upper arms in greeting. I use the excuse of grabbing my bag from the table to arch away. I sling the strap across my body.

'Why? Cancel it. We'll just go to my place afterwards,' he says.

Damn! Damn!

'But it's already paid for. I want tonight to be special! It's what I was planning for Valentine's Day before we broke up. They'll bring up our drinks. I already ordered your favourite!' I trail a finger down his partly open polo shirt.

His breath quickens. There's naked longing in his eyes. And something deeper that I don't have time to analyze just then.

'There's been no one else. I'm so sorry for what happened. Oto doesn't even live with us any more. Mother kicked him out and it serves him right.' Every word is bitter in my mouth.

He takes my hand. 'Okay, babe.'

He locks the door. He's kind of smiling. It looks more like a grimace in the dim lighting. His hand is tight on my upper arm and he's dragging me straight towards the bed.

'But what about our drinks? They'll be here any minute!'

'You want me so bad, we do it my way.'

'But won't you let me welcome you properly first?' I dig in my heels, trying to regroup. Slow us down. Worrying my wig will fall off despite tons of pins.

'Look, Wura, just drop the pretence. I don't know what game you're playing but I'm not stupid. You're up to something, and I will find out. I've had enough screwed-up shit in my life!'

I didn't bargain for this. He's bigger than me and relentless and each step sinks the heels of my buckled-on shoes into the plush carpet, making me clumsy. I can't kick them off. It's the worst part of a plan that looks dicier by the minute.

I wrench away but his arm locks around my waist, hauling my back flush into his body.

'I really liked you, for real.' He sounds broken.

Shock and surprise make me freeze.

'God, I'm so sick of this crap!' His voice is breathy, almost tearful. Then his hand roughly clasps my breast and a growing hardness pokes into my lower back.

Hell no! Suddenly I can think again and, praying it's not the last thing I ever do, make myself go slack while bending my knees so I'm sliding down, then in one swift move I break his hold, swing back my cocked elbow and catch him such a blow in the goolies they'll have to be excavated back out. He's dry-retching on the carpet and I'm sitting on his back holding his arm at an angle that leaves him clenching his teeth between heaves.

Swiftly, I reach one-handed into the handbag slung across my body and bring out a few items. When he sees and draws breath to shout for help, I stuff his mouth with a scarf. After all, I learned that terrific move from his cousin. Except I make sure he can still breathe.

I shift to kneel on the arm behind his back, which makes him yelp in pain but frees my hands. I quickly tie up his wrist, then slip a knot around his opposite ankle and pull it in. I do the same on his other side. I rise, leaving him lying on his side, hobbled. I thank Derin in my head for insisting I practise tying secure knots. He typically left nothing to chance, and was dead set against me doing this alone. But how else would Elijah buy into my act? And Mr D would have flat out barricaded the door had he known what I planned to do.

I let him struggle crazily for a while, mumbling through the scarf, till he understands the rope is secure and I'm in charge now. Then his jaw clenches and he stares fixedly at the wall.

On the table is a candle, giving the room a jarring romantic glow. Over its steady flame I start heating the tip of a knife. The curved, slender kind used for scaling fish. Elijah's eyes meet mine, incredulous at first. Then terrified. He dated Wura long enough to know she went for the kill when she got truly mad. It flares suddenly within me like I've caught on fire from that candle, the rage she'd feel if she only knew the truth about this lying lowlife at my feet. Anger I should have felt long ago had I not been raised voiceless. Elijah flinches from the madness in my eyes. I take a calming breath, then lean forward so he feels the heat of the blade near his face.

'Fun fact!' I say. 'Did you know a hot blade cauterizes as it cuts? You and your cousin chose a really nasty line of business to be in. Rape is not cool. It is pure evil. I think it is time to take away your equipment. Know what I'm saying? You won't bleed much. I might even throw in a few tribal marks, knowing how much you admire your own face.' It's as if someone else is inhabiting me, saying those words. Someone perfectly capable of slicing him into bloody ribbons.

'Grrnnn. Ompph . . .' he says, wrenching in wild jerks.

'I guess that means you're not happy about my plan.'

His head shakes vigorously.

'I'm going to remove the scarf so you can answer my questions. You scream, I cut your face.'

I slide the soggy scarf from his mouth and he coughs.

'First, what is Bayo planning, and second, what does he have on Principal Akiolu?'

Elijah shrugs and stays silent. I want to squash him like he's nothing. *Patience*, I tell myself.

'Okay. Answer me something. If Bayo was in your place right now, would he rather die than rat on you? You both messed up my innocent brother's life to where he attempted suicide. I nearly lost him. *Do you understand?* Yet that wasn't enough for you.'

'I never wanted any of this,' Elijah mumbles. 'Once I heard Bayo was in trouble again, I just knew it would somehow find me.'

'Oh, so you only pull the occasional rape job on his behalf?' I'm about ready to use the hot knife.

'I didn't rape anyone! I never intended to. It was only to get back at your brother for causing Bayo trouble!'

'And that's worth all the heartbreak and grief you caused?'

'Well, if you two hadn't been so damn gullible . . .' he mutters.

Not that again. My knuckles sting, I've punched his face so hard. He doesn't get to insult us. Not on top of everything else. Plus, I owed him one.

'Fine! No more rape after I cut it off!'

'No!' Elijah jerkily strains his bound hands, desperate to cover his front.

'I'll count to three. One ...'

'You wouldn't dare!' Tears seep down his face. His clenched teeth are chattering.

'Guess what? Fun fact two. My brother's stomach had to be pumped out to save his life.' I'm undoing his belt, face hard, teeth bared. I realize then that I am not acting. No innocent young boy will ever fall prey to Bayo or Elijah again if I can help it.

'No! No. What do you want? Anything. I'll do it!'

'I already asked. What is Bayo up to? What does he have on Akiolu?'

'I don't know! His father is trying to get him into some bogus London college where they don't look at things too closely. St Wexford or something.'

'Why did you do such a terrible thing on his behalf? And don't tell me it's just because you're cousins!'

Elijah hangs his head. 'No, it's not. I didn't want to do it. I didn't even plan on how much I'd like you,' he sighs. 'It's just ... he used to do things to me ... back when we were younger.'

For a moment I can't quite grasp what he's saying. Then I'm staring open-mouthed.

'Bayo was always much bigger than me. He said he'd tell my parents if I didn't keep my mouth shut. He hounds young, good-looking boys, especially if they seem soft. Like Oto. I don't enjoy harming people. Not like him.'

It comes out in a gasping sob. Like a dam bursting in him to finally say this out loud even to Wura.

'As soon as I could, I lifted weights and bulked up my body so he'd stop pestering me. But he's made me do too many things my parents would kill me for. And if he ever knows I told you this, my life is over! He's a high member of the SeaHawks confraternity. His father was one of them. That family is not quite right in the head. You've no idea what he's capable of!'

It's there now in the droop of his shoulders, the shame and

self-loathing no longer hidden behind a handsome face and confident swagger. Elijah was a tortured kid. How can Bayo have been so twisted from childhood?

'You must know something about the principal!' I hiss, steeling my heart. This is no time to go soft.

He's marble-still, eyes on my hand, hovering dangerously above his open fly, thin boxers the only protection between his precious manhood and my scaling knife.

'Look, Chief Keji is not somebody to mess with. Especially when it comes to his only son. He slapped a nun at Bayo's previous school when she told him they couldn't deal any more with Bayo's behaviour, then made a big donation to their charity to keep it quiet.'

'Consider me warned. Now talk!' And I thought I couldn't get any angrier. For sure it took a certain type of man to batter an old nun at St Christopher's. A man who raised sons like Bayo.

'Principal Akiolu never graduated from university. His certificate is fake. Chief Keji found out somehow and used it to make him accept Bayo at ISS. He's been making the man grant favours to his rich and famous friends ever since, but it's not always easy to get past the teachers.'

'Oto told me about a boy that killed himself, Godwin. What did Bayo do to him?'

'Guess?' Elijah bitterly says. 'He just wouldn't leave that child alone. Really messed him up. He was such a nervous little thing.'

'And the principal knows this?'

'I guess. Godwin's parents were neither rich nor powerful. He won a scholarship to ISS from some bush primary school in the Delta swamps. Bayo threatened he could get Akiolu to revoke the boy's scholarship if he said anything.' Elijah gives a mirthless chuckle. 'Bayo used to enjoy telling me all about his latest victims. Remember Udo, from New Year's Eve? He was one. I was gladly out of Bayo's game till your brother came along. Then Bayo roped me back in.'

It's hard to keep hiding my shock. I hope both tape recorders I set up earlier are working.

'I'm going to let you go for now. One word – especially to Bayo – about what happened here and I'll broadcast exactly where I got my information. And I'm not working alone.'

'Look, just leave me out of whatever you're planning to do and I swear I'll keep my mouth shut. Trust me, I want him gone worse than anyone. He's the only reason I joined the EagleLions confraternity – for protection.'

I blindfold him with a piece of cloth and order him not to move or make a sound. Silently, I grab the tape recorders from underneath the bed and leave.

Downstairs, I tell the receptionist my boyfriend is sleeping but could someone go up and wake him in a couple of hours. He'll have a job explaining why he's lying on the floor, trussed up like an *ileya* goat.

Outside, I lean against the closed door for a moment, my heart pumping hard, my legs shaking in my high heels. It is only the first part, but I feel that somewhere, Godwin might be smiling.

Back home, I ask Mr D to please not get mad at me, then give him the information he's so crucially needed. He's speechless for a long moment, shaking his head as emotions chase across his face – shock, horror, fear, anger, back to horror.

'I'm torn between hugging you and shaking you. I never would have advocated such a feat,' he finally says.

'I know. It's why I didn't tell you.'

'Yet you just might have saved me and countless others!' He springs up from his chair. 'There's so much we can now set to rights! See how brave and special you are?' My ears tingle at his praise.

We decide he'll keep a distant eye on Bayo in school and quietly update the parents of both boys Bayo assaulted. They'll then pretend to halt all enquiries into Bayo's crimes, while Mr D uses trusted contacts to dig up information from the university Principal Akiolu supposedly graduated from. It will take precious time, and I'm having to trust that Elijah, for his own safety if not mine, will keep quiet as promised. *A viper's head*, says my proverb book, *though separated from its body, remains venomous.*

I stay home to keep my head down. Derin spends a big chunk of his pocket money on a phone card that gives us ages to talk. Being Derin, he's done some research with his mom's help and tracked down an article from the letters section of a magazine, written by a person like me! It says the word pseudo-hermaphrodite is not only inaccurate but should be replaced with something better, intersex, which is described as *'a person existing between the sexes, having unique variations in reproductive or sex anatomy'.*

'Intersex.' I whisper, my cheeks heating up to say aloud a word with sex in it. It sounds good, though. Solid. A right feeling word that lets things be what they are – fluid and unchained to expectations. I am Lori but I can also keep some of Oto. I can be the whole of me, Otolorin. I need not cut off one part at the expense of the other. It feels wild. I can practically hear Derin's smile over the phone. 'Yep!' He says, 'There is even a whole intersex society!'

Joy fills my heart. People like me! I *cannot* wait to meet them! Derin and I speculate and make plans. I drowse on the living room sofa, the handset cradled at an awkward angle to my ear, grateful for the sound of his voice telling me his latest, marvellous story.

42

1993 (AGE 16)

Needing some air, I venture out to check in with Mrs Ladipo. There's no news yet.

As I walk the last stretch towards home, cars whizz past me. I'm so lost in worry about what might happen next, it's a while before I notice one, a Jeep, slowing to a crawl, keeping pace with me. Others honk behind it. The windows are tinted dark so I can't see who is inside. I walk faster, cursing my carelessness. People have been kidnapped in broad daylight, with no one batting an eye. The Jeep pulls ahead then swerves to park on the shoulder.

Bayo! is all I can think. *He's come for me!* I skid to a stop, desperately seeking a chance to cross over, but the trail of zooming cars leaves no safe opening. I turn to run but see a couple of young men loitering with intent mere footsteps away. What if they're part of his confrat? Behind me is a high wall topped with barbed wire.

A back door slides ajar, and leaning out is the last person I expect to see. She lifts her sunglasses and regards me with the dark-eyed sharpness of the hunting bird Mother once accused her of being. My legs feel rooted, yet when she beckons with an impatient hand, I find myself walking towards Maami Akinro.

'Get in.'

I don't move. Has Father sent her?

'Stop malingering. We have things to discuss.'

Does she have news? Is Wura okay?

I enter, shutting the door, but leaving my hand on the handle.

Useless, because the driver presses a button and with a sliding series of clicks I'm locked in.

The Jeep merges back into traffic.

Maami is watching me steadily. It occurs to me that there's some sort of test going on. 'Eye-talking' is like a whole other Yoruba language and every well-raised child knows it's extremely rude for a young person to look an elder in the eye beyond the space of a blink. I focus on the seat ahead as if it holds mysterious secrets to hidden treasure. What fresh hell is life about to unleash?

Maami starts peeling an orange as precisely as though performing brain surgery, her sharp knife coiling each strand of peel off the white at exactly the same length and diameter as the last. I watch, mesmerized, from the corner of my eye. It's a bold thing to do on these Ibadan roads. Some potholes are big enough to bury a grown man in.

'So your mother thinks I'm a witch, eh?'

Startled, I begin choosing my words with care, then give up. 'Yes. And she believes I'm in league with you. A delusion I've found somewhat useful.' I chance a sidelong glance at her, surprised by my own daring.

Her knife swerves. She lets out a choked sound that could be a cough. Or laughter.

'Did Father send you?'

'I heard you've been involved in some trouble with very bad people.'

'Who told you?' How does she know? What has she heard? Does that mean Father knows? Surely Mother didn't tell him. Wura wouldn't be so vengeful ... would she? My head begins to pound. Maami is acting like the tree in a thunderstorm. I've no idea which way she's blowing or what she aims to crush.

'That was why you left that boarding school you so desperately wanted to go to?'

'How do you know all this?'

'Just answer my question.'

'What do you want, Maami?' I want out of this car already. It has the horrible feel of Father's presence, his power. A trap.

She holds out half the orange. For a long heartbeat I hesitate. Then I take it and eat. She bites into her half, looking as if some unasked question just got answered. If I've just become a witch, I definitely look forward to the flying part.

'Laitan is my son. He is also one of the most ruthless men I know. It's past time for me to tell you about your father.'

I'm convinced I'm either dreaming or I've fallen into some alternate world. While a part of me questions why she'd do this, another sits up at the prospect of knowing something, anything, about the man who chose to unsee me from the day I was born.

'When I married your grandfather, I'd hoped for twins, but had only Laitan. No other children came but your grandfather stayed with me. We were very poor, but he was a good man, with a plan to start a cocoa farm and make our lives better. He borrowed a large sum of money from a man named Aluko, bought seedlings and leased some land. Then he developed elephantiasis. It was a merciless disease that caused his limbs and private parts to swell grotesquely.'

'That's terrible.'

'Laitan had to leave school to work for Aluko and repay the loan. It's called *iwofa*, an ancient system by which a person is indentured to pay off a debt. It is illegal, but it still goes on in one form or another. Aluko was rich and powerful, and left us no choice. It was all I could do to care for your grandfather full-time and keep a roof over our heads. One by one friends and relatives vanished; it was such a shameful and ugly disease. My husband drank away his sorrows and my son became deeply embittered.

'A condition of *iwofa* was that Laitan lived in Aluko's house, at his beck and call. His children tormented Laitan. *Son of dragging balls,* they taunted him, *when will yours become like melons, too? We know you're poor,* they said, *so we'll buy you a sack to carry them in.* He was always angry and fighting. They tortured him till the good inside him died. My mistake was that I didn't realize how bad things were till it was almost too late.

'Your grandfather died. Laitan paid off the loan. He began

collecting, cleaning and reselling plastic jars and bottles. I helped him, and also cooked and sold food by the roadside. He soon had other people working for him and eventually leased some machinery to start manufacturing plastic bags. He scraped and scratched and single-mindedly dragged us out of poverty. He's been obsessed with wealth and power and perfection since.'

I try to re-imagine the heartless man I know as an embittered young boy and fail. He's always loomed so large. I can't fathom how Father's suffering could possibly justify him turning around to wound others – especially his own children.

'Perhaps I'm betraying him, telling you this, but it's time you knew. Laitan worships physical perfection, which is why he succumbed to Moji's wiles. It is unoriginal, as her mother-in-law, for me to say this, but she was utterly wrong for him. Given a bit more time, I'd have helped him realize it. Anyway, you were born, and to him you were a snub. Your imperfection brought back the ghost of humiliation that could drag him back down to that place he'd struggled so hard to escape. I had to tread softly for all our sakes.'

It's painful to hear her confirm how my existence really picks at the scabs of some festering, locked-down wound inside Father.

'When Laitan sent word that Moji had given birth to twins, I was elated. You see, in the olden days children died all the time for no obvious reason, so they made *ere ibeji* statues for twins. If a mother could mourn and appease the departed soul, then maybe the one left behind would agree to stay. I was one of those left behind.'

'You had a twin?'

'Yes. My Kehinde lived for eight years. Her *ere ibeji* was passed on to me after my mother died. You never stop feeling the loss of a twin.'

I can't imagine what I'd have done if Wura was taken from me so soon. If she's *ever* taken from me. Maami's sharp eyes miss nothing.

'But instead of inviting me to stay with her and care for my first grandchildren as tradition demands, Moji asked me to stay away, insisting her mother would take care of her. I respected her wishes, though I perceived the manipulative hand of Mama Ondo. When I eventually went to Ibadan for your naming ceremony, I took my *ere ibeji* to honour my lost sister, hoping now our family was once more blessed with twins, Moji and I might find some common ground.'

I can't help my widening eyes. I've heard a different version of this story before.

'Laitan revealed that you were born with a difference. I watched your parents turn away and knew if I paid you any attention, it would only backfire. Moji's fear and hatred of me had only worsened for reasons you already know. I kept up the pretence of visiting Ibadan to buy gold so I could see you but as you know, she ended that, too.'

'But why didn't you do something? My life could have been so much better if you'd stood by me!' I'm left with the bitter taste of *if only*.

'Ah, but it is the baby on its mother's back that doesn't know the journey is long. I have been watching out for you as best as I can. Maybe if I'd handled Moji differently, things would be better but that woman afflicts my last nerve.' Maami sighs.

I barely stop myself nodding in agreement.

'Your father forbade me to interfere. Convinced Moji trapped him into marriage, he couldn't be reasoned with. It was you or him and I chose him, fearing for his mind and what he might do to you if he thought you had turned me against him. Perhaps it was wrong, but he is only this way because I failed him, and that is my cross to bear. I might be the only conscience that he has left.'

I can barely take this all in. Maami abandoned me to save me and keep her son's love and protect his sanity. No doubt all families have participants in the craziness Olympics, but mine just won the gold medal.

'That alone might not have kept me from you,' Maami continues. 'But when I consulted the *Ifa* oracle, I was told the path your *ori* predestined must be allowed to unfold so you can acquire what you need to fulfill your destiny. I accepted Laitan's terms on the condition that you were taken to Babalawo at least twice a year, hoping that would keep Moji's cruelty in check.'

'That was *your* doing?' No wonder Babalawo would never answer many of my questions. Maami had sworn him to silence!

Maami calmly nods. I'm anything but calm. It all makes so much crazy sense now. I don't know whether to laugh or cry. 'Now I know why he once suggested I should come and live at the shrine. How terrible would it have been for you to have me stay with you even just for the holidays?'

'I'm not going to pretend I've been a good grandmother or that if the choice ever came down again to you or your father, I'd not still hesitate. I'm only hoping you'll understand I've had to make hard choices; that all families are imperfect, and we could spend generations finding fault. As our elders say, the sieve never sifts corn by itself.'

'So I should just forgive and forget?' My temples throb so hard it's like this overload of information will leak my brain out of my ears. My hands are clasped to my head and I'm not even aware I've moved.

'That is your choice, Oto. I'm offering an apology and making no excuses. I'm also too old for regrets. Tell me, have you never felt or done something that made you ashamed to look at your own face in the mirror?'

I think about Elijah and stay silent.

'Exactly. You see, we all come into this world with our *ori* partly pre-determined. What we make of the rest is up to us. We can choose to do right or wrong. Your mother, in her ignorance, chose to torture you. I, to keep my son, left you at her mercy. Laitan, desperate to hide his shame, rejected you. You, in your confusion, coveted what belonged to your sister.'

'How on *earth* did you know that?' For one sharp, jolting moment, I'm certain as Mother that she has supernatural powers.

A mischievous light enters her eyes. 'I do have my spies . . .'

It's suddenly obvious. 'Emily!'

'Yes. I send money to her family, and she's kept an eye on you in return. That was how I knew to persuade your father to let you go to boarding school so you could escape those rats that call themselves Wolis. Your mother would, of course, lose her mind if she knew.' The almost-smile that tips Maami's lips can only be described as sly. 'It's unfair, but I knew no other way. Emily still calls when she can, from the home of a friend of mine. Usually on her way to the pepper grinder.'

Inside Maami's Jeep my whole world rises, shakes itself hard then flips upside down to settle into new, unfamiliar lines. In the cascade of information I don't know what to seize on first. The reasons for Father's twistedness? Maami and Babalawo? Emily the master spy? I think back on how she's always been kind but distant. The innumerable times her discreet warnings kept me out of trouble with Mother.

'It took a while for Emily to contact me about the threats from confraternity boys, as I was away travelling. I only heard yesterday and realized your situation had become grievous, and it was past time to help you understand the forces you've been fighting even before you existed. So much is set in stone before we utter our first cry that we must become like water in order to reshape the future. That, as you can tell from my own failings, is not easy to do.'

'So it wasn't grievous enough when Mother left me for dead in the hospital?'

'She did *what?*' Maami looks shocked. I realize even Emily didn't know why I went to Mr D's. She just assumed I chose not to return home and was safer living with my art teacher. Mother told no one.

I realize there's no point heaping on to Maami's guilt. Better to figure out how she can be helpful to me right now. She can't demand Father protect us. Plus, his twisted mind might see a convenient opportunity to rid himself of me for good.

'Never mind. Okay, so can you offer any practical help?' I can't hide the anger that hardens my voice. She could have stood up to my parents for me, and she didn't. Because Laitan must always come first. 'I've applied to go to university in America. I'm hoping I get a full scholarship. If I don't, I'll need money. Can you help with that?'

To see Maami's shamefaced expression feels like suddenly seeing her naked. I look away. The terror and bane of Mother's life suddenly looks like exactly what she is – a tired old woman who has had a hard life and made some questionable choices. And haven't we all?

She has no money, she quietly admits. Father never wanted her to work another day in her life after he became rich. But he also never lets her forget she owes it all to him. He owns her house and car. With her, Father has the added advantage of control via guilt.

I've one more test for her, just as she tested me with half an orange.

'Maami, I know I'm a girl. I have seen a urologist who confirmed this. I want to live as a girl. Can you accept that?'

'Ah, yes, you people and your *oyinbo* medicine! It was one of the things Babalawo already counselled. In these modern times we have lost so much understanding of our own true *ijinle* ways. You see, when the *Odu-Ifa* falls, there is always a story that comes with it. Babalawo received and translated your story with a pure and open heart. They do not meddle with the message of the gods, and neither will I. You are what your *ori* says you are with my full blessing, but remember people will persecute what they do not understand.'

No shit, Sherlock, I think. But my heart begins to open to her. I press for more information and Maami explains how Babalawos have always been our doctors, therapists, peacemakers, soothsayers and philosophers in Yorubaland. How they've seen and heard it all, and for centuries, too, which is why they are called the Fathers of Mysteries. How the *Odu-Ifa*, which is like a mathematical mystical system of divination that tells an *odu*, a story, guides them in their divine duty of helping all who come their way, whatever situation they face.

When we're at the turnoff to Mr Dickson's house. Maami tells her driver to stop. 'Your parents have worn me to my bones with the way they treat you. Here's my number in Ijebu. Call me if you have questions. Forgive me, all I can do is answer them,' she says, pressing a few naira notes into my hands before dropping me off, my head whirling with the insanity of the last few days. Not least of it, that Maami manages her son as much as she mothers him. Like a ringmaster and an unpredictable predator.

43

1993 (AGE 16)

Days later I pop out to get the *Daily Herald* and nearly drop it when I see the headline.

CONFRATERNITY MURDER

The University of Ibadan recently witnessed an unprecedented clash between suspected members of two secret cultist groups, the EagleLions confraternity and Sea-Hawks confraternity. The only fatality has been identified as Bayo Keji, son of the prominent Chief Keji. He was identified wearing a black T-shirt bearing the skull and crossed guns insignia of the SeaHawks. Police suspect he was stabbed by none other than his own cousin, Elijah Jegede, a member of the EagleLions. Although he denies the murder charge, investigations are still continuing. Meanwhile, Chief Keji is rumoured to be in intensive care, having suffered sudden cardiac arrest upon receiving news of his only son's death. Anyone with information is urged to contact the police.

I race home to Mr D.

'Yes, I saw the news! And this part is not public yet, but after I made my disclosures to the vice principal and the International School Board, they contacted the university abroad where Akiolu was supposed to have graduated from and found no record of him. That big, shiny certificate hanging in his office is fake, never mind summa cum laude! Once confronted, he sang like the proverbial canary! He's on a sudden leave of absence pending investigation by the school board. Once everything comes out he should be facing some quality jail time!'

'Wow! So Bayo must have heard, realized that Elijah ratted him out and decided to do justice the confraternity way. Except Elijah was ready to snap. I don't doubt he killed him.' The Eli I'd cornered in that hotel room was a desperate guy.

I can't be sad Bayo is dead. If I have an ounce of sympathy for either of them, it's for Elijah, who is now in police custody. The grim history of those two is like that of two snakes that strangle each other. One because it's simply his nature, the other out of pain.

'Godwin's parents are finally ready to talk. Turns out he kept a diary which they hid out of shame and intimidation. He wrote nightly in it, talking to God, describing a bullying and abuse so systematic and terrible that if Bayo wasn't already dead, someone else might have gone for him. Akiolu has a lot to answer for.

'I've asked the vice principal to FedEx your transcript and references to the US Center. Your application will proceed as it should, and your ISS records will now reflect what a sterling student you were.'

'God! Is this nightmare truly over?'

'Yes, Lori. And your courage made it happen.'

'You taught me how to be brave.'

'A pleasure, daughter of my heart. In so many wonderful ways you were reborn in my presence.'

His words fill me with the sense of peace and belonging I've craved all my life.

I wait and wait, hoping once Wura hears the news about Eli's arrest for Bayo's murder, even though the details of Godwin's story are not out yet, she'll realize he wasn't a good person and forgive me at last. I'll never stop longing for the familiarity of my sister's presence, her headlong joy for life, my smile reflected on her face. I stand at my bedroom window, close my eyes, imagining it is New Year Day. I see the cooking women, hear the clanging of pots and pans filling the air. Smell the ghost of woodsmoke, see Wura wander into my room, impossibly pretty even with a sleep-lined face. But my eyes snap open. Because even in my sad, lonely daydream, her rage glows white-hot. It's not only about what Elijah did. She just can't forgive that I wanted her boyfriend.

Mrs Ladipo tells me three letters have arrived for me. I rush there as fast as I can. I've been accepted by all three universities but with partial tuition scholarships. It's one of the most contrary moments of my life. I'm honoured to get three acceptances but I've hoped and prayed for just one full scholarship.

Since I couldn't provide my parents' financial records, Mrs Ladipo explains, we were unable to prove a need. In order for me to accept the offers, and to ultimately get a student visa, Father and Mother must sign my acceptance form, consenting to pay for my living expenses for the duration of my studies. Not to mention that I'll need my passport renewed. It comes around again, exhaustingly, to my parents. Seeing my crestfallen face, Mrs Ladipo says I can always try again next year.

Mr D congratulates me. He says as far as he's concerned, giving me this hope kept me among the living, and that alone was worth it. That this is a huge achievement. And he trusts that where there's a will, I'll find a way.

I dread calling Derin. Our weekly chats have been full of plans for all the places he can't wait to show me, like Central Park, and Times Square, which he says will blow my mind. I've longed most of all for the day I'll look into those cat eyes again. I can't bear to think this is it. But I've learned my lesson, so I call him and share the joy of being accepted and sob out my pain at being stalled. He's heartbroken but calm and consoling. We discuss and discard possible solutions. He tells me far or near, he knows exactly where his heart is.

44

1993 (AGE 16)

The phone shrills, knocking me out of sleep. *Wura!* I know it as surely as I'm breathing. My heart wants to trip out of my chest, she's so agitated. It's as if our channel of communication suddenly blew wide open. My bedside clock glows 1 a.m. I rush to Mr D's living room to snatch up the receiver.

'Oto, I have to leave this place now!' she whispers.

'What's wrong? Why are you whispering?'

'Because Mommy mustn't hear me! I'll catch a bus back to Ibadan first thing in the morning. Can you come and meet me, please?'

'Of course! I'll be waiting at Alakia motor park.' It's where Mr Driver always went to get Mama Ondo after picking us up from school.

There's no question of sleeping. Whatever has sent Wura fleeing all the way from Mother's side in Ondo has to be terrible but I'm grateful she's running to *me*.

Wura emerges from the bus carrying a small travel bag, looking wrung out. It is depthless and wide as the universe, the love that wells in me to see my sister, my twin, once again. I drink her in with my eyes. In the taxi, Wura insists we head straight home. That Emily needs to be there for what she has to say. Then she leans back and closes her eyes. I swallow my increasing alarm and curiosity and just breathe her in.

When we arrive, she waves me right past the gateman and a startled Emily and we go up to her room.

'Do you want some water? Are things okay? Are you sick?' Her distress is like a living thing. I'm fluttering around her like a moth around fire, unsure what this is, desperate to comfort. Uncertain if it's welcome.

'No. Yes! Oto, stop fussing. I'm fine.' She stares at me for a long time, then, wonder of wonders, cups my face in her hands, touches my chin, my forehead, staring all the while as if I might disappear.

A smile trembles its way to my lips. My Wura is back! By some miracle I'm yet to discover, I have my sister back.

'This is so hard to say.' Wura is shaking. I pull her to sit on her bed and hug her close, wipe her tears with the sleeve of my shirt. Stunned all over again that she's right here and I can touch her.

'Why did you run away? What happened?'

'I c–can't believe ...' Wura stutters silent, her eyes fill with tears.

'What?' I'm on the balls of my feet, ready to run for help, to do whatever, because she's terrifying me.

'She wanted to kill you. She actually attempted to kill you when you were a baby,' Wura says.

'Mother? I'm more surprised she *didn't*. I tried to tell you. Remember that day on the playground you muddied Bayo's shorts? I was heartbroken because I'd heard her tell Aunty Abiye that I was a changeling out flying with Maami at night! She called me a thing put in her womb to replace her real son!'

'*What?!* And you're just now telling me?'

'It just never seemed to be the right time after that. I didn't know if you could deal with it, or even wanted to hear it.'

'I'm sorry, I let you down so much!' She clasps her hands to her face, sobbing softly. 'But I wasn't talking about Mommy. It was Mama Ondo!'

'*What?*'

'And it wasn't her first time, either. Those two babies she had before Mommy? She killed them both!'

My head shakes from side to side. Surely I'm not hearing right.

'They were born like you, Oto, and she secretly stuck needles into that soft place in their heads. Thankfully, Mommy was born fully a girl.'

'How do you know this?' Has Wura gone crazy? Mama Ondo never hid her dislike of me but *killing babies*? It's too horrible to be true! And yet . . .

'Oh, sweet goddess! The urologist! She said if what I had was this syndrome that causes partial insensitivity to androgens, it is an x-linked disorder, meaning it's inherited from the mother's side of the family. That's why she wanted my family's medical history.' Thrilled to finally have information, I've read the articles she gave me so thoroughly I could recite them backwards.

'What on earth are you talking about?' Now Wura looks at me like I'm crazy.

'Oh Wura, I have so much to tell you, but please carry on.'

'I overheard her confessing to Mommy because she's dying. She's been doing that for days, rambling and begging forgiveness from people who aren't there.'

'How come I survived?' From what I've heard, Mama Ondo was around a lot when we were babies.

'Maami Akinro apparently protected you. I've no idea how, because Mama Ondo kept babbling all sorts of crazy talk about Maami. Something about one night when Maami Akinro was visiting, and she had a terrible dream about a creature with sharp teeth that led her to the side of a river and told her to leave you alone.'

'Seriously? Maami didn't tell me this part!' She's no more a witch than I am. She just, like me, uses her imagination in situations where she has little power or control. At least that's what I plan to believe.

'You've spoken to *her*?'

I tell Wura about my encounter with Maami. Narrate our Father's life story.

'Holy bananas! This is one crazy family!' Wura is up pacing, shaking her head. 'This means that somehow, Maami and I were protecting you. See, Mama Ondo confessed she once tried to "accidentally" drown you in bathwater but I screamed as if *I* was being murdered, which brought Emily running in.'

Wura goes to the door.

'Emily!' she calls.

'You don't have to fear Mommy any more,' Wura says, when Emily arrives. 'We know you've been secretly working with Maami Akinro, and I for one am grateful. Now tell us everything.'

Emily looks wary, like someone who knows the game is up but won't be first to confess. She sighs. 'Maami hired me to watch out for you as best as I could but it wasn't enough. It wasn't till Babalawo told madam that if one twin dies, the other will follow that Mama Ondo stopped trying to kill you. Maami Akinro did her best to put all sorts of fear into both of them.'

Wura looks shocked.

'It's true,' I add. 'I overheard Mother saying she saw Maami Akinro sleeping like a witch with her legs up against a wall!' There's so much to tell Wura about all the awful things Mother said that terrible night.

Emily shrugs. 'Maami suffers from restless legs, and sometimes putting them up is the only way she gets some peace.'

I'm so grateful for this wide net of protection when I was a mere infant: Wura, Maami, Babalawo. Yeyemi, even. And now Emily! All from the real hidden enemy I've been fighting all along. It's incredible that one of my grandmothers plotted to kill me while the other fought from the shadows to save me.

'How did you and Maami become close?'

'It was after that time Mama Ondo tried to drown you. Even I wasn't sure if what my eyes saw was real. All I know is that you were lying in the bathing bowl when I rushed in and Mama Ondo's hand was on your chest holding you down. Then she saw me and brought you out. You were already limp. I snatched you from her and turned you upside down and you started coughing water. I turned around and Maami was right behind us. Mama Ondo ran out as if the devil had arrived! Later, Maami called me aside and said she would help my family, put my sister and brother through school if I looked out for you but made sure nobody knew.'

I don't know what to say, so I go over and take her hand. 'Thank you, Emily. Thank you for my life.' Now I know why I was so terrified of the Woli's baptism. Maybe somewhere my body still remembered my grandmother trying to drown me in a tub.

'I'm glad to help. Maami said I can come and work for her once you're safe. I think it's time and I will leave when madam returns. It has been too many years and I'm truly tired of her Temple people.'

'Ah, Emily, so are we,' Wura sighs. 'Thank you so much.'

'It's okay. I stood to gain, too. My sister is going to polytechnic now to become a nurse.' Emily smiles a rare smile of pride, pats us both on the cheeks and leaves.

I wait for Wura to say something about what she's just learned about Father's miserable childhood. What has it changed for her? Will she defend him? Then I know within our silent understanding that this is a wound too tender for her to examine just yet. So I leave it alone and allow myself to bask instead in the wonder of her existence.

45

1993 (AGE 16)

I return to Mr D's and pack my few belongings so I can be at home with Wura while Mother is away. For some ridiculous reason I feel wobbly inside.

'You do know wherever I am is always your home, don't you?'

He's saying this because I was about to get in the car so he can drive me back to Mother's house and I've just flung myself at him sobbing – which I hadn't planned to do. It's just this sudden feeling that things will change yet again.

'Yes,' I sniffle.

'Good.'

He hands me his pristine handerchief to wipe my face and we get in and drive off.

Wura and I talk and talk. I've longed so much to be with her that despite the circumstances, it seems a sort of miracle to wake up and there she is. We simply live and breathe each other's presence. Like me, she feels both loathing and pity for Elijah, knowing what Bayo did to him and made him do.

'I hoped so much you'd call once you heard about Eli and Bayo.'

'I only found out two days ago. You know how slowly news reaches the village. I was trying to untangle how I felt. To figure out what to say.'

'I've been so desperate to say sorry. If I hadn't been so stupid about Elijah, none of this would have happened and—' Wura puts her fingers to my lips, silencing me.

'Stop. That's the other thing.'

'What other thing?'

'In one of her rambling confessions, Mama Ondo said she'd seen Eli come to your room and followed, then pressed her ear to the door. She heard you saying no and telling him to stop. And all this time she never said a word in your defence. How can anyone be so full of hate?'

I remember the sound of shuffling slippered feet. The sinking realization that help was not coming. Wondering if in my terror I'd only imagined it. And that was Mama Ondo. Yes, she's certainly full of some ugliness. I guess I'll never know what happened to make her that way. I wonder how she became involved with the Temple and decide I don't even want to know.

'But I still wronged you. I was attracted to Eli.'

'But you said no. You thought of me and said no. I don't know if I can ever look Mommy in the face again. Would you believe after Mama Ondo said how she'd failed to kill you, Mommy said it would have solved many problems? I felt so sick I ran to the bathroom. Then I hid in my room till she went to bed and I called you. Oh God! I keep seeing those babies, cold and silent and dead. Oto, if they'd killed you, I'd have died too.'

But we're both here, alive. I pull her close and hold tighter than I should. I just want to stop any pain from ever touching her again. She hugs back even tighter.

'I felt you gone,' she says, in tears, when I tell her about swallowing those Panadol. 'Half of my heart was desperate to find you but then I'd picture you again with Eli and just erupt with anger. I was so torn. All our lives you wanted what I had. All our lives it scared me, because I didn't know how far you'd go, where you'd stop. And it seemed you'd stop at nothing. It took hearing Mama Ondo's confession to know that's not true. God! The heartbreak she could have prevented.'

I sigh. It's no good to hate a dying old woman. Best to move on. I summon up my courage.

'Wura, I know you always wanted a real brother but you've done your best with what you got. Now I must show you something.' I need her to see. To acknowledge. To be sure.

Wura looks apprehensive, but nods.

I stand and unbutton my shirt. When she sees the binding on my chest, her mouth drops open. I take it off. 'I'm your sister, Wura, I've always been. And my name is Lori.'

'But . . . but down there, you have . . .'

'Yes. I have a little bit of everything and parts that look somewhat different. It's caused in the womb by a condition that makes my body unable to process male hormones. At least that is what the urologist thinks based on tests she did. I'll give you some paperwork and magazine articles that explain it better and hopefully you'll never need, because this is passed down the female line of the family. It all made so much sense when you told me about Mama Ondo's evil deeds. Anyway, this is me, and I love you with every beat of my heart. I always have, no matter what.'

Wura gets up and walks around me, shaking her head in wonder.

'Wow! Those are truly for real? Like mine?'

'Yes.' Her words make me giggle. 'They're for real. You can touch and see.'

'Eww. Put your boobs away! My God, Oto . . . I mean, Lori. You really are my sister!'

'Yes.' I put the bindings and my shirt back on.

'All this time!' Wura is tearful, dazed, regretful, and many other things all at once.

'To trick Elijah, I became you, Wura, just as I'd always wanted.'

'No, you fought to become who you should always have been, my beautiful sister. So brave! I'm so sorry for the mean things I used to say.'

'It's okay. You did your best.' All that matters is that we're no longer lost to each other.

She looks so proud of me, I cry happy tears. Babalawo would be proud of me, too. I've shaped up to be quite the eagle!

And yet I cannot truly soar. The deadline for me to accept a university place is ticking closer. When I tell Wura, she's torn between pride in my achievement and pain to know I'll be separated so soon from her if I get what I want. Still, she vows to do whatever she can to help.

*

The phone is on speaker when Wura calls Mother.

'Wura. Oh, thank Jehovah! How are you? I've been so worried.'

'I'm joyfully reunited with my twin, so I'm doing just fine.'

There's a long silence. Mother's voice quavers. 'I heard your footsteps as you fled and realized you heard some things. I'm so sorry. I can't leave your grandmother right now. She could go anytime. Please come back so I can explain.'

'Explain what? That Mama Ondo tried to murder Oto and that would have been just fine with you? You've always blamed others for your troubles, which, as it turns out, come from your own vicious mother.'

'Ah, Wura! Precious child, if you'd stayed and heard more, you'll know I didn't excuse what Mama did. I swear I didn't.'

'I don't believe you. Anyway, it's not me you should be apologizing to. Your other child who you left for dead in the hospital is right here and she urgently needs your help.'

There's a long silence that stretches. I can almost hear the word *she* bouncing around, finding no resting place within Mother's brain.

'Goodbye, Mommy. Call me when you decide to treat my sister right.' Wura hangs up, drained and tearful.

She comes to sit beside me, gently rubbing my back. I didn't even realize I'd bowed my face into my hands. I thought I was beyond weeping. Mother couldn't even bring herself to ask what I needed, never mind helping me. I've done everything that it was in my own power to do. My hopes of studying art in America and gaining better understanding of my body are fading into the mirages they've often seemed. Yet, inside me burns a flame that refuses to be quenched. I've fought so hard, and so many hands and hearts have helped keep me safe and lifted me up and kept me going.

That night I open my my well-worn proverb book to a random page, seeking guidance. *It is only through fire that the audacity of the dehinko-run plant is freed.* It was one of Babalawo's prophecies.

46

1993 (AGE 16)

The fire flares, red hot and throwing wild sparks. The forest is aflame. Everywhere creatures flee. Rooted to the ground, the plant burns and burns but doesn't die. It grows stronger and bigger. How can such a thing be? I'm filled with wonder. What is this marvel happening? And then I know. Because I hear the roar and swell of water, and feel no fear. It arcs over my head and I'm no longer a *dehinkorun* plant but myself and I'm sitting on a chair of moss in a brightly gleaming room made of glassy water and Yeyemi stands across from me. On her head is a crown of stars. Her tail is covered in jewels, her body wrapped in shawls of radiant sea flowers. She begins to undress. First the shawls float off by themselves, then the silky binding around her chest flutters off like a small flag. As if pulled by an invisible zip, her waist-high tail splits slowly apart and settles in soft folds at her feet. Before me stands a woman, and yet she is not. Between her long legs, she looks exactly like me.

Lori, she says, without speaking, *go now. You know what to do.*

When I wake up, I do know exactly what to do. And everything I've been through has given me the courage to know and face it.

First, I call Maami Akinro.

'Long ago, Babalawo gave me words he said I would one day need.'

'Yes?'

'*If you remain fixated on where you fell, you'll never figure out where you slipped.*' I'd always thought he was referring to Mother, but Maami, those words are for you. Father is now a grown man responsible alone for his choices.'

'Ashé, my granddaughter,' she says. Meaning, So be it.

I set out early, telling Wura I need to go and sort out some paperwork to do with studying abroad. I tell her I want to make some enquiries for her, too, so I get a recent passport photo and her thumbprint on a blank stamp. I hope our renewed shared intuition won't tell her it's a lie, because I don't want her worrying. Maami's driver meets me at the Lagos motor park. The last time I saw Father was nearly five years ago, and Mother was telling him to get lost. In my worst nightmares about the twists and turns my life could take, confronting Father had the same level of possibility as being hit by lightning and might prove just as fatal.

After telling the gateman that Maami had sent him to deliver a package to Father, Maami's driver enters and parks. While he distracts Ajibade, the gateman, I sneak out from where I'm concealed under a blanket in the back of the Jeep, tiptoe to the ornate door and lift the heavy lion's-head shaped brass knocker.

James, father's houseman, opens the door and I'm inside before he has time to reconsider. It's all going as Maami planned and described. I tell him who I am.

'M . . . make I go fetch madam,' he stammers, sensing, I guess, that this could be bad.

'No. Don't fetch madam. Tell Father I'm waiting for him.'

James reluctantly leaves. He tried to choose the lesser evil by fetching Father's wife, Mama-Ibeji, so she'll be responsible for passing the bad news of my arrival to Father, who has no scruples about crippling the messenger. Maami had made sure he'd be home.

James returns straightaway and with a quick, 'He dey come,' makes himself scarce so fast, he seems to move on wheels. I don't blame him. Unlike the grass in the forest, he has the choice to not be underfoot when elephants clash.

Rampant with gold-trimmed paneling, Father's colossal living room whispers wealth. Above me, a chandelier drips icy crystal. The bottoms of my shoes have vanished into an opulent rug. I've never before seen a TV as wide as the one on the claw-footed gold stand, beside which hangs a huge studio portrait of Father, his wife and two little boys, my half-siblings, acknowledged and displayed like me and Wura never were. It all adds fuel to my fire.

At the sound of doors slamming within the house, my spine stiffens. My heart thumps but my hands stay dry and steady. I'm ready for him.

'Good evening, sir,' I say, alert to any sudden move.

'I explicitly told your mother to keep you out of my sight if you both want to live, or don't you imbeciles understand plain English any more?'

'We do. Perfectly. I, however, have a compelling request that necessitates this conversation. Comply and you need never see nor hear from me again.' It's all part of my plan, turning his intimidation-by-colossal-word habit on him.

Father's eyes turn red. 'Have you lost all sense of self-preservation?'

'Just give me what I need.' It gives me courage to remember words from my proverb book. *However red with anger a man's eyes may burn, he cannot use them to light a fire.*

Father's lips curl into a smile that holds no humour. 'And what, your highness Otolorin, might that be?'

'I've been accepted to study at an American university. I know you can afford to pay. Do so and I'll vanish from your life.'

Father slowly shakes his head. His pitying look promises that when he's done with me, I'll wish I was dead. I return it with a measured look of my own. In the past, I've wished the same. Now I have every intention of living. On my terms.

'Let me be clear,' Father says. 'I have two sons. Healthy, intelligent and, most importantly, *normal*. Born of a meticulously selected woman of excellent lineage. Unblemished children a man can be proud to call his own. They and, God willing, their siblings, will inherit everything I built up with my two hands. You, on the other hand, are the erroneous result of one careless night with a woman of low pedigree. Yet you have the audacity to come here making demands.'

'I don't care what you think. I and the people who matter to me know I'm no error. Refuse me and see what happens to your precious Akinro name, you and your perfect sons.'

Father strides to the door, opens it and bellows, 'James! Ajibade!'

With Yeyemi's image giving me courage, I take off my shirt. Then my trousers. My thumbs are hooked into the elastic band of my briefs when Father turns around. His eyes bulge. His mouth unhinges.

'Are you crazy? What in God's name are you doing?' He forgets to speak quietly.

'Undressing. And won't it be great to share this delightful moment of revelation with your yes men! I'm sure they'll gladly gossip with all of Lagos and beyond about your so-called son. Don't get me wrong, I have no problem with myself, but imagine what all those narrow-minded people like you would say! Your precious boys will forever have to prove their lineage is not, how did you put it? Oh yes! Of low pedigree.'

I pull off my binding. My breasts spring free. Father's eyes snap shut. His lips move as if he's swearing – or praying. I smile.

Footsteps sound outside. Father slams and locks the door. Bars it with his body as if James and the gateman might break their way in. He sees the windows and, despite the privacy blinds, runs around frenziedly jerking the curtains closed. He even locks the door to the inner passageway so Mama-Ibeji can't come in. So she doesn't know! This makes things *a lot* more interesting!

James yells from outside, '*Oga*, sir, you call me?'

'N . . . no.' Father's voice cracks. James bangs harder on the door.

'No, James!' he barks. 'Both of you get back to work right now!' Father doesn't move till their footsteps fade.

'Please get decent.' His voice is shaking.

He said *please*! My smile widens as I unhurriedly dress.

Father opens his eyes. 'You think you're smart? You think you can use your deformity to blackmail me?'

'I'm only demanding my birthright.'

Father wipes his sweating face and neck with the edge of his *agbada*. I've barely fired my first shot!

'And what did they accept you for?'

'Studio Arts.'

'What? You want to waste my hard-earned dollars to become a use-less *ayaworan*? You didn't even have the common sense to apply for something worthwhile, like Medicine or Engineering?'

'You know that Bible story about the three talents? The person that buried his talent instead of using it was the one that God punished. I intend to use mine. Imagine if Sunny Ade's parents had refused to let him be a "mere" musician or Pelé's father had denied him the chance to play football.'

I open my travel bag. Put on the table between us my painting of Yeyemi. His eyes fly from it to my face, as if he can't believe I've accomplished this. But he knows.

'What stops me from making you disappear?' he whispers, looking like he's already measuring me for a coffin.

I'm aware of how, when he's cornered, dead bodies tend to turn up.

'Maami said you shouldn't even think about it.'

Father's jaw drops again. 'My mother said *what*? Is she now in league with your madness?' His fingers rub his temples. A mother's betrayal. I know every sharp, cutting facet of it.

'She said for too long she's been guilty of looking not where she slipped but where she fell, and if you harm me, she'll make you curse the day you were born.'

'She said that,' Father states flatly, teeth clenched. His mother is his idol. Maami perhaps underestimated herself. His stable anchor through life has suddenly floated belly up. He's adrift. His knee starts to shake. If it wouldn't be showing weakness, I suspect he'd sit right down.

'I'll also be going as Otolorin Akinro, *female*, so you'll need to get me a passport that says so. And while you're at it, I'll want Wura's passport renewed, too.'

'Are you out of your mind?' Father tries to roar but it comes out more as a croak.

'Nope. And you can make it happen. It's actually legal. Not like you haven't done things that aren't for lesser reasons.'

'And what about your school certificates? Don't they list you as a boy? You think you can fool that university?'

'I saw a well-respected doctor who certified that I was born with indeterminable gender but should ideally have been raised female. The agency in charge of my application knows. That's all taken care of.'

'You really are crazy.' Father looks as if he's being washed away with not even a stick to cling on to.

'I'm actually surprisingly sane, considering what you've put us through. I went to the passport office and got the application forms. See? You simply tick male or female after you present sworn affidavits affirming the birth of your twin daughters. Everything you need is in there, including the document signed and notarized attesting to my birth gender error, our passport photos and our fingerprints.' I had a photo taken after Wura had plaited my hair, wearing a pair of clasp earrings and light make-up. It was virtually indistinguishable from Wura's except for that slight difference in jawline if you knew to look for it.

He sits heavily on the sofa.

'Look, just do your part, and I'll leave you and your children in peace.'

'I'll want to see that letter of admission and details of the full cost.'

'Of course.' I fetch both documents from my travel bag.

Father gasps when he sees the cost of tuition and living expenses.

'Ridiculous! Do you think I'm made of money?'

Pretty much, and you have no soul. I know from Maami that the exclusive international nursery the twins attend costs double what my school fees did. 'Just do it and I'll never again ask you for one *kobo*.'

'This is too much, too much!' His foot taps rapidly on the rug.

I play my last hand. 'They offered me a full tuition scholarship, conditional on your agreement, in writing, to be responsible for my living expenses for the duration of my studies. They'll require your signature and Mother's.' I hand him the scholarship award letter. 'If we factor in rising costs, a cheque for double that should rid you of me for life.'

'Moji will never agree to this!'

'I'm sure you can think of a way to persuade her. She's in Ondo with her sick mother.' His protest sounds exactly like Mother's last stand when I argued for going to ISS. That's when I know I've won.

'If I do this, will you swear on your twin sister's head that you'll never again trouble me or my sons?'

'I swear on one condition.'

Father looks ready to spring up from the sofa and strangle me. I'm like the bird taunting the hyena only because it's already sighted a convenient high branch within reach.

'You will write a second cheque for the same amount, which will go directly into an account for Wura. You will also transfer ownership of the house in Ibadan to her name. She'll never need to come and beg you for anything.'

'Have you quite finished issuing orders?' Father pretends calm but his hands are shaking. It feels amazingly good to have the tables turned, even as I pity his lack of a heart. I've read about people in concentration camps who, despite untold suffering, showed great humanity and shared their meager crusts of bread, while others plundered what little their fellow sufferers had. No question which he'd have been. Suffering is no excuse for cruelty.

'Yes. I'm done.'

'Why does Wura want her passport?' he throws out, a last grasp at commanding a situation he's lost.

'Since when do you care? It's not as if you've asked after her since you abandoned us for your perfect new family. Just do this and we'll leave you alone. Don't, and you'll have to silence us both. Except, you harm one hair on Wura's head and nothing on earth will stop Mother from castrating you.'

Of all the most unexpected things, he laughs. It's a cruel sound. At the same time I realize, *this man will always be profoundly unhappy. Something fundamental inside him broke and never got fixed. His existence is its own punishment.* I needn't wish him worse nor excuse his heartlessness.

'You know, Otolorin, you have some guts. I do admire guts. I'll get your passports and set up your visa appointment with the American

Embassy. I'll find a way to make Moji sign where necessary. Once you're ready to depart, I'll write a cheque for the full amount. I will want to see evidence of Wura's account. And you will keep your part of this bargain.'

'Sure. And just for your information, certain photographs of me – naked – and all sorts of other juicy, eye-opening information has been stored in safe hands. Nobody you can harm or buy off. Should anything unfortunate happen to me, it will all go straight to the press. I feel really sorry for those children you're raising. Bye, Father.'

I've pushed him further than I ever thought I could. *And I won!*

47

1993 (AGE 16)

Back in Ibadan, Wura is in the kitchen with Emily. I grab her hand and we hurry to her room.

'I ... um ... wasn't entirely honest about why I went to Lagos.'

'Tell me something I didn't know.' She rolls her eyes.

I can only laugh. I love her like *goody-goody* sweets. 'I've ... um ... persuaded Father to get us both our passports. He's also agreed to pay for my living expenses in the US and convince Mother to sign my acceptance forms.'

Wura shrieks and flies at me, tumbling me onto my back. It's *so* good to hear her bell-like laughter again.

'How on earth did you do that?' She's propped on one elbow, looking at me with something like awe.

'I threatened to run around Lagos naked and show everybody the daughter Laitan Akinro insists is a son. Plus, Maami backed me up.'

'God, I wish I'd seen that!' She starts to laugh.

'Oh, he was pissing himself nearly!' We fall into each other's arms, helpless with laughter till we're hiccupping. Which sets us off again. It's cleansing like rainwater sweeping away all the muck and pain that Laitan Akinro has spilled all over our lives.

'Thank you for showing that man correct pepper! I put him on a false throne for far too long.' Wura wipes tears from her eyes. 'So what are you going to do now? Even in America, won't it be strange for a boy to have breasts? Won't people point at you and say nasty things? You can't wrap your chest forever.'

'That's the other thing. I also persuaded Father to swear a birth affidavit and get a passport that says I'm female. I'll be going as Lori Akinro.'

Wura gapes for a good few seconds. For maybe the first time in our lives, I've left my sister speechless.

'Holy flying cows above! You know, when Mommy hears this, she's going to think you pulled some major witchery on him.' She cackles, then sobers. 'I don't even know what she believes any more. She simply can't justify hating you now.'

I don't care. Once Mother signs my forms, she can go bury herself in an extra sandy part of sacred land. I don't tell Wura yet about her cheque or that this house will be hers. I want to make sure it all comes through first. I'm hoping it will help ease some of the pain she's been through, to know she's provided for, that her future is hers to shape however she wants. I've no doubt it will always be Mother's home for as long as she wants, too. However Wura feels right now, she'll always need her mother.

Wura sits up against the headboard and pats the space beside her. When I sit, she tugs me sideways till my head is in her lap. She reaches across, grabs the comb on her side table and begins to part and oil my hair, which I've been growing out. 'Jonpe, jonpe, o!' She calls me into song.

'Jonpe!' I answer, smiling wide.

'E b'an paja yi o, kowa l'anje omo, jonpe ...'

The last brick in the wall that grew so tall between us tumbles down. My heart finds peace.

Wura insists on mailing Mother a copy of one of the magazine articles, along with a simple explanation about how what I have is a hormonally induced condition, insisting she's smart enough for it to make sense or, at least, to get her questioning her beliefs. Wura, the eternal optimist-ostrich, still wants to believe Mother can change. Knowing her expertise at burying her head in the sand, I simply hold my peace. One lesson I've finally understood is that you love someone not in spite of, but along with their faults.

'Did you get what I sent you?' Wura calls Mother some days later.

'Yes.'

'And?'

'Wura, just come back, please? I'm begging you, my daughter.'

'You didn't answer my question.'

There's silence. Then a sob, tinny through the speakerphone.

'Please, Wura. It's just . . . your grandmother passed away last night.'

'So?'

'I know you don't mean that. I'm sorry, precious one. She was my mother. She had my best interests at heart, just like I have for you. Please come back to Ondo. Don't leave me to mourn alone.'

I sense Wura's heart tug at the pain in Mother's plea. Sense her harden herself. I take her hand. Squeeze gently.

'Best interests are obviously a matter of opinion. Just ask the grandchild she tried to murder as a baby. Listen, I need you to do something for me.'

'Anything.'

'Daddy will contact you about swearing our affidavits of birth so that he can apply for both our passports. Can you sign the papers he brings without giving any trouble?'

'Both of you? But why? Where are you going?' Mother's voice sharpens with fear. She bursts into fresh sobs.

'Never mind that. If you want me to even begin to forgive the terrible things you did, just sign whatever he asks you to. If you don't, I promise I'll never again talk to you in this lifetime.' Wura hangs up.

It really hits me then. Mama Ondo is dead and gone for good. I remember her wig. The one that started it all. The one I'm now certain she burned on a flaming pyre because she believed me evil. Wura's tears are silent. We hold each other for a long time.

48

1993 (AGE 16)

Father calls weeks later to say our passports are ready and a date is set for my visa interview. I spend two days in Lagos, staying in a hotel that he pays for. The interview is quick and I walk out with my visa by noon. Father hands me two certified bank drafts, each for the full amount I demanded. They feel like an impossible fortune. More than Mr D has been paid for a lifetime's worth of work. And for Father, it is at most five per cent of all he owns. I hope never to see him again.

When I return to Ibadan, I tell Wura we're going on a surprise outing. I lead her to the bank and help her open an account and then deposit her cheque. She's dazed and babbling as if her mind has packed up and gone. I can't stop laughing. I remember her aged ten, throwing her pocket money on the floor in a fit when she realized Mother had given her double what she'd given me. I'm filled with a fierce gratitude that she's now provided for and no longer subject to Father's whims and manipulations.

We have only two weeks more together before I leave for New York. We're inseparable, except for when I visit Mr D. Mother keeps calling and Wura keeps hanging up on her unless she talks to me. It's a strange turnaround from when it was me at the receiving end, like that unfortunate proverb that says, *the new wife rejoicing to see the stick that is used to beat the older wife should remember that it only patiently awaits its next victim.*

A couple of days before I'm due to leave, Wura tells me Mother asked which urologist I saw, so Wura told her and they talked for a bit.

I'm glad more for Wura's sake than mine. I've used up all the hope I had that she'll ever change. In return, as a concession, Wura agrees to return to Ondo in time for our grandmother's funeral, after which she and Mother will both return to Ibadan together for good. Emily plans to be gone by then. Her work, she said, is done. We've all agreed Mother never needs to know about her double-agent status in our home all these years. It will just cause unnecessary grief.

Wura decides she wants to spend our last day together out celebrating and shopping with her sister. She dismisses my worried objections that people might see and give her grief after I'm gone. 'I've denied you long enough,' she says. 'Besides, you need a top-to-toe knock 'em dead outfit to meet Derin, and you can't try things on dressed like a boy!'

I feel my face warm. She teases me non-stop about Derin's phone calls and mimes me floating on air afterwards. We're so far away from the days when her teasing was of the hurtful kind. Now she's planning to dress me up to dazzle him!

When we're finally sitting resting, sipping cold Fanta, I concede with awe that I will never attain my sister's Olympian levels of clothes shopping. Beside our high-heeled white-sandal-clad feet sit a mountain of bags. Some young men a few seats away keep giving us sidelong glances. One of them is ridiculously cute. Wura and I turn to each other with identically sly grins. We both thought it at the exact same time! She makes a show of lifting her wrist to glance at her watch but she's undercover checking him out. I might have a lot to learn about the fine art of flirting but I'm catching on fast. My heart melts as I look down at my own matching watch. I got hers repaired and bought new straps for both. Inside, we wrote each other's names, just like before. Only this time, inside her heart, Wura wrote 'Lori'. She's my twin, my sister now in every way. My heart aches to know we'll be going our separate ways soon, though we'll never again be apart in spirit. I'll always know if she needs me, and I intend to be there. It was Babalawo's third prophecy. Now I am my true self, Wura, the other half of my soul, is truly safe with me.

A woman pauses beside our table to retie her son's shoelaces. 'You're both so pretty,' she says, 'your mother must be proud of her twin daughters.'

We thank her, and I feel lit inside with a joy that reflects on Wura's face.

'Pwetty, pwetty!' the little boy echoes, as his mother tows him away.

Our eyes meet and we collapse into giggles, then sober up fast.

We've walked around the shops, tried on perfumes and admired jewellery, revelling in sisterhood, delaying the inevitable.

That night, though we're too old for it, we sleep curled together like a pair of commas in womblike closeness.

Morning comes too soon. Mr D has arrived to take me to Lagos airport while the sunlight is still watery in the early dawn sky. Wura uncharacteristically fights tears upon seeing him. I see her chin wobble, then firm as she bends her knees in greeting but he pulls her up and she just hugs him, and whispers something in his ear. I think she's thanking him for saving my life. For everything. He nods and pats her pack. My emotions are all over the place like spilled rice. Elated. Terrified. Happy. Sad. I'm leaving them behind. I'm going to where Derin is.

'Will you help Wura with her SATs and TOEFL if she wants to join me one day?' I ask Mr D. I'm secretly hoping that's what she'll use her money to do. There's already been talk of Business Studies. She's amazing with numbers. It's also so they'll have an excuse to keep in touch after I'm gone. This matters very much to me. I think Wura could really use his wisdom in her life, too. Plus, he's partial to her cakes.

'Of course!' He smiles. I think he understands what I want.

'Thank you.' Wura dimples a smile so like mine I see Mr D start slightly then shake his head in wonder. He's not used to seeing two of me. One in lilac, one in pink. We're dressed like a photoshoot about to happen. Wura did my make-up with a deft and light hand. I've never looked so fabulous. On our wrists clink matching brass bangles – an *ibeji* gift from Maami.

My few things are soon in the car. Our journey to Lagos is filled with stories, catching up, revelations, and by the end of it, I've no doubt that Mr D and Wura have formed a true connection. She plans to talk Mother into letting Mr Driver take her to the weekly karate classes he teaches at Ibadan University.

'Heh! Like she'll say no to anything you want for the next twenty years! Better milk it!' I grin wickedly. Wura pulls a face. She's not as amused as I am. 'Remember Mother loves you no matter what, Wura, and you do need her.'

'I know. But until she accepts who you are and apologizes, I can't forgive what she's done to you. To us. I can't even forgive myself.'

'I've forgiven you. Like you forgave me. To love is to forgive. Again and again and again.'

'Wise words, Lori,' Mr D says.

'And Mr D is the best teacher! You'll soon be kicking serious arse, just like your sister!' I crow, to lighten her mood.

They both laugh. Mr D lets me get away with what he'd normally reprimand as sloppy speech.

Murtala Mohammed Airport is crowded, heaving with touts young and old trying to wring a living out of those arriving and departing. We're at the security gate, beyond which they cannot go with me. All around us people embrace loved ones they won't see for a while and parents weep over children who might never return home to live. It all comes crashing in. The reality that I'm leaving. That these two people I love more than life are not coming with me. Yet, on the other side there is Derin, waiting. Life is full of holding on and letting go. This is a hard lesson to learn.

'Well, daughter of my heart, we are here. You have done it,' Mr D says in that practical way he has when there are emotions involved.

'Yes.' I swallow and swallow.

'I want to hear from you minimum once a month!'

'Yes, father of my heart. At the very least.'

'Good.' He pulls out his handerchief and dries his eyes. Then he hugs me. And I know he'll always be my father. Because we chose each other. Family happens in different ways.

Wura's hand is light on my back. I turn to her.

'I wish we didn't have to part.' She's trying to be brave.

'Me too.'

'It seems to be our destiny.'

My chin quivers.

'Don't you dare!' she says. 'That's a first-class make-up job you're about to ruin!'

I laugh and then have to not cry. How do I leave her?

'I'll visit as soon as I can. Maybe even join you one day.'

'That would be all my dreams coming true.'

She holds my face, looks into my eyes. I do the same. We touch foreheads.

'Bye for now, sis. Say hello to Derin from me. I love you.'

'I will. I love you, too.' I smile back, though my voice cracks. We rarely say those words. I vow to tell her every single time I call.

It feels impossible to let go. She clings just as tight for a long moment then steps away. Chin raised, she smiles, and I see all the fiery determination that makes my sister a fighter. I've no doubt she can and will succeed in whatever she sets her heart to do. She'll bloom and shine and find her way. As I walk through the security gates, I can still feel her heart beating in time with mine.

49

1993 (AGE 16)

When my turn comes, I hand over my travel documents to the man at the counter. He squints at my passport, stares for a long time at my photo, checks and rechecks my visa stamp and my admission letter and begins to flip through the pages of my passport again. I tell my roiling stomach to be still. Remind myself that with my braided hair swinging free to my shoulders and my full-skirted pink dress, I look like any young woman he's seen that day. He waves me right through.

It's strange, this feeling like vertigo and happiness. I want Mr D to tell me once more all the ways it's going to be all right and how I now hold in my own hands the power to shape my destiny. Impossible as it seems, I'll soon see Derin, who fits in my heart like a key in a lock. He'll meet me at the airport and I'll stay with him and his mom till I move onto campus. Has America already changed him in subtle ways? For one thing, he'll get the shock of his life when he sees me, because knowing in theory that your beloved best friend is now a girl will still be mind-blowing in reality. I hope it will be a good shock. A new beginning.

 In the waiting lounge is a large fish tank. I'm drawn to it like a magnet and then bubbles begin to dance and rise out of the water and I'm whirling and surrounded by tiny, shimmering fish. Yeyemi swells out of the depths and flows up into the sky, its dark blue becoming a velvet background for myriad twinkling stars that swirl like smoke yet hold her shape. Their movement becomes a deep humming song. The song is old, and its strands weave the web of life. I know this song; I've always known it because the words are mine also, even as they belong to every being that lives. With no words, Yeyemi says, *I am the strength and fire in you, I am everything that is and was and ever will be. You are the stuff my stars are made of. I am you and you are me.*

I open my eyes wide. At last I understand. The goddess is real. The goddess has always been me.

My flight is called. I straighten the crimson belt around my waist. The ruffled hem of my pink dress whispers against my legs as I step through the departure gate and, in my strappy white heels, take the first step into my new life as Lori Akinro.

A pretty lady hovers above me, graceful in her red and blue air-hostess uniform.

'Please fasten your seatbelt,' she says and, for a second, I imagine she's referring to the life ahead of me and the bumps in the road as yet too far to see. She smiles, though, and I click the metal tongue into its groove. The plane glides forward and I feel as though my will alone can lift us into the air. Soon, beneath me, the dollhouse roofs of Lagos lie scattered like shards of broken pottery. When the clouds finally swallow us, I tilt back my chair and close my eyes, the better to peer into my future.

Epilogue

He stands tall, *dada* locks tied back, a single orchid flower in his hand. It's my favourite colour – all shades of pink deepening to lilac. For a moment he hasn't yet seen me. I luxuriate in his height, his long arms, the beautiful plate of his chest in a white T-shirt. The warmth blankets me and yet it is electric, sending tingles under my skin. Then he sees me and his eyes widen. And he's striding forward, mouth softly open in an *oh!*

We stand face to face and there is no time, no airport, nothing but this. Us. He takes me in – one long sweep from the crown of my braided hair to my toes in strappy white shoes. And his lips remain parted in wonder.

'You're so tall,' I whisper. It means he's so handsome and so vital and so much a universe I can't wait once more to explore. But he gets it. He hears all that, too.

'Welcome to America, Lori,' he says. 'I've missed you so much.'

His voice wraps round and round me. My hand cups his face, like I wanted to do a million years ago. His lips land lightly on mine, part and then it is like drinking sunshine and madness and nectar and a freefall into joy. We come up for air and he's smiling dazedly.

'Let's go,' he says, taking my hand. 'I have so much to tell you, so many amazing places to show you!'

I smile. I always knew I'd follow him anywhere.

In this land where people all the time do great things that once were considered impossible, where you can break bread with a man who trod the surface of the moon and still returned to walk the earth, I know I will become everything – the woman, the artist, the *wonder* – I was born to be.

Postscript

Dear Reader,

If you'd like to learn more and support intersex people and advocacy groups worldwide, please visit the InterACT website and the Intersex Campaign for Equality website, find and read books written by intersex authors, and remember to celebrate and amplify intersex awareness day on 26 October!

Thank you!

Acknowledgements

My greatest gratitude goes to Juliet Mushens, agent extraordinaire and all-round superhero goddess for believing in me and loving my writing. You said you were here for the long haul and you meant it. I am so lucky to have you! Many thanks, also, to Liza DeBlock.

Thank you to Mrs Udenyi my secondary school literature teacher for lending me a mysterious new book called a thesaurus at age twelve and opening up a world of magic where yellow was also sunshine and gold and butter. To Miss Lamb, my other literature teacher for encouraging my idea, also at age twelve, of composing a 'soliloquy' (see thesaurus above) to be read aloud on the school stage, and for telling me here was a thing I was good at. To Mr Austin, my A-Level literature teacher, for so loving poetry that his classes became a sumptuous banquet of words.

Many thanks to the Lesley University Creative Writing MFA (past and current) program directors, faculty and staff, and my MFA graduating cohort and fellow alumni. I am infinitely grateful for the talent and generosity of my semester and thesis mentors: Laurie Foos, Tony Eprile, the late Wayne Brown, and especially Michael Lowenthal, in whose class the fuzzy nucleus of *An Ordinary Wonder* got its first ultrasound, and whose immediate and wholehearted enthusiasm lit a forever flame.

I am grateful to the writers conferences, residencies and workshops which, with grants and scholarships, gave my craft the opportunity to breathe and grow; The Key West Literary Seminar especially for the opportunity to meet the late great Timothy Seldes (who read my work and told me I had something special and my feet barely touched the ground all week!); Miles Frieden who gave me some sage life advice;

and The Parrot Fish Crew. (Who still has San Carlos the writing fish? Maria-Elena Montero or Lorenna Sparling?) Many thanks to The Fine Arts Work Center in Provincetown for being like a fairy-tale land for writers, Vermont Studio Center where I got work done and met wonderful artists and writers who became friends, and the VONA Voices founders, mentors and fellow alum. To Grub Street in Boston and the Cambridge Center for Adult Education (CCAE), thank you for classes both taken and taught.

Special thanks to the Community Committee for International Students at Stanford University, and all the wonderful friends I made at Friday Morning Coffee – I wish I could name you all – and Gwyn Dukes and John Pearson and Lynn Kroner and Brian Groves and Kayleen McDonald and the entire Bechtel International Center Staff of 2002/2003. Thank you, CCIS and Gwyn, for saying *your dreams matter too*, to the lost and bewildered spouses trailing their partners to a new country, often sacrificing their own aspirations and careers. The Bechtel I-Center literally gave me room to dream and The CCIS Spouse Education Fund sponsored the very first writing class that started me on this wonderful journey.

To all my friends and writing partners and everyone who read drafts and gave support and advice at various points along the way, I appreciate and thank you with all my heart and wish I could name each and every wonderful one of you. Special thanks to Jennifer Gilman-Porat; we knew we were kindred writing souls that night we snuck into a closed bar after meeting in Key West and talked till dawn. Belle Brett, the loveliest of neighbours and beta readers. Amy Caldwell, for being that lovely neighbour who was an early reader of my words and kindly gave me a reference. Jennifer Kircher-Carr, for reading and celebrations. I'm so glad we met during that One Story class! The Quills for being superstars and so much more than a writing group – thank you for feedback and support through the ups and downs. Ailynn Collins and Melissa Hill, my early beta-reading angels. Joxy (surprise!) for our way-back history and friendship that always thrived on a shared love of words and for the hilarity we got out of every possible way to use *in flagarante delicto* in a sentence! Michael Graves, thank you for reading early drafts, giving invaluable feedback, and years of an exceptional friendship. Keep shining!

No words can encompass my thanks to my beloved family; my mom & dad, Margaret and Samuel Olajide, for unsparingly doing your utmost always to make a good life for your children, and also for that spare room filled with giant boxes of books that never got unpacked each time we moved, where I spent many hidden hours inhaling tomes far above my age. My siblings; Mubo Farukanmi, Jumoke Ishola, Muyiwa Olajide and Molara Oshinuga; my auntie Victoria Mope Adeleke; my uncle Michael Teju Ishola; and all of your spouses and children – you are super precious and I thank you for putting up with this often perplexing but always loving relative you got saddled with, *aka* me. If I've made you even a little proud, it will all have been worth it.

Finally, and most importantly, to Julien, for being that sweet French boy who stopped to help that exhausted Nigerian student in Hull University carry her moving boxes to her dorm room many lovely moons ago (Reader, I married him!). Thank you from my deepest heart for your love and immeasurable support and enthusiasm and inimitable, wonderful *you*-ness. For *pot-au-feu* and *pâté en croûte* and joy and laughter. This could not have happened without you, my darling.

Buki Papillon was born in Nigeria, studied law at Hull University in the UK, and obtained her MFA in Creative Writing from Lesley University in Cambridge, Massachusetts. She has received writing scholarships and awards from Key West Literary Seminar, Vermont Studio Center, Fine Arts Work Center and is a VONA alumnus. Buki has been at various times an events organizer, travel adviser, librarian and chef. Her work has appeared in *Post Road Magazine* and the *Del Sol Review*. Buki lives in Boston, USA. To learn more, visit www.bukipapillon.com and follow her on Twitter at @bukipapillon.